AGENT OF DOOM

"The police let you go?" Laika asked. "But . . . why?"

Because I have to kill you. Because walls can't keep out the one that wants you dead.

And then the gun was in his hand, and he was pointing it at Tony, and Laika was saying something, saying no, no, fight it, you can fight this. We're your friends. Just put it down.

But he could hardly hear her, and he knew it didn't matter what she said. He couldn't fight it. He could only obey.

I have no will. I have no choice. He is fire, I am water. I have no choice but to boil . . .

THE
SEARCHERS

—— BOOK THREE ——
SIEGE OF STONE

CHET WILLIAMSON

AVON BOOKS ◆ NEW YORK

AVON BOOKS, INC.
1350 Avenue of the Americas
New York, New York 10019

Copyright © 1999 by Chet Williamson
Inside cover author photo by Ron Bowman
Published by arrangement with the author
Library of Congress Catalog Card Number: 98-93540
ISBN: 0-380-79189-7
www.avonbooks.com

First Avon Books Printing: March 1999

AVON TRADEMARK REG. U.S. PAT. OFF. AND IN OTHER COUNTRIES, MARCA REGISTRADA, HECHO EN U.S.A.

Printed in the U.S.A.

WCD   10 9 8 7 6 5 4 3 2 1

To the McDonalds:
T. Liam, Elizabeth,
and Brendan Redmon (newest of the clan)

O, beat away the busy meddling fiend
That lays strong siege unto this
    wretch's soul . . .

—SHAKESPEARE, *Henry VI, Part II*, II, iii, 21

Blood shall drip from wood,
    and the stone shall utter its voice;
The peoples shall be troubled,
    And the stars shall fall.

—2 ESDRAS 5:5

Chapter 1

Joseph Stein looked into the gaunt, wizened face of the man. He had been dead a long time. The turnscrew that pierced the top of his skull was hung over a metal rod, and the rod was fitted into one of a row of vertical brackets attached to the paneled side of the case.

Metal wires ran from the turnscrew down to the man's arms, holding them aloft in an attitude of mid-air crucifixion. The chest had been split open and the ribs folded back, exposing some of the internal organs. Those had been dried, and painted in various colors. The red heart was still connected to the main artery that snaked down from the neck.

Joseph slowly drew closer, until his face was only an inch from the glass that separated the exhibit from the patrons of the Mutter Museum of the College of Physicians of Philadelphia. Others might have turned away, but Joseph had seen far worse. Besides, he could appreciate the painstaking artistry with which the physician who had prepared this specimen had worked. That same kind of patience and attention to detail had earned Joseph the repute in which he was held in the Central Intelligence Agency.

Unfortunately, it was that same reputation that had brought him to his current situation. He was hiding out in a safe house in Philadelphia, along with Tony Luciano and their team leader, Laika Harris, while Richard Skye was cozily tucked in back at Langley, probably trying to decide what new madness to unleash on them. Skye had interrupted their much needed R&R in San Francisco to send them to Philadelphia, supposedly to keep them closer to Langley, but also, Joseph suspected, to keep them from being in one place for too long, which only increased their odds of getting spotted.

As far as everyone in the Company knew, except for Skye and a few above him, Joseph, Laika, and Tony were on individual missions in the Balkans and elsewhere in Asia. But in actuality they were performing black ops within the United States, in direct violation of the CIA charter, first in New York City, and then in the deserts of the high southwest.

Skye had assured them that the creation of their group was the result of a direct presidential request. The President, however, didn't seem to have shared the news with any other government agency, if the FBI man who had insinuated himself into their party in Arizona had been any indication. He had treated them like dangerous fugitives and had wound up dead as a result. You didn't fire a gun at Tony Luciano if you wanted to stay alive.

Even though it had been many weeks before, the three operatives still wondered when the dead federal agent's masters would send more of their dogs out on the hunt. Though they hadn't seen anyone suspicious in the two weeks they had been in Philadelphia, that didn't mean the feds weren't looking for them. After all, the ops had killed one of their agents, and they weren't too forgiving about things like that.

Joseph tried to push the thought to the back of his mind, and concentrated on the exhibits. He and Laika and Tony had seen most of the tourist attractions in the city, including the Liberty Bell, Independence Hall, Christ Church, Betsy Ross's house, and the Philadelphia Museum of Art. Tony had been disappointed that the statue of Sylvester Stallone as Rocky was no longer out front.

Joseph had even talked Laika into going to the Poe house, but she had been disappointed to find it completely bare, since none of Poe's furniture had survived. Joseph applauded the Park Service's decision not to fill the rooms with period pieces. The empty chambers were, for him, far more evocative of Poe's haunting presence.

He felt, as he walked through the low-ceilinged, white-washed rooms, that he had somehow come home. It was Poe's stories that had enthralled him as a child, and led him into his lifelong interest in weird and supernatural literature and films. As he stood in the dirt-floored basement of Poe's house, he had found himself wondering if this place was what Poe had pictured as he wrote "The Black Cat," if those basement stairs were the ones down which the narrator's wife had tumbled, dead, or if that wall was the one behind which he had entombed both her and the cat. It was as close, Joseph thought, to looking through Poe's eyes as he could ever come.

In a sense, he owed Poe his vocation as well as his avocation. Joseph's love of popular fiction had led him to the spy books and movies that had intrigued him as a teenager and eventually brought him to the CIA, the ideal place for his precise, logical, and encyclopedic mind.

It was also an ideal place for a person fascinated by the macabre, as was the Mutter Museum. In retrospect, however, Joseph thought the museum was a bad choice for a place to *forget* what he had been through in the past few months. The first few rooms were innocuous enough, with a turn of the century doctor's office, and some circumspect displays of glass X-ray tubes and presidential artifacts, including Grover Cleveland's jaw tumor.

However, the cases on the wide gallery and those in the large room below held the things for which the Mutter was notorious. Hundreds of human skulls were carefully labeled with the names of the subjects, their occupations, and causes of death.

The Soap Woman, whose body, buried in chemical-rich soil, had turned completely to adipose tissue, looked up at Joseph. Her mouth was open in a silent and eternal scream, as if shocked by the glass-cased display her remains had become, a momentary thrill for curiosity seekers.

Jars filled with preservatives held the raddled heads and

limbs of syphilis victims. Next to them were molds of other victims' faces, the decay of their flesh preserved perfectly in multihued wax, like 3-D color photographs.

In the room at the bottom of the stairs, a massive dried colon reared up like a sandworm from *Dune*, and the shared livers of Barnum's Siamese Twins, Chang and Eng, sat in shadow in a pan. A number of wide metal cabinets held thousands of items that had been either accidentally swallowed or aspirated by human beings, and a well-worn book detailed the circumstances of every nail, tack, buttonhook, and shard of glass.

Joseph spent twenty minutes studying the various invaders, and when he looked up again, he saw that he was alone in the museum. There had been only a few other people to begin with, and now they were gone. The solitude did not bother Joseph, even in the midst of so much evidence of human frailty. He knew that there were far greater things to fear in this world than the dead.

The Prisoner, for one. Joseph and the other ops thought he had been responsible in one way or another for every bizarre occurrence that had taken place since Skye had assigned them to their current job of debunking supposedly paranormal phenomena.

It had all started with a mass suicide that they had later found out was a mass *assassination* of a group of men, the last Knights Templar, assigned by the Roman Catholic Church to investigate acts possibly caused by a strange prisoner. And things became stranger when they found out that the church had apparently been keeping the Prisoner captive for centuries.

The situation had shaken Joseph to the very roots of his skepticism. He had always gloried in his materialism, but now every bit of evidence, and his own experiences, pointed to an ageless prisoner, somehow bound and weakened by lead, who nevertheless had the power to communicate to others with his mind alone.

If what they had seen was true, the Prisoner had spoken in

dreams to a sculptor in Manhattan, to a fat and loathsome guru in Arizona, and to Joseph himself, cajoling, ordering, demanding his freedom. And now, at last, he had gotten it.

Michael LaPierre, a billionaire and religious right demigod, had assumed the Prisoner was none other than the Antichrist himself. Joseph still didn't buy that story, but LaPierre figured he could stick a real feather in his holy cap by sending the "Antichrist" straight to the flames of hell.

Unfortunately for LaPierre, it hadn't quite worked out that way. LaPierre had been the one who had gotten burned, along with the small army he had put together, and the rest of his followers. It had only strengthened the "Religious Right = Nut" equation that was hurting the Republican party while strengthening the Democrats.

But the worst thing that had resulted from LaPierre's arrogant coup attempt was that the Prisoner was no longer the captive of the church. He or she—or *it*—was free now, maybe still walking the American desert, or maybe cozying up to Saddam Hussein, for all Joseph knew. And that was a bad thing. No, that was the *mother* of all bad things, because the Prisoner had an incredible and frightening power, one in which Joseph had to believe, for he had seen its results.

The Prisoner had the power to enter certain people's minds and use them. He could point them like guns at each other, making them kill or torture or sabotage or commit suicide or whatever else amused him. And from what Joseph had seen, amusement took an awful lot of blood. If the Prisoner wasn't the Antichrist, then at least he was Superprick, or Badass Supreme, with the potential to become Nasty Master of the Universe, now that he was free of his leaden prison.

Still, several weeks had gone by, and the ops hadn't heard of any new wars or mass acts of violence. If the legends that the church had passed down were true, the Prisoner could take an entire town and turn it against itself. True, some people were immune to the Prisoner's commands, but not enough for comfort.

Every morning, Joseph dreaded waking up, fearful that he

would hear the news of an outbreak of mass violence for no conceivable reason, or receive a report from Skye that some dinky burg in Ohio or Missouri or West Virginia was being swept by a wave of murder-suicides. But nothing had happened, and the more time went by, the more apprehensive Joseph grew.

Laika and Tony weren't nearly as jumpy as Joseph, but then, the damned thing hadn't touched them. It hadn't crawled inside their heads while they slept, pretending to be Jesus or some other near-perfect entity, begging with all its tender-hearted might for freedom so that it might live and love and bring all mankind to the truth.

The truth of blood and death. The truth of mass destruction. That was the only truth that would satisfy it.

Joseph closed the file drawer filled with things that foolish people had swallowed or breathed into their lungs, his mind fully on the Prisoner now. *Forget it*, he told himself. *Forget everything that's happened so far. You're on R&R now, so just enjoy yourself in your little macabre museum. Now, what else is there to gawk at?*

That was when he saw the babies. There were dozens of them. Some were tiny skeletons braced upright, showing the huge skulls of hydrocephaly. There were larger ones, too, who had survived until the toddler stage, if indeed they had ever been able to toddle with those monstrous heads bearing them earthward. There were others in preservative, babies born with trunks instead of noses, or brains on the outside of their skulls, some with no head whatsoever, or with no limbs, or with flippers instead of arms.

But what lanced through Joseph Stein was a specimen on a bottom shelf, an infant fixed eternally in a standing position it could never have known in life. Its dried skin was as brown as leather, and its eye sockets had been filled with blue glass eyes that looked disturbingly alive in the midst of that parchment-like flesh. It was looking toward the side of the case, away from him, as if denying him the grace of its gaze.

It would not look at him, because he had killed it.

Chapter 2

*N*o. No, that wasn't right. He hadn't killed any baby, and certainly not this poor child, who must have died a hundred years ago. He had shot that other baby, yes, had *thought* he had killed it, but it was already dead, starved to death, still held by its mother, who had come at Joseph with a knife in some wretched tenement back in New York.

He had shot at her, in self-defense, and the bullet had passed through the baby and into the mother, killing her, sending the madwoman to wherever her child already was. But when Joseph had thought he had shot the baby, it had been the worst moment of his life. The feeling would never fully leave him, and now, crouching among these cases, filled with children who had never had a chance to live free of agony, the feeling came flooding back. He felt guilty, sick, and empty, and the thought occurred to him that maybe the Prisoner had been able to speak to him inside his head because he was evil, because he was a man who would shoot a child to protect himself.

The Mutter Museum lost all its interest and novelty, and he stood and walked up the steps and through the exhibits, his eyes on the carpet to avoid the evidences of mortality.

Outside on the street, the early autumn day had grown chilly, and he shivered and took several deep breaths of cool air, then started walking back toward the safe house. He had thought he might be able to clear his head of some of the things that were bothering him, all the questions and enigmas

7

yet to be explained. But the questions weren't nearly as bad as the guilt that he had hoped to forget. It hung around his neck like a dead albatross, so viciously demanding that he didn't even notice the man following him until he had walked several blocks.

The man was on the other side of the street, twenty yards behind Joseph. He was carrying a shopping bag for cover, but he couldn't hide the posture and attitude indigenous to feds. Despite the leather jacket and jeans, the man was a little too upright, alert in more than a street-smart way.

Once he had made him, Joseph tried not to notice him any more. The man didn't want just Joseph, he wanted all three of them, so he wouldn't try and pounce on his prey until he reached its den. And then it could get very ugly.

Three rogue CIA agents working inside the United States, agents who had capped an FBI man when he'd tried to arrest them in their illegal activities, agents who had been at the scene when Michael LaPierre had begun his unsuccessful war against the government. No, definitely not a scenario the ops wanted to get in the middle of.

And Langley wouldn't want them there, either. Skye would let them twist in the wind. Rogues. Outlaws. Not pretty, but it happened, despite the best efforts of the agency.

Hell, maybe he was just being paranoid. Maybe the guy was just an Al Gore–type wooden stiff who just happened to be walking in the same direction as Joseph.

And maybe not. Paranoia could be your friend. It had saved a lot of lives over the years, including his own a couple of times. No reason to doubt it now.

Joseph turned right at the corner, taking the man away from the safe house. The man followed about as innocently as a pit bull ripping open a cat. Joseph smiled to himself. He would take no more turns until he was ready to lose the man for good.

A possibility presented itself after he had gone another few blocks. A covered alley ran down between two townhouses, and Joseph, not changing his pace, entered it. It could have been a dead end, but instead it cut across to the next street.

He darted through and found himself on a street with a number of small shops. He quickly entered a coffee shop, sat near the back, where he could still see through the window, and watched as the man following him trotted by, glancing around as he ran. Joseph ordered a sandwich and coffee, and spent a half hour over his modest meal.

The man was nowhere in sight when Joseph stepped back onto the street. He started walking away from the safe house. Several blocks later, when he felt sure no one was following him, he flagged a cab and had it drop him off seven blocks north and two west of the apartment, and walked the rest of the way back.

When he got there, Tony was in the kitchen cooking home-made cheese ravioli and Laika was at one of a row of three computers on a long table against the living room wall. They both took the time to greet him. "You're pretty late," Laika said. "I was starting to worry." A smile of concern creased the café au lait skin of her face.

"Not me," Tony said, coming in from the kitchen. The full chef's apron he wore made his stocky frame look even more solid. "I just figured you'd gotten all wrapped up in those stiffs and pickled body parts. You've got strange tastes, Joseph."

"Somebody tailed me," he said without preamble.

"What?" said Laika, rising. Tony's face grew equally grim.

"I lost him. He picked me up outside the museum. I think he might have been a fed. At least, he moved like it."

"You led him away?" Tony asked.

"Of course. He was easy to lose. I just nested for a while, and he was gone."

"You're sure?" Tony asked. Joseph gave him a look. With over twenty years in the Company, he knew when he had lost a tail. "Okay, sorry." Tony shook his head as though he wished he hadn't said anything.

"One or tandem?" asked Laika, and Joseph held up a single finger. "That's good. Maybe he stumbled onto you then, recognized you. They've got to have our photos out there. Eyes only for field agents, in the hopes that one of them gets lucky."

"Like Brian Foster did out west," Tony said. It was the name of the man he had had to kill. "So you think the town's gonna be crawling with agents by tomorrow?"

Laika looked thoughtful. "How close was the guy to you?"

"Twenty yards away," Joseph said. "He may have been closer when he made me, though."

"Young guy? Or old?"

"Pretty fresh-faced. Looked right out of Quantico."

"He'll report it, then," said Tony.

Laika shook her head. "I doubt it. If he could've tracked you down, he would've, but odds are he lucked onto you. Then his luck changed. He probably doesn't feel positive enough about his ID to report that he found you and lost you. It'd make him look bad, and why risk that if he's not sure it's you to start with?"

"So what do we do?" Tony asked.

"We stay put," Laika said. "But we'll report the incident to Skye. If he wants to relocate us, he can. But this is a big city, and he picked you up a couple miles from here. Let's just stay away from that part of town from now on."

Tony headed back toward the kitchen. "Suits me. I never wanted to see any babies in jars anyway."

Joseph felt Laika's gaze on him, as hard as hail. "You okay?"

"Yeah. Just tired. Think I'll lie down a little bit before dinner." Joseph went into his bedroom and sat on the bed. It was after six o'clock, and the sky outside was lit only by the lights of the city. He left the blinds open and lay down, looking out at the sky from which all the stars had been washed by the millions of bulbs that shone from the earth below.

He closed his eyes, and felt the albatross again, pushing down on him, its weight made heavier by the mysteries he could not explain and by his being a fugitive in his own country. Although he doubted he could sleep, only minutes passed before he was dreaming.

He dreamed of darkness, thick, dense, cloying. He was breathing it, aspirating the black, and it felt gummy, tarry in his lungs. His eyes tried to pierce it but it was no use. He could see nothing except the flashes, fire against velvet, within his eyeballs.

Joseph brought up his hands, and they pressed against soft cloth, with hardness behind, like the lining of a heavy box, and he knew that it was a *buried alive* dream. He had had them before, and although the inability to breathe easily was disquieting, he was not afraid, for he *knew* it was a dream, and that nothing bad would happen to him in reality.

Still, for the life of him, he couldn't remember *where* he was sleeping. Was it one of those damned motels out west? The apartment where he had lived in New York City while they were investigating the death of the sculptor? But no, that was long ago. His townhouse in Alexandria? Hell no. That was even longer ago, when he worked at Langley. Oh Christ, that must have been a hundred years or more.

Or was it over a hundred years since he had been lying in this casket?—yes, that was it. He had been in here for centuries, sealed inside and buried down under the earth, and it was goddamned well time that he got out. He *had* to get out. He didn't know why, but it was important, not just to him, but to others, too—to Laika? Tony? He remembered them all right. So if he was going to get out, he was going to have to yell, just scream as loud as he could, like that screaming woman in the Ray Bradbury story, the one the little girl heard screaming under the ground. Maybe a little girl would hear and go get help, someone to dig his casket up and open it and let him out.

So Joseph screamed. Inside his dream, he yelled and shouted and called to whoever might be standing over his grave. He screamed, and the blackness that rolled down from his nose and clogged his throat spewed from his mouth with

the words, incomprehensible even to him. The sounds were
the shrieks of his soul, the demands of a prisoner, held long
and hard against his will.

Laika and Joseph did not hear them, but someone else did.

Chapter 3

*T*om Kerr came from a long line of treasure hunters. Eight generations of his ancestors had been ship salvagers as well as sheep men. *Ships 'n' sheeps* was how his father, Old Tom, had always put it. But things had changed precipitously for his son, who was still addressed as *Young* Tom, although he was sixty and his father had been in the ground for twenty years.

Young Tom Kerr still hunted treasure, all right, but there were no more ships to salvage off Scotland's rough western coast. Ships hardly ever sank anymore, and if they did, the salvage laws had changed drastically. Gone were the stormy nights when the Kerrs prayed for the failure of the lighthouse at Rubha Reigh.

The current Tom Kerr did his treasure hunting with a White Eagle Spectrum metal detector. He didn't find trunks of goods the way his fathers had, but he did find his share of coinage, some of it dating back to the fifteenth century. He had also found metal cups, tools, and on one occasion, the blade of an authentic claymore that Dr. Byrne over in Ullapool said was old enough to have belonged to Robert the Bruce himself.

While Tom sold most of the coins he found to a dealer in Inverness, he kept much of the other booty for himself, and had a nice little collection of artifacts that nearly filled the shed behind the sheep barn. His wife occasionally complained about the "rusty rubbish" that Tom had accumulated, but because the money from the coins he found nearly equaled the amount they made from crofting, she never pressed it.

Tom didn't usually hunt at night, but he didn't want to be seen on this jaunt. He had learned in some old books in the Gairloch Library that there had been a small village back in the seventeenth century, half a kilometer east of Castle Dirk, and there was no place to find coins and artifacts like the site of an abandoned village.

The problem was that the area was within the property owned by Mr. Scobie, the never-seen landlord of the castle. Tom's wife had said that Scobie probably was ashamed to show his face, owning a castle with a name like that. It was true, it was a stupid name. Most castles were named for the families or clans who owned or had owned them, and others were named for Gaelic place names. But Castle Dirk? It sounded like something invented by a boys' book writer. Why not Castle Adamant, or Castle Braw? Castle Dirk, indeed.

Yet maybe it wasn't Scobie's fault. The castle had borne that ridiculous name ever since Young Tom could remember, and he knew that Old Tom never called it by any other. Still, Scobie, whoever he was, should have changed it to something more Scottish. Even Castle Scobie would have been an improvement.

It seemed in pretty sad shape. Tom had heard it had been built in the late fourteenth century, but nearly all of the outer curtain and its towers had fallen, and most of the stones had been hauled away for use elsewhere. The inner curtain, the wall that surrounded the castle's apartments and the inner ward, was mostly still erect, however. It appeared to measure fifty meters wide on each side and ten meters high. Tom recalled when the castle was partly reconstructed when he was a boy. Even from a distance one could see the difference in the color of the stone used in the newer sections.

Some of the workmen had told him about the castle, and had filled his head with stories of the ghosts that were reputed to haunt it. Most of them were joking, he thought, but one night he heard Robbie Douglas telling Old Tom that he had really seen something one day at dusk when he was the last to leave the work site. He said it looked like a white robed figure with a face so smooth there were hardly any features to it at all. It glowed and seemed to hover just above the ground, looking at him. Then it disappeared in a wink. Old Tom told Robbie he'd had too early a start on his evening's drams, but Robbie swore he hadn't touched a drop, and what he'd seen, he'd seen.

His story was enough to give Young Tom nightmares for a week. When he'd finally told his father about overhearing the tale, Old Tom had scoffed and told him there weren't any such things as ghosts, and he should know. While salvaging, he and his had robbed the dead themselves, washed up on the shore, and never a bogle had haunted his house or his dreams afterward.

That had made an impression on Young Tom, and he had never seen a ghost himself, though many times he had hunted around graveyards and ruins where they were reputed to dwell. So he had no fear of any ghosts in the vicinity of Castle Dirk, nor was he afraid of being seen by the caretaker, who went into Gairloch once every two weeks for supplies and was never seen outside the castle walls at any other time.

What did make Tom hesitate was the fear of getting caught trespassing by the local constabulary. Inspector Molly Fraser had been with the district police for three years now, and she seemed to have an uncanny nose for sniffing out lawbreakers. She was a handsome woman in her early forties, originally from Torridon, but had spent her youth down in London, doing what nobody knew, though some folks said it was government work.

Still, the odds of getting hobbled by her tonight were as long as they were that he'd actually find anything, digging around in the dark. A fine, misty rain was starting to fall, and that would help to curtain his light from the road two hundred meters away, should anyone actually pass by at eleven o'clock.

Tom Kerr walked through the drizzle until he reached what he figured was the site of the old village. As far as he could determine, this land had never been crofted, and he wondered just what it was that whoever had lived in Castle Dirk had done with the land around them. As far as he could see, it was just brush and gorse, dotted by the occasional tree. All the better, he thought, that no ploughs had ripped up the soil, and plunged whatever treasures he might find even deeper.

He turned the dials to no discrimination, which meant that the machine would alert him if it detected anything at all metallic. Then, since he could not see the display in the darkness, he slipped on the headphones whose varying tones would tell him when the machine scored a hit. Tom kept the flashlight off and moved slowly, as he always did when he searched, sweeping the big platter of the machine scarcely an inch from the ground.

Five minutes later, he got his first sound. He could tell it was something small, a coin, he hoped, from pinpointing the tiny area which yielded the sound. He set down his machine and stuck his probe, a thin, eight-inch awl with a wooden handle, into the ground at the sweet spot. He moved it up and down in the earth until he felt the gentle contact of the point with metal. Then he turned on his flashlight and dug with his small one-handed shovel.

The moist ground was soft, and four inches down he uncovered a nail. It was worthless, but it was a carpenter's nail, not a horseshoe nail, and from its shape he knew that it was eighteenth-century or earlier. At least he seemed to be on the right track.

In the next half hour, he found innumerable pieces of ironmongery, but also turned up three coins from the era of the Stuarts, and another example of Tudor coinage. He also found the heavy iron head of a blacksmith's hammer, and what he suspected were the surviving parts of a brace, the handle and bit having long vanished.

It was nearly midnight when the tone in the earphones began again and continued to sound, even when he swung the detector in a foot-wide swath. There was something big here, larger than a coin or an ax head. And then the other sound crept through his earphones and into his head.

It lasted for only a second, but Tom could have sworn that the steady beeping tone of the metal detector twisted into a human voice, a man's voice that screamed so loudly Tom staggered. He yanked off the earphones and shone his flashlight all around, certain that someone had just shouted nearby. But the only sound was the soft patter of raindrops on the earth, and not a soul was in sight.

Ghosts? he thought. But then he shook his head. Ghosts were for gowks, and bogles were bull shite. It had been his imagination, that was all, or maybe the machine had malfunctioned. Tentatively he brought one of the earphones back to his right ear, swung the machine over the place that had sounded before, and listened.

There now. Just a good, strong, steady tone, the way it should be. His imagination then, nothing more. Relieved, he set down the machine and knelt on the wet earth. No need to probe, he thought. He was bound to hit whatever was buried here.

He dug, trying to be patient, not to go too fast or thrust the blade of the tool in too violently. Doing so could scratch soft metal like gold, or break whatever the metal that had sounded might be attached to.

He was eight inches down now, and still there was nothing. But he kept digging. He wouldn't have gotten a strong sound like that for nothing.

Finally, at a little more than a foot in depth, the blade scraped a rough surface. Tom shone his light down into the hole and began to clear the dirt away. His heart jumped in his chest when he saw what he had found.

It was a box, nearly a foot long and nine inches wide. It was made of a dark wood, and brass fittings covered the four corners that Tom could see. He cleared the earth around it, and saw that a padlock was slipped through a brass hasp. There was no need for it. The nails that had held the hasp had loosened, and he easily pulled off the lock and hasp.

Tom knew that he should wait, should get the entire box

out of the ground before he opened it. But he couldn't. Here it was, begging to be opened, begging for hundreds of years. He wouldn't make it wait any longer.

He held the flashlight with one hand, and brushed as much dirt away from the edges of the box as he could, so that it wouldn't fall in when he opened it. But when he tried to lift the lid, he discovered that it was somehow sealed around the edges with a soft gray substance.

Lead.

All right then. He'd dig it up and chisel it open.

Getting the box onto the surface took another fifteen minutes of digging, as it proved to be nearly a foot high. But at last he lifted it from the hole, and was surprised and alarmed at the feel of it. It seemed heavy enough, but there was no mass to it, and the thought of it being filled with coins and jewels was fast vanishing. Still, there must be something of value inside. Why would anyone bury an empty box?

The flashlight he had set on the ground illuminated the box as he scraped away the lead from around its edges, the bits falling off like strips of putty from weather-worn windows. When there was enough lead chiseled away, Tom opened the lid.

Inside was something made of cloth, pale yellow in color, the threads glistening metallically. Loosely woven silk, Tom thought. But then, what made it glisten so? And what did it conceal?

He carefully folded back the first layer of cloth, but there was only more of the garment, if that was what the thing was. He pressed on it, but felt nothing beneath but a yielding mass of fabric. Still, he peeled back every layer, just in case.

No. Nothing but the cloth. He stood up, holding it, looking down into the now empty chest, feeling somehow betrayed. Well, he thought, the cloth seemed to be in decent shape for all its time below ground. Being sealed up had probably helped. There couldn't be many cloths this old that had survived so nicely.

He began to open it up, and was further disappointed to

find that it wasn't any type of garment, but seemed rather to be a blanket or coverlet, a meter wide and two long. What was worse, there was a large piece missing from the one corner. Grand. There went any real collector's value.

Tom shook the thing out the way his wife did when she was shaking the dust out of blankets, first up and down, then side to side, as though he were waving a flag. He saw no dust come from it in the flashlight's glare. It had been sealed up well.

He gathered it in his arms again, and bent down to put it back into the chest, thinking that maybe he could get some money for the container, if not for what it contained. It was a strange box, brass cased, but lined with some dark material. He scraped a fingernail across it and guessed, from the softness and weight of it, that it was lead, the same metal that had sealed the damned thing.

Tom had just closed the lid, turned off his flashlight, and picked up the box when he heard a gentle voice speak to him from out of the darkness.

"Nice soft night, eh, Tom?"

Chapter 4

Tom Kerr's heart jumped up into his throat, and he felt the hair stand on the back of his neck. He froze, afraid to turn around. Then a light hit him from behind, and he knew it was no ghost, but something that inspired even more fear. He turned, and in the bright flashlight's peripheral glow, he saw the round and lovely face of Inspector Molly Fraser. Her head was cocked to one side, and she was smiling like a mither who's caught her son at the sweets jar. Her long brown hair seemed to pour out from under the knit tartan tam she wore.

"Aye, Inspector," Tom stammered. "A wee bit cold, though."

"And what've you got there, Tom?" The inspector shined her light on the box he was holding. "An old box? And what's in it?"

"Oh, just an auld cloot, that's all."

"Mmm-hmm. Let's have a look." Tom opened the box, and held it toward her so she could see. She shined her light on it, then turned it off. "A strange old cloth, though, Tom— you've got to admit that. Aren't many cloths that glow in the dark, are there?"

Tom looked down. He had always had a light on the cloth before, but now that it was in darkness, he saw that it was indeed glowing dimly, with the same pale yellow color. He was so startled he almost dropped it, and the first thing that came into his mind was the childish fancy that it might be a fairy cloth.

"And what's that lining the box, Tom?"

"I think it's lead, Inspector."

Molly Fraser looked at the bit of lead lying on the ground. "Sealed with lead, too, was it?" Tom nodded. "You know what lead does, Tom?" He looked at her dully. "For one thing, it doesn't allow radioactivity to pass through it," she said. "Now you've got something glowing there in a box that's lined and sealed with lead, Tom. What might that lead you to think?"

His eyes grew wide and he slammed the box lid shut, set it quickly on the ground, and backed away from it. "Do you . . . do you think I'm all right?" he asked her, thinking of all the horror stories of what large doses of radiation could do.

"Don't know, Tom. Did you handle it?"

"Well, I . . . I took it out, shook it, opened it up—you don't think . . . ?"

She shrugged. "You might have taken a pretty strong dose, Tom. I suggest you have the doc take a look at you. I'd better take that box with me. And you'd better fill in that hole. You're on private ground here, you know. At least I *assume* you know, otherwise you'd have been here during daylight. Am I right?"

"Uh, yes, ma'am . . . Inspector."

"Now I won't cite you, Tom, but I will confiscate that box, and whatever else you've found out here. So come on, carry it over to my car."

Tom picked up the box gingerly and held it at arm's length during the long walk to the Inspector's little English Ford. There, he put it in the boot, and handed over the coins and tools he had found. "Give you a lift back to your car, Tom?"

He looked skittishly at the closed boot lid and shook his head. "No thanks, mum. I'm fine."

"All right then. Stay off private land from now on, you hear? Next time you'll visit the magistrate."

Molly Fraser put her car into gear and pulled out onto the one-lane road. Between her threat and the radiation scare, she doubted Tom Kerr would be digging the castle's land anytime soon.

She had been out tonight, driving the lonely roads of the Gairloch peninsula, for the usual reasons. She couldn't rest, and figured she might as well tend to her flock as sit in her cottage and stew. Ninety-nine nights out of a hundred, she found nothing amiss, but when she had seen a quick flicker of light far across the fields, she'd known something was afoot. The old caretaker of Castle Dirk never would have been abroad at midnight.

Sure enough, Young Tom Kerr was scavenging again, this time on private property. At least he hadn't been on any land held by the National Trust. Then she would have had to hobble him sure.

She had already caught a few people hunting for treasure over at the Mellangaun Stones, on the eastern side of the peninsula. When she'd found them, they hadn't uncovered a thing except for some modern coins and ginger beer can tabs. Still, she'd had to arrest them.

No worries about the Stones now, though. There was an archeological bunch up from Edinburgh University doing a full dig all around the stone circle, and about time, too, Molly thought. Though not as impressive as Callanish, the Mellangaun Stones still had the power to awe. The stones, like those at Callanish on the Isle of Lewis, were sharp edged, alarmingly vertical stone teeth, canines as opposed to the ground-down molars of most stone circles.

It was to these university nobs that she would take the box in the morning, along with the tools and coins. Mr. Scobie of Castle Dirk had no claim upon them, for they were now archeological treasures, property of the government. She wondered what they would say about the cloth. It probably wasn't at all dangerous, as she had led Tom Kerr to believe. She knew that all things luminescent gave off some sort of radioactivity, but most at very low levels. Still, why had the thing been sealed in lead?

It might, she thought, be something that her old bosses in

MI5 might be interested in. Then she dismissed the thought. After all, she had come on her drive to forget MI5. God, it was hard enough. Nearly fifteen years she had spent in the British Security Service, coming in under Sir John Jones and leaving with relief after Mrs. Rimington's tenure as director-general had ended.

The game had changed too much for Molly's taste. The great majority of the service's resources were spent combatting counterterrorism. The divisions in which Molly had gained her expertise, counterespionage and countersubversion, had become, with the downfall of Soviet communism, poor relatives. Although an official statement from MI5 in 1993 said, ". . . the old threat no longer exists, but it is equally true that spying continues," you'd never have known it from Molly's assignments.

In 1996, when Stephen Lander took over from Mrs. Rimington, the writing was on the wall. Lander had previously been MI5's director of Irish counterterrorism, and had every intention of expanding his war against the IRA and its splinter groups, using every MI5 resource available to him.

Molly Fraser did not share his passion. Although she was appalled by the renewed spate of IRA bombings that had so incensed Lander, her heart was in espionage. When they asked her to go undercover, using her gift for dialects and her red-cheeked cherubic face to pose as Irish and work her way into a cell, she declined, and then turned in her resignation.

Though Molly did not approve the tactics of the IRA, neither could she bring herself to fight against them. There was more kinship between her and them than language, however; they'd had their country stolen as well.

Ten years before she might have done it, but those ten years had been spent in the pursuit of, among other things, history, the history of not only the Irish and the English, but the Scottish as well. Though she had known the history of her homeland, she had learned it from an English perspective. When she looked at it from a purely Scottish point of view, it became a scenario in which one country had used its superior

military strength and numbers to first conquer and then sub-
due a proud and noble land, then allied itself with the greed-
iest natives by promising wealth for those few in return for
obeisance from all.

Over the years, she had learned how England had used the
Scots. They had used the technological brilliance of the finest
Scottish minds, and sent their English dullards to Scottish
universities; they had formed Scottish regiments of the brav-
est soldiers in the empire, and then marched them into
cannons' mouths or set them upon native peoples in Africa
and Asia, allowing the conquered to conquer, but only for
their English masters; they had taken the resources of the
North Sea, and allowed only a small portion of those billions
from suboceanic black gold to filter back to Scotland.

The more she read and the more she learned, the louder
the songs of English betrayal and domination rang in her ears:
Falkirk, Glencoe, Culloden, the highland clearances. True,
they had happened centuries before, but present-day Scots
were still living with the results of their ancestors' defeats
and deprivations. If she, as a Scot, felt this resentment, how
much greater anger then would the Irish feel, with England's
far more recent injustices toward them?

So she had resigned. The director of counterespionage had
offered to clear her way into MI6, the foreign intelligence
service, but Molly had politely declined. She had had enough
of the government. She did accept his offer, however, to assist
her in finding the police job that she sought in her native
Scotland.

As luck would have it, there was a chief inspector's opening in the Gairloch district on Scotland's northwestern shore,
not far from her hometown of Torridon. The pay wasn't
much, but with her MI5 pension she didn't need much. The
director had provided her with an unbreakable résumé, which
included police experience in London and Australia, as well
as exemplary letters of recommendation from several highly
placed police officials in London and Sydney.

In the three years she had been living in Gairloch, she had

come to love the job and the people. There were hardly any acts of violence except for the occasional pub brawl, and few major larcenies. The primary crimes were petty thefts and vandalism, most of which she and her two deputy inspectors were able to solve readily enough.

Her mother and father still lived in Torridon, and she spent many of the weekends she wasn't working with them, helping around their house. The modest needs of her love life were met by Alan Keith, a fifty-year-old widower who owned a gift shop in Gairloch, and whom she dined with, and afterward circumspectly slept with, every few weeks. All in all, it was a pretty boring life, and extremely satisfying, although every now and then Molly hoped for just a little excitement.

Maybe, she thought, the glowing cloth in the boot would provide a little interest.

The first ghost was seen the next day. At six o'clock in the morning, the driver of a delivery truck on his way to Melvaig ran off the B8021 and got stuck in a ditch. When the tow truck arrived to pull him out and the garageman asked what had caused him to slide off the road, the driver said that he had seen a glowing white shape floating above the roadway, like a man without a face.

It didn't take long for the story to spread down to Gairloch, where the young people laughed at it and the older ones frowned. A ghost made more sense, thought the elders, than blaming it on drink at the crack of dawn.

They were proved right quickly enough. A crofter came into the pub in town that evening, anxious to tell his tale. He claimed he had been looking for a lost ewe, and was driving her back from the steep gully in which he had found her, when he heard a sound like the wail of a woman, and when he looked behind him, he saw, only a few feet away, but a foot or two in the air, the figure of a woman in a long white dress. She had a face like something out of a nightmare, all smooth and almost featureless, and her arms were reaching out for him.

When he finally got over his shock and knew that he could move, he left that ewe in his dust, but she came running along behind him until they had both outdistanced that bogle. And the funny thing was, he finished, it was broad daylight, the sun shining, for a change, as bright as you please.

The crofter was believed, since his description pretty well matched the truck driver's, and the crofter hadn't been in town to hear the driver's story. But what kind of ghost, the drinkers wondered, would show itself in daylight?

That night, four people discovered that the ghost or ghosts had no exclusivity on sunshine, nor did they seem to be limited to certain places. A fisherman on Loch Ewe, bringing his dory in at dusk, saw a luminescent humanoid shape fifty feet in the air above the waters of the loch. It too had no discernible face, but the fisherman continued to watch instead of flee, and swore that he saw the shape rise higher into the air until it vanished. "Soared up like an angel," he said. "I wasnae a bit afraid of it."

A hiker and his wife from Glasgow who were planning to spend the night on the gentle summit of Cnoc Breac changed their minds when a throbbing sound awakened them shortly after midnight, and more gleaming shapes than they could count seemed to be standing all around them before they vanished into the trees. When they told their story later, the husband said they looked like ghosts, but the wife held out for aliens, "Like in that *Close Encounters*, *wee* fellas."

And in Kenley House, her Gairloch bed and breakfast, Mrs. Ross was helping a young English boy's parents to clean up him and her carpet after he'd wakened in the middle of the night and thrown up the lovely salmon, brown potatoes, and carrots she had cooked them for supper, along with three helpings of raisin pudding. She was taking the sodden paper towels out to the rubbish can in the alley, when two shapes appeared on either side of her, "Burning like hell's fires," she said later. She screamed, and fainted dead away, for the first time in her life. When she came to, the only detail she could remember was that "They didn't have faces ... not proper faces, anyway."

Chapter 5

When Chief Inspector Fraser heard the next morning about the multiple hauntings, her first thought was to attribute it to a hoax. So she and Ian and Kevin, her Deputy Inspectors, set out to visit some of the locals who specialized in such shenanigans, but found all of them sincerely puzzled about what had happened.

When she got back to her office in the late afternoon, there was a message on the machine: "This is Martin Leech calling for Inspector Fraser," the man said. He then gave a number and requested she call back.

Now, what the hell was this all about? Martin Leech had joined MI5 several years before Molly'd left. He had been very unlike his name, a gentle young man eager to learn, and to serve his queen and country. A bit *over*eager, she had thought, like a puppy rather than a leech.

Then she thought about the possibility that his call might have something to do with the glowing cloth she had confiscated from Tom Kerr. The day before, she had driven over to the Mellangaun Stones and given the box and cloth to a Dr. Ewing, the head of the dig, but had cautioned him that it was glowing and might be radioactive. He had tentatively identified the box as fourteenth-century, and had said that he would send it directly to the university for examination. Molly had asked that she be informed of whatever was learned about the cloth, and Dr. Ewing had promised her she would be. But what, she wondered, might MI5 have to do with it? And so quickly, too?

She dialed the number, identified herself, and was put through to Leech. "Molly," he said. "How are things in Scotland?" His voice sounded jovial enough, but she sensed an undertone of tension.

"Fine, Martin, just fine. So tell me, is this about the cloth?"

There was a moment of silence, then a small laugh. "I'm sure your detection skills are proving useful up there. Yes, it *is* about the cloth. They called us from Edinburgh University just about an hour ago. For the past twenty-four hours they've been mucking about with this blanket or cloth or whatever it is, and they've found some rather . . . amazing things. It is indeed radioactive, and it seems to have been inside the box for the past five hundred years, at least. Now, I don't pretend to understand all this scientific terminology, but the gist of it is that at first they thought it was emitting gamma rays, because the electromagnetic waves had a very short wavelength. Apparently these gamma rays are very dangerous, but when they did whatever they do to measure this sort of thing, they found that they *weren't* gamma rays, because they didn't seem to harm . . . oh, what's the word? . . ."

"Ionize," Molly said.

"Yes, *ionize* any atoms. And they found something else very odd indeed. Gamma rays travel at the speed of light. *These* rays, well, they tested again and again, and far as they could determine, these travel . . . *faster* than light."

"That's impossible, isn't it?"

"Apparently not. There are these things called tachyons that they believe might exist that go faster than light and can't be slowed down, but nobody's found them. Yet."

"If they can't be slowed down, how could lead contain them?"

There was silence for a moment. "I don't know. Maybe they just bounced around faster than light inside the box. I'm not really a scientist, Molly, and I don't pretend to understand everything that I've heard today, but that's about the gist of it.''

Bull shite, Molly thought. There was more to come. Leech wouldn't have spilled all these secrets otherwise. She waited, and Leech spoke again.

"Now, all this is very top secret, of course. But the reason I'm telling you is because we need your cooperation."

"In what way?"

"Well, if these tachyons could be found and somehow harnessed, it would change the history of the world . . . or of communication, anyway. Imagine, instantaneous communication to anywhere in the universe. There's a feather in the cap for England, eh? Now, the cloth came from the area in which you're CI, and you'd sniff out an MI5 investigation as soon as one of us popped up his head. So the powers that be figured it would be better to have you with us from the start. And let's face it, we *know* that there's no security risk involved with bringing you onto the team."

"Wait a moment, Martin. What do you mean, 'onto the team'? I resigned from MI5, you know. Not retired, *resigned.*"

"We understand that. You would merely be our local police liaison, but you would assist us in maintaining our cover."

"Which is?"

"An archeological team. To all intents and purposes, we'll be part of the group from the university that's over at . . . Mellangaun Stones, is it? We intend to investigate the area where this artifact was found. And at the same time anything else of a suspicious nature that may crop up."

Molly thought about the three alleged ghosts that had been reported. "You might have your plate full in that department," she said, and told him about the sightings.

"No worries," Martin replied. "Just sounds like the usual backwater foolishness. No offense intended."

"None taken. When will you arrive?"

"It'll take a week to get the team together and the bona

fides all in place. Needless to say, this is for your ears only. Not a word to anyone about our teams' connection to MI5, not even to your friend Mr. Keith, yes?''

She didn't respond to the slight teasing in Leech's voice. Of course they would still know everything about her. Once you were in MI5, you never fully left their surveillance. "Of course not," she said shortly. "I *have* learned to keep a secret, Martin."

"Right then. We'll be in touch."

Martin Leech and MI5 were not the only things to be in touch. Within a half hour after she hung up the phone, she had received four more reports of sightings during that day and the night before of ghosts or aliens or spirits. Molly Fraser was pretty much a staunch materialist. Still, she had seen her share of horror movies on the telly, and the thought naturally came to her of that creaky plot of the reemergence of something that should remain in the ground, and its cursed aftermath.

The thought left her as quickly as it had come. Whatever was happening with the unearthed cloth, it smacked of science. And as for the purported ghosts, fraud was still the most likely answer. After all, the work of the crop circle hoaxers might have been considered alien for decades had they not come forward and shown how it had been done. The ghosts were probably nothing more than a well-organized bunch of scrub footballers looking for a cheap laugh.

Besides, why would ghosts bother to show themselves and scare crofters and housewives and truckers? Just for the fun of it? It was too preposterous. Surely ghosts would want more than that.

He wanted blood. But not the small amounts that had flowed from the individuals he had met while wandering in the desert. It had at least been entertaining, however, when he'd come across backpackers and hikers. Of the half dozen he had confronted, there were only two of them whom he had not been able to control.

Fortunately, one of them was a man hiking with his wife, and the woman had been all too susceptible to his desires. She had attacked her husband with the strength of the madwoman that she temporarily was, and had torn clean down to the jugular with her teeth. Then she had taken out a folding knife and disemboweled herself, precisely the way in which he had requested of her.

The other person whom he had met had been untouchable, his mind as impregnable as if there had been a foot thick layer of lead between them. Ah well, he had thought, as he'd smashed the man's head into a pulp with a rock, sometimes blood *didn't* tell. Actively killing wasn't nearly as rewarding as directing the mayhem, but it had to be done. He couldn't let the man go and tell of meeting a wanderer in the desert who looked like Jesus and was dressed like John the Baptist.

But he was bored, this creature who had been known by many names. The Roman Catholic Church had called him the Antichrist; a motley assortment of pilgrims seeking truth, power, and self-justification had proclaimed him the Divine, the Holy One, and the Lord; and Laika Harris, Joseph Stein, and Tony Luciano referred to him only as the Prisoner, the one behind the disappearance of a sculptor in New York and the dehydrated bodies in the desert. They had come close to finding him in New York, and were tracking him down in Utah, only to be outdistanced by Michael LaPierre, who, in releasing the Prisoner from the lead-lined Anasazi kiva, let the bestial genie out of his bottle, and died for his efforts.

It was good to be free at last, the Prisoner thought, after so many centuries of captivity. But he had wandered enough. This world's only true charms were the billions of intelligent creatures that bestrode it, creatures that he could anger to violence, and watch as they tore each other apart. What he had been doing was like stepping on ants when he could, with the proper planning and aid, raven cities, and turn countries against each other until this world ran red with the blood that flowed in its inhabitants' veins.

But he could not do it alone. There had to be others that

he would control, those who would take the risks and orga-
nize the chaos, while he sat back and relished the sights and
sounds of carnage, until the red madness that had exiled him
here had spread like a plague among the dwellers of earth.

And those who would most easily fall under his control
were those who sought him. Most of them were willing to be
disciples in exchange for the power he could give them, like
Swain, whose ability to touch the Prisoner's mind, even
through his lead prison, had been far greater than most humans.

Swain, however, was dead. He had died, and yet the Prisoner's hold over him was so strong that he had called him
from his sandy grave and Swain had come, though he had
been useless to the Prisoner, a fat corpse bloated with other
men's fluids. It was a pity to lose such a potentially powerful
ally.

The only human in recent years who'd surpassed Swain's
talent of mental contact with the Prisoner was the man Stein,
to whom the Prisoner had appeared in dreams. His strength
was formidable, and the Prisoner knew the blood must be
strong in the man. But unlike Swain, there was no desire to
worship in Stein. There was fear and denial, but also great
knowledge, knowledge the Prisoner could use if he could persuade—or force—Stein to join him. If he could not, then he
would destroy Stein.

Stein, however, was far away. East. It was a great distance,
and the Prisoner wondered if there were any others closer who
had been searching for him, for good or ill. If there were, he
should seek them out. If they proved to be allies, that would
be beneficial. But if they wished to find him to destroy him,
then he would destroy them, were he not able to bend them
to his will.

He reached out then, with the tentacles of his probing mind,
trying to find not those whom he could contact, but those
who wished to contact him. If they were untouchable by his
mind, if the blood link was weak or nonexistent, they would

remain unknown to him. But if the link was there, and their desire was strong, then he would know.

The Prisoner felt her. She was the foolish one, the one who had the strength to reach him but not the strength of will necessary to accomplish it. Swain's sister.

He had known that she and others were seeking him after Swain died, and he had called to her, but she had heard his shouts as if they were a whisper from the bottom of a great canyon. Still, she was the closest of those who had sought him, so he would go to her and find what power she had, to whom she was bound on this earth, and if she would be an effective partner in his reign of terror.

Effective, if temporary. Eventually, all would die. His purpose was nothing more nor less than universal destruction.

He did not have the patience to breed humans so that he might enjoy their torments and deaths indefinitely. If he could, he would rather destroy everything now, and then live alone in misery on a world empty of all but himself.

He could not help it. It was his nature.

Chapter 6

Jezebel Swain sat alone in her cell, grinding her teeth and scratching her arms. It was the same damn thing all the time, just sit and stare at the goddamn walls, and wait and wait and wait. And then, every few days, one of those bastards in white would come and take her to see Dr. Ross again, and the sonofabitch would talk to her and ask her the same dumbass questions, and she would tell him the truth and he would shake his head and look sad and ask her again, and then she would get pissed off and tell him to go to hell and then start to scratch her arms again.

She was up to her arms now, because she had scratched the backs of her hands and her wrists raw already, and they were bandaged up. But she had to scratch something, because she couldn't keep her hands still. Dr. Ross had told her that if she continued to hurt herself, they'd have to put her in restraints. Then she would stop, and wait until she got back to her cell, because for Chrissake, she was already restrained *enough*, wasn't she?

She knew what he wanted to hear her say, but she wasn't about to say it. She was going to tell the truth, and she *had* told it, time and again, and it was so simple an idiot *child* could understand it, but they didn't believe her, so they kept her in this *nut*house.

She went over it in her mind again, her closely clipped nails digging at her arms, burrowing in the soft spot inside the bend of her elbow, reddening the flesh. They had been in that Indian roadhouse on the reservation, and those moronic cowboys had started on Damon, who was trying to lead them to the Divine now that Ezekiel had disappeared into the desert. Then Rodney, the big ex-biker who was with them, went for one of the cowboys, and all hell broke loose.

Before she knew what had happened, Jezebel had rammed a shard of glass from a broken sugar container into the throat of a cowboy, killing him deader than dirt. She and Damon had gotten out and driven away, but their van got stuck, and the next thing she knew, Ezekiel, her brother and lover, was there, a mummylike walking corpse, enveloping Damon and somehow sucking all the juice out of him. In a minute, Damon's body was as dried as Ezekiel's had been, and Ezekiel, now full of Damon's fluids, was standing there, looking happy and satisfied, come back to life.

Then the cops had come, or at least some people she *thought* were cops, some black bitch and a white guy. They took Ezekiel and put him in their trunk, along with Damon's body, and told her to say that Damon had run away. That was the story she had told the *other* cops when they came, and they had taken her and charged her with the murder of Arthur Griffith, which was the name of the shit-for-brains cowboy she had stabbed.

For a while, she had given them the story the first cops had told her to tell, but then, after days of being in her cell, she told her court-appointed attorney to go screw himself and gave the authorities the dope on what had actually happened. When none of them believed her, she got a little violent, and then started scratching herself. That was when they'd put her in the nuthouse.

She didn't give a damn, though. Those cops who'd taken Ezekiel away hadn't come back or done shit for her, so why should she tell their bullshit story? And when it came right down to it, the nuthouse was better than the jail. The cells were cleaner, for one thing, and she'd rather be locked up with crazies than with the trash she'd been with in jail.

But Jesus, she *hated* that Dr. Ross. If they let her nails

grow out, which they wouldn't, she'd try and scratch his eyes out. She was already in for murder, so what else could they do to her?

She had just closed her eyes to try and get some sleep when she heard a weird sound, like somebody had ripped a really big piece of cloth. She sat up quickly and opened her eyes, and saw him.

She had never set eyes on the Divine before, nor had she spoken to anyone who had ever seen him, but from the electricity that filled her entire body, she knew this being in front of her could be no one else. He was wearing a loose white shirt and light-colored trousers, and he smiled at her as though he were an angel come down from heaven. A light brown beard wreathed his strong jaw, and his soft hair fell straight down to his shoulders. His unblemished skin was a perfect bronze shade, and his blue eyes looked into hers with a promise of paradise.

"Jezebel," he said, and her name had never sounded more beautiful in her ears. "I've come to free you." Then he held out his hand, and she stood up and put her bandaged right hand into his. There was a further tingle at the contact, and she laughed out loud at the sensation. "Come," he said, and he stepped through the wall.

She didn't pause to wonder at it. Of course the Divine could pass through walls if he wished to. He could do anything, couldn't he? She watched as her hand in his vanished through the white-painted cinderblock wall, and then she just stepped through it as well.

Instantly, there was a feeling of compression. It was as though all the atoms in her body had suddenly shrunk, and the pain was so great as to be beyond the release of a scream. But it lasted for only a moment, and then she and the Divine were standing in a dimly lit hall, and he was leading her down it, and she was moving along with him, the pain gone, but the memory of it still pounding at her mind.

This part of the facility seemed to be deserted. She could hear no screams or moans from inside the rooms they passed.

At the end of the hall, they came to a heavily locked door, but again, the Divine simply passed through its steel surface. Jezebel wanted to try and pull back, but was helpless. Had the Divine walked into flames, she would have gone with him, as long as her hand was in his.

This time the pain was even worse. The steel was far less yielding than the more porous cinderblocks that had walled her cell. As she came out on the other side, she felt shredded, slashed apart, and put back together with will alone.

But they were outside now, and it was the first time she had felt cool night air for many weeks. Or was it months? She had lost all track of time, and the pain she had just experienced muddied her mind even more.

The Divine didn't look back, nor did he acknowledge her pain. He only walked with the certainty of a god toward the back wall of the facility, and then through it, and she followed, her soul screaming one last time at the pain, and then they were through, and a dry plain made silver by moonlight lay before them, as far as Jezebel's burning eyes could see. They continued to walk, the Divine still clinging to her hand. It wasn't as though she was *holding* his hand, or that he was holding hers, but as though they were one creature, half-man, half-woman, joined at the ends of the arms, grafted together so that their hands became one, a shared fusion of flesh.

Although the memory of pain stayed with her, it faded after a time, and she was amazed to find that she did not grow weary as she walked. It was as if her contact with the Divine strengthened her, as though he were an inexhaustible battery from which she drew power through their contact.

They walked all through the night, away from people and buildings and roads, straight into the desert. At last, just as the sun was starting to lighten the eastern horizon, he suddenly stopped, whirled about, and looked at her, his gaze piercing her like a butterfly on a pin. She tried to draw back from the ferocity in his face, but their hands still clung together.

"*Why?*" he said. The power of the single word was like a

slap in her face. Jezebel shook her head, not understanding. The Divine pulled his hand away from hers, and the release left her weak. She staggered and fell to her knees in the dust, her right hand throbbing. But when she looked at it, it appeared unchanged, the bandage still wrapped around it.

"Why did you seek me?" the Divine said, and his voice seemed more gentle.

She tried to think, and then to make her mouth form the words her mind spoke. Everything seemed suddenly, terribly complicated and difficult. "I . . . because . . . you are the *Divine*. Because you know . . . all the secrets. And you have . . . all the power."

"And what power," the Divine said softly, "do *you* have, little one?"

"I . . . I don't know, not much, I mean . . ."

"Are you not involved with a group? The group that Ezekiel Swain led?"

She felt tears pool in her eyes. "Ezekiel's dead . . . they're *all* dead now. I tried to find you after he died, but I couldn't. Then I . . . then everything fell apart."

"You are his sister, yet you couldn't find me? The blood should have been strong. His blood was your blood, yes?"

She shook her head dumbly, trying to explain. "My mother was Ezekiel's father's second wife. I was born after they were married."

"Half siblings, then," said the Divine thoughtfully. "Still, the same father . . ."

"No. My mother . . . had a lover. *He* was my father."

"Ah," said the Divine sagely. "That explains it, then. Why you couldn't reach me. Why even now it takes me great effort to peer inside your head. Our connection is so . . . tenuous."

"Oh, don't say that, my lord!" Jezebel took the Divine's hand again and held it tightly. "I've wanted so much to be with you . . . Ezekiel told me everything about you, your powers, your desires, what you could do for those who served you . . ."

"For those who serve me with more than themselves, my

child. But you have nothing. I am free now. I need allies with connections. I need warriors. You I do not need.'' He held her right hand, and then ripped the bandages from it. She gasped at the pain. "You scratch yourself. So much so that you bleed." Then he nodded, as if in satisfaction.

The Divine took both of Jezebel's hands in his, so that her fingertips rested against his palms. Then he began to stroke her fingers with his thumbs. He did this several times, and then closed his hand over her fingertips and held them for nearly a minute. Jezebel could feel something changing in her hands, as though insects were crawling from the tips of her fingers.

Then the Divine opened his hands, and Jezebel saw that her fingernails, which had the day before been trimmed so short that she could barely scratch herself at all, had grown until they rose a full inch past her fingertips, curving inward like ragged and spatulate claws.

"Ah," the Divine whispered. "A miracle. Now you can do what you've been wanting to do, Jezebel. You can really scratch now. Scratch *hard*."

He looked at her, and the look would have told her what she had to do, even if she hadn't already heard the command inside her head. Maybe she wasn't the perfect channel for the Divine's will, but with him here, right in front of her, she knew precisely what he wanted her to do. And she had no choice but to do it.

She lifted her hands to her neck and she began to scratch the skin at the hollow of her throat, just below the spot where, she remembered, she had rammed the dagger of broken glass up under Arthur Griffith's chin. She scratched with both hands at once, so deeply that the nails started to cut right through the skin.

She scratched until she felt blood start to trickle down her fingers, across her palms, and onto her wrists from her torn exterior jugular veins. In another few minutes, she had dug deeper, so that her jagged nails severed her interior jugular, and her blood, wet and warm, start to rhythmically pulse against her hands. After that, she lived only another three minutes, and died wondering how all this had happened, and hoping that she would come back to life the way that Ezekiel had, and that she would see him again.

"Don't count on it," said the creature who watched Jezebel Swain's eyes go dull, and who read her last thought before her brainwave activity ceased altogether. "There's no coming back for you," the Prisoner said softly.

He watched for a while longer, until the blood had ceased to pulse. It had really been all over when the blood had stopped its flow to the brain, but there was still some residual flavor, and he had been without such nourishment for so many centuries.

At last he stood up from where he had been crouching, looking into the woman's eyes as life left them. He looked at the eastern horizon and breathed deeply, relishing the smell of her blood that was soaking into the sandy soil. Then he looked down again, and wondered if perhaps he should have let her live and mated with her instead of enjoying her death.

No, he thought. This was no time to start new generations. There were already enough of his blood. His ability to wield over half of Michael LaPierre's troops was proof of that. Amazing, how a mere score of seeds planted over a millennium ago could bear so much fruit.

Yet maybe not so amazing after all, when one considered the remarkable evolutionary advantage those with his blood would have. Genetic strengths that would enable them to survive plagues and deal with hunger more effectively than other humans. Add to that the fact that they could not help but be more intelligent and hardier workers, and it was no surprise that his progeny should have spread so widely.

Now it was another of those descendants that he would seek. This woman had been so feeble and useless that it was time to reach out to one who had proved himself a repository of data about the governments of this world, the governments that the Prisoner would have to use against each other.

The Prisoner had appeared to Joseph Stein in his dreams, and had found him a vibrant conduit for his will. The bond between them had been strong, and now he sent out the tendrils of his mind, firing brainwaves like missiles into the open sky, heatseekers searching for Stein's genetically sympathetic thoughts.

He reached far, and at last sensed the man's mind. But it was far to the east, across this continent. He would have to close that distance before he could hope to bring Stein under his control. He had in the past achieved mastery over souls, even through the lead that had bound him and through which he had learned to pierce, with great effort. But distance diminished his powers considerably. At several hundred miles, he had been able to touch Ezekiel Swain, and the weaker mind of Martin Reigle, who, at his order, had dynamited the Dead Horse Dam, in an unwitting effort to free the Prisoner from the kiva in which the Catholics had held him.

But Joseph Stein was several *thousand* miles away. From that distance, the Prisoner might give him dreams and visions, as he had when he'd wanted Joseph to come and free him. But there would be no point. It would only warn Stein of his approach.

No, better just to proceed, to go east and find him. Then he would use Stein's knowledge as best he could, to spill as much blood as he could.

Chapter 7

It was a few hours after dawn when Joseph awoke with a shout. He heard footsteps coming across the small hall that separated his bedroom from the others, and Laika and Tony opened the door and looked in at him.

"You okay?" Tony said.

Joseph nodded. "Another goddamned dream," he said, falling back against the headboard. "Hope I didn't wake you guys up."

"We were both up," said Laika. "What was the dream?"

"Him. The sonofabitch himself. Mr. Antichrist-Prisoner–Bad Guy Supreme. It was like he was standing right there at the foot of the bed, just looking at me. I opened my eyes and for a second I swear I still saw him." Joseph rubbed his eyes. "Dream after-image, probably."

"Maybe not," Laika said. "We know he's out there somewhere. Maybe he's getting into your head again."

"Why would he?" Joseph said. "He's free now."

"I don't know. But I think he's coming. He's getting ready for a move. To what or on whom we don't know. The other dream you had a few days ago, the one where you were in a box?"

"That was *just a dream,*" Joseph said. "The Prisoner wasn't in it at all. I'd expect to have a dream like that, thinking about the Prisoner being held in boxes and caskets as much as I have."

Besides, he thought to himself, there had been no punchline

to the dream. He had screamed, the box had opened, and he had surged into bright light and woken up. That was it. No Prisoner, no priests, no nothing.

"Still, he's out there somewhere, Joseph," Laika said. "And I don't think it unlikely that he would try and get into contact with those people with whom he knows he has a link."

"It takes two to make a link, Laika. And I don't want to play."

During the next few days, the Prisoner moved eastward. He amused himself as he went, careful not to do anything too splashy or obvious.

It was very easy to hitchhike. All he had to do was to command a driver of an oncoming car to stop for him, and one out of every three or four would, often acting surprised and telling him that they normally never stopped for hitch-hikers. He would smile and say that it must just be his honest face, and then he would talk to them until they had come to their destination. He did not try to force them where they didn't want to go, nor did he implant any killing commands in them. That way, he felt, he would not be connected with any violent acts. Those he saved for the evenings.

He found that families in campgrounds were ideal for his purpose. He would simply walk into one after dark and feel about mentally until he came across a trailer with a family whose members he could control. He preferred trailers over pop-up campers or tents. The sounds of slaughter carried too easily through canvas. Sometimes he afflicted the father, sometimes the mother, sometimes a grown son, and some-times all. It really didn't matter. Everyone inside would be dead within minutes, the last person by his or her own hand.

He did this every few nights, when the hunger was great and the opportunity perfect. Afterward, he would walk into the night, with no connection between him and the family who would be found dead the next morning, victims of a tragic murder-suicide. There was no danger of his being discovered. He never set foot inside the trailers, and after all, how could there be such a thing as a serial suicide? Copycat killings, that was all. Sometimes people just went mad, and sometimes it was contagious.

And sometimes, when people who knew what to look for were looking, a connection, a pattern, a modus operandi, were all too obvious.

"It's him," Colin Mackay said, setting down the sheets of paper that showed a definite eastward progression of the murder-suicides that had been taking place in campgrounds. "Copycat killings, my arse. Only reason they say that is because they don't know what we know. Look . . ." The other three men in the room looked over Colin's shoulder as he punched his finger at different points on a map of the United States. "First one in Farmington, New Mexico, then three days later outside of Denver, then Omaha, then Davenport, Iowa. He's not going fast, he's taking his own sweet time, and he's having his fun along the way."

"What the hell's he goin' east for?" asked Angus Gunn. His voice rumbled within his massive body.

Rob Lindsay clapped a hand on his big friend's shoulder. " 'Cause there's something or someone he's after there. So what we've got to do is intercept him."

"How we gonna do that?" Angus asked.

Colin Mackay leaned back in his chair and looked at Angus. "Well, lad, we could put a man in every single campground on the main motorway between Joliet and Pittsburgh, say, but being that there's nae but the four of us, I think we'd better depend on our secret weapon. How about it, James?"

James Menzies, perpetually glum, nodded in agreement. Colin knew that James hated to use the damnable link that he shared with the Deil, which was how they referred to the one Colin's father, Sir Andrew Mackay, and his fellow Knights Templar had believed to be the Antichrist. He was not that, surely, but he did have the potential for great evil, so the "Deil" or devil he had become for them.

Over the past few months, James had begun to feel, tentatively at first, and then more certain of it, that he could tune in to the Deil's thoughts somehow, something that they all knew was possible from what Sir Andrew had told his son over the years. James had so far felt them only in bits, glimpses, and shreds of presence, brief and faraway.

"I think it's him," he had told Colin, when he had first become aware of it.

"How?" Colin had asked. "How do you know it's him?"

"Because it feels . . . bad. It feels *sick*."

"Would it be stronger—if you were closer?"

"Aye. But Colin . . . I don't want to get that close."

"You may have to, brother. For the cause."

"Aye. I'd do it for the cause. But for nocht else."

And now it was time for James to do what he had said he would.

The four Scots drove out of New York City within the hour, heading west. If the Deil maintained the direction and the relaxed speed at which he seemed to be moving, they could expect him along routes 80–90 on the Ohio-Michigan border. They went nonstop, driving in shifts, and finally got off and back on near Toledo, so that they would be in the eastbound lanes, the ones in which the Deil should pass by.

They pulled off at a rest stop with a picnic table, and there they waited, with a food chest full of sandwiches and several thermoses of coffee. The main task would be to keep James awake until—and *if*—the Deil came within sensing distance, for want of a better term. And James had to be not only awake but alert all the time.

They sat there for twelve hours. At 4 A.M., they heard a story on the car radio about a man who had murdered his wife, then taken his own life in a campground in South Bend, Indiana. "Not too far away," Colin said, consulting the map. "He'll probably hole up somewhere for the night, then grab another ride in the morning. I think you can get a few hours of sleep, James."

Colin woke James up at 7, and they sat together as the day

brightened. If it was tedious for Colin to watch the traffic roll by, how much more so, he thought, must it have been for James, who stared at and studied every approaching vehicle.

Shortly after noon, James stiffened in his seat, and although Colin looked down the road, he could see no cars approaching them. "What is it, lad?" he asked. But James only shook his head slightly, as if trying to throw off an unpleasant thought.

Angus and Rob in the backseat leaned forward, and Angus shook James's shoulder. "You all right, then?" Still, James did not respond.

Then his eyes widened, and Colin could actually see the hair on the back of his neck stand up as if from static. Down the road Colin saw the approaching vehicle. "There . . ." James whispered. "He's in *there* . . . "

"Hell almighty," said Rob softly. "A police car."

The black-and-white markings and the bubble top made it unmistakable. It shot past them at 70 mph, and Colin got a glimpse of the people riding inside. He started their car and pulled it onto the highway, following the police car.

"What are ye doin'?" Angus asked. "Colin, that's a *police* car, for God's sake. They've *arrested* the bastard!"

"If they'd arrested him," said Colin, "he'd be in the back. But he's riding up front, as gay as you please. He's just bummed a bloody ride, that's all—with a state trooper."

"That's just stupid," Angus protested. "Coppers don't give hitchhikers rides here, they *arrest* 'em."

"Well, maybe the Deil was just a little too persuasive for the copper to refuse," Colin said.

It finally dawned on Angus. "Y'mean the Deil *took* him?" He shook his head in admiration. "Quite a lad. But what you goin' to do, Colin? Ye cannae pull over a copper!"

"If the Deil did, then so can we," Colin said, stepping on the accelerator. When he caught up with the police car and was directly behind it, he turned on his flashers and honked his horn several times. When it continued on, he pulled up into the passing lane beside it, and glanced over.

The policeman behind the wheel was looking straight

ahead, but the man in the passenger seat was watching Colin and his colleagues with what looked like amusement. He was smiling, and Colin smiled back. After all, he wanted cooperation from the creature.

Colin took his eyes off the road again, just long enough to look over at the Deil and lift his left hand, middle fingers down, thumb and little finger extended, and waggle it. It was the horns, the sign of the cuckold, but also the sign of the devil, and he hoped the Deil would realize that they knew who he was. Then he turned back to the motorway ahead, ready to flank the police car all day, if need be.

In the police car, the Prisoner's decision took only a fraction of a second. Here were some who knew who he was, and weren't shooting at him, or blasting flamethrowers through their car window. He was intrigued, even more so when he had shot out a bolt of pure thought at the driver at a range of only a few yards and felt no contact whatsoever. Such men were rare. Most he could at least touch, if not affect, but there was a barrier around this one.

"Pull over here, please, Officer," he told the policeman, who obeyed immediately. The Prisoner got out of the car, as did the four men inside the other car. The policeman merely sat there, waiting.

"Is it him?" the driver, a tall, red-haired man, asked another in his party, a man shorter than himself.

The little man nodded. "Aye, it's him, all right."

"You're Scots," the Prisoner said, hearing the burrs in the Rs. Scots, like the twelve Scots who had dogged his contacts, followed his works over the centuries, the Templars.

The red-haired man nodded. "Aye. And we have a proposition for you, Deil."

"What kind of deal?" said the Prisoner.

"No. Deil as in devil."

"Ah. You'll forgive my ignorance of the vernacular. It's been a . . . *lang* time since I've had any contact with Scots. Eighteen-oh-four, when I was held in Inverness for a few months. A wet and nasty country, I recall, but picturesque. At least, that was the feeling I got from those whom I could . . . communicate with. Physically, I was . . . incommunicado.''

He shot thoughts like quick bullets of lights at the other three men. It took only an instant for him to realize that he could easily control two of them, and reach the third with some slight effort. There was nothing to fear then. ''Perhaps,'' he said, ''we could continue this conversation as we ride.'' He nodded toward the Scots' car. ''I see you're also heading east.''

''We'd be glad for your company,'' said the tall man, who then nodded toward the policeman. ''And what about him?''

''Well, normally,'' said the Prisoner, ''I'd have him wait a few hours and then blow his brains out with his service revolver, but since some passing motorists might have noticed your car here, I'll just have him drive on.''

''He won't remember you? Or us?''

The Prisoner smiled at the thought. ''No.'' He went back to the police car and spoke to the officer, who drove away. ''He won't remember his own name. Nothing. He's born again as of today.'' He looked at the car. ''Shall we?''

Chapter 8

*C*olin Mackay loathed the creature sitting next to him. He thought that he had never before been in the presence of any man who seemed so completely amoral. He had spoken of killing the copper so casually that it made Colin's skin crawl. He couldn't understand it. Life was a gift, and death was a tool that you could use to further your ends, to advance your cause, and under those conditions you had to be callous. But to kill for bloodlust alone, to kill because you could, was the act of a barbarian.

But somehow, he was going to have to talk this barbarian into killing for him.

"My name is Colin Mackay, though it's not a name I go by," he began. "And I know who you are because of the things my father told me. He is Sir Andrew Mackay, and I don't know whether he's alive or dead at this point. Frankly, I don't much care. But he told me who and what you were, and what you could do."

"And what did he tell you I was?"

"He said you were the Antichrist, and that he and the rest of the twelve surviving Knights Templar were supposed to try and keep the world from your ill effects while the church kept you prisoner."

"And did you believe him?"

Colin thought for a moment. "When you know your father has lived for eight centuries, you tend to be pretty accepting toward things other folk would call fantastic. I believe it all except for the Antichrist part. You're not the Antichrist. There's no such beastie.''

"Yet you call me the devil—or the *Deil*."

"That's because we don't know what else to call you. You have a name, then?''

"I do. But I believe you would find it unpronounceable. I'd have trouble myself, with this . . .'' He paused. "Well, I'd have trouble. But you should have some name for me. What about . . . Mulcifer?''

It was an ugly name, Colin thought. It sounded like a rotten fruit. "And where did that come from?'' he asked.

"From Dr. Weyer's *Pseudo-monarchia Daemonum*, which was kindly given to me in 1590 by a thoughtful priest. He hoped that if I read the chronicle of all the devils in hell, it might assist in my conversion. Actually, it was very funny, and quite entertaining.''

"So, uh, who's this Mulcifer?'' Angus asked from the backseat.

"The architect of hell,'' said the person or being that Colin Mackay would now try to think of as Mulcifer. "So tell me what picking me up was all about, and also how you found me, if you don't mind.''

Colin told Mulcifer how they had tracked him down, and then turned to the more delicate subject of their collaboration. "I know what your powers are, how you can affect people, turn them against each other. I also know that you like your dirty little tricks, and the bloodier, the better. But all alone, just moving about the country, you don't have much opportunity to tackle a big score, a real coup. For that you need . . .'' He nearly choked on the word. ". . . Friends. Colleagues. Collaborators. You need a network of some sort to protect you and work with you. And that's what we can offer you. Your . . . expertise, to benefit our cause. We both profit.''

"Your cause. What *is* your cause?''

"Scotland. We're Nationalists. We believe that Scotland should be fully independent of the English Crown. It is a separate country. England stole it centuries ago, and we want it back. Oh, aye, we've a devolved parliament now, but the United Kingdom's Parliament is still the supreme authority. We want *all* of Scotland's money to stay in Scotland, we want our oil and our fisheries and our electronics and other industries to benefit our own families and children alone. We—''

"Enough," Mulcifer said, looking out the window as though he were bored. "You could have answered me in one word, and it would have been enough."

Colin could have answered him in thousands, and there still would have been more to tell. He could have talked about the Nationalist upsurge of the late twenties, when he had first begun to learn of the injustices done against his country. He could have told of the voices he had heard over the decades— of Neil Gunn and Hugh Macdiarmid, of Maxton and Mackintosh, of all those who spoke in the hot tongue of home rule.

But London had ignored those voices, or tried to still them by doling out occasional sweets of political favor, the same way in which Edward I had satisfied the Scottish nobles nearly seven hundred years before. Some had said that the recent devolution and the resulting Scottish Parliament would be the next step on the road toward full autonomy, but England still controlled monetary policy and employment legislation, and would continue to do so. No, there could be no slow, gentle slide into independence. Freedom had to be taken from a government as grasping and imperialistic as England's. Ireland was proof enough of that.

"You want to make England bleed," Mulcifer said, "and you think that I'm the one to do the job."

"Aye, in a nutshell. We're all set up to harass and terrorize England. The better job of it we can do, the faster they'll be willing to grant total sovereignty. And you'll have all the English blood you can spill, so long as you restrict your actions to government targets—English military and police. We don't want civilian casualties. And we sure as hell don't want slaughtered families."

The creature turned and looked at Colin, and his grin made his dark and handsome face seem like a skull. "I'll try not to disappoint ye . . . brother.'' The voice was an exact rendition of the highland dialect, but even more, it rang in Colin Mackay's ears like the echo of his own voice, though neither Angus nor Rob nor James seemed to notice.

Colin tried to concentrate on the road ahead, and asked Mulcifer, "So where were you headed, going east like you were?''

"I was going to try and find another friend,'' he said. "But then you lads came along, and I think you'll prove to be far better friends than ever I had before.''

And I'll prove a far greater enemy than any you've ever known. I'll make your English foes look like little girls in lace. But first I'll twist your soul and make you wish you'd never even heard of me from your damned father . . .

This was ideal, Mulcifer thought, for that was how he would think of himself as well. The architect of hell, the one who would turn this earth into a slaughterhouse where souls were forgotten, where men and women and children were only meat, pure flesh to suffer and feed his hungry spirit.

The havoc would be wonderful, but equally grand would be his revenge upon Sir Andrew Mackay through the destruction of his son. The man would know all the torments of the damned and more, before Mulcifer finally struck him down.

As they were driving on the Pennsylvania turnpike late that evening, there was a call on the car's cell phone. Brian, back at the New York headquarters, had received a letter from an Inverness firm of solicitors. The letter had been shuttled through the usual channels before it had arrived at their Manhattan mail drop.

"Open it and read it to me,'' Colin told him.

The letter stated that as Mr. Francis Scobie's father, Alister Scobie, had not been heard from by the firm of Dingwall, McCord, Pollock and Herrie within the time period set forth by the elder Mr. Scobie, that all his accrued wealth and the ownership of Castle Dirk in County Ross and Cromarty settled upon the younger Mr. Scobie. The letter further requested Francis Scobie to report to the solicitors' office and take possession of the property.

"Thank you," Colin said, and ended the call. He took a deep breath. The news meant that his father, who had owned Castle Dirk for centuries, and for the past thirty years under the name of Alister Scobie, was dead. He was to contact the solicitors every six months, and were he to miss such a contact, Colin was to be alerted by the solicitors, and to assume that Sir Andrew was dead.

Colin had thought it likely his father had perished in the mass deaths in upstate New York. But since only eleven bodies had been found, he thought it possible that his father might have survived. If he had, he was gone now. It was possible that whoever had killed the other Templars might have done for Sir Andrew as well.

Colin was ambivalent about the news. He had no tears for his father. After almost a hundred years of life, he had no tears for anything. And how could one truly mourn the death of a man who had lived nearly a millennium? His father'd had his fill of life, Colin had seen that in his eyes the last time they had met, fifteen years earlier.

Although Colin didn't particularly believe in the god his father had defended since the reign of the Bruce, he saw some guiding hand here, some act of destiny that, within hours, provided him not only with a terrible new weapon, but also with a stronghold from which he might wield it. He had sworn to go back to Scotland only when he was ready to free it, and that time had come. What better center of operations than a castle?

"We're going back now," he said to the others. "And we have a place to go back to." He told them about Castle Dirk, but not about the death of his father. They knew his real name, but not his ancestry, and not the truth about his age. Angus had said many times, "Ye're wise beyond your years, Colin," but he didn't know that Colin Mackay's years numbered 98.

"It'll be grand to see the old land again," Angus said softly, or at least as softly as he could speak, with his growl of a voice.

"Aye," said Colin. "We'll take a few days to finish things up here and have the place prepared for our coming."

"Like Prince Charlie coming back over the water," Rob said, recalling the Jacobite dream. "But we'll have better fortune than poor Charlie."

Colin hoped so. Charlie might have had a better chance had *he* had a devil beside him, thirsty for English blood.

Chapter 9

Several days after Colin Mackay drove to New York City with the being known as Mulcifer, Laika Harris received an encrypted message in her e-mail. It instructed her, Joseph Stein, and Tony Luciano to come fully packed to the front door of their building at 10:30 that evening, where a white van labeled ''Portobello Limo Service'' would pick them up. That was all.

The van was there at the appointed time. Following standard operating procedure, they had transferred all the files on the desktop computers with which they had been supplied onto their laptops, then used a special Company program to completely destroy the hard drives of the desktops. Not that it mattered, since Laika knew that Company cleaners sent by Skye would come in to do a sweep of the place only minutes after the operatives had departed.

The van driver said nothing, nor did they speak to him. He took them to one of the private hangars at Philadelphia International Airport, where they took their luggage into a small waiting lounge with no windows. There, seated on a chair covered in gray cloth, was Richard Skye. He still looked like an underfed water rat, Laika thought, with his little brown mustache over his pursed lips. Those lips drew up in a purposefully insincere smile as he gestured to them to sit down.

''You're leaving the country for a time,'' he said without preamble in his tight, prissy voice. ''Your recent activities in the wild west have gained you some notoriety among some of our . . . investigatory colleagues in the government." He paused, as though he expected one of them to say something, but they all only looked at him. "Do you know who Joshua Yazzie is?" Skye asked flatly.

Laika was glad to see that her colleagues' faces were unreadable masks. "Yes," she said. "He was a tribal policeman who assisted us in Arizona."

"He was Brian Foster," Skye said. "An FBI agent."

Laika made her eyes widen slightly. "Sonofabitch," she said softly.

"Mmm. He also seems to be missing. From a deep-cover FBI file that we intercepted, I learned the last anyone heard of him was when he was heading for Utah, apparently on your trail, Agent Harris."

"We were unaware of any such surveillance, sir."

For a moment, Skye looked at her as if he wanted to call her a liar. But instead he took a deep breath and looked up at the fissured ceiling panels. "At any rate, I've also learned that the Federal Bureau of Investigation is very anxious to confront you three. I don't really know whether your usefulness in this country is at an end, or if this is something the gray-suited shits will get over shortly. But I'm sending you abroad just the same, out of their jurisdiction.

"Frankly, I would have done so anyway. This is a very intriguing situation. It sounds like Ghost Central." Skye handed her a thick, sealed dossier. "To be read in transit. Surprisingly, news of all this hasn't yet begun to leak to the tabloids over here, possibly because of the general isolation of the area and the attitude toward outsiders. So it should be some time before they're running ghost excursion flights to your destination. However, as always, the sooner you come up with an answer, the better.

"You also have new covers for this assignment. You are an archeological team from Princeton University. Agent Harris, you are Dr. Brown . . ."

"Foxy or Jackie?" said Laika under her breath.

"I beg your pardon?"

"Nothing, sir."

"Dr. *Frances* Brown," Skye clarified. "Agent Stein, you are Dr. Charles Witherup, and Agent Luciano, being the youngest, you are a graduate student, Mr. David Angelo."

"And if anyone checks with Princeton?" Laika asked.

Skye gave her an angry look again. "Agent Harris, do you know of any cover from my division ever being broken?"

". . . No sir."

She had hesitated just a bit too long, and Skye jumped on it. "Are you implying something?"

"Sir, it's just that . . . I've heard there have been cases where your agents have been left in the cold. But if true, I would assume those incidents were due to the agents' own carelessness rather than faulty covers."

"You would assume correctly," Skye answered curtly. "Now I think you should board the plane. You'll find your covers quite adequate. Have a pleasant trip."

The way Skye said it, it sounded more like, "Go to hell." He turned and stalked through the door to the outside.

The plane was a ten-seater, fast and comfortable. "I thought the Company's budget was going *down*," said Tony when they were on board.

"This isn't a Company plane," said Joseph in a whisper, probably thinking about bugs. Laika knew what he meant. It damn well wasn't a plane of *the* Company, anyway, and Laika wondered who Skye called in a marker from to get this bird.

An uncomfortable silence fell on the three of them as they waited for takeoff. After the episode in the southwest, they had talked long and hard about whether they could trust the man who was running them, and come to the conclusion that Skye was holding out on them major league. They felt certain that he knew about the existence of the Prisoner, even though they had not told Skye about it, due to their lack of trust in him. He was using the ops to hone in on real paranormal occurrences caused in some way by the Prisoner. Laika, Joseph, and Tony were Skye's hunting dogs, but they were not as ignorant as he had hoped.

Someone was running Skye the way he was running them, she felt sure of it. But while they were following orders, she was afraid that Skye had been turned, the same way that Michael LaPierre's money had turned Popeye Daly, a CIA agent who had tried to kill the three of them. But who, if she was right, was behind Skye?

She thought there might be a clue in the plane, but there were no identifying corporate logos emblazoned on the leather seats, nor any annual reports stuck in with the magazines, none of which had subscription labels. She had noticed the exterior was equally anonymous, except for the registration number that was required by the FAA on every plane. They could check on that later.

The steward came back into the cabin before Laika got settled enough to open the dossier. There was something about him, a lack of intensity perhaps, that made Laika think he wasn't Company. "Mind telling me where we're headed, or is it a secret?" she asked.

"Oh no, ma'am, not at all. We'll be landing in Inverness Airport in Scotland."

"Scotland again," said Joseph. "Wonderful. I just love rain and lake monsters." Laika smiled at the memory. Skye's first assignment for them had been to debunk a phony psychic in front of his audience. The psychic had set his demonstration in Drumnadrochit on Loch Ness, but the only monster anyone had seen was the psychic when the operatives got through with him.

Afterward, they had met with Richard Skye on western Scotland's Isle of Skye, a meeting place whose name proved unconditionally the size of Skye's ego. There he had explained to them the purpose behind their continuing mission. They had believed it then, but were less gullible now.

"So what are we up to?" Joseph said. "Finding Nessie, or laying the ghost of Glamis Castle?"

Laika opened the dossier and began to read. "You've got the ghost part right, Joseph. It seems that the Gairloch peninsula, up on the northwestern coast, has been auditioning for

Ghostbusters III. There's been sighting after sighting of manifestations of some sort. Some of the witnesses do indeed call them ghosts, others say they don't know what the manifestations are, but they glow in the dark.''

"And where and when do these hauntings occur?" Joseph asked.

"Day and night," Laika said, her eyes scanning the report. "Town and country, inside and out. There doesn't seem to be any pattern."

"The lack of a distinct pattern," Joseph said with mock solemnity, "often signals the presence of the most meaningful pattern of all."

"*The Book of Joseph,*" Tony said. "Chapter nineteen, verse eight. Over how wide an area are these things being seen, Laika?"

"Apparently the whole peninsula. About ten miles north to south and another five or six across."

"That's nothing," said Joseph. "A few hoaxers could cover a territory like that easily enough."

"These things have also been seen floating thirty feet in the air," Laika added.

Joseph snorted. "Never underestimate the skill of a determined hoaxer—*or* the imagination of a terrified witness."

"There's one thing that makes the sightings a little more complex," said Laika, "and that's an MI5 report the CIA intercepted and Skye got ahold of. It states that the night before all this started, a treasure hunter uncovered a luminescent and radioactive cloth that had apparently been buried for several hundred years. The next night the manifestations began. Curiouser and curiouser. But here's the kicker. The rays emitted aren't like any known radioactivity."

"Of course not," Joseph said. "They're obviously *ghost*-producing rays. I suspect what was opened here was Pandora's box." He chuckled. "Look, there's no such thing as scientific infallibility, any more than there is *papal* infallibility . . . no offense." He nodded deferentially to Tony, and

Laika hoped he wasn't going to rise to Joseph's Catholic-baiting.

But Tony didn't. "None taken," he said in a chilly voice.

"As long as human beings are running the tests," Joseph went on, "mistakes are going to be made, and I suspect that's what happened here. They just got the results wrong. The glow and the radioactivity are probably just from a phosphorescent mold, or something."

"You think scientists at Edinburgh University would make that simple a mistake?" Tony asked. "Not recognizing *mold?*"

"Well, whether they did or not, we're going to be doing some archeological investigation during the next few days," Laika said. "There's a partly ruined stone circle on the peninsula that's called the Mellangaun Stones. It's what's known as a number three status for these things—'ruined but recognizable.' However, there's already an archeological party doing a dig there. But two miles west there's another circle. This one's in far worse shape—a number four. 'Badly ruined.' The MacLunie Stones, named after the farmer who discovered them. There was a dig done there, but in the late eighteen hundreds. The current MacLunie has been given enough money to persuade him to allow a small team from Princeton to do a dig there, without disturbing the stones."

"I don't know squat about archeology," Tony said.

"There's a small box of books on the subject with the luggage," Laika said. "Also, I had a course in it in college, as Skye reminds me here."

"One of your native American culture courses?" Joseph asked.

Laika nodded. "We should be able to fake it well enough. After all, it's only a cover. One of us stays at the site, while the others investigate the phenomena. There'll be tools and supplies when we land in Inverness."

Chapter 10

*W*hen they touched down at Inverness Airport just before noon, they found a van waiting for them. It contained archeological tools and supplies, along with detailed notes on how to use them and how to construct a dig site that would pass investigation by experts. Along with the gear was the usual assortment of weapons, covert operations equipment, and communications devices the operatives had come to expect.

Beside the van, there was also a small Peugeot similar to the one they had used before in Scotland. Its compact size made it perfect for the narrow, twisting roads of the highlands, and the engine had been modified so that it would accelerate quickly and powerfully up the country's steep hills.

The maps showed that it was nearly 300 miles northwest to the peninsula. Most of the roads were one-lane, with passing places. With luck, they might be able to get there before dark.

Joseph got into the Peugeot while Laika joined Tony in the van, and they headed up the A9, Tony in the lead. It was a sunny, welcoming day, and the highlands wore autumn hues of pale yellow and brown, highlighted by the green of the Scots pines that covered much of the hillsides.

Tony was quiet, more so than he had been before their trip to the southwest and his involvement with Miriam Dominick, who had accidentally died in a shootout between the ops and some of LaPierre's hired thugs. Laika noticed that he still wore the silver cross that Miriam had given him. It dangled from a chain around his neck.

She had tried to talk to him about it, thinking that if he opened up it might be easier for him to live with the loss. But he hadn't wanted to talk and she hadn't pushed him. Now they sat in silence, until he finally spoke.

"This day reminds me of the first time we came here. But up here it's more like the Isle of Skye than Loch Ness. Hardly anybody around."

"Sort of like the desert," Laika observed, thinking of the isolation of the southwest.

"I like it better here," said Tony after a moment. "Trees and lakes instead of just desert. I don't know how anybody can live out there." Then he gave a short, barking laugh, and Laika knew he had just thought of all the deaths they had seen. And she knew whose death he was thinking about most.

It was eight in the evening when they drove into Gairloch. From there they went another three miles up the west coast of the peninsula, and turned left onto a dirt road that took them to the cottage that had been rented for them. It was a large, white, two-story house only a hundred yards from the rocky beach that looked out across the Minch, the body of water separating the mainland from the Isles of Harris and Lewis. There was not another cottage in sight.

They went into the house first and looked it over. Downstairs was a large living room with a television and sparsely filled bookshelves, a smaller parlor, a kitchen, and a dining room. Three computers sat waiting for them on the long dining room table. "Guess we eat in the kitchen," Joseph said.

The refrigerator and pantry were well stocked, and the closet just inside the front door was filled with rain gear in their respective sizes, as well as several pairs of rubber boots. Upstairs there were four small bedrooms and two baths.

Then they unpacked the van, taking the weapons, explosives, and covert supplies down into a windowless cellar accessible only from the kitchen. Once locked, the heavy door to the cellar would need a well-placed charge to open it.

Afterward, they had a supper of sandwiches. Laika and Tony had tea to finish, and Joseph helped himself to the single malt Scotch thoughtfully provided by whoever had prepared the place for Skye. Joseph smacked his lips after the first sip. "I'd forgotten how much I liked Scotland," he said.

"Better be careful," Tony warned him. "You'll have bad dreams."

It wasn't a bad dream Joseph Stein had that night, but a good one. Joseph dreamed that he awoke in the middle of the night, and saw his father standing next to his bed, tall and strong, as he had been when Joseph was a boy. He seemed to be illuminated from within, and was smiling at Joseph.

His presence was comforting, and Joseph thought how nice it was of his father to come back from wherever it was that people went when they died. He probably wanted to reveal to him that there was life after death, and Joseph found that reassuring, despite the fact that he knew he would not believe it in the morning, no matter how real it felt now.

Then his father started to change his shape. His arms joined his body, becoming one with the torso, and the features of his face faded into a pale plain. The entire figure became taller and cylindrical, losing all detail and definition, but still the sensation of comfort and benignity remained in Joseph's mind. There was a touch of frustration as well. Joseph had the overwhelming feeling that his father, or whatever seemed to be his father, very much wanted to tell him something, but could not, not yet.

The glowing figure ascended slowly, and the ceiling of the bedroom melted away, so that Joseph could see the form rising into the sky, gaining speed and diminishing in magnitude as it went, until it was only a dim dot against the black night, and then was gone. The sky's darkness became the darkness of his bedroom ceiling, and Joseph realized that he was lying in bed, his eyes open, looking up at it.

He was awake, all right, but his father's ghost had been nothing more, he was certain, than a hypnopompic hallucination, a half-dream, half-vision sprung from the mind just before waking.

So the next morning, when Tony jokingly asked Joseph if he had had any nightmares or seen any ghosts, he simply smiled and said he had not. After breakfast, they drove to the MacLunie croft.

Dennis MacLunie was a thin, sunbrowned man, seemingly made up of flesh and ligament alone. The house out of which he came, however, was big and broad, made of whitewashed stones. Its thatched roof made it appear to be wearing a wig, an illusion strengthened by the net that kept the individual rushes from blowing away in the gusty wind. MacLunie introduced himself and then invited the three inside, "out of chill."

His wife, Mary, as round as he was thin, brought tea and homemade scones, and they all sat by the fire in the main room. Although the house had looked huge from outside, the stone walls were so thick that the room felt cramped. "So you're from Princeton, then?" MacLunie asked. "Never been to the States m'self, but had a cousin gone over there. You'll be wantin' to know about the stones, won't ye? They're over on the croft next to this, I own 'em both. Have three of 'em altogether, four acres of inbye land each."

" 'Inbye' land?" Laika asked.

"Aye. Means the land's good for farming. Not all rocks and cliffs and such, that's all."

"What do you farm?" Joseph asked, curious to know what this rough land might yield.

"Oh, corn and barley, mostly, and then I've got my souming on the common land."

Joseph chuckled. "You lost me again. What's souming?"

"Souming—how many sheep I'm permitted to graze on the land where the other crofters graze their sheep, too. Anyway, the stones are right near the castle."

"There's a castle?" asked Laika.

"Aye, Castle Dirk. Stupid name. Man called Scobie owns

it, but haven't seen him in years and years, though folks say he comes to the castle time to time. Just an old caretaker in there now, lives in a cottage right by.''

"So, Mr. MacLunie," Laika said, in the brief silence during which MacLunie took a bit of scone and dipped it in his tea, "you're not concerned that our little dig might stir up any . . . ghosts?''

"Achhh," MacLunie growled. "Ghost are shite, ye'll pardon me. Lived here all my life and never seen one."

"We've heard that other people are claiming they have."

"I've heard that, too, but it's foolishness. The only ghosts these drunkies see is when they've had one too many drams." He looked thoughtful for a moment. "Though there must be a lot of whisky and lager goin' down lately." He tossed back his tea and set down the cup with a rattle. "Shall I show ye the stones, then?''

The croft that held the MacLunie Stones was another mile north. Laika went with MacLunie in his truck while Joseph and Tony followed in the Peugeot. MacLunie turned off the rough road into an open field and gestured for the two men to hop into the back of the truck. "Your wee car won't do so well here," he said, and proceeded up a steep hill. Although Laika couldn't yet see the Minch, she knew they were heading in that direction.

MacLunie stopped when they were fifty yards from the top of the hill, and they got out. The MacLunie Stones were nothing to write home about, Laika thought. There were three of them, all heavily weathered. Two were lying flat on the ground, nearly covered by vegetation, while the third, only two feet high, stood barely upright, leaning like a tired gravestone. Moss and lichen clung to its gray surface.

"Nae much to look at, are they?" MacLunie said. "Don't think I'll be puttin' in a souvenir stand soon. Dig all you like, lang as you don't dig up the stones. I won't be botherin' you. Can't farm here, too rocky. And bad grazin' land, too. The bees like the heather, though. I've got some hives nearby. Anything else you'll want, then?''

"I don't think so, Mr. MacLunie. We'll look around up here a bit, then walk down to the car."

MacLunie tipped his wool cap, went back to his truck, and drove down the hill and onto the road. Laika and the others surveyed the site. The land sloped down to the south and east, where they could easily see the road, and rose to the north and west. They walked northwest until they came to where the hill stopped rising.

The earth fell away from them down to the narrow strand that hugged the waters of the Minch. But what captured their gaze was not the sea, but the broad and heavy shape of the castle that sat upon a crag not five hundred yards from where they stood.

It seemed ancient and majestic and grand in its partial ruination. The tumbled stones that remained of the outer wall lay as though flung by the hand of Fingal the giant. But the inner wall and the four towers at each corner still stood, defying the centuries of war and harsh elements that must have stormed around them. The castle sat on the edge of the sea, and though not as high as the spot where the operatives stood, it held a commanding view of the Minch. Though Laika could not see its northwestern wall, it appeared to drop straight down to the strand, making it a formidable foe to attack by water.

Several outbuildings stood around the main pile. Laika could see smoke rising from the chimney of the largest one, and assumed it was the caretaker's cottage of which MacLunie had spoken. A rusty English Ford sat next to it, the only vehicle in sight.

A low stone wall separated the castle grounds from the rest of the peninsula, going down all the way across the strand and into the Minch itself. She wondered how far under the water the defenders of the castle had piled the stones. It seemed more symbolic than practical, for an attacking force could easily climb over it.

"Wish we were digging *that* up instead," Tony said. She barely heard him over the sound of the wind blowing up the cliff from the sea. It was cold on their faces, with the sun at their backs.

"It's a pretty small castle, though," said Joseph, "you come right down to it. It looks impressive, but most of that's the location. I wonder if it was really designed for defense. What little is left of the outer curtain indicates that it wasn't very high, or even very thick. But it *is* old, not a Victorian reproduction—see where they replaced missing stones with new ones? There's a difference in color."

"It's bigger than my apartment back home, anyway," said Tony, as if miffed that Joseph was minimalizing such a romantic vision. Laika knew how he felt.

"Well, we'd better get down to work," she said, "or *none* of us will ever see our little hovels back home again."

They walked to the car, drove back to their cottage, and returned to the site in the van, bringing all the equipment with which they would develop their archeological cover. The van made it easily up the hill to the stones, and they parked it so as to most effectively block their activities from view of anyone passing on the road.

Then they set to work with stakes and yellow plastic ribbons that reminded Laika of crime scene markers, setting them in a gridwork pattern around the stones. Next to them they placed wooden frameworks of plastic webbing through which dirt could be sifted.

With flat-bladed tools they cut through the turf, first marking off a six-by-six-foot area and then removing square-foot-sized slabs, placing them carefully in piles, the way the Scots cut peat. At last they began to dig with small shovels, removing only the first six inches of dirt, sifting it through the webbing, and finding only pebbles and bits of rock.

Even though they were only creating a ruse, Laika still looked carefully at what they were doing. Once, possibly millennia ago, men had worked here, placing these now worn stones in patterns that meant something deeply significant to them. It was altogether possible that they might unearth something of interest.

After a few hours of work, they had found nothing, but at least there was physical proof of their cover, should it be required. They drove back to the cottage and had lunch. Afterward, Laika and Joseph took the Peugeot into Gairloch to buy groceries and investigate the spectral reports.

Tony returned to the MacLunie Stones in the van, and continued digging. Another few hours of excavation would add to the verisimilitude of their facade. But he had worked only for a half hour when he had a visitor.

He had seen the black-garbed figure coming north on the road on a bicycle. At first Tony had thought it was a woman, because of what he mistook for the hem of a long skirt flapping around the man's ankles as he rode. But when the man stopped and began to walk up the hill toward him, Tony could see that it was a priest's cassock, black and buttoned nearly to the feet. The priest was wearing a very nonecclesiastical burgundy-colored beret, and was panting by the time he reached Tony. He was thin to the point of gauntness, and appeared to be in his early sixties.

"Good day, *m'sieu*," he said with an unmistakable French accent, looking anxiously at the three large stones. "These are the MacLunie Stones, *n'est-ce pas?*"

"*Oui, père*," Tony said, continuing the conversation in French. The priest, who said his name was Father Alexandre Coisne, was delighted to find someone who spoke his tongue. As his fatigue from climbing the hill vanished, he grew more garrulous. He was, he told Tony, finishing a three-month bicycle tour around England and Scotland.

"I am trying," he explained in rapid-fire French, "to see as many of the British stone circles as I can in that time."

"Even these?" Tony said, gesturing with mild contempt to the trio of sorry boulders.

"Oh, I did not come especially for these, but they are only a few miles out of my way as I travel to the Mellangaun Stones. And I wanted to see the Templar castle."

Tony suppressed his reaction to hearing the word. The Knights Templar had been the key that had opened this mystery back in New York. The eleven men found poisoned and burned in an upstate hunting lodge had, in all likelihood, been Templars, either a newly formed group, or, as the evidence seemed bizarrely to suggest, men centuries old, who had somehow retained their youth and survived all those years. Tony smiled and looked at the priest with what he hoped appeared to be only slight interest. "Templars, Father?"

"Yes. Certain studies suggest that this Castle Dirk was built as a Knights Templar meeting place rather than a fortress."

"I'd never heard that."

"Oh, my reading takes me into obscure corners, my son. There are many books and old manuscripts concerning the Templars in the *Bibliothèque Nationale*."

"I'm afraid you'll be disappointed, Father, but the castle isn't open to the public."

"Ah well," said the priest, looking forlornly at the three stones, "I have had other disappointments on this trip." Then he brightened and looked back at Tony. "So what is it that you are searching for here, *m'sieu*?"

"Whatever may be left after so many centuries, Father. Tools, hopefully. Anything to help explain how and why the stones were moved and put into place."

"May God grant you success in your goal," Father Alexandre said, and bade Tony goodbye.

To maintain the illusion they had created, Tony resumed digging, but he carefully watched the priest walk down the hill to his bicycle. Several cars passed, and he found himself hoping the old man would be careful on the narrow roads. When the priest had pedaled around a bend, Tony dropped his shovel and walked up to the ridge of the hill, where he looked down at the castle.

Templars. My God, what were the chances that they'd have come across a Templar connection again? There seemed to be a synchronicity at work here, a guiding hand of some sort. Or maybe it was all connected. Maybe the sightings here somehow tied in to the Prisoner, and since those same Templars had watchdogged that same Prisoner for centuries, it made sense that there might be a Templar connection here as well.

As he looked at the castle, he knew that something was different. Then he had it—the rusted Ford was missing from beside the caretaker's cottage.

Had Tony been in his normal, cautious state of mind, he would not have even considered going to the castle alone. But losing Miriam Dominick had made him ravenous for action and involvement. When he was merely digging a trench, there was too much opportunity for memories and regrets to come to him. If he did not keep his mind constantly busy, the sight of Miriam's face, the sound of her voice, the touch of her hand haunted him.

Here at last was a chance to banish her for at least as long as it would take to enter the castle and see what might be found. There was no denying that it was a long shot to take on the casual word of a wandering priest, but priests had proved to be effective guides before, both spiritual guides through his life, and guides to the mystery in which he and his colleagues were immersed.

He jogged back to the van, stuffed what equipment he thought he might need in a backpack, and trotted back over the hill and down toward the castle.

Chapter 11

Joseph had never seen a town as much on edge as Gairloch seemed to be. As he and Laika entered the grocer's shop, the man looked startled and forced a smile at the strangers. When they took their selections to the register, he avoided eye contact as he tallied up the bill.

"Beautiful day," Laika observed. He glanced up and nodded, then went back to his sums. "Is there a pub in town you might recommend?" He would have to talk now, Joseph thought.

"Black Bear," he said, not looking up.

"Is anything wrong?" Laika asked.

"Wrong?" Still he looked down.

"When we came in, you looked as though you expected to . . . see a ghost."

Now he looked up, gave a sickly smile, and forced a laugh. "Oh no, not *me*." The implication was obvious.

"Others have, then, eh?" Laika said, as though she knew.

"I wouldna know anything about that." He straightened up. "That's thirty-three pounds and forty-seven pence."

Laika paid, and they picked up the bags and walked out. The grocer kept his gaze fixed firmly on the floor.

"There's a man who's hiding something," Laika said outside, as they put the groceries into the trunk.

"Or maybe it's just a bad case of acid reflux," said Joseph.

Laika speedread the newspaper she had bought in the shop. "Nothing much in here except births, weddings, and deaths, jumble sales, auction records, crop yields, and the weather.''

"I was expecting newsboys to be on every corner, shouting 'Ghosts haunt peninsula! Citizens panic!' ''

"Let's try the Black Bear," said Laika. "Maybe people will be more talkative there."

"Great. I've been dying for a lukewarm beer."

The Black Bear was only a few storefronts away. On one side was a bar with small tables for drinkers along the opposite wall. A door led to a dining room. Laika and Joseph chose a table near one occupied by three men in work clothes who, Joseph guessed, worked on a croft. He got two glasses of lager at the bar, and he and Laika sat and drank and chatted of nothing, trying to overhear the conversation of the crofters.

But the men spoke in low voices, and when Joseph tried to make conversation, they were polite but unresponsive. Laika and Joseph finished their beers and left.

"I think we need to find the local shoeshine guy—slash-informant and slip him a twenty. Or maybe a cabbie—'You know where we can get some good ghosts around here?' ''

"No. Let's pay a visit to the *Gairloch Gazette*," she said.

The newspaper office was housed in a Victorian building complete with a corner tower. Inside, a round-faced man and a thin woman, approximately the same age, were working at two desks. The man got up, introduced himself as Samuel Trotter, and asked how he could help them. Though he seemed affable enough, there was a sense of guardedness about him.

Laika told him that they were archeologists from Princeton digging at the MacLunie Stones. "Since, as a newspaperman, you're certainly familiar with the area and the people," she said, "I wonder if you could think of anyone who might recall any of the other digging on the MacLunie site."

"Well, there's surely a lot of digging about these days," he said, his face momentarily sour. "But as for the MacLunie Stones, I doubt there's anyone living who'd recall the last time there were any archeologists up there. I believe it was back in the 1890s—I'm interested in local history, you see. As far as I know, they didn't find a thing."

"Well," said Joseph, "our methods are a bit more advanced now, and you never know what might have been missed. There is one thing that I'd like to ask you about, though. Some rumors we've heard."

"Rumors?" Trotter looked ready. The man was dreadfully inept at hiding his emotions.

"We've heard people have been seeing . . . well, *things*. Ghosts or visions or . . ." He chuckled. "I guess some folks even said aliens. True?"

"I, I don't know anything about any ghosts."

"That's a relief," Joseph went on. "We were concerned because a lot of the older people, not just in Scotland, but in other countries in which we've worked, are a little . . . superstitious about archeologists. They seem to feel that we dig up things that are better left undisturbed. My colleagues and I have had our share of blame for raising plenty of ghosts, and I just wanted to see if there was any of that feeling here."

"Not that I know of, sir. No." He said nothing more, and from his expression, Joseph didn't expect him to.

"We're sorry to have disturbed you," Laika said. "Thanks for the information."

Trotter nodded, looking at them apprehensively, as though he couldn't wait for them to leave, and they obliged him.

"This town is scared shitless," Joseph said, "and I don't think it's of ghosts."

"Ghosts, or what *look* like ghosts," Laika said, "have got to be part of it. Skye's intelligence told us that much. And it's obvious that Trotter wasn't telling all he knew. He was covering up, but I don't know why."

"Maybe there's something they're scared of *more* than ghosts," Joseph suggested.

"Publicity?"

"Oh yeah, the paparazzi are just swarming, aren't they?"

"No, and the cover-up may be why. But you can't tell me

a whole town would cover up multiple sightings on their own, just to keep busybodies out.''

"You thinking the government?"

"I don't know what I'm thinking. But I do know that I'd like to find out a little more about our fellow archeologists up at the Mellangaun Stones.''

Tony Luciano went to the door of the caretaker's cottage and knocked. He didn't expect a response, and received none. The car was gone, so why wouldn't the caretaker be gone? If anyone had answered, Tony had a story ready, but it wasn't necessary.

What was left of the outer wall of the castle lay in ruins, and he passed through the opening and walked up to the inner gatehouse. The giant door was visible from the cottage, and he didn't want to have to open it when the caretaker returned, so he went around the back. Near one of the towers, the wall had crumbled enough so that he could clamber up the rubble and climb the remaining ten feet up the angled wall by using the cracks in the mortar that held the stones in place.

After only a few minutes, Tony pulled himself up onto the inner curtain wall of the castle. A stairway was close by, and he descended it into the inner ward, the open area around which the rooms of the castle had been built. It seemed the owners had foreseen that intruders might enter over the wall, for all the inner doors were securely locked, and Tony saw the traces of an old-fashioned wire-based alarm system around the door frames.

With the alarm evasion kit in his backpack, it took him only a minute to incapacitate it. He was delighted to see that the lock on the nearest door was not even a pin-tumbler, but a decades-old warded lock, which yielded quickly to his skeleton keys. The owners, he thought, were either naive or had little fear of being invaded, probably both.

He pushed the door open slowly, listening carefully. But he heard no response to his approach, and went inside, pushing the door closed behind him. The light passing through the grimy windows that looked out onto the inner ward gave the room a twilight glow. It was a kitchen, and the old sinks and cupboards made it obvious that it had last been renovated in the 1940s. An icebox, its cooling coils on its top, stood silently in the corner. Outlets on the walls showed the place had been wired for electricity. There was no food anywhere in the large room.

Tony moved through a wide doorway into what he supposed was a great hall, used for dining. A long table sat against the outside wall, and chairs were placed randomly against the wall opposite. He turned a corner and found a row of sleeping apartments, with an unmade bed in each. The mattresses were made of straw and ticking. When he lifted them, he saw there were no box springs. Each mattress rested on a web of ropes that crossed the wooden frames of the bed. The only other things in each room were a small chest of drawers, a clothes tree, and a wooden chair. There were six such rooms on the ground floor, and six more above, with a bathroom on each floor.

Twelve rooms. Twelve Templars?

Tony tried every door he came across. Most were closets, empty or nearly so. But on the side of the castle beyond the kitchen and opposite the bedrooms, in what seemed to be a storage room, was a closet filled wall to wall and nearly to the high ceiling with old cardboard boxes.

Tony, curious as to what might be inside them, tried to lift one, marked *Bovril* in faded letters, from the top of the pile, and was surprised to find that it was empty. So was the one beneath it. Why, he wondered, have a large closet filled with empty cardboard boxes, unless to disguise the fact that it was more than a mere closet?

He removed enough of the boxes to reach the back wall, and discovered that it was a pocket door. He slid it open, and found himself looking down a narrow, circular staircase that wound into darkness. There was a light switch on the wall, but nothing happened when he flicked it. The power was probably off everywhere but in the cottage. Taking a bright flashlight from his backpack, he turned it on and started down the stairs.

The stairs were steep, and there were fifty of them, so that Tony suspected he was thirty or forty feet beneath ground level when they ended in front of a door. He opened it and shone his light into the darkness.

The room was vast, and he suspected it sat under most of the castle. Rows of great stone pillars ran the length and breadth of the room. Tony could count twenty-four of them, and there seemed to be more stretching back into the deeper darkness beyond his flashlight's beam.

Three broad slate steps took him down to the level of the room, where a long oak table stood. Five massive chairs sat on each side, with one more at each end. The table was bare, and there was nothing else in the room except for a large wooden crest affixed to the stone wall near the table.

It appeared to be a coat of arms, and showed a fist clenching an upright dirk, the source, perhaps, of the castle's name. Two words framed the heraldic device, but the letters were too worn for Tony to decipher. He stepped closer to the crest, but it was so high up on the wall that he could not quite reach it.

He walked around the room, looking into the dark corners and behind every pillar, but there was nothing else to be seen. The place was surprisingly dust free, and he figured there was no breeze to stir it. With the door shut, the chamber might be literally sealed. He turned off his flashlight to see if any light was coming into the room at all, but he found himself in pitch blackness and turned it back on.

Tony was only a few feet from the door, ready to go back upstairs, when he heard the sound. It was a high-pitched, machine-like hum, but unlike a turbine's whir, or any machine he had ever heard before. The sound seemed to be coming from behind him, and he wondered for a second if there were a generator down there that he had somehow overlooked. If so, perhaps the caretaker had returned and started it. The thought made him tense, but when he looked over his shoulder, the tension grew into something as close to panic as Tony had ever felt.

There in the subterranean room, less than ten feet away from him, something was glowing in the darkness. It was a vertical shape, seven feet high, and seemed to hover in the stagnant air of the cellar two feet above the stone floor.

Chapter 12

*T*ony Luciano wasn't afraid of anything human, but what he saw before him didn't fit any mortal parameters. He didn't move. He never even thought of reaching for the weapon beneath his jacket. He could only stand and watch, fascinated and afraid, as his eyes adjusted to the manifestation's light, and defined its features more clearly.

It appeared to be a shrouded, slightly bent figure, as Lazarus might have looked, risen from his grave. Near the top there was a face, but a blank face, devoid of features, that was more frightening than any hollow eyes and gaping mouth. On this empty canvas of a face, one saw what one's own mind projected, and Tony saw it soften into the soft lines and gentle features of Miriam Dominick.

A smaller column of light broke away from the whole, but remained connected near the top. It was as though Miriam's arm was coming up, reaching out for him, and he had the chilling sensation that this woman who had loved him enough to die for him was now asking him to reciprocate, to take her hand and join her in death.

Then he made himself blink, and the face was gone, blank again. And in another second the vision itself blinked out entirely, leaving the pupils of Tony's staring eyes to widen as he stood in only the light of his flashlight hanging forgotten in his hand. The sound that had accompanied the glowing form had ceased as well, and Tony could hear only the pounding of his own heart, and his stifled, shallow breaths.

Somehow he managed to lift the flashlight and shine it around the room, but it illuminated only those things he had seen before the glowing shape had appeared: chairs, table, pillars, walls. He crossed the short distance to the door by stepping backward, the flashlight held in front of him as though it were a cross warding off a vampire. Then he ran up the stairs, and at the top, closed the door behind him with a sigh of relief.

But as he leaned against that door in the back of the closet, he heard the unmistakable sound of someone moving in another part of the castle. There were several sets of footsteps echoing down the stone halls, and soft voices. When he crossed to just inside the door to the hall and listened, they seemed to come from the kitchen.

Tony thought about running, but instead he decided to replace the cardboard boxes that had hidden the cellar door. That way, those in the castle would not know that someone had found the meeting room below.

It took him only a minute, and the voices sounded no closer. He assumed that the caretaker and someone else had driven the car through the inner gatehouse and into the open inner ward, where they were bringing supplies into the kitchen. Perhaps the master of the castle was returning.

Tony had shut and locked the door through which he had come, so the caretaker would not know anyone had entered, but he had also disengaged the alarm system, and unless he enabled it once again, the traces of his handiwork would be evident to anyone who looked. Before he left the castle, he would have to remove the small clips that had intercepted the electric signal that probably ran to the caretaker's cottage.

And that meant he had to find a place to hide until whoever was in the kitchen had gone. The storage room was no good, as they might come in to retrieve some of the furniture stored there.

Tony took a small mirror and held it at floor level so that only a half inch protruded into the hall. He could see three different people moving through the kitchen door at the end of the hall. He waited until all three had moved toward the inner ward, and then he dashed silently out of the room and down the hall away from the kitchen.

He followed a stairway upward to the top of the inner curtain. Crouching so that he would not be seen from below, Tony moved down the walkway until it passed by the northeast tower of the castle. Looking down he saw, in a small open area between the buildings and the tower, a stone well ten feet across, covered with wooden planks cut and joined in the shape of a large disc.

Another stairway wound down the inside of the tower, and he followed it down to the well. A short, narrow passageway led from there to the inner ward, but halfway down it was another door, slightly ajar.

Tony could open it without being seen from the cars, so he slipped inside. From the two anvils and stone fire pit, he assumed that he was inside a blacksmith shop, and thought the likelihood of them bringing any new horseshoes into it was slim. The fact that it was unlocked proved its uselessness, and from it he could easily hear the vehicles when they left.

If they left, he thought grimly. They would eventually discover that the alarm had been turned off, but not necessarily today. If they remained in the castle, there was a chance that he could restore it anyway, long after dark.

As he sat on the earth floor and waited, he thought with a shudder about what he had seen. Tony could not say that he believed in ghosts, but neither was he a complete disbeliever, as Joseph was, or perhaps "had been." The experiences that they had gone through, the things they had seen and learned, would have convinced Carl Sagan, God rest him, of the existence of something beyond science.

Of course, Joseph still held out for the theory that science had to be at the bottom of all they had seen, a science that was merely beyond their current powers of understanding. And maybe that was true.

But Tony didn't know what kind of science could make what he had seen in the cellar appear to him, or what kind of science could enable a being like the Prisoner to send his thoughts across hundreds of miles, make people kill each other, or bring them back from the dead afterward, as he had with Ezekiel Swain.

He understood all too well, however, how Miriam had achieved her psychic miracles: through subterfuge, hoaxes, and tricks. And at the end, her love for her twisted image of God had made her send him to what she thought was certain death.

But her love for Tony had made her come with him, and she was the one who had died, not him. She had met death, beyond any reason for lies, loving him.

He pushed the thoughts away and settled into the mode he had rested in so many times before, waiting. Waiting for the time to be right, to steal or flee or kill.

Chapter 13

"**T**hey were screwing around in there for another half hour," Tony told Laika and Joseph. "And then they left. I rewired the alarm and went out the way I'd come in, over the top. But I couldn't go back the way I came, so I found a steep stairway down to the beach. Then I headed south, and when I figured I was out of sight of the cottage, I climbed back up to the Stones." He sat back in the lumpy old easy chair in their cottage's living room and sipped his tea.

Laika scowled. "First of all, that wasn't smart. You should've waited for us before you tried a recon like that. What if they'd had a dog with them? It might've found you and you would have had to fight your way out. Oh, I have no doubt you'd have made it, but our cards would have been spread out all over the table."

"Along with your bowels," said Joseph, "if there were a *number* of doggies."

Laika gestured him to silence. "There's no denying, though, that you may have come across something here. Let's look at the Templar connections first. All we have is an old priest's word, and the French are pretty Templar crazy. The whole Merovingian dynasty connection came out of France, along with its Templar connections."

"But we *know* there were twelve Templars following the Prisoner's influence," Tony said.

"Twelve is a pretty common number," said Joseph. "Most large dining tables seat either ten or twelve."

"What about the twelve bedrooms?" Tony asked. "And they were austere, just as plain and sparsely furnished as the room that MacAndrews guy lived in. And we know *he* was a Templar."

Joseph shrugged. "Along with being homes, castles were also military barracks. Frankly, I'd feel a lot more convinced if that coat of arms you saw on the wall had been the Templar symbol." They had all seen that symbol—two knights riding a single horse—branded on the dead MacAndrews' chest.

"It more than bears looking into, though," Laika said. "We'll try and find out what we can about the castle's history, who this Scobie is who's supposed to be its owner, and who the previous owners were. I doubt we'll get much help from the locals. What I'm really *more* concerned with is this thing you saw in the cellar, Tony. You can think of no possible explanation?"

"Light shining down from the stairway?" Joseph suggested.

"The stairway was black as hell," Tony said. "The only light down there was from my flashlight. I turned it off for a few seconds to make sure, before I saw the thing."

"From what you said," said Laika, "it could have been identified as a ghost, a saint, a vision, even an alien, right?"

"It could've been Jesus, for that matter. I had the feeling that anybody could've seen anything in it, a dead father, or wife, or . . . anything," Tony finished quietly.

"We have to assume, then, that you've seen what a lot of other people have been seeing . . ."

"But that nobody wants to talk about," Joseph added. "I saw one of the things myself last night." Laika and Tony looked hard at him. "Don't sweat it, it wasn't real, just a dream."

Laika, relieved, turned her thoughts back to the castle. "It looks like the caretaker and a few others are getting ready for some occupation," she said. "The MacLunie land extends slightly beyond that ridge that overlooks the castle. So tomorrow we'll start another dig up near there, give us some camouflage so that we can keep an eye on the castle. After we get the site prepared, Tony, I'd like you to do the surveillance, since you're the only one who's been inside it.

"Joseph, you and I will check out the libraries, historical societies, museum holdings, and whatever else we can find, to try and find out more about the castle. Frankly, I'd like to rule it out as a possibility of any connection with the Prisoner. If we find no Templar connection, all well and good. If we do, well, we'll see where it takes us."

"One thing bothers me, Laika," Tony said. "Since the inception of our team, every single thing that would have been otherwise inexplicable—and most of it still is—has been connected to the Prisoner. And what I saw in that cellar, as far as I'm concerned, was pretty damned inexplicable, along with being pretty damned scary. I think he's here. I think that somehow he's behind what's going on, all these sightings of ghosts and demons and aliens.

"So I guess what I want to know is, are we following him, or is he following us?"

The following morning, they drove the van further up the hill and parked it just on the other side of the ridge from the castle. They began digging again, an area ten feet by ten feet square, removing the turf and sifting through the topsoil. Then they ran ribbons across the site, and dug up several of the square foot areas that resulted. They expected to find nothing but stones, and their expectations were fulfilled.

At noon, Joseph and Tony stopped for lunch, but Laika wanted to finish the small piece of earth on which she was working. The two men went over the ridge to watch the waters of the Minch as they ate, leaving Laika alone.

She saw a car pull off the road down below, and a woman started to walk up the hill toward her. There was nothing threatening about her, so Laika didn't call the others. When the woman was fifty feet away, she waved a hand, and Laika waved back. "Hi," the woman said, coming up to Laika. "I'm Molly Fraser." She had a Scots accent, but one less broad than most, and Laika guessed that she had spent some years in England. "I'm with the Edinburgh U. team over at the Mellangaun Stones. Thought I'd come over and give our counterparts from the States a welcome."

"Nice to meet you," Laika said, wiping off her hand before she shook Molly Fraser's offered one. "I'm Frances Brown. We're from Princeton."

"So I've heard," said Molly. "We were a wee bit curious as to why you're doing a dig here at the MacLunie Stones."

"Well, it's pretty much virgin territory. Just sort of a shot in the dark, you know? We probably won't spend much more than a few weeks here."

"And why so far from the stones themselves?"

"Oh, this one's just a sampling, really. Dr. Witherup, one of my colleagues, theorized that this would have been a likely place to have set a watch while the measurements were taken and the stones were being set in place. And the watchmen are more likely than the workers and planners to engage in . . . well, in activities that might empty their pockets."

"Gambling," Molly Fraser said. "It's possible. But I'm puzzled as to why you'd use a Flannery subsurface before you did a magnetometer survey."

Laika felt a twinge of warning. This woman was fishing. Laika didn't know what the hell a "Flannery subsurface" was, although it was probably just the term for the type of excavation they had made, but Fraser couldn't fool her with that magnetometer stuff. Laika had boned up on her old college subject. "Well," she said, "since a magnetometer measures magnetic anomalies that are produced by major disturbance of the soil, we didn't think we'd get anything here. Nobody's dug any pits or ditches on this spot, if indeed they ever did anything. So there wasn't much point."

Laika saw Tony and Joseph coming back over the crest of the ridge, and waved to let them know everything was all right. The woman glanced over her shoulder at the two men, gave her own wave, and then looked back at Laika.

"Just one more question?" Molly Fraser asked. "What possible interest can America's Central Intelligence Agency have in a decidedly minor Scottish prehistoric site?"

Chapter 14

Joseph got only a glimpse of the woman's face from some distance away before she turned her back on him again and said something to Laika. He couldn't hear what it was, but it made quite an impression on his team leader. He didn't think he had ever seen her usual poker face so unguardedly surprised.

There seemed to be something familiar about the tall woman Laika was talking to, but he didn't really know what it was until she turned and smiled at him and he heard her voice. "Hi, Joe."

Jesus God. ". . . Molly?"

"You *know* each other?" Laika said.

"Come on, Joseph," Molly Fraser said. "I haven't changed that much, have I? I identified *you* at fifty paces." She turned back to Laika. "That was the giveaway, Dr. Brown, if that's really your name. Although I started to doubt you when you didn't ask what a Flannery subsurface was. I made that up, you see." She turned back to Joseph. "So you're still a Company man, Joseph? Haven't gone in for archeology, have you?"

"No more than you, Molly. I don't suppose you'd believe me if I told you I was Dr. Charles Witherup of Princeton, so I might as well not bother."

"All right," Laika said. "You two want to can the Nick and Nora Charles routine and tell me what's going on here?"

"This is Molly Fraser, of MI5," Joseph said, trying to keep

his head from spinning by sticking to hard facts. He felt thoroughly disoriented. How could Molly be here, and the two of them be chattering away like this, completely disregarding the secrets with which they had lived their lives? Simply put, no secrets remained between them.

"*Ex*-MI5," said Molly. "But I assume," she went on, gesturing to the excavated earth, "from this carefully woven cover and the fabric of lies I've detected, that you are *not ex*-CIA. And please be careful how you answer. I *am* the chief law enforcement officer of this district."

"Oh, Christ," muttered Laika.

"Molly and I worked together for several weeks back in 1982," Joseph said, "in a joint anti-Soviet intelligence mission."

"And we got the bad guy, too, didn't we?"

"Yes, we did." Joseph sighed. "So now what?"

"Now you three tell me all about why you're here. The only alternative is terminating me and tossing me into the Minch, and I'd advise against that, since the other team at the Mellangaun Stones knows I've come to see you."

"You mean the MI5 team?" Laika asked.

Now it was Molly's turn to look surprised. "No, the Edinburgh University team, as I told you."

"You lied," Laika said. "It all fits together now. The people around here aren't saying a word about the manifestations they've been seeing, and the newspaper isn't reporting them because they've all been cautioned by agents of the government, none other than MI5, probably under function number four, protective security."

"You're very good," Molly said with a grudging smile. "Almost as good as I am."

"Well, you've got a few years on me."

"Ladies," Tony said, calming the waters. "It seems that since everyone's cover has been blown, I may as well introduce myself to the charming Inspector Fraser. I hardly think she's going to buy the fact that I'm a grad student from Princeton. My name's Tony Luciano, and I'm very pleased to meet you." He extended a hand, and Molly shook it.

"You're right," she said with a warm smile. "I wouldn't have bought that grad student thing for a minute. You deserve at least a full professorship."

"And my name's Laika Harris," said Laika, shaking Molly's hand hesitantly. "I'm the team leader, and I think we need to have a long talk before you inform anyone of our presence here."

"Agreed. Your cottage is near here, I believe."

Laika nodded. "We can go in our van if you like."

"I prefer that we go in my car. I'll bring you back here when we're done. Or wherever else you may want to go."

As they walked down the hill to the road, Joseph realized why Molly wanted to go in her own car. It would cause them more of a hassle if they decided to make her disappear.

He could not imagine ever wanting to make Molly Fraser vanish, unless he could vanish with her. They had been lovers as well as partners back in 1982, when their mission together had been to expose a pair of Soviet moles. The tricky bit was that the moles were working in tandem, one of them within MI5, and the other within the network that the CIA had put together inside England, of which the British government was officially supposed to remain unaware.

It was a delicate situation, to say the least, and when it was completed, Molly and Joseph had decided that they could never see each other again. Joseph had always thought that their decision, the only rational one, had been far more painful for him than for her. He had wondered many times over the years if she had felt the loss as deeply, but had simply behaved more professionally than he. After all, the English, and he supposed that included the Scottish, were more stiff-upper-lip than Americans, who were more likely to wear their hearts on their sleeves. And Jews, of which he was one, were very talented when it came to suffering. God knows, he thought, they had enough experience.

Though rational humanism had always courted him, it was only after the episode with Molly that he had fully embraced it. It seemed to ease the pain, and eventually became his way of life. And he had been content, until the current madness of these shadow operations for Skye had begun and made him doubt not only his atheism, but also his sanity.

And now here again was Molly Fraser, to remind him of those days when emotion had played a much larger role. He was sitting in the front seat with her, and he had to look hard to see any sign of the years in her face. There were a few strands of gray in the mass of dark brown hair, and maybe some lines in the corners of her eyes and her mouth that hadn't been there before, but she still looked wonderful to him. She had kept in shape, something that he had been lax about, although she probably couldn't notice his slight belly under his loose-fitting jacket.

Christ, he thought, here his cover and that of his colleagues had just been broken by a policeman with MI5 connections, their mission stood in jeopardy, and they had been theoretically *captured* by an operative of a foreign, if allied, government, and all he was thinking about was how good his gut looked. It was time to bring back the practical Joseph Stein, and figure a way out of this mess.

"Now," said Molly Fraser, when the four of them were sitting in the living room of the cottage, and Tony had put water on for tea, "suppose you tell me exactly what your mission is, and the reason behind it. If you don't, I promise you that I will report your presence to MI5. If you do and it's not destructive to our government or its security, well, Agent Stein and I have peacefully coexisted despite our two organizations once before. Possibly it could happen again."

A promise like that was as good as they could expect, so Laika put the three of them firmly into Molly's hands. She told her about their mission, basically repeating what Skye had told them at the onset, how orders had come down from the top echelons of government that a small, deep-cover team be established to thoroughly debunk any reports of supposed paranormal activity or powers. The purpose of such debunking was to bring a much-needed rationality back to the American people, both the New Agers on the left, and those on the right who clung to miracles and angels.

Langley had received reports that there had been multiple sightings of purportedly paranormal phenomena on the Gairloch peninsula, and their superior had sent them to investigate, using the Princeton team cover. However, Laika did not mention their previous missions, or anything about the Prisoner or the Knights Templar or the Roman Catholic Church.

"If you want to check our story," she concluded, "contact Richard Skye in Counter-Intelligence Operations at Langley. I recommend, though, that he should be the *only* person you contact. You'll receive denials from anyone else."

Christ, Joseph thought, she'd probably receive a denial from Skye, too. *Then* where would they be? A loud whistle told them the water was ready for tea, and Tony went into the kitchen.

"Question," Molly said. "Why were you digging where you were—up higher from the stones?"

Laika glanced at Joseph, then looked back at Molly. "We thought it possible that the source of the manifestations might be the castle." Molly raised her eyebrows, and Laika went on. "Look, our goal is to debunk. That means we can't believe in any supernatural mechanisms here. Whatever these forms are that people are seeing, they're not ghosts." She smiled. "Okay, maybe they're aliens. That, at least, would have some scientific validity. But we don't believe that, either. Despite all the tabloid blather, no evidence of extraterrestrial life has been presented, and believe me, the Company would know. There isn't much they *don't* know."

"So what are they, then?" asked Molly. "And why the castle?"

Joseph had to admire how Laika could create spin on a moment's notice. Of course, she did have time to flesh out the story in her head as they drove to the cottage. "Our theory," she went on, as Tony returned with the cups and saucers on a tray and passed them around, "is that whatever is

creating these images has to be a machine of some sort, probably wireless computer imaging. We assume that the builders
and operators of such a device require a certain amount of
space and a large amount of privacy. Castle Dirk is about the
only place on the peninsula that meets those criteria.''

"So," Molly said, "we have a desolate Scottish castle
filled with mad scientists out to terrorize the populace with
their ghost machine, is that it?''

"I admit it sounds a little farfetched—"

"It sound positively outlandish," said Molly, "like one of
those stories Joseph used to relish.''

"No," Joseph said. "I never cared for the stories where
the ghosts were illusions created by some mad scientist. I like
my ghosts real—in fiction, anyway.''

"I stand corrected," Molly said. "Your theory still sounds
absurd.''

"If MI5 can come up with something more rational,"
Laika replied, "I'd be happy to hear it.''

Molly pursed her lips. "No. They haven't yet.''

"And would you tell us if they had?'' asked Laika.

"Possibly not. I'm certainly under no obligation to.''

"And we are?'' Joseph said.

"You're American agents found operating on foreign soil.
In case you didn't know it, Joseph, spies are supposed to be
clandestine.''

"Well, spies usually don't run into other spies who happen
to recognize them after seventeen years.''

"You're the only person who ever actually saved my life,''
Molly repled. "One tends to remember that.''

"Like the lion remembered Androcles?'' said Joseph. "We
could use a favor. Are you required to report our presence?
Because if you are, it's very possible our government will
hang us out to dry.''

"What's the phrase?'' Molly said. " 'Twist slowly, slowly
in the wind?' As for your question, no, I'm not officially
required to report your presence, or to do a damned thing for
MI5. I told you the truth. I'm a police inspector now, and I'm

'cooperating' with MI5. You were correct, Agent Harris, they *are* at the Mellangaun dig, doing the same thing as you—trying to find the reasons behind these sightings.'' She took a deep breath. ''Frankly, I think the three of you would be more use to us as unofficial colleagues than as exposed foreign agents. We all want the same thing. And I, especially, want my district back to normal. These things have caused quite a reign of terror. And,'' she added in an undertone, ''MI5 hasn't made things cheerier for my flock.''

''They've warned them, haven't they?'' asked Laika. ''The newspaper, the shopkeepers, everybody—they're not supposed to say anything.''

''That's right. Not to outsiders. Magna Carta or no, certain offices of our government can still behave like an absolute monarchy when it suits their purposes. So now the people have two things to be frightened of—the ghosts, and the government bullies.

''Listen,'' Molly went on, ''I won't contact this Skye you mentioned, and I won't inform MI5. As far as they're concerned, you can be legitimate archeologists from the States, and I doubt they'll bother you, because they think that you'll find *them* out as fakes.''

''Just the way you did to us,'' said Laika.

''Just like,'' Molly agreed. ''I'd be foolish to discard a valuable resource like you three. So if we can agree to work together—independently but cooperatively—I'll walk away, and you can carry on.''

''That sounds acceptable,'' Laika said.

''Well, I don't see that you have much choice.''

Molly smiled at Laika Harris. She liked the woman. There was a toughness about her, a refusal to back down or show weakness, the same qualities that Molly had had to develop to move up in MI5. They were the qualities that got a woman labeled a hard-nosed bitch among many men, but a hard-nosed bitch couldn't let that bother her.

''So,'' said Laika. ''We've shared what little we know with

you, and you've got our fates in your hands. Are you going to reciprocate? What have your people learned so far?''

Molly thought for a moment before replying. She damn well wasn't going to tell them about the possibility of tachyons, but she could at least tell them about the cloth itself, and she did, including the fact that it had been discovered on property belonging to the castle. She also told them about its luminescence and radioactivity, and that a large piece was missing from its one corner. Then she shared with them the information that had been received only that morning.

''One of the technicians who was into history came up with an interesting link. Have you ever heard of the Fairy Flag of the MacKenzies?''

''Yeah,'' said Tony. ''Isn't that an old cloth that this clan used to use as a battle flag? They've got it displayed somewhere.''

''Partly right. The casket that holds it is on display at Castle MacKenzie in Sutherland County. There are several legends behind it. One is that it was given to the head of Clan MacKenzie by the queen of the fairies, who was smitten by him. She told him to wave it when he went into battle, and he would be invincible, but it would only work three times. Supposedly it's been waved twice, and the MacKenzies won the battle both times. Now it sits inside a *lead* casket, until it's needed again. But photographs of it are widespread.''

''I've seen them,'' said Tony. ''It's just pretty much a rag, isn't it?''

''Yes,'' Molly said. ''It's in rough shape. It appears to have been cut or torn from a larger piece of cloth, and the technician analyzing the radioactivity of the cloth found near here noticed its similarity to the Fairy Flag, and thought that possibly the MacKenzies' flag might have been taken from this larger cloth. Some MI5 people went to Castle MacKenzie this morning with Geiger counters and a paper pattern of the larger cloth.''

''The larger cloth glows in the dark,'' Joseph said. ''Is there any account of the Fairy Flag doing the same?''

"No," Molly answered, "but battles are fought in daylight. Maybe no one ever happened to look at it in the darkness."

"And if somebody had, say, centuries ago," Tony said, "maybe it wasn't worth mentioning—a Fairy Flag would be *expected* to glow. After all, it was magic."

"You may be right," Molly said. "We should hear shortly if it matches and if it's radioactive. That would give us a connection, but I'm not sure what we do with it. What's *your* next step?"

"I think we'll move further toward the castle," said Laika. "Creep up on them. There was some activity there yesterday, as though the caretaker was getting ready for someone to stay there for a while. Maybe we can force their hand, find out how they respond to an archeological incursion."

Molly shrugged. "It beats sitting on our thumbs. We're just basically marking time, trying to gather the data from everyone who's been . . . visited by these bogles."

"Bogles?" asked Tony.

"Ghosts. Old Scots word." She stood up, setting her empty tea cup and saucer on an end table. "I'd best be getting back."

"One more question," said Laika. "Are you going to let the owners of the castle know that you found the cloth on their property? And will you return it?"

"The hole's been filled in so that not a trace remains," Molly said. "Nobody found anything there at all."

Chapter 15

Molly drove the ops back to the MacLunie land and headed north, promising to keep in touch and receiving the same promise in return. When they were alone, Laika shook her head regretfully. "All we need. Our covers shattered like glass."

"It could be worse," Tony said. "You look at it one way, we're in better shape than before. Now we've got British intelligence feeding us information."

"What's this woman like, Joseph?"

He hoped Laika couldn't see everything in his face. "A good agent. Thoroughly professional." Except for making love to her colleague. "I trust her."

"You really saved her life?" Tony asked.

"Yes."

"Come on, don't be shy, what'd you do?"

"I got between her and a knife."

"Disarmed the attacker, huh?"

"No. I got stabbed."

Tony chuckled. "Next time, disarm the attacker." Then his smile faded as he remembered the last time Joseph had been attacked with a bladed weapon. He had disarmed the attacker, all right. He had killed the madwoman in that ruined townhouse in New York City. And now the scar reopened again, and Joseph could see that Tony was sorry for reminding him.

"Okay," Laika said, trying to change the subject, "before

96

we set up the new site, any thoughts or revelations about the cloth?''

"Just that it seems strange that the Fairy Flag was enclosed in lead," Joseph said, getting back on track. "I can't think of lead without thinking of the Prisoner, and the lead-lined caskets and rooms the church kept him in."

"I think we need to wait, though," said Laika, "until we learn if there's a connection between the flag and this cloth. If the flag proves to be radioactive and the same kind of weave and material as the cloth—"

"Hey," Tony said quietly. "I just had a really weird thought, and I know you're going to think I'm full of crap, but you know that deal about waving the flag and the clan would get help in battle? Well, what if that's what happened here, but on a bigger scale?"

"You want to expand this thesis a little?" Joseph said. "I'm still in the dark."

"What if the old guy who found this cloth waved it? You know, just opened it up and spread it out? And what if it worked the same way as the Fairy Flag?"

Joseph's frown of disbelief grew deeper. "You mean, what if he beckoned the fairies? You're saying that all these ghostly manifestations, including the one you saw yourself, are *fairies?*"

"Shit, I don't know *what* I'm saying. It's just an idea, okay? I mean, maybe they were never fairies to begin with, but something else."

"Pixies," suggested Joseph. "Or elves?"

"Look, after everything we've seen, you're gonna draw the line at a radioactive cloth producing simple images? Joseph, that's kid stuff compared to some of the things we've actually *experienced.*"

"I wouldn't rule anything out, Joseph," Laika said. "But until we hear any more from Molly, I suggest the most productive use of our time is to get closer to that castle and whoever's in it, especially since the cloth was found on their land." She started walking toward the van. "Dig we must."

Tony drove the van up over the crest of the hill, past their second site, and down toward the Minch and Castle Dirk, parking only a few yards from the stone wall that surrounded the castle. It was a spot where they would be sure to be seen from both the castle and the caretaker's cottage. Then they got out and began laying out a site grid with stakes and ribbon, and removing the turf.

"I'm getting sick of this," said Joseph. "Why can't we do surveillance in a town where we can sit in a sidewalk café and peek over a newspaper? I never yet got calluses peeking over a newspaper."

"Yeah, but you don't see any fairies at sidewalk cafés," said Tony, hoisting a shovelful of dirt. Joseph considered a comeback, but found it politically incorrect and remained silent.

Around 5 o'clock, just as they were talking about calling it a day, Tony called out, "Incoming." Two vans and a car were coming down the long dirt drive from the road to the castle. It was growing dark, and at a distance of 200 yards, the ops were only able to see that there were several people in each vehicle. They felt sure, however, that they had easily been seen from the dirt road.

"Keep working," Laika said. "Maybe we'll be lucky and get some company." The vans and the car followed the road as it passed through the rubble of the outer curtain, and then wound through the opening of the inner gatehouse and vanished from sight. "Let's just play it cool, boys."

"Duh-deeeeeeee-*dah!*" Tony sang, snapping his fingers rhythmically afterward.

"A loose rendition of *West Side Story*?" asked Joseph.

"Yeah. I'd dance, but I'm too tired from this damn digging."

"Who in bloody hell were they?" asked Angus Gunn.

"That's what we'll find out," Colin Mackay said.

Angus shook his head. "Naebody good, I'll wager. You think police?"

"No, not police, Angus. Probably just some damned treasure hunters. See a castle and they think there's gold buried all over."

"Would you like *me* to talk to them?" said the man they knew as Mulcifer. "I'm sure I could put a stop to whatever it is they're doing. Permanently."

Colin ignored him. The man was teasing, playing his little games. He'd made such suggestions whenever they ran into a spot of difficulty, which hadn't been very often. The trip from the United States to Scotland had been surprisingly trouble free, all except getting through customs with Mulcifer, and that had been the creature's own fault.

His false passport had been perfect, in the name of Philip Braxton, an American traveling on business, planning to stay in the United Kingdom for two months, the time divided between northern England and Scotland. The contact with the customs officer was the first Mulcifer had had with anyone outside of Colin's organization since joining them, and Colin suspected that Mulcifer had been waiting for such an opportunity.

Colin had been several spaces behind Mulcifer in the customs line, and tensed slightly when the officer had asked "Mr. Braxton" to please open his luggage. There should have been nothing to worry about. The fake samples of "Mr. Braxton's" product line were as they should be, and the clothes were neatly packed. Then something strange happened.

The customs officer took out a very conservative regimental striped necktie, and looked quizzically at Mulcifer, who then simply nodded. The officer removed the tie he was wearing, and then tied Mulcifer's about his neck, closed the suitcase, and beckoned him through, as if nothing had happened.

Colin joined Mulcifer as they left customs, and asked what the exchange was all about. The man shrugged. "He simply liked my tie better than his own. In fact, he liked it so much that tonight when he goes home he'll hang himself with it." He flashed a smile like a light blinking on and off, and kept walking.

There was no way that such a minor incident at Glasgow Airport could be traced to them, Colin decided, and tried to stop thinking about how quickly and easily Mulcifer could take a life. But when the thought would not depart, he started to think how that talent might best be used for their great cause.

He had returned to Scotland with a monster at his side, but that monster, if properly controlled, could bring him what he wanted for his country, total freedom from the English yoke. Why, then, did he feel, as he entered what had been his father's castle and was now his own, that he was doomed to failure, that this was a mistake, a great and tragic one?

No. It was a mistake only if he allowed it to become so. He knew how this creature could be contained, and there were enough men who served him to bring down Mulcifer by sheer strength of numbers, regardless of the great power his father had claimed he had. Colin had called some of his men who were still in Scotland and told them to have a leaden casket made in Glasgow that would hold a man. Were Mulcifer to grow too hard to control, they would simply force him into that, and there would be an end of it.

But first there were the strangers on his land to take care of. Exploring his castle for the first time would have to wait. The vehicles parked within the great square of the inner ward, and they all got out. Colin asked Rob Lindsay to see to the unpacking, and walked back out the way they had entered and across the field toward the strangers.

He easily hopped over the stone wall and walked up to them, two men and a woman who all looked tired and dusty. "Good afternoon," he said without a smile. "May I ask what you're doing here?"

The woman answered that they were archeologists from Princeton University, and were searching for the site of a seventeenth-century village that was reputed to be in the vicinity.

"Then you'd better search somewhere else. This is my land you're on."

The woman looked puzzled. "But I thought the wall marked your property line, Mr. . . . ."

"Scobie. Francis Scobie. Believe me, madam, I've just spent two days in a solicitors' office in Inverness concerning this property, and I do know my boundaries. You're over them, and you're not welcome. I have plans for this land, and digging is not among them."

"Then I apologize, Mr. Scobie. We'll remove ourselves from your property immediately. Where does your line stop?"

"Along the crest of that rise." He pointed and moved his arm in an arc that spanned the darkening southeastern horizon. "On this side of it about twenty yards."

"We can replace the soil and turf first, if you like," the woman said, nodding at the pile of earth and the stacks of turf.

"Not necessary. I'll see to it myself. I shouldn't want to keep you here after dark." Then he turned on his heels and strode back to the castle.

"That went well," Joseph said when Francis Scobie was out of earshot. "Let's get our tools and get out of here, boys and girls, or that Celtic warrior might be after us with his claymore."

"He was a big one, wasn't he?" mused Laika, watching the retreating form. The man's red hair gleamed in the dying light, and his tall body moved effortlessly.

Tony began gathering tools. "The bigger they are . . ." he said.

"The harder they swing their claymores," Joseph finished.

"We'll pull back to the ridge again," said Laika. "We can still see the castle from there. I want it kept under surveillance from now on. Did you see the way he looked at us?"

"And it got worse when you said we were from Princeton," Tony said. "I don't think he likes Yanks."

Laika kept watching the man walking back toward his castle. "The man's a firebrand. And whatever his name is, it isn't Scobie."

"What makes you think that?" asked Joseph.

"Because he didn't say it with enough pride."

Chapter 16

"**N**ow, O master, what is it you would have me do?"

Mulcifer eyed Colin Mackay over steepled fingertips. The Scot was sitting in a plain wooden chair, sipping from a cup of tea sitting on the chair's wide, flat arm. They were alone in the first bedchamber on the ground floor, which had been turned, by the addition of furniture, into a small meeting room.

"We want to strike against the English," Colin said. "The targets must be the British government and trade and not the Scottish people. No stores, no public places. Only government and military facilities and British business offices in Scotland."

"And would you like to restrict the victims to men only, and of a certain age group? No one with families, of course, for we can't have any orphans or widows, can we?"

"Don't be absurd."

"No, don't *you* be absurd, Colin Mackay. You want to be a terrorist, you have to spill blood, you know. I believe that's how it's done. Now you tell me specifically the kind of target you would like. What organization? What building? What man?"

He thought for a moment. "All right, then. The executives of British Petroleum, who take our North Sea oil. The British education officials who've funneled funds away from our public schools. The English monarchy itself—let their country cry for *all* their dotty, inbred rulers, not just their precious princess of hearts.''

''Ah, you'd like me to extinguish the little princes then? Just like Richard the Third? Smother them in their beds?''

''I don't care *what* happens to that damned bloodline! Windsor, my arse—Saxe-Coburgs and Battenburgs and Tecks is what they are, as much German blood as English. And even if they weren't, what right have the English to rule us, anyway? They *stole* our land from us—''

Colin broke off when he saw Mulcifer's sneer. When he spoke, Colin heard the timbre of his own voice. ''And the '45 and Bonnie Prince Charlie, and William Wallace and the Bruce, and Culloden and Glencoe and the Clearances . . . oh, *please* . . .'' The voice returned to Mulcifer's own soft, velvet tones. ''Spare me the lectures. I know all about the history of poor, bleeding Scotland. Now if you're finished spewing your chauvinist bile, may I present a plan of action that should accomplish what we both desire?''

Colin nodded. The man made him feel like a damned fool all too often. He mocked Colin's passion for his country the same way in which he would mock any passion for anything held dear.

''First, how many men do you have in your little shock troops? A dozen?''

''Fifteen here at the castle. Across the Isles, nearly a hundred, and they've all got mates—foot soldiers. We've men, *and* women, in Edinburgh, Glasgow, London, and in Belfast, too—anywhere the British can be hurt.''

''And are they professionals?'' Mulcifer asked, leaning toward him. ''Have they set bombs under the Houses of Parliament? Picked off prime ministers through sniper scopes? Sliced the throats of dukes in public loos? Have they done, or do they have the *capability* to do, all these things?''

''I think . . . I *know* they have the capability.''

Mulcifer sat back and crossed his legs. ''Then what do you need me for?''

Colin held his mocking gaze. ''Because you're *more* than

a professional. You exist for violence, you feed on destruction. Your capabilities alone are far greater than my entire company of patriots.''

"Which isn't too great a company at all . . . in number, at least. I take it you've heard all about me from your . . . *late* father.''

"Yes. He told me a good number of things about you.''

"And did your . . . *late* father tell you I was the Antichrist?''

"Yes.''

"And did your . . . *late* father tell you I was the epitome of human and nonhuman evil?''

"He implied that. Look, why do you keep referring to him like that?''

"The answer puts me in mind of a story, probably apocryphal, that I once heard about a very much disliked jazz musician, a violent man who had made a lot of enemies with his temper and his bullying, a man after my own heart, in fact. It seems his widow received a telephone call asking for her husband, and she told the caller that he was dead. The next day she received another such call, and again told the caller that her husband was dead. The third day she received still another call, and was sure from the voice that it was the very same man. She said to him, 'Look, I already told you he's dead—why do you keep calling?' And the man said, very gently, 'I just like to hear it.'

"You see, Colin, that's the way it is with me. I just like to hear that your father, Sir Andrew Mackay, and the eleven other hounds who tried to undo my handiwork over the centuries are dead. Dead. Dead and gone, not to that heaven for whose blessings they so nobly strove, not to that hell whose lord and . . .'' He raised both hands in self-recognition. ''. . . Supposed minions they so despised. But gone to nothingness. Oblivion. Non-existence, from which they can never return, from which no sweet and mewling Christ can raise them. Thus, your . . . *late* father. I just like to hear it.''

"Fine. Refer to him as you like.''

Mulcifer raised an eyebrow. "I take it there was little love between you."

"We're not here to talk about me. Why don't you tell me your brilliant plan?"

"Oh my, do I detect a note of hostility? Well, politics does make strange bedfellows, and as your . . . *late* father might add, he who sups with the devil had best use a long spoon. But as for my *brilliant* plan, as you so foresightedly put it, let me explain what I have in mind.

"I prefer to use other people to do my work. I don't care for making bombs and aiming guns myself. So the question becomes where to *find* those people. Now, being a prisoner for so long has given me a true empathy for other prisoners, particularly for those imprisoned for political and religious reasons. After all, I myself was cruelly confined because of . . . religious intolerance. My soul is not entirely devoid of sympathy, now, is it? At one stroke, I could aid your cause and satisfy my own needs while freeing these poor souls. What did Jesus say? 'I was in prison, and ye came unto me.' " Mulcifer grinned, and stage whispered, "Yes, that suits my purposes. Anyway," he went on, "I shall do more than simply come unto them. I shall free them, on the condition that they use their very specialized skills to advance our joint cause."

"And how do you intend to free political terrorists from the most well-guarded prisons in the British Isles?"

"Oh, I have my ways. Believe me, it will be quite simple, and the results will be nothing short of spectacular. You see, I intend to just walk into the prisons, introduce myself to the prisoners, and walk them out again."

"Ah," said Colin. The creature was insane after all. "And who's going to open the doors for you then?"

"Doors? Did I say anything about using *doors?* But don't you worry your head about that. You just make a little list for me. You list all the Scottish terrorists now in prison that you would like on your side."

Colin frowned. "That won't take long. There frankly aren't

all that many . . . imprisoned Scottish terrorists.''

"But you were just bragging about this wonderful network you have.''

"Aye, we have the network, but there's been little activity. A couple of nutters who went off on their own, calling in reports of bombs under motorway bridges and in train stations, copycatting the IRA, mucking up the transport, and messing about with the tourist business.''

"Ah, phone pranks. Dangerous men, indeed.''

"A few planted bombs,'' Colin said defensively, then admitted, "Some didn't go off, some did, but to little effect.''

"So do you want them freed at all?'' Mulcifer laughed, and Colin felt his face grow red. "They sound like more trouble than they're worth. I'll tell you what, why don't I free some of these Irish boyos? They sound like they've got more experience than your little soccer hooligans.''

"And why would IRA men do any favors for Scotland? We're bloody Protestants to them.''

"For gratitude,'' said Mulcifer. "The cost of their freedom is one job for Scotland, and then they're on their own to bomb Belfast to their little hearts' content. Again, you leave that to me. As you know, I can be . . . persuasive. What I want you to do is make a wish list of, say, a dozen men in Irish and English prisons who you'd want working for you, in the order of their relative desirability—in terms of terror, that is. I know you're a man's man all the way.''

"And assuming you can get them out of prison without getting caught, then what?''

"What do you *want*, O laird and master?''

"I'd not want them brought here to the castle. They could be given their directives elsewhere.''

"A good idea. That way they can't ever betray their former emancipator. I don't know if their fabled loyalty extends to Scots. I'll also need to know where these men are held, and I'll need plans of the prisons along with the locations of the cells, so I won't have to wander around until I find them. Can you do that?''

Colin nodded sharply. "But I can tell you right now the single man I'd want most on our side. His name is Liam Riley, and he's held in Maze Prison in Belfast. He's an artist with explosives, and absolutely ruthless."

"Good," Mulcifer mused, as if talking to himself. "Bombs are good. Lots of deaths with bombs." Then he brightened, beaming at Colin. "We'll start with Mr. Riley. I assume you and your men can get me over the water to Northern Ireland."

"Aye, but Belfast is riddled with checkpoints, and they only get worse as you get closer to Maze. It's not like no one's ever tried to break someone out of there before."

"You let me worry about the checkpoints. As I said, I'm persuasive, and that goes for English soldiers, too."

"The security's tighter than hell, man."

"I *am* hell, man. Now . . ." He rubbed his hands together. "You get your little wish list together and Saint Mulcifer will make your wishes come true. We'll take the first man you want out of Maze and then go on to the next prison, spring someone else, and so on and so forth, romping back and forth through Ireland and England."

"It'll take time. We'll have to plan an itinerary. I want to be able to send messages to the government, received just after each escape so that they'll know what faction is responsible, set up safe houses for the prisoners . . ."

"Trivia. I leave all that in your more than capable hands."

Colin thought for a moment, then shook his head. "I'm committing a lot to this. How can I be sure you're not just leading my men into a trap, that you can do what you say you can?"

"Don't ever doubt me." The smile vanished. "Don't you know what I am? Don't you know the things of which I'm capable? Did your father keep you so ignorant of my powers? I can make your men kill and eat each other. I can even make them kill *you*, if I wish it."

"Which brings up the question," Colin said, refusing to be cowed, "why haven't you, then?"

"Because it does not suit my purposes."

*   *   *

At this time, thought Mulcifer. *Not until you see your dreams go up in the smoke of burning Scottish children. Not until your precious land weeps its way through a thousand Dunblanes. Not until your countrymen curse your name as they would a plague, until Colin Mackay becomes vileness in their mouths and poison in their ears. Scotland will be the heart of my new darkness that will engulf the world, and your home and the home of your damnable father and his fellow jackals will become another name for hell.*

Chapter 17

*I*t all seemed absolutely suicidal, and Colin told Rob Lindsay so, but Rob was still willing to head the team to get Mulcifer into Ireland. "The crazy bastard wouldn't do it if he didn't think he could get away with it," Rob said. "But I don't see how the shite we're going to be driving away from Maze through British checkpoints with Liam Riley in the car."

"That's why I'm telling you it's suicide. I won't blame you, Rob, if you don't want to do it."

"Ah Christ, if it doesn't work I'll be a martyr, and if it does I'll be a legend. How can I lose?"

Together, Colin, Rob, Angus Gunn, and James Menzies created a list of six men who, once freed, had the knowledge, talents, and ruthlessness to strike hard against England. Three were IRA, two INLA, and the last was a Scottish Nationalist. Two IRA and the INLA men were held in Maze and Maghaberry, but the Scot was in Edinburgh, and the other IRA man, Kevin Brady, was in a small, maximum security prison in northern England. "Brady's crazy as shite," James Menzies said. "They put him in Maze, and the first month he was there he killed two loyalists in his block."

"They put the IRA in with the loyalists?" Angus asked.

Colin nodded. "Same block, but separate wings. I guess they figure they'll be so busy watching and hating each other that they won't have any energy left to make trouble with the

110

prison officers. Seems to work pretty well . . . unless you're a prisoner.''

"Or unless you're Kevin Brady,'' James went on. "Solitary didn't do a thing to him. Soon's he got out, four loyalists jumped him. He crippled two and would've killed them all if the guards hadn't gassed him. They moved him out of Maze, then to Hixton Prison, near York. You don't see another prisoner's face there. Pure solitary.''

"Is the bastard too crazy to be of use to us?'' Colin asked.

"Depends on how effective you think this Mulcifer is. But I suggest we put Brady last on the list. Ultimate weapon kind of thing, aye?''

The plan went into high gear. While the other men handled the logistics of getting men and vehicles into Ireland and England, Colin wrote the letters that would be sent from remote mailboxes around the United Kingdom when he received word that Mulcifer and the crew were in position for the next jailbreak. The letters did not credit the breaks to any named group, but only stated that they would continue if the demands in the letter were not met. The demands ran on for six pages, but the gist of it was that the English government should extricate itself immediately from any and all Scottish affairs, and an interim government should be appointed by the nominating committee of the Scottish Nationalist Party.

It was remarkable, Mulcifer thought, how people let politics direct their lives. Countries, governments, rulers—none of it meant a thing when compared to the true meaning of existence, the shedding of blood and the causing of pain.

He walked alone in the night along the stony beach. The moon shone brightly in the water of the Minch, and he watched the way that its reflected light shimmered with the motion of the waves. Everything certainly seemed to be working out for the best. First had come freedom, after all those centuries, and then the son of his greatest enemy had fallen into his hands, and given him a great game to play, presented him with a convocation of fools that he could use to deepen the pools of blood he would cause to be shed. Things could scarcely get any better.

Now he stopped and stood looking at the water. There were, he thought, other sources of beauty in this world besides blood and death. He gazed up to the moon, looking like a great gold eye shining down, watching him.

Then the moon seemed to tremble, and for a moment he thought that somehow the water had gone up into the sky, and that he was seeing the reflection above him. But then he realized what an impossibly foolish thought that was, and that he had been around human beings too much, that what little facet of his mind that he had called imagination was working overtime, as they put it.

Then the moon trembled again, and seemed to lengthen vertically, and he froze, feeling true fear for the first time in a millennium. No, he thought, this could not be. There was no way they could know, no way they could have learned.

The shape formed directly in front of the moon, its own pale glow blotting out the yellow light behind it. He could only stand and watch, not daring to move, as it took on form. It remained motionless for a long moment and then vanished instantly, so that the sky showed only the moon again.

He watched the sky, but there was no other movement except for the stately drift of the moon and stars and planets. Had they seen him, he wondered, and if they had, how close were they? Far away, no doubt, for if they, rather than their searching images, had been there, they would have taken him immediately.

No, he thought with relief, however they might have learned of his freedom, they were still far from him. There was still time.

He turned away, thinking how much he suddenly wanted to draw blood again, to hear a scream, and see the contortions that pain could bring a man.

*   *   *

They were on their way. Rob and Angus had gone with Mulcifer, leaving Colin and the rest of the men behind at the castle. Rob would call Colin when Mulcifer was ready to go through the final checkpoints and enter Maze Prison.

Then Colin would have the message to the government, already in the hands of a man in Aberdeen, put into the mail. The first prisoner would be freed and placed in a safe house, and Colin's shadow group would receive the credit. Then they would move on to a man in Maghaberry before returning to Maze, continuing to go from one prison to another until all six men were freed.

At that point, Colin would meet them and give them their assignments—half a dozen blows against what was left of a pitiful empire, simultaneous blows that would shake England to its core. Colin had already chosen three targets: the Tower of London, accomplished by a well-placed boat on the Thames; the Houses of Parliament, which necessitated a huge charge and the use of subterranean engineering, and, most outrageous of all, the island on which the darling Princess Diana was buried. All could be accomplished late at night, insuring the fewest casualties.

But such audacity did not come without a price. MI5's counterterrorist division was skilled and tenacious and as ruthless in their pursuit as their quarry. It was altogether possible that the full weight of the law could come down on Colin Mackay and Castle Dirk and all those in his organization. The more people involved, the greater chance there was for informers and quislings. And it was because of that risk that Colin put into effect the plan he had discussed with Rob and James and Angus.

It took Colin and James and two other men two trips to carry enough C-4 into the cellar. They piled it against the stone wall on which hung the worn coat of arms of the Mackays. That would be the right place. That wall, on the landward side, held up half the structure of the castle.

Once the charges were set, Colin attached a manual triggering device. Once thrown, there was no hope of reprieve, no cutting wires, as in the movies. The device would allow whoever threw the switch five minutes to evacuate the castle, or, if the enemy outside allowed no escape, five minutes to sit next to the pile of C-4 and think about what you were going to die for.

When that was finished, Colin at last found himself with some time on his hands. He went to the small study that had been his father's, a bedchamber like the others, but with a small desk. Colin sat down, undid a seal on some papers, and read what his father had left for him with the Inverness solicitors.

They were all written, probably years before, in his father's broad hand, and said what Colin had thought them likely to say. They stated that since Sir Andrew had now been missing long enough to be considered dead, it fell to his son to carry on his work. And if it so happened that all of Sir Andrew's "brothers" were also gone, then it was up to Colin Mackay to assemble a new group of men, totaling twelve.

These men should be of the highest moral character, and should come from pure Scots stock, with no traces of any Mediterranean bloodline whatsoever. Even then, they would not be approved for their task until they met within the confines of a place chosen by the Vatican and brought face to face with the Antichrist himself, to ascertain that his wiles would not be effective against them.

There could be no exception. One man among the twelve that the Antichrist could touch with his evil mind could mean doom for the entire group, and for the world itself, were his influences to remain unchecked. "My son," Colin read, "you are pure. Both I and your mother, my cousin, are in a direct line untouched by the Antichrist's hateful blood."

Goody for me, Colin thought, as he read on. "And as you know, the cup has made you as immortal as I—but not invulnerable. We can die, but not by disease or the ravages of age. When you find the men to make up the Twelve, find where my body lies, and there you will find the cup. In the Holy City, after the confrontation with the Antichrist, have all the chosen drink from that cup as you did, and you and they shall then be made Knights Templar, and protect the innocent from the wiles of Satan and his servant.''

There was more, equally superstitious and overwrought. At least it explained to Colin why his mind and will were untouchable by Mulcifer. But as for finding others with a similar heritage, it would be damn near impossible. The original twelve had been established in the 1300s. Colin would have had seven centuries more of mingled breeding to deal with. In a way, it was remarkable that every person on the earth was not somehow related by this time. Surely Mulcifer's progeny must be widespread if not universal by now.

Of course, those concerns presupposed that Colin was actually interested in following his father's directive, while he had no intention of doing so. The whole Templar/Antichrist/ church affair was absurd, the remnants of an older and more foolish age. Whatever Mulcifer was, he was not the Antichrist, and Colin refused to allow his father's beliefs to infect him.

What was his father so enthusiastic about preserving innocence for in the first place? Even though he was a classic example of religious mania, he had ruined the innocence of Colin's mother by taking her virginity when they were unmarried. He had married her once he had learned she was pregnant, taking a ship back from South America to ensure that he would arrive in Scotland in time to prevent his son's illegitimacy. That was the last thought that Andrew Mackay had ever had for his son's welfare, except perhaps for his giving him the immortality of the cup.

Still, in both cases, Sir Andrew's thoughts had been more on himself. The offer of the cup had had behind it the ulterior motive of the preservation of his precious Templars. And making Colin's birth legitimate was born of Catholic guilt. Yielding to his lust had been a sin, but having a bastard child would have been a greater one.

Besides, what did marriage mean to an immortal, anyway? The woman would be old and dead soon enough. Sir Andrew had never offered his wife the cup, and that omission told Colin that he had never loved her.

Colin knew that his father had never loved him, either. His constant absences told him that. Of course, Sir Andrew gave his excuses that business kept him away from his family, but Colin's mother had told him the truth about what his father's business was. The seeming romance and mystery of it were what had seduced her in the first place, like Othello's tales of adventure had seduced Desdemona.

His father had told him the entire story when Colin had become a man, and when he had turned thirty, Sir Andrew had offered him the cup. Colin had taken it less for the promise of immortality than because it was the first thing his father had ever truly given him that meant something. And having just seen his mother die slowly of cancer was another spur to a disease-free longevity.

Nearly seventy years had passed since then, and he had seen his father less than once a decade. Sir Andrew had provided him with money, large amounts of it, and had shown him during their infrequent meetings how a man who lives long enough can become very rich indeed, even by investing conservatively. Colin had grown rich quickly and had become even richer. He still received a hefty sum every month from his father's trust funds, funneled through a number of international accounts designed to hide both father's and son's true identities.

That was something else his father had taught him, that governments tended to look with suspicion upon people who lived for several hundred years without dying or aging. Sir Andrew changed his identity every generation as a matter of course, and Colin had done the same. His closest associates still knew his true name, and thought that the Francis Scobie alias had been created simply to evade the attention of England's counterterrorist division.

And now "Mr. Alister Scobie" was presumed dead, and the wealth accrued over seven hundred years had come to Colin. It was not, however, as much as might have been supposed, for no bank could have been expected to remain solvent through seven centuries of changing political climates. Still, it was an amount more than sufficient for Colin's purposes. It would buy explosives and weapons and cooperation. It would feed and house his men. And when the time came, it could help to finance a new, free Scotland.

But first Mulcifer would have to fulfill his end of the bargain.

Chapter 18

While Tony watched the comings and goings in Castle Dirk from the ridge above it, Joseph and Laika traveled to the county town of Dingwall, where the public records of Ross and Cromarty County were kept. Their Princeton credentials gained them admittance, and they told Mr. Douglas, the young man in charge of the records, that they were looking for information on the ownership of a certain castle and adjoining lands, back as far as the thirteenth century, if those records existed.

"Oh, they exist, all right," the young man said. "County deeds date back just that far, in fact. After the defeat of Edward I, the Scottish nobles wanted done with Scotland what William I had done in England centuries before with the *Domesday Book*—a complete record of land ownership. It was attempted during the reigns of the Bruce and David II, but was never completed. Still, Ross and Cromarty historians were fortunate in that our county was pretty accurately recorded."

"But the *Domesday Book* was written in a clerical Latin," Joseph said.

"Which hardly anyone is capable of translating today, yes, I know," said Douglas. "But we were fortunate in having the Reverend Stewart translate the whole of the records a century ago." He pointed toward an identically bound set of thick volumes sitting in a glass-fronted lawyer's bookcase. "They were published in the 1890s by the county record society. You'll find both the translation and the original Latin, should you need it.''

"I doubt it,'' Laika said. "My Latin's a bit rusty. Where would we find more recent records?''

"Everything from 1400 to 1900 is in the record society's volumes on that far wall. And after 1900, there are only individual deeds in filing cabinets. Those I'll have to get for you on request.''

There was no mention of Castle Dirk in Reverend Stewart's translation, so they searched for any large properties on the Gairloch peninsula. But since the entries were listed in alphabetical order by the fourteenth-century names of the land holdings, they found themselves having to examine every one to see if its location matched that of Castle Dirk's.

After two hours, Joseph finally said, "Bingo,'' and read:

Andrew Mackay Knight holds SRON EILEAN *near* GAIR LOCH. *Neilson has there 3 ploughs; and 40 petty burgesses, 12 cottagers, 12 villagers and 5 smallholders who have 15 ploughs. A castle is there and a church and a priest. 1 fishery, two mills, which pay 26s.*

Joseph broke off his reading. "There are some more details about how big the pastures and woodlands are, along with what's taxable, but the key is Gair Loch and the castle.''

"But where's 'Sron Eilean'?'' Laika asked. "I haven't heard of that.''

"Names don't last forever,'' Joseph replied. "Let's see if we can find some old maps.'' As it turned out, they didn't need very old maps at all. As late as the 1960s the area of coast near Castle Dirk was referred to as "Sron Eilean an Air.''

"Must be it,'' said Joseph. "Andrew Mackay, Knight. Templar, do you suppose? Now that we've got an owner, let's see who else the castle of Sron Eilean belonged to.''

It took the rest of the day to glean the information. In the intervening seven hundred years, there were twenty-three individual owners of the property from a dozen families: Mackay, Pollard, Magee, Nelson, Macphail, Bayne, Paulson, Allen, Morgan, Williamson, McQuaid, and Scobie, the most recent owners, according to the deed, which had been amended only a week earlier to reflect the ownership's passing from Alister Scobie to his son Francis.

"Twelve families," Laika said thoughtfully. "Could they be the names of the twelve Templars?"

"I suppose it's possible, but I don't know. Sometimes a dozen is just twelve." He looked over the list and dates again. "This is a long record of owners, but there's a consistency to it. In 1353 the property passed to Andrew Mackay's son Peter. Then, fifty years later, it was sold to Simon Pollard. Went to his son in 1451, then sold in 1498 to Richard Magee, and so on until the 1700s, when the changeovers start every thirty years or so instead of every fifty. But it's still the same—a sale to a different family, the son of that family inherits, or here and there a nephew, but that might have been just to obscure the transitions a little, and then he sells the property some years later . . ."

Joseph sat silently for a moment, then got up and went over to young Douglas's tiny office and asked where the family and clan histories were kept. It took only a minute for Douglas to find a history of the Mackay clan.

"This look familiar?" Joseph asked Laika, when Douglas was back in his office. He pointed to a gold coat-of-arms stamped on the front cover cloth. The picture was of a fist holding a dirk upright, and the words on either side read, "*Manu forti*."

"This is the coat-of-arms Tony saw in Castle Dirk," Laika said. "But '*Manu forti*'?"

" 'With a strong hand,' " Joseph said. He opened the book and found in an appendix a list of clan septs down which he ran his fingertip, smiling. "Every one of the twelve family names who have owned Castle Dirk," he said, "is a sept of the clan Mackay."

"So what's a sept?" Laika asked.

"An associated family. Sometimes it's just a variant of the clan name, like Mackay produced MacCoy and Mackie and Magee, to name one of the castle's owners. Other times, as in the case of Nelson and Pollard and Allen, they're families who would fight with the Mackays and also claim that clan's protection."

"So what's the big deal? Maybe they just kept the castle close to the family."

"Or maybe," Joseph said slowly, "the family never got rid of it at all. Look, we know . . . or *think* . . . that the Templars, including this McAndrews, had abnormally long life spans. What if all these sales and transfers were just a cover? What if every single person listed here, fathers and sons, were all Sir Andrew Mackay?"

"There's no way to prove that, Joseph."

"Maybe there is." He made a list on a piece of paper, approached Douglas again, and asked him where the actual deeds were kept, the ones that would bear the buyers' and sellers' signatures.

"They would be in the archives, sir," he answered. "I'm afraid they're classified as historical documents, and are not accessible to the public."

"Do you have them on the premises?" Joseph asked.

"Well, yes, but . . ."

"There's no one here but we and thee, Mr. Douglas, and of course, the ever popular Sir Walter." Joseph took a roll of Scottish currency out of his pocket and fanned it so that Sir Walter Scott's face looked up from its pink background multiple times. "If you can allow me to see three of those actual deeds on that list, from any three different centuries, a number of Sir Walters will be happy to make a new home in your pocket. You can even hold the deeds for me so that I won't have to touch them, if you like."

Douglas rubbed his right thumb with his fingers, and then took the roll of bills from Joseph. "Madam," he said to Laika, "if you would keep an eye on things up here, I'll take the gentleman down into the archives for a moment."

The archives were a temperature and humidity controlled room in the basement. Douglas searched for several minutes, then opened a document case, took out a quarto-sized paper in a mylar sheet, lay it carefully on top of the case, and, with a charmingly antiquated gesture, invited Joseph to view the item.

It was the deed of sale from 1353. The writing was barely legible, but Joseph could see where Peter Mackay had signed to claim his father's estate. He took detailed notice of the signature and nodded that he was satisfied.

The procedure repeated itself twice. Joseph viewed the 1498 deed in which James Pollard had sold the property to Richard Magee, and the 1832 deed in which Robert Allen had sold it to Brian Morgan. Then he nodded his thanks to Douglas, who returned the third deed to its case, and they returned upstairs.

Joseph and Laika left, with a final expression of thanks to Douglas. It wasn't until they were in the Peugeot that Joseph answered Laika's anxious inquiries. "The deeds spanned nearly five hundred years," he said. "I'm not a handwriting expert, but I'd bet my life that those signatures were written by the same person."

"The lawyers must have been in on it, then," Laika said.

"Back then lawyers weren't as prevalent in every aspect of life as they are now. But even in the 1400s, I'm sure there were lawyers whose silence could be bought. We have to break that silence, though."

"I don't think the townspeople are going to be very helpful."

"Then we'll talk to somebody else—a neighbor." He glanced at Laika. "How about Mr. and Mrs. MacLunie?"

"Of course," Laika said. "They've lived near the castle for years. We can show them McAndrews' picture, the one we got from the Sûreté."

"The ninety-year-old one," Joseph said, thinking of the first time they had realized that "Robert Gunn," "Kyle McAndrews," and whatever other aliases he might have used

had been around since at least the beginning of the present
century.

"Yeah. Maybe they'll recognize him."

By the time they stopped at the cottage and picked up the
photo, it was nearly dark, and Tony had returned from his
surveillance. He told them that the van that had left the day
before had not yet returned, and they told him what they had
learned about the castle and its possibly long-lived owners.

They made dinner, and afterward Laika telephoned the
MacLunies. She asked if they could come over to ask them
some questions, and Mr. MacLunie agreed without a moment's hesitation.

Both the man and his wife were waiting eagerly at the door
when they arrived. They immediately offered tea and cakes,
and would not take no for an answer. Mr. MacLunie asked if
they had found anything yet, and they said they hadn't, and
then told him that they had become interested in the castle.

"Aye," MacLunie said. "Someone's come back, then.
There's young men there. I've seen them goin' in and out of
town."

"But it's not time yet, that's what puzzles me," said Mrs.
MacLunie, her first words since she had offered them cake.

"Not time?" said Laika. "What do you mean?"

"Oh, well, it's every ten year, isn't it?" Mrs. MacLunie
said shyly, as though she shouldn't have spoken at all.

"Every ten years for what?" Laika pressed.

"Well, till they *gather*, isn't it? Every ten year they come.
But it's nae been that lang now. And they look different, too,
not as gentlemanly as before. I think there's more of them,
too."

"Wait a minute, Mrs. MacLunie. You're saying that every
ten years there's been a gathering of men at the castle?"

"Oh, aye," her husband interjected. "Ever since lang as I
can recall."

"What do they do?" asked Joseph.

"That's what we never knew," MacLunie said. "But
around here we're not ones to go pokin' our noses into things.

I recall once when I was just a lad, though, I seen some of them close up. Me mates told me they'd heard from their parents as how they was a bunch of deil worshippers, and dared me to climb in and take something from the castle to show as how I'd been there. Well, I was a braw lad back then, so I did. I'd seen the motors arrive and knew they was all parked in the courtyard inside, so I decided to steal me somethin' off one of 'em.

"I waited till night and then went in right through that front entry, bold as you please. And dumb as I was, I was caught right quick by a rough dressed fellow, I guess a servant. He drags me into the kitchen by the ear, and a couple of gentlemen all dressed in tweeds come in and look at me like they were preachers and I'd just pissed on a Bible, and the one says to me as how I don't belong there and I'd better go and never come back or nobody'd see me ever again. Then that servant drags me out by the ear and lets me go. I ran, I'll tell you."

"What did your friends say?" Laika asked, not wanting to push too fast. "Did they believe you?"

"Ach, as scared as I was, they believed me all right, even the next day."

"Mr. MacLunie," Laika said slowly, as though she'd just thought of it, "do you think you'd remember the men's faces?"

"I'll never forget them. Burned like a scar into my brain, they were." He laughed. "Why, seen 'em around?"

Laika reached into her purse and took out the photograph of Kyle McAndrews. "We were doing some research into the castle today and came across this picture—it's just a copy." She handed it to MacLunie. "Ever seen him before?"

MacLunie looked at the photo and his face went blank. Then he murmured, "Shite . . ."

"Now, now," Mrs. MacLunie said reproachfully.

"Aye, I'll never forget *that* one. He's the man I saw, told me to go or die. Christ, what a cold one he was." He looked up at Laika. "Where'd you get this?"

"Over in Dingwall," she lied. "When would this have been, Mr. MacLunie?"

"Well, I'm sixty-three now, I must've been around nine or ten then, so that's fifty-some years back." He snorted. "Like it was yesterday. And do ye know, I've stayed away from that damned castle ever since."

Chapter 19

"*I* think we have our Templar connection," Joseph said on the ride back to their cottage. "A mysterious group meeting every decade, a castle that's had the same owner for seven centuries, the French priest's story, *and* the fact that Kyle McAndrews, aka Robert Gunn, one of the twelve departed Templars, was one of the group at a meeting fifty years ago."

"I hate to jump to conclusions," Laika said, "but you know what else I think about Kyle McAndrews?"

"You think," said Joseph, "that he was Sir Andrew Mackay, because that's exactly what *I* think."

"Me too," Tony said. "And Andrew Mackay was every owner of Castle Dirk, father and son, all through the centuries. Just one thing, though. Andrew Mackay—also known as Alister Scobie—is dead now. So who's this Francis Scobie who's supposed to be his son?"

"If I had to guess," said Joseph, "I'd say that Francis Scobie is his *real* son—the young Mr. Mackay."

"It's as good a theory as any," said Laika, "with the information we've got. Maybe he's leading a new bunch of Templars, with a more contemporary look, as Mrs. MacLunie implied. I think we should just maintain surveillance for the time being, if you don't mind being outside in the Scottish mist, Tony. They're calling for rain this week."

"Goody. I'll pretend I'm Mel Gibson."

"And Joseph," she said, turning toward the back seat,

"you and I will just—" But her words were broken off as Tony jammed on the brakes. "*Jesus*, what the . . ."

Laika turned and looked through the windshield. There, ten yards away, was a glowing, upright form like a man or woman shrouded in white. She felt her breath lock in her throat as she watched it hover several feet above the surface of the roadway.

There was no face, just a smooth plain of white, and as Laika's mind struggled to see features there, a gaunt, terrible face began to take form upon the empty canvas. Then, just as she thought she saw the eyes start to open, the image vanished utterly, leaving not even a nimbus of light behind to mark its passing.

"What the hell," said Laika slowly, "was *that?*"

"That," Tony replied, "was what I saw in the cellar of the castle."

Laika took a deep breath, then took a flashlight from the glove compartment. "Turn off the engine, but leave the lights on," she told Tony. She opened the door and got out. The men followed. She walked to where the manifestation had appeared, shining the light down on the road and to either side, and up into the air. "Let's check the brush," she said.

With their flashlights they explored the area to either side of the road, but the vegetation was low, and no trees were in view. There seemed to be no haven in which anyone might have hidden a projector or other device to create an illusion.

"Well," Joseph said, his voice trembling slightly. "I didn't find any spiritualists lurking in the heather, so what *was* that thing?"

"Tony, was that exactly what the other one you saw looked like?" Laika asked.

"Absolutely. Only it was a little closer in the castle. I think. Kind of hard to judge size and distance with the damn thing."

Laika cleared her throat, wishing the fear would dissipate. "Did any of you see any kind of face?"

"Not I," said Joseph. "Not really. I think maybe I started to *imagine* one the longer I looked."

Tony nodded. "Same with me. I could swear something started to form both times, but when I look back, I think that maybe it was just my imagination."

"The human mind demands order," Joseph said. "We'll imprint what we expect to see on whatever blank screen comes along." He smiled. "Reminds me of M. R. James's 'face of crumpled linen.' "

Laika couldn't place the name. "Who?"

"The English ghost story writer. His most haunting image was a face of crumpled linen that formed out of the bed sheets. I always wondered if James intended that face to be real, or just a projection of the protagonist's fears."

"Well, if I'd want to scare the greatest number of people," Tony said, "I'd use a blank face myself. You see whatever frightens you most."

"Did either of you hear anything?" Laika asked. "Because I didn't. Not over the sound of the engine."

"No, not this time," Tony agreed. "But in the castle I heard that high-pitched humming. Like a machine of some kind."

"Sure it wasn't the sound of glowing ectoplasm?" Joseph asked, then held up a hand. "I'm not baiting you. I've seen it too. I know it's real, unlike my dream about one of the things, and I know we've got to find out what's causing it, especially in light of the Templars in the castle. This has all got to tie together somehow."

"And the more we learn, the stranger the connections get," Laika said as they walked back to the car. "Let's just keep on keeping on. Something else has to happen sooner or later."

Chapter 20

*L*iam Riley had to take another piss. He'd been up once already at one. And here it was two-thirty and he had to go again. Shite. He knew he'd just dribble a few drops and wake up again around four.

His prostate had to be the size of a bloody potato, but the goddamned Social Services doctors told him there was nothing to be done, just stuck their fingers up his arse and prodded around until he thought he was going to scream, but he never did. "Nothin' wrong there, Liam," they'd say. "Right as rain." Then he'd ask them, "Then why do I have to piss every five minutes?" and they'd say, "Maybe it's just nerves, Liam, me boy. Would you be wantin' to see a therapist, get your head back on straight?" Then he'd tell them where they could stick their bloody fingers and go back to pissing.

At least there were no locks on the cell doors in HM Prison Maze, or the Shitehole, as Liam called it. He was free to come and go to the pisser, or the precious *sanitation*, anytime he wanted. He was also free to crack a few loyalist heads, were he so inclined, if he could get past the circle, the area between the two wings that the prison officers supposedly controlled, and into the opposite wing where dead Billy Wright's so-called Loyalist Volunteer Force was housed, along with the UDA and UFF boys.

But that was a mighty big "if." Both the Republican and Unionist "officer commanders," prisoners themselves who controlled their respective Catholic and Protestant wings, would order even a guard badly beaten if he came onto their wing without permission. No, as lovely a fantasy as it was to sneak into the opposite wing and kill a few of the Orange bastards, it was far safer to drain one's prick and go back to sleep.

As he passed the cells, everyone was sleeping except for the men on watch, to whom he nodded and spoke a word or two of greeting. He passed his pitiful amount of water, then returned to his cell, only to find that some bastard was in it.

Liam Riley stiffened and stayed outside the doorway. He didn't recognize the long-haired bearded man, who was wearing a dark shirt and trousers. A Loyalist bastard, maybe? But which of them would have the guts—no, the *stupidity*—to come into the IRA wing in H-block 8?

Still, Liam didn't call out, for fear of being shot down instantly. Shooting him would have been suicide for the stranger sure as hell, but that was nothing new. Some of these crazy shites would welcome the attack, taking down as many Republicans as they could before they were killed themselves.

But as Liam looked more closely, he could see the man had no gun. In fact, his hands were empty of even a shank or a cosh. And he looked peaceful enough, standing there against the back cell wall with that soft smile on his calm face. "What is it, then?" Liam whispered.

"Do you want out?" asked the man, and his voice sounded strangely like Liam's old da, first kneecapped and then killed in the troubles when Liam was a boy.

"What are you talkin' about?" Liam asked, shaken by the vocal similarity to his father.

"Do you want out of here?" the man said. "Do you want to be free?"

Well, Christ on a crutch, of *course* he wanted to be free. He was looking at another fifteen years at least, and by the time he got out, he'd be pissing every three minutes. Besides that, he didn't do shite for Ireland sitting in the Maze. But what could this bastard do about getting him out?

"I can do a great deal, Liam."

Liam's eyes widened. It was like the man had read his mind, answering questions before he'd even asked them, just the way his da used to.

"I can get you out of here, if you'll come with me. Freedom, Liam, for you—and, if you play your cards right, maybe for Ireland, too. All you have to do is do one little job for me, and then you're on your own. What do you say?"

"I say . . . how are you goin' to do it? Get me out?"

The man held out his right hand. "We're going to have to hold hands, Liam. And whatever you do, don't let go of my hand. Then we're going to walk right out of here. Right past the guards and the soldiers and through the walls."

"Ye're fulla shite."

"So what are ya then, Liam, a *nancy boy?*"

It was just what his father had said to him when he was afraid of something, back in the old days when he still could be afraid of something other than his da. Hearing it now put steel into his backbone, and he decided it would be worth dying to try and get out of here. Christ, if he stayed, his piss would probably back up into him and poison him anyway.

"You're right, Liam," said the man. "Better to go down bravely in a hail of gunfire. But don't worry, you won't die today." The man spread the fingers of his outstretched hand, and Liam reached out and grasped it. Then the man turned and proceeded to walk into the wall, right into the frigging wall. Liam gasped, but before he knew what was happening the man had pulled him along so that his hand and then his entire body was entering the painted cement blocks. He opened his mouth to say "*Jay*-zis!" but the wall entered it before he could speak. It felt as if someone had slapped every cell in his body with a palm of fire. It went through him even more deeply than when his da had slapped him for being a nancy.

Then the darkness that had claimed him when he'd entered the wall was gone, and bright fluorescence burst upon his aching pupils. Christ, they were in the circle, and two prison officers were coming down upon them with clubs. Liam tried to draw back his arm to defend himself, but the stranger held onto it so that he could not, and before he knew what had happened, one of the officers was swinging hard at his mate, whaling him on the side of the head and then jumping on him when he went down, and swinging the club again until the skull shattered and only wet sounds followed.

Liam followed the stranger, taking him right up to and through the locked door that led into the Loyalist wing of H-block 8. "Hell, no!" Liam roared. "For Christ's sake, not in there!"

"Be a man," his father's voice said, and then the stranger vanished and Liam hit the steel. He was through it in a flash, before the hellish pain could drive him mad, and out the other side.

And there they were in the Loyalist wing, the middle of the fire for an IRA man. Life expectancy was five seconds if the bastards wanted to shoot you, a minute to stab you, and too damn long to think about if they decided to have some fun and beat you to death. And there were three of them now, glaring at him and the stranger as if they'd been priests with bombs.

The three men gave out with cries intended to wake up the entire wing, if not the dead, and then came at Liam and the stranger. But as the UDA, UFF, and LVF pricks came pouring into the hall to stomp his and the stranger's arses, something strange happened, even stranger than what the guard had done. One of the three boyos hurled himself into another one, leaving only the third, a huge, nasty bloke, to come at the stranger, who threw him aside as though he were a bum boy. Then things *really* got weird.

The Loyalists, dozens of them, who had only had hunger for Republican blood in their eyes, suddenly turned on each other like rabid wolves. Some of them looked surprised to be attacked by their political brothers, but the attackers were like berserkers. Those who had knives were using them, and then the guns came out, dropping the men dead upon the floor.

"Just stay behind me," the stranger said to Liam.

"Wouldn't want you to get hurt." Liam did as ordered, and they made their way down the corridor of bleeding and dying men. None of the men attacked either him or the stranger, but once a stray bullet caught the stranger in the shoulder. Liam saw it rip his shirt and enter his flesh.

But the stranger only laughed and kept walking slowly, as though he were enjoying the slaughter going on around him. Liam had to admit he enjoyed it, too. It was like being in the eye of a hurricane, untouched, as the world toppled into chaos and your enemies fell around you.

In a few more minutes, they had reached the end of the corridor. The stranger looked at Liam, winked broadly, and then went through the wall. Liam followed without even thinking.

Damn, but the bugger was thick. He seemed to feel his brain weeping in agony, because no tears could come from his eyes, which were one with the wall. Just when he thought he was dead, that he and the stone were one forever, he came out into a place where the air was cold on his face and the light was low and soft.

They were outside in the yard, and the high concrete wall lay ahead of them, its top rimmed with razor wire. But they weren't going to have to worry about the top, were they? They'd just go right through the damned wall.

Then Liam heard someone shouting at him to halt, and when the stranger started running, the gunfire began, and bullets started biting into the blacktop, whining off its surface. He thought he was hit, for something burned in his upper left thigh, and he nearly stumbled, but then he felt the pain rush through his body and down his arm to the hand the stranger was holding, and disappear, as though the stranger had absorbed the wound.

They hit the wall at a sprint and went through. This time he scarcely felt it, their speed was so great. They exploded out onto the other side, still running as if the thick wall had never been there at all. Liam thought they might have gone through more, and he later recalled a great silver thicket of razor wire. But the rest of it seemed like even more of a dream.

The hardest part was convincing himself that it was real. Like every prisoner, he'd had fantasies of such a miracle, of some angel from God coming to his cell and taking him out right through the walls or up into the sky and flying over the walls of the Maze, while turning his enemies against each other. It was the classic prisoner's dream. But this time, he was convinced that it was truly happening, even though walls opened and bullets caused no harm.

After what seemed an eternity of running, of shouts and sirens and gunfire and lights that rose and fell, he was sitting in the back of a moving car, the stranger's hand still in his, and finally it was dark and quiet. But then they came to a checkpoint and one of those damned English soldiers, his rifle pointing at them inside the car, was telling them to "Get out! Get out of the car right now and keep your hands where I can see them," and two other soldiers were behind him with guns, and they looked just as panicked and angry.

But then the stranger said something to him, and one of the soldiers behind him shot the first soldier in the back, and then turned and shot the other one as well. Then he just stood there looking at them, while the car drove right through. In the rearview mirror, Liam could see the soldier who had shot the other two just standing there, as though he were waiting for something. Christ, he wouldn't have long to wait.

They drove for what seemed like a long time, and then got out of the car, the stranger finally letting go of his hand. They were out in the country somewhere, far from Belfast, and the stranger and the two men with him went into a small cottage. Liam followed. There was never the suggestion that he wouldn't.

Now that he was free, Liam knew he should be reporting back to his unit as quickly as possible, and begin once more his trade of building death from explosives and timers and fuses. But he also knew that he had to follow this man who could do what angels did, this man who could perform miracles, and learn why he, Liam Riley, out of all the men in the Maze, had been granted this blessing. He knew that he had been doing God's work, but so had all his brothers.

The room into which he was led was quiet and cozy. One of the men built a fire in the fireplace, while the other got him a glass of whisky. Then, when the two of them were alone, the stranger leaned toward him intimately, and told him, with his father's voice, what it was that he wanted him to do.

It was then that Liam Riley knew the price to be paid for miracles, and that it would be a long time, if ever, before he saw the lads of his unit again.

Chapter 21

"*T*he plans have changed," Rob Lindsay said into the pay telephone.

"What do you mean?" Colin Mackay said. "I know you got him out—Christ, it's all over the news." He was careful not to mention any names. There should be no reason they would be tapped, but you never knew.

"Yeah, we got him out all right. God, what a bloodbath. But we're not bringing him back."

"Why the hell *not*, man?"

"Because M is doing things his own way."

"Well, we're doing things *my* way. Now, you bring that man back here so he can be given instructions!"

"Can't do it. He's gone already. Ordered and—"

Suddenly Colin heard the voice of Mulcifer. "You seem to be upset."

"You're damned right I'm upset! You were supposed to bring that man back here or leave him in a safe house until—"

"He's safe. Not in a safe house, but safe as houses. As your friend was just saying, he has received his orders, and he will lie low until the time comes to carry them out."

"*What* orders? You weren't supposed to give him any orders, goddamnit!"

"My friend," Mulcifer said, "you will get what you want, trust me. And you will get it in great quantities. And if you have been sending out your missives as planned, your precious cause will receive full credit. Trust me. If there is one thing with which I am familiar, it is terror. In fact, I've changed the plans a bit more. I'm freeing the prisoners, all right, but they won't be doing anything until one certain day. And then all the rain will come down at once."

"That's what I'd planned—one huge strike."

"We'll have half a dozen huge strikes. A day that will live in infamy. When we return, I'll tell you when that day will be."

Colin's mind was filled with a dozen different emotions, not the least of which was betrayal, not only from this creature for whom perfidy was the norm, but from Rob and Angus, who were like brothers to him. "One question, damn you," he said. "Rob and Angus had their orders, and they think as I do. How did you get them to go along with this?"

"As I said . . . I can be very persuasive. You'll have to excuse us now—we're off to Her Majesty's Prison Maghaberry to free a jolly young sniper on remand. Ta-ta . . ."

The line went dead. Colin set the phone back in the cradle, his teeth clenched. The gall of the bastard, to take over their operation for his own purposes. But then, after all, their purposes *were* the creature's purposes. They wanted to shed blood and cause terror, with the purpose of making the English Crown and government see all too clearly that the Irish problem would be as nothing compared to what they could expect from Scot patriots.

We are greater than any group. We are everywhere. We are Scotland.

That was how he had signed the letter to 10 Downing Street, the *London Times*, and the BBC, claiming credit for the breakout of Liam Riley. He knew that it was possible that MI5 would get to the *Times* or the BBC and ask them not to make the story public, so he had also sent the letter to four tabloids as well. British tabloids, with their lack of respect for just about anything you could name, including the government and its MI5 lackeys, made the ideal delivery system. They should be receiving the letters first thing this morning, bearing postmarks of the day before from several different Scottish cities.

Christ, he certainly couldn't fault Mulcifer for the style of the first escape. According to the BBC news, the toll was one freed IRA bomber, two dead prison officers, nine dead Loyalists, two dead checkpoint soldiers, and the raving lunatic who had shot them. Twelve more prisoners and six more officers had also been injured in the melee afterward. All in all, a very profitable night.

And just how was all this accomplished? The government was blaming the IRA for a paramilitary assault on the prison the likes of which had never been seen before. That would change soon enough when Colin's letters were published.

BBC news at noon ran the story, and said that although early reports indicated that the escaped prisoner had gone through no locked gates or doors to make his escape, it was now certain that those gates had been unlocked and locked again behind the prisoner, but who was responsible for opening them was not known. Nor was it known why the Loyalist prisoners had attacked each other when Liam Riley, the escapee, came into their wing with an unidentified man. There was as yet no description of that unknown man, since "every surviving witness described him somewhat differently." The witnesses were still being questioned in the attempt to come up with a composite drawing.

Damned Mulcifer, Colin thought, worse than the Shadow when it came to clouding men's minds. He didn't know what the creature was, but he was glad it was on his side. So far, at least.

At last the reporter mentioned the letters that had been posted the day before, but said only that an "unidentified militant Scottish nationalist group" was claiming responsibility for the break, although officials expressed puzzlement as to why Scottish nationals would be freeing IRA bombers.

That confusion was partially cleared up later in the day when the *Times* ran the full text of Colin's letter. Still, officials stated that even though Scot nationals might have been the liberators, they could not believe that Catholic terrorists would cooperate with them in any way.

Colin didn't give a damn whether they believed it or not. If they didn't, it would just make the ultimate strike all that much more unexpected. Everything would be fine as long as they could take the credit, first for the impossible escapes, and then for six huge blows against the empire. It would seem almost supernatural to England, as if God would never again be on their side. And then, when they saw there was no stopping Colin and his movement, a free Scotland.

Free. He trembled at the thought, and then smiled as he thought of how England would tremble next.

Chapter 22

Richard Skye sat in his office in Langley, Virginia, and read the printouts of the intercepted MI5 memos forwarded by the London office. The one that interested Skye most was the one sent by MI5's head of counterterrorism to the deputy director general of operations concerning the recent spate of terrorist jailbreaks.

There had been five escapes within the past seven days, two from Maze, two from Maghaberry, and the most recent from HM Prison Soughson in Edinburgh. Security had been increased exponentially after every escape, but that didn't seem to stop the team that was breaking the prisoners out.

The press was being informed that the escapes were carried out by large teams of men disguising themselves as prison officers to infiltrate the prisons, and British soldiers to facilitate the escapes once the prisoners were free of the walls. The government was taking an enormous amount of flak over not being able to secure the facilities properly so that impostors could not intrude.

But that was nothing, the memo said, to the amount it would take were it to be discovered that the escapes had been carried out by a single man and a getaway car. The counterterrorism head apologized abjectly for having to make this report, but the facts were that of all the witnesses questioned, and they numbered in the dozens, all reported the same details.

All the escapes had occurred between midnight and

4:30 A.M. The escaping prisoner was suddenly seen by the witnesses in the company of another person, showing up in whatever wing of the prison housed their political and religious rivals. They were always holding hands.

There was no good description of the accessory to the escape, because even during the same event, some men reported him to be short and stocky, others tall and thin; some dark-haired, some blond. There was not even any consensus on the accessory's race or sex. Some prisoners and guards saw a woman, and some a black woman. One saw an Asian man.

Admittedly, it sounded insane, but the reports existed, and there was absolutely no evidence of collusion between witnesses. Besides, such a conspiracy would surely not be possible between prison officers, prisoners, and soldiers located in and around three different prisons on two different islands. But as strange as the different descriptions were, there were stranger things to come.

The prison officers had tried to restrain the two men, and the escapee's enemies had naturally tried to attack them for intruding into their areas of the prison, but both groups found themselves fighting and in many cases killing each other. Some claimed that they had simply been overcome with the urge to turn on their fellows, and those who had not been so affected had had no choice but to defend themselves against their former allies, so the escapees were never interfered with.

However, soldiers outside both Maze and Maghaberry had sworn that they had hit both men with gunfire from the walls, and during the second Maze escape, a number of witnesses had claimed the two had been struck repeatedly, but had showed no ill effects from the gunfire.

As for how they actually got out of the prisons, that was the most bizarre circumstance of all. Again, there were several dozen witnesses, consisting of officers, inmates, and soldiers, who claimed that the two men passed directly *through* solid concrete block walls and steel doors, as well as through spiraled enclosures of razor wire without the least hesitation or any signs of injury.

Hundreds of inquiries had been made, and informants among the IRA and the few known Scottish paramilitary groups had been consulted, but as yet there had been no trace of the five escapees. Watches had been placed on all known family members, but this too had proved useless. Wherever the men were hiding, it was not with their former comrades, as far as the counterterrorism division was able to ascertain.

As for the claims of responsibility from the unnamed Scottish nationalist organization, they had to be taken seriously. Multiple letters had been received by the government and the media, postmarked the day before the escapes, giving the name of the prisoner who had been freed. The letters had been printed on a common white bond on the most popular laser printer sold in the United Kingdom. The Courier 12 typeface offered no indication of the word processing program with which it had been written.

The philologists stated that the voice of the letter writer was certainly Scottish, and the psychologists studying the texts felt that the writer, although showing a great deal of maturity (he might, they claimed, even be an elderly man), was in some ways very naive about the political climate he and his organization were so anxious to change.

Operations were now under way in every major Scottish city to infiltrate nationalist movements and so apprehend the terrorists. Security had also been increased in every British prison, and the most notorious terrorists had been placed under twenty-four-hour guard, despite the reactions and threats of the IRA inmates.

The memo ended with the assurance that the deputy director would continue to be informed of any further information pertaining to the incidents. Attached was another memo from the deputy director confirming receipt of the original memo, along with a directive for the head of counterterrorism to appear at a meeting with the prime minister, the director-general, and both deputy directors, during which a cover story least harmful to the government could be developed.

Skye neatly stacked the small sheaf of papers on top of his

desk, then leaned back, breathed deeply, and closed his eyes. When he opened them, he reached for the executive toy upon his desk, pulled back the end steel sphere on its string, and let it fly, striking the others and starting the back-and-forth motion of the five balls. He never ceased to appreciate how one affected all the others, how movement and purpose in one place created a similar motion elsewhere.

Men walking through walls, unharmed by bullets. Political comrades closer than brothers suddenly becoming the deadliest of enemies. A man who looks different to everyone who sees him. And all these things had been confirmed by the highest levels of MI5, whose members, as Skye's experience had shown him, were far from imaginative. It meant one thing, as far as Skye was concerned.

It meant paranormal activity of the most bizarre kind. He naturally would have thought of assigning his three shadow operatives to look into it, but the fact that they were already in Scotland when the motivation for the escapes had a strong Scottish connection was fortuitous. He wondered if there was a connection between the ghostly sightings on the Gairloch peninsula and the paranormal aspects of the escapes. Probably the Gairloch sightings were a hoax, but another intercepted memo had told him that MI5 was also investigating the spectral reports. Surely between them his operatives and MI5 should have come up with the culprits by now.

The long arm of the mysterious Prisoner might easily be involved. But had he then somehow been freed? Skye's suspicions that his operatives had been holding information from him had grown stronger than ever. He would set them onto the prison escapes as well. If they were indeed familiar with the Prisoner's methods, they should learn something within a few days.

Then he would step in—physically this time—and squeeze the truth out of them, if need be. But one way or another, he would find this man he was looking for, this man of mysteries and miracles.

Chapter 23

Richard Skye's three operatives were feeling particularly ineffective. They gathered back at the cottage at the end of the day, and Tony was the first to report.

"I stood, sat, and lay up on the ridge all day, watching the castle. The van that had left last week returned, but I couldn't see who was in it. I did see Francis Scobie—or young Mackay—taking a walk, disappearing down over the cliff to the beach. I didn't follow. I didn't think I could bear the excitement of watching somebody walk on the beach, especially in such a lovely drizzling rain. And now I think I'll have another cup of tea to drive the chill out of me bones."

"You sound Irish, not Scottish," Joseph said. "*I* happened to learn something of great import today. In our never-ending search for ghosts, I spoke to a retired fisherman who lives in a cottage up near Rubha Reigh lighthouse. I'm doing archeological work, any sites of prehistoric stones about that he'd know of, worked the topic around to local legends, blah blah, ever see any ghost, heh heh. And for some reason, this guy didn't clam up. Maybe MI5 hadn't gotten to him yet. Anyway, there is, only two hundred yards from him, another cottage, long deserted, and he told me with great certainty that it was haunted, and that people who had the nerve to stay there overnight—and many who just visited during the day— saw a man with a sailor's cap, high sea boots, and a coat with brass buttons. Naturally I explored the cottage and found a lot of dirt, three empty beer cans, and a used condom. Laika? Your turn.''

"Two little villages on the east coast of the peninsula. Inverasdale and Midtown. As with the good folks in Brae and Naast, which I visited yesterday, I can see in their eyes that they either have seen an apparition or know someone who did. But when I ask them, they know nussing, they see nussing.''

"*Hogan's Heroes*?'' Joseph guessed, playing Spot the Allusion.

"Yes, and I'm feeling about as competent as Colonel Klink.'' She shook her head as she set down her cup of tea and booted up her computer. "I know that half of police work is waiting for something to happen, but God, it's hard.''

They sat in silence, sipping their tea, while Laika checked her e-mail over the encrypted line. "Well,'' she said after a time. "Seems that something may be happening after all. Mr. Skye sends a message.'' She read it aloud.

First came the directive from Skye that depending on the potential of the Gairloch sightings, they add to their investigations the recent prison breaks taking place in Ireland and Scotland, centering on the Scottish escape.

"What?'' Tony said. They had heard the official news reports about the escapes on the BBC, and read about them in the newspapers. "That's an internal British situation, Laika. What are we meddling in it for?''

"Yeah,'' Joseph agreed. "Did Skye read something in the tabloids about IRA aliens using an escape-o-ray?''

"Just wait,'' Laika said, and read to them the attached MI5 memo that the CIA had intercepted.

"Holy shit,'' Joseph said softly when she was finished. "Sound like our boy? Especially that part about turning people against each other.''

"The same thing that happened to LaPierre's men in Utah,'' Tony said. "And bullets don't hurt him. And he walks through walls.''

"As long as they're not lead, eh?'' Joseph added. "Well,

considering that we've been striking out with the ghosties around here, it makes sense to follow Skye's directive and get cooking on this thing . . . if we can do it without getting in the British government's way. Christ, they've got to be pouring all their energies into this one.''

"And that's why we're not going to go whole hog on it," Laika said. She had been looking quietly at the computer screen, but now she turned and fixed Joseph and Tony with a hard look. "Everybody got it all?" she asked, and they nodded. The details of all she had read to them had been committed to memory. With a few keystrokes she deleted Skye's message and the accompanying document completely. "One person, and it's going to be you, Joseph. You'll attract the least attention. Tony looks too Italian, and I look . . ." She smiled. ". . . Too Jamaican. But your accent is impeccable and you look British."

"I'm Jewish."

"So was Disraeli. In a dim light, you look like Sean Connery."

"A *younger* Sean Connery, I hope."

"Of course. Anyway, Tony and I will stay here. I think it's more important than ever that we keep an eye on the castle, since it's supposedly Scottish loyalists behind these escapes." She shrugged. "A Scottish castle filled with men, and with a possible link to our Templar Mackay, along with the fact that currently the only two paranormal events in the British Isles have Scottish connections. I think we're starting to see a pattern, and it's altogether possible that our old friend the Prisoner might be at the core. Joseph, you realize this is going to be very dangerous. There's no cover provided for this. If you should get yourself into a position where you'd be questioned by MI5 or the police, there's no using your CIA status. You're on your own, unless Skye decides to bail you out."

"And that's not likely, I know. Don't worry, Laika, I know the rules." He sighed. "And just think, a year ago at this time I was lodged in an office interpreting intelligence data, thinking how boring it was. God . . .'' He chuckled. ''What I'd give to be bored again.''

''Five men you've released,'' Colin Mackay said to Mulcifer. His voice was controlled but angry, like the sound of a boiler just starting to overheat. ''Five terrorists, five of the most violent and angry rebels ever seen, and instead of bringing them back here, you let them go. And then you refuse to tell me just what you're having them do.''

Mulcifer sat back in his chair, his arms folded, that devil's smile upon his face. ''Trust me.''

''*Trust* you? For centuries people have called you the Antichrist, your only pleasure is in causing pain, you disobey me at every turn, and you keep telling me to *trust you?*''

''We want the same things, Colin. Besides, what choice do you really have? Those five men are infernal devices, as they used to so colorfully call bombs. And all five devices are set to go off at the same time, four days from now, and the cause of a free Scotland will receive all the credit. And there's more.''

''Kevin Brady.''

''Oh yes. The mad dog himself, the jewel in the crown. Without him the lovely six-pointed star becomes a mere pentagon. We'll motor down to England and free him tomorrow, set his little clock ticking. Believe me, Colin, you will be delighted with the boom. Look on it as my surprise for you—my little thank you for giving me such splendid opportunity.''

Mulcifer stood up and stretched. ''Ah, I don't know why I feel so tired. After all, I never have to sleep. I do believe I'll climb one of the remaining seaward towers and watch the Minch. After so many years of confinement, it's such a pleasure to observe nature in all its glory.''

''It's raining buckets,'' Colin observed.

''Even better.''

As Mulcifer left the room, Rob, Angus, and James came in, edging past him as though they feared to get too close. They heard his low laughter as he went down the hall. ''Shut the door," Colin said, and the four men were alone in the small room.

"Christ, Colin, I'm sorry," Rob said. "I tried to keep him from letting them go—so did Angus, but we couldn't say shite against him. He'd get them out of earshot, tell them what he wanted them to do, and that was it. We'd drive them where he told us, and let them out into the night."

"What do you mean, Rob," Colin asked, "you couldn't say shite? Did he threaten you, or what, then?"

"Well, the first time I told him that letting them go wasn't what you wanted, that you wanted them brought back here for instructions, he just looked at me and he said, 'I don't want to hear any more from you,' just that, and I thought the hell with you, you bastard, and I opened my mouth to tell him so, but no words come out."

"Aye," Angus said. "Same with me. I was fixin' to tell him to go and fook himsel', and he just looked at me and shook a finger and said, 'No no,' and hell, Colin, that was it for me. But you think *that* was somethin', you shoulda seen the bastard at checkpoints. He was like that damned Obi-Wan Kenobi fella in those *Star Wars* movies. Sometimes he'd tell 'em to just let us on through, and they did, but other times one of the soldiers said hell no, and then he'd get another soldier to start in beatin' or shootin' the one said no. Weirdest thing you ever seen."

"Aw, shite, Colin," said James Menzies, "I knew something like this was going to happen. Maybe we should have just let this bastard alone and tried to get ahold of the nerve gas after all."

"Hell we should," Colin said angrily. He had thought this argument was behind them. "First off, all we know about the nerve gas is that the English buried canisters full of the stuff somewhere in Scotland. *Naturally* in Scotland, because they wouldn't want to put their own population at risk, but if a few thousand Scots died, well . . ." He gave his head a furious shake, trying to get back on track. "But we've got a mighty big country here, brothers. Only way we'd find out where the shite is would be to crack MI5 files, and that's not going to happen.

"But the main reason is that chemical and biological weapons are too bloody dangerous. They're too hard to target, and first thing you know, children wind up dying, and I will not have that. So forget the damned gas. You know how that shite Mulcifer didn't want to hear another word? Well, neither do I!"

But Mulcifer heard far more than Colin Mackay thought he did. He was standing on the northwest tower overlooking the Minch. The dark water was being peppered by heavy raindrops, and the sound of all the drops striking the stones all around him made a ceaseless roar, a unity of sound born of individual specks of water, so weak on their own and so strong when combined.

Still, over the sound of the rain and distant thunder, Mulcifer heard what was being said within the room by the four men. He also heard the other men moving about the castle in their separate rooms. And he heard footsteps slogging through the mud that coated the dirt road to the castle.

Someone new was coming. A stranger. Someone who didn't belong.

Chapter 24

*T*aylor Griswold cursed under his breath, though he knew
that in this storm no one would hear him if he shouted
"Sonofabitching rain!" at the top of his lungs. But instead
he cursed softly, first the rain, then the cold, then that Scotty-
boy that he'd followed all the way over to wet, rainy, cold,
shitty *Scotland*, for Chrissake.

Griswold was a reporter for an American tabloid newspaper, *The Inner Eye*, which covered more stories about angels,
aliens, UFOs, channelers, Satan, and the efficacy of horo-
scopes, seances, and Ouija boards than it did stories about
celebrities. The exception, of course, was Princess Diana.
Only the *Eye*'s stories concentrated on the many manifestations of her aggrieved spirit and the conspiracies regarding
her death—the wilder, the better.

Griswold had also been a paid agent for a group in America
headed by the man he had finally followed to this castle. He
knew now that the Scotty-boy went by the name of Francis
Scobie, but he was sure that was bullshit. In the States, they
had paid Griswold to tip them off when it had looked like
something actually paranormal was going down, and not the
usual phony-baloney crappola that made up 99 percent of the
whole.

The reason, as far as Griswold could figure out, was that
there was somebody these guys were looking for, and they
weren't the only ones. There was this trio of government
agents (at least, that was what he *thought* they were) who

kept popping up whenever what could be the genuine article lifted its fishy head. All Griswold knew for certain was that undeniably real phenomena were taking place here and there, and that it was somehow connected to this dude who the Scots and the spooks were looking for.

And what was happening on this Gairloch peninsula looked as real as any of this stuff could be. He had heard about the mass sightings of ghosts or aliens through his usual channels, and had made the usual inquiries, only to find out that everyone who was supposed to have seen the things said (when they said anything at all) that it was a crock, and they hadn't seen anything and nobody understood what all the fuss was about, because *nobody* had said anything lately about seeing any ghosts or anything strange at all.

That would have driven most of the reporters off the trail, and probably *had* discouraged some who used sources similar to Griswold's. But Taylor Griswold knew something that the other reporters didn't, and that was that Francis Scobie and a number of his friends had flown to Scotland and were headed right to the spot where all these supposedly *rumored* ghost sightings had been made.

That was enough for Griswold. He had come over as soon as he had found out about Scobie and had tracked him down to Castle Dirk. Christ, what a great headline *that* was going to make: "HORROR AT CASTLE DIRK!" After all, he might as well expose whatever there was to expose. Scotty-boy had cut him off the payroll, so there wasn't any reason to avoid pissing him off. Of course, the death threat Scobie had made when he had last seen him made Griswold tread a bit lightly, but Scobie probably hadn't been serious, and even if he did catch him snooping around, Griswold felt confident enough to talk his way out of anything.

As if all this wasn't proof enough that some heavy shit was coming down, Griswold had spotted one of the three feds in the town, proof positive that there was going to be a paranormal convention pretty damned soon. It was the tall older guy Griswold had seen from his car, and he was sure the guy hadn't spotted him. He had thought about following him, but they had nailed him before when he had tried to tail them, and he didn't want to take the chance again. Besides, he wanted to find out what Scobie and his fellow kiltie-boys were after.

So here he was, making his way over a pile of fallen stones into Castle Dirk. He'd have felt like Errol Flynn if he hadn't been so damn cold and wet and pissed off. But he had always said he'd go anywhere for a story, and damned if this wasn't proving him an honest man . . . at least about his word.

He couldn't turn on his flashlight here, but the light coming through the castle's grimy windows was bright enough to let him see an opening that led between the buildings and into the inner courtyard, or whatever they called it. He moved through, hugging the wall, thinking that no one could see him in the darkness, and that if anyone did, the rain provided so much motion in the air, they might not even realize he was a man.

Now he was inside the courtyard, and there were a number of windows that were lit up. Still, he saw no sign of motion from within. Keeping his head down, he moved to the closest window, crouched below the bottom of the frame, and listened. He thought he could hear, over the rushing sound of the rain, men's voice coming from somewhere, probably inside.

He slowly raised his head until it was at the bottom corner of the window frame. Then he tilted it and moved it up diagonally so that as small a segment of his head as possible might be visible from inside. At last he could see inside, and there in the dusty glass was his own reflection, lit from inside, his own eye looking back at him.

But then that staring eye blinked when he didn't.

When his eyes went wide with shock, the eye on the other side of the glass narrowed like that of a predator about to strike. Then suddenly men were grabbing him and pulling him away from the window, and he felt himself falling back onto the wet stones and being dragged through the rain while men cursed around him.

Then there was light, and the rain stopped, and he was hauled to his feet and pushed down a corridor and into the room into which he had been peering. There was the man he knew as Francis Scobie, and some other men he recognized, the ones who had blindfolded him and taken him to see Scobie in the States. The room was large, but furnished spartanly. Plain wooden chairs, a large table, and a small desk. The only sign of decoration was two crossed claymores attached to the stone wall.

"Taylor Griswold," said the big, red-haired Scot called Scobie. "Christ, I should've known you'd show up like a bad penny sooner or later. What do you think you're doing here?"

Griswold tried to smile winningly. "I'm a reporter—I come to where the story takes me." Then he chuckled. "See, I'd heard about the sighting of ghosts around here, and then when I found out that you had come over here, well, I knew there must be more to it than just speculation. I came in here trying to find out how much you knew about all of it. Just wanted to touch base and see if you could fill me in, being as how I've helped you so much in the past."

"And you wouldn't say a thing about us being here, now, would you?"

"You kidding? Of course not. My lips are sealed."

"If you wanted to talk to me, how come you were skulking at the window like a burglar?"

"Well, I just wanted to see who might be with you. Didn't want to walk into . . . an uncomfortable situation."

"You've already done that, laddie, and no mistake. So who else knows we're here?"

Griswold considered telling him about the spook he had seen in Gairloch, then decided against it. The Scot was already pissed enough at him, and he was sure it would be news he didn't want to hear. "Nobody, far as I know," he said.

"And who knows *you're* here?"

"Still nobody. I keep my contacts confidential, you know that."

Griswold had been watching Scobie all this time, so the voice speaking right in his ear was such a shock that he could not help but flinch. "The only true silent ones are the dead."

He turned and looked into the eyes of the man who had been looking at him through the window. They were cold eyes, humorless. Griswold hated people he couldn't joke with, and he felt an intense distaste and discomfort as these dead eyes bored into him. He tried to keep smiling. "*And* truly professional reporters, like myself. We're *quieter* than the dead, believe me."

"There is no reason to believe you, no reason to trust you, no reason for you at all," the man said.

"Hey, c'mon now, pal," said Griswold, still smiling. "I mean, I've done a lot for Mr. Scobie here." He looked at Scobie for reassurance. "Steered a lot of real good leads your way, didn't I? Huh?"

"We don't need your leads anymore, Griswold," Scobie said, shaking his head. "We've found what we were looking for."

"Yeah? Yeah? What was that?"

Scobie looked at the man with dead eyes. "Him. You're no longer useful to us."

Griswold's mouth was so dry that he had to work up some spit in it before he could talk again. "So what's that mean?"

"It means that you're going to spend some time under lock and key," said Scobie. "We can't afford to—"

"We can't afford to let you live," said the man at Griswold's shoulder. Another man who had not spoken quickly removed one of the heavy claymores from the wall.

"Whoa whoa whoa!" Griswold turned on the man with dead eyes, while carefully watching the one with the sword. "Who's running the show here? Are you?" He turned back to the Scot. "Or are *you*, Mr. Scobie?"

"I'm running the show," Scobie said. "James, put that sword down. Angus, Rob, take him down to the—"

"No," said the other man gently. "Kill him, James."

Almost faster than Griswold could follow, the man with the sword was next to him, the claymore over his head. Then it came straight down upon him. Griswold was just able to put up both arms to defend himself before the blade struck.

It did no good. The sharpened edge of the claymore sheared through both of Taylor Griswold's wrists, so that for a split second he saw his severed hands suspended in mid-air. The sword cleaved his skull before they began to fall.

"What the bloody hell!" Colin Mackay bellowed, as he leapt to James Menzies and smashed the sword out of his hands. The claymore clattered on the stones as James staggered and went down on one knee, then fell headlong into the gore that had run from Taylor Griswold's cleft skull. Even a fool could see that the man was dead beyond recall. "Why did you disobey me?" Colin shouted at James, who looked up groggily and shook his head, as if he had no realization of what he had just done.

"He could not help himself," Mulcifer said quietly. "I told him what to do, and he did it. Had his own mother and father and whatever God in which he might believe . . . or better yet, had the Bruce and Bonnie Prince Charlie both told him to restrain himself, he could not have done it. So don't blame him. Blame me." He grinned. "I *like* it when people blame me."

Colin knew that he might be making a terrible mistake, but he couldn't help himself. He backhanded Mulcifer with a closed fist, and felt a surge of joy as he saw the man's leonine head snap back, and heard a grunt escape those sneering lips. Though he might not be able to kill him, if what his father had said was true, he could still cause him pain. Then he grabbed the front of Mulcifer's shirt and pulled the creature to him until their faces were only inches apart.

"You don't tell my men what to do," Colin growled from deep in his throat. It was all he could do to keep his hands from encircling Mulcifer's neck. "You keep your filthy thoughts and your bloody will out of their minds, do you hear me?''

Mulcifer started to chuckle, and when Colin could no longer bear touching him, he pushed him away. ''Colin, Colin, Colin,'' Mulcifer cooed. ''I wanted this slug dead, yes, I did, but I'd scarcely even thought about it when James reacted.'' Mulcifer looked at Menzies, who was still half-lying on the floor, his clothes soaked with his victim's blood and brains, his face still puzzled, as if trying to comprehend the reality of what he had just done. ''So malleable,'' said Mulcifer. ''My wish is his command.''

''Then stop wishing, God damn you!'' The thought of challenge rose into Colin's mind, and he decided that this was the time. If he relinquished any control of his men now, he would never get it back. And if he had already lost it forever, he might as well know now as later. He could not bear mockery. ''Or would you like to try *me* out, you damned brute?'' he asked.

''Be careful now,'' Mulcifer replied, his voice low and dangerous. ''Be careful what you ask for, boy. The deaths of thousands were on my hands a millennium ago.''

''Oh, I'm so frightened. Look, I'm quivering. Why don't you make *me* pick up that wee sword, Mulcifer, can you do that?''

The creature's eyes narrowed and stared into Colin's, and a frown of intense concentration came over his long, angular face. But Colin gave him back stare for stare, and felt nothing but the adrenaline rush of a contest that he had to win.

For all of Mulcifer's Svengali postures, Colin's mind was untouched. It wasn't even as if anyone was scratching weakly at the door. There was nothing at all.

At last he relaxed, and smiled at Mulcifer, who knew well enough what the smile meant, even if his own inability to make contact had not yet told him. The tension in Mulcifer's face slowly vanished, and Colin fancied he saw there a grudging respect that bespoke compromise. ''Colin Mackay,'' said

Mulcifer, as if he were pronouncing the name of a prince. "You are indeed your father's son."

He knew he was. His blood, pure and untainted by Mulcifer's, had been his father's greatest gift to his son, with the possible exception of the drink from the cup. "All right, then," Colin said. "That's settled. James, you clean this up. Rob, Angus, help him get rid of the body." Colin turned and walked out of the room.

Yes indeed, boy. You are your father's son, Mulcifer thought, as he watched Colin Mackay go. *And because of that, you will suffer unimaginable anguish. Watching this fool die was just the beginning. I may not be able to touch you, but there's scarcely a man among your loyal crew into whose mind I cannot slither as easily as a serpent into Eden.*

Chapter 25

"They've released the cream of the crop," said Joseph, his eyes fixed on the computer screen. "Two are INLA—Irish National Liberation Army—and two are IRA, both connected with the Continuity Army Council, a splinter group. There's one Scot, and he's linked to a very small paramilitary Scottish independence group. They're not taken very seriously, or at least they weren't until this laddie's sniper attack left three Scottish MPs dead. That's members of Parliament, not military police."

"I figured," Laika said. "Is there any pattern involved?"

"Well, aside from freeing the absolute worst of the worst, they went from Maze to Maghaberry to Maze to Maghaberry to Edinburgh."

"I bet they're nervous in Maze tonight," Tony said. "There's one thing that's mildly interesting in reference to our Templar castle. The one van left the castle two days before the first break, and returned the day after the last one."

"Could be coincidence," said Laika. "If this bunch in the castle are a new crew of Templars, why would they be freeing terrorists?"

"I don't know," said Joseph. "Maybe we're barking up the wrong tree entirely. Just the same, it might be a good idea to see when that van leaves again and where it goes." Joseph leaned toward the monitor and peered into it. "If by any chance they're behind it, I think they'll be on their way to Hixton."

"Where?" Laika asked.

"Hixton Prison, near Carlisle, just over the Scottish border. That's where the British government's holding Kevin Brady."

"I read about him," Tony said. " 'Mad Dog' Brady?"

"That's the boy. Responsible for a series of bombings that killed a total of eighty-five people, a good number of women and children among them. Couldn't keep him in Maze Prison—he kept trying to kill his fellow inmates. He's in solitary in Hixton. His M.O. would be right in line with the fine character of the rest of the freed terrorists."

"Well, we can't stake out an entire prison," said Laika.

"No. That's why the best thing might be to just keep watching what's in our own backyard."

"That's a *real* long shot," said Tony.

"It's an even longer shot for Skye to think that three covert agents can do what the British government can't," Laika said. "I think it's just wishful thinking on his part."

"Yeah, but we've got one advantage the British government doesn't," said Joseph. "We know about the Prisoner, and what he's capable of. And we've linked him with the castle. And since we can only be in one place at a time . . ." He shrugged. "But I suggest a twenty-four/seven on the place starting now. When they go, I'll follow alone."

"Why alone?" asked Tony.

"Joseph's the one who can pose as a Brit," Laika answered. "Anything happens to him, maybe the two of us can bail him out. Wherever he goes, there are going to be hordes of British police." She turned to Joseph. "If they head toward Hixton, or any other prison, I want you to stay uninvolved. Observe, but not too closely. You can't prevent an escape on your own, and I don't want you captured as an accessory."

"Me neither, believe me. I've got no cover on this, so I won't be taking a damn thing in my pockets except money. The Peugeot's untraceable, if I'd be stopped."

"Don't think negatively." Laika smiled. "I'll take first

shift on the ridge. I'll call on the cell phone if a van leaves tonight."

"Fine," Joseph said. "They'll have to come by here to get off the peninsula. I can pick them up easy enough."

"You're not used to pursuit," Tony said. "I think I should go along."

Laika shook her head. "Joseph's a big boy. He can stay on them without being spotted. Besides, we can't risk losing both of you, not that I'd expect that to happen."

Their heads all turned as one then to the front of the cottage as they heard the sound of a car coming into the gravel driveway. Tony went to the window and looked out. "Inspector Fraser. She's alone." Joseph hit a few keys, and the monitor's screen went black. Then they let in Molly Fraser.

"So," she said as Joseph took her dripping mack and hung it by the door, "just thought we might compare notes . . . if there's anything to compare."

"I'm afraid we haven't come up with much," said Laika, as they entered the living room and sat down. "We've been to a number of libraries seeing if there's been anything in the peninsula's past or its geological or climatic makeup that could spur any theory concerning the sightings."

Molly Fraser raised an eyebrow. "What about your 'ghost machine' theory? I thought you were going to investigate the castle."

"Well, frankly, we haven't had much luck there. How has MI5 fared?"

"You don't know about Mr. Scobie and his friends?" Molly asked, an eyebrow raised. "He just inherited the castle from his daddy, who died and was buried over in the States. Son Francis came up from Glasgow with a batch of his chums, and they've been playing lord of the manor. Or maybe *lady* . . ."

"Meaning?" asked Laika.

"Meaning from what was learned in Glasgow, that they're a pretty well outed group of gay men. People who knew them down there said they were nothing but idlers, living for the night life and little more. They hardly sound like the mad scientists that you envisioned."

"To tell the truth," Laika said, smiling, "they haven't done much of anything, as far as we've been able to see, and we've kept pretty solid surveillance on them. So I'm afraid we've been striking out so far. How about your group? Any news about the cloth you mentioned?"

Molly paused for a moment, as if trying to decide how much to tell. Then she closed her eyes and shrugged. "The cloth that was found is not the larger piece that the Fairy Flag of the Mackenzies came from. The piece didn't fit. But surprise, surprise, it *is* radioactive, and the Mackenzies were *really* surprised to find that it does glow in the dark. One more detail to brighten its legend and draw more tourists. MI5 has . . . *requested* possession of it for the time being, but Lord Mackenzie is already planning a darkened display room in one of the towers. And he'll sell those glow-sticks in his gift shop now."

They chatted a bit more without giving each other any additional information, and Molly said goodnight, reminding them to contact her should they learn anything of value, and promising to do the same for them. The ops agreed, all of them knowing that the promise was conditional.

"So," Laika said, when the car had vanished into the night, "did we learn anything?"

"The Fairy Flag glows," said Tony. "And if it's not a piece of the cloth found here . . . that means there must be more than one of those cloths. Maybe we should start hitting the flea markets. But what's this stuff about Scobie—or Mackay's—men being a bunch of gays?"

Joseph shook his head. "If this group is who we think they are, whether Templars or terrorists, that was planted, you can be sure of it. A network of false informants to throw off the police. If you want to appear nonthreatening—at least to non-Baptists—just get yourself labeled a bunch of homosexual dilettantes. It's right out of the fin de siècle period, Oscar Wilde and the boys playing knights and ladies, just sitting

around reading poetry to each other. Hardly prime suspects
to free any terrorists. No, MI5 thinks they're exactly who they
want them to think they are. A bevy,'' he finished in a Monty
Pythonesque voice, ''of bloody *poofs*.''

''You're probably right,'' Laika agreed. ''Scobie—or
Mackay—struck me as a tough nut when he ran us off his
land.''

''Don't think in stereotypes,'' Tony reminded her. ''Remember Adam Guaraldi?'' Guaraldi had been the lover and
assistant of Peder Holberg, the sculptor who had, under the
direction of the Prisoner, created the huge iron sculpture in
New York. Guaraldi had been a man's man all the way,
strong and rugged, who had handled iron pipes as easily as
though they were wooden dowels. And he had died like a
man.

''Yeah,'' said Laika, who knew of the friendship that Tony
had shared with Guaraldi. ''You're right. But so's Joseph.
The gay thing is a cover.'' She picked up a waterproof raincoat and slipped on a muddy pair of Wellingtons. ''I'd better
get up there and keep an eye on the castle. Tony, relieve me
at, say, 5 A.M.''

The relief wasn't necessary. The phone rang at 4:30, waking Joseph. Tony was already up, getting ready for his shift.
He said ''Okay'' into the phone and hung up. ''They're on
the move,'' he told Joseph, who was already slipping on his
clothes.

While he finished dressing, Tony got the Peugeot started
and put Joseph's unmarked bag that held a change of clothing
into the car. Then Joseph turned the car around, kept the
motor idling and the headlights off, and waited for the van
to pass the driveway, heading south.

Soon he saw its headlights, and after it passed he waited
until it was several hundred yards down the road before he
pulled out. He would leave as much distance as possible between them. The road was nearly empty at this time of the

morning, and he could regain visual contact later in the day, when the roads were more traveled.

Joseph turned on the radio until he found a station with some music, and tried to keep his mind on it. He might as well try and relax, he thought, particularly if they had to drive all the way to Carlisle.

Chapter 26

*A*t 2 o'clock the following morning, squadron leader Richard Greene sat in the back of the disguised British army van and waited with his mates. The van was parked across the road from the walls of Hixton Prison on the outskirts of Carlisle. It had two flat tires, and its windows were cracked. The hubcaps were missing, and the windowless sides had been spray painted with graffiti.

His six men crouched inside, all of them wearing riot gear, although they held their gas masks and helmets in their laps. It was too bloody hot in there to keep the headgear on. The earphone/mike headpiece that Greene had to wear was bad enough. They'd only been there two hours, and already it smelled like a musk ox convention.

They sat in absolute silence, lest anyone driving by hear their curses or remarks. It was altogether possible, the old man had told them, that these blokes might have sophisticated noise detection devices "that they might aim at such abandoned vehicles to determine whether or not they are occupied by you lot."

Greene wondered who had come up with the bright idea that these terrorists were planning to target Hixton next. They had sat in this bleeding shithole of a van for the past three nights until dawn, as had four other teams around the prison. Greene suspected, however, that similar army teams were undergoing the same exercise in every other prison in the United Kingdom where anti-British terrorists were being held.

The government wanted, more than anything else, to lure these bastards in, and the way to do that was to make them think that the prisons were doing business as usual. In truth, beside the teams stationed in abandoned vehicles and behind the walls of deserted warehouses, there were dozens of soldiers on alert inside the prison. Just let these arseholes try an escape here, and they'd be shot down before they'd be able to try a skeleton key.

Oh, Greene had heard the stories about the walking through walls and the guards attacking each other, but the official story was that these jailbreak artists had used some kind of gas on the guards that had made them a little crazy. All the soldiers inside and outside Hixton had gas masks, so the Scottish or Irish or whatever-they-were buggers would get a little surprise if they decided to pay an unscheduled visit to Kevin Brady.

Oh yes, he was the one they'd want, all right. A mad dog bastard with the sweetest face you'd ever want to see, but a goddamned mass butcherer for all that. If there was one shite that Hixton Prison wanted to keep within its old stone walls, it was Brady.

"Hoy," whispered Davis, the soldier looking through the eyepiece which was connected to the inset scanning device on top of the van. It gave them visual access in all directions. "Somethin' comin'. A van."

Vans were suspicious. They hid too much, like a half dozen soldiers, Greene thought to himself, and smiled in the dark.

"Goin' past," Davis said softly. "Turnin' right at the corner."

Greene whispered into the ball mike of his headpiece. "Gamma team, van headed toward you."

There was no reply, which was standard for a dead quiet situation. Greene knew gamma team leader had gotten his message.

"Another one," Davis whispered a minute later. "Dark sedan, a compact . . . it's slowing down . . . passing the corner . . . okay, it went past, straight ahead. Now it's pulling over . . . parking. Its lights just went off. One man getting out. Over six feet, slim build. He's crossed the street, walking back toward us . . . stopped at the cross street, looking down after the van.''

"Gamma team, do you have that van in view?'' Greene asked.

"Didn't show up on this end,'' came the reply. *Shite*, Greene thought. That meant it must have stopped against the southwestern wall, the one place they hadn't stationed a surveillance squad. The old man had said there was no need, since the wall was forty feet high, topped with razor wire, and eight feet thick, the last surviving wall of the medieval stronghold that had once stood there. "Need a bloody H-bomb to blow through that,'' the old man had said.

All right, then, if these bastards were the jailbreakers, they'd have to come around to one of the observed walls. Greene pushed Davis aside and looked through the eyepiece.

The man was still standing looking down the street in the direction the van had gone. There was a tension in his attitude, and Greene could see that his mouth was partly open. He started walking slowly until he disappeared past the outer wall of the prison, and out of Greene's sight. Greene did a visual 360 degrees, but saw no other vehicles or persons.

"Get ready,'' he told his men. They put on their gas masks and helmets, and placed their weapons across their knees. Two men on either side turned and set their hands on the pushbars that would drop both sides of the fake van.

They sat there, tense as hell, for seven minutes. Then, suddenly, the sirens began to howl, and through the eyepiece Greene could see swirling lights. ''*Go!*'' he barked.

The sides fell away from the disguised bivouac, and the men jumped out and rushed toward the corner around which the van and the man on foot had gone. There was no van there, but the man was about fifty yards away. He saw Greene and his men, and started running in the opposite direction. The sirens continued to blare as they charged after him. Then lights shone on them from a vehicle that had swung around the far corner and was advancing upon the fleeing man, who stopped and dived to one side.

In another second the vehicle was on Greene and his men, who had to leap to the side to avoid being crushed. It was the van they had seen earlier, and Greene ordered his team to fire at it, but by the time they picked themselves up and aimed, the van had turned the corner.

In the meantime, the man on foot had scrambled upright, and was once more running toward the far end of the street. "*Halt!*" Greene yelled, and fired a burst of bullets that chattered off the surface of the street two yards to the man's right. "Continue to run and you will be fired upon!" The man stopped, his hands in the air.

Greene and his squad secured the man, patted him down for weapons, and removed his wallet. There was no identification in it whatsoever. "Look," said the man in a midlands accent, "I'm really afraid there's been a bit of a cockup here. I was driving about and happened to notice that van, and I—"

"Put a cork in it," Greene said, jamming the barrel of his weapon under the man's chin. "What you driving around for with no identification papers? Suppose you give me your name, and damn quick."

"I, uh, I'd really rather not say, uh, officer."

"That's Sergeant-Major—Sergeant-Major Greene. And maybe you'd rather not say, but you'd better."

"Look, Sergeant-Major, I was just out for a bit of fun, you know . . . and if I was caught at it, I preferred not to have my identity known. Very embarrassing. So I figured I'd give a false name, and no one would be the wiser, see?"

"Yeah, I see all right, but that was if you got nicked for soliciting a prostitute, which, as you damn well know, does not constitute a crime. However, aiding and abetting a prison break does."

"Aiding and . . . you mean you think *I* have something to do with . . . with whatever's going on here?"

"Very much looks to me like you're the lookout," said Greene. "You're under arrest on suspicion of terrorism, mate.

You can either tell us your name now, or we'll get the information from your car registration.'' He nodded back toward the corner where the little car was parked.

The man look startled, then shook his head. ''I'm sorry, Sergeant-Major. I'm afraid I can't tell you who I am.'' He smiled. ''My marriage means a great deal to me. More than my freedom, even.''

Somewhere in the distance, they heard gunfire, short sharp bursts over the howling of the sirens.

Chapter 27

Joseph was immediately remanded to Hixton Prison, which in itself would have been a nightmare of bureaucracy, but was made far worse by the violence that had swept through the facility as the result of the escape of Kevin Brady, the IRA terrorist. Though Joseph did not hear the story of what had happened, he had seen a number of dead and wounded men, guards and inmates alike, carried past the remand area on stretchers to waiting ambulances.

Though no one made reference to it as he was being processed into custody, he knew all too well what had happened. The Prisoner—*his* Prisoner—the one who they had nearly found in New York and then again in Utah, had been here. Joseph had actually seen him for the first time, down that dark street where the British government's trap had been set. The man hadn't looked in Joseph's direction, but Joseph had known him nonetheless. He had been in profile, standing across the street from the parked van, and in the street light's glow Joseph saw his face, the same Christ-like face he had seen in his dreams.

And then the van had driven around the corner, and the man had walked into the wall.

At first Joseph couldn't believe that he had seen it. He looked at where the man had disappeared, but there was no door, no opening into the thick stone. He felt all around the mortar holding the heavy rocks in place, but there were no crevices at all.

Through the wall? Could the man actually have gone through the wall? Joseph stood there, staring at the solid wall, thinking about Newton's laws of motion and Lavoisier's law of conservation of mass, about entropy and density and the possibility of molecules in one solid object passing through and around the molecules of another, and thinking that maybe he was going crazy and hadn't seen this after all, and that it was just another one of those stupid dreams, when the sirens started blaring, and the soldiers were around the corner and on top of him.

He had tried the bullshit looking-for-sex story, but they hadn't bought it, and now here he was, remanded, fingerprinted, photographed, deloused, and garbed in a prison jumpsuit, being walked to a cell through one of the oldest and grimiest prison halls he had ever had the misfortune to see. The two guards with him were pissed as hell, yet somehow delighted to have gotten their hands on one of the blokes who had aided in the assault on their prison, and possibly left several of their comrades, maybe even their best friends, dead.

"We've got a right special cell for you, Mister John Doe, terrorist extraordinaire," the more talkative of the pair said, giving "extraordinaire" an outrageously phony French accent. " 'Cause of all this fuss your goddamn pals made, we can't put you in with the general population, so we're gonna put you in Longneck Peter's cell. Not a soul down in that wing, not in years. You'll be all by your goddamn self, just you and Peter."

"And who's Peter?" Joseph asked in his impeccable accent.

"Peter's the little Irish pansy who hanged himself in there eighty years back with his two shoelaces. Stretched the bastard's neck somethin' awful, it did. Finally had to quit puttin' prisoners in there."

"Why's that?" Joseph said, anxious to move the story along and ingratiate himself in the hopes that the two prison officers wouldn't kick him to sleep.

" 'Cause they kept hangin' themselves. Peter would come

to 'em at night, y'see, and tell 'em to. Leastways, that's what one of the poor bastards said who we found before he'd choked. He was the only one as survived. So say your prayers before you shut your eyes, you poncy shite.''

The wing was damp and chilly and smelled of bad drains, and Joseph saw no other prisoners in the darkened cells. Longneck Peter's cell was all the way at the end, down a steep incline, and Joseph had to step through several puddles of water before they arrived at the cell door.

It was not a solid steel door, as were on the cells in the other parts of the prison, but thick iron bars. The distance between them was scarcely wide enough to slip a hand through. The silent officer unlocked the cell, and the other one pushed Joseph inside. There was a wooden stool, a toilet and sink, and a cot with a stained and mildewed mattress.

"Sorry about the accommodations, but you know how things are." The officer pointed toward the ceiling, where a large black timber ran the width of the cell. "That's where they generally hang themselves from. Pretty handy, isn't it?" The officer looked down at Joseph's prison issue slippers. "Too bad, no laces. You could always tear your clothes into strips, though. A lot of them did that."

"I don't think I'll bother," Joseph said. The last thing he planned to worry about was some moldy ghost story. "I'm sure I'll sleep very well indeed." He spread his blanket on the cot. Fortunately it was big enough so that he could lie on it and fold the rest over to cover him. He wouldn't be warm, but he probably wouldn't freeze.

"Well, we hope you enjoy your stay," said the officer. "And if you yell, yell loud—you're a long way away."

They shut and locked the cell door behind him, and the light from the hall diminished. There was no bulb in the cell. Joseph sat on the cot and listened as the officers' footsteps receded up the hall. When he could no longer hear them, he got up and looked around his cell in the semi-darkness.

There wasn't much to look at. The cell was below ground level, and there were no windows, only a wall of heavy stone.

Despite its age, the mortar was secure, as Joseph found when he attempted to dig some away with his fingernails. There would certainly be no escaping from Hixton for him, not unless, he thought bitterly, the Prisoner returned and walked him through the stone wall.

Try as he might, Joseph couldn't imagine himself in a worse situation. If he revealed himself as a CIA agent, their entire cover would be blown, and he would return to the States in disgrace, *if* the Company and Skye confirmed his story in the first place. If he kept silent, he was a terrorist, and Hixton might turn out to be the most hospitable prison in which he was kept.

At least they wouldn't be able to trace him through the car. It was Company, and was spotless. It didn't even exist. That in itself might lend credence to his story if he decided to go the "I'm a spy" route. But the success of that might be decided for him. He was sure that his photograph was already winging its way toward the CIA and FBI for possible identification. For the time being, there wasn't anything he could do except sit in the cell and think about which lie to tell next.

The next day he was given two dreadful meals, and went through seven hours of questioning. He held to the story that he was a resident of Carlisle who had been looking for a prostitute when he had found himself in the middle of the breakout. Then why don't you tell us who you are? they asked him. Why does your car have a false registration and serial number? Don't you think it's better that your wife knows you've been catting about than that she sees your picture in the paper as a terrorist?

He knew they knew he was lying, and by the end of the day their frustration had led them to minor physical assaults, the kind that would leave no marks. They clapped their hands over his ears from behind, and twisted his ears, along with a number of other minor tortures in their repertoire. Still, Joseph did nothing but howl his innocence, as any wrongly accused burgher would. They threw him back in his cell and gave him his second meal, a piece of unidentifiable meat and a boiled potato. At least they were hot.

He pushed the metal plate into the hall under the narrow bottom of the cell door, and lay down on the cot. He had been remanded just before dawn, had not slept in all that time, and now was exhausted. There was nothing to do but sleep. Maybe he would dream of someplace much nicer than Longneck Peter's cell in Hixton Prison.

So Joseph closed his eyes and breathed deeply, trying to center his thoughts on rest. He fell asleep and dreamed of himself in Hixton Prison, and of Longneck Peter hanging from the black beam across his cell, his face in shadow.

Sometime after midnight he awoke, his eyelids fluttering open. And there, a yard above him, was a figure dangling in the air, twisting and turning slowly, its face coming around to look into his with open and knowing eyes.

Chapter 28

*F*BI deputy director Quentin McIntyre was working later than usual tonight. He usually liked to leave the building before 7 o'clock, since he always came in at 6 in the morning, but there had been more things to take care of than usual, and too many damned meetings for his liking. Things never got done in meetings, they got done by people painstakingly working one or two at a time the way he and his assistant, Alan Phillips, did.

McIntyre had just put some files in his briefcase to read before he went to bed when Phillips entered his office with some papers. "I know it's late," he said, "but this is something you're going to want to see."

It was a request from the counterterrorism division of MI5, asking the FBI to cross-check their photograph and fingerprint files for an ID on a terrorism suspect. McIntyre recognized the man in the enclosed photograph immediately.

It was Joseph Stein, one of the three CIA agents who had been working inside the United States against the CIA charter. McIntyre had been unable to find out what exactly they had been up to, but he knew that they were being run by Richard Skye, a petty bureaucrat who, to McIntyre, demonstrated the seediest aspects of the Company. From earlier run-ins, he had good reason to dislike Skye, and this new team he was running didn't further endear him to McIntyre, who thought that the three had been responsible in some way for the disappearance of Agent Brian Foster, who had found them in Arizona.

And now here was one of them, out of McIntyre's jurisdiction, admittedly, but still at his mercy. What was that bastard Skye up to now, over in England?

McIntyre considered the situation. If he informed MI5 that their suspect was CIA, they would let him go with a caution to the U.S. government to keep their nose out of Great Britain's internal affairs. It would certainly do Skye no good, but it would also be an embarrassment for the country.

Better perhaps to stay silent for the time being. That way Stein and the other agents would stew, as would Skye, not knowing if his whole operation was going to fall. And if Skye had to cut Stein loose, it would serve him right. He'd have a lot of explaining to do to his superiors, and depending on what the other two members of the team reported when they came in . . . well, it could be a real mess for Richard Skye, and that was something that Quentin McIntyre would dearly love to see happen.

"Let's run it through our files," McIntyre said, handing the photograph and copy of fingerprints back to Phillips, and looking at him knowingly from under furrowed brows. Phillips smiled, getting the message. They both knew that Stein, having no criminal record, would not be in their files. The search would turn up blank, and Stein would remain in a British prison, a wonderful liability for Richard Skye.

And it was Richard Skye at the CIA to whom MI5 had sent the photograph in a sealed envelope. When he saw it, he came as close as he ever did to panic. But then he made himself relax, and tried to see how this situation might be worked to his advantage.

When he found no way, he considered his options. Claiming Stein as one of his agents was out of the question. Apparently Stein had not revealed his CIA connections to his captors, so that made things easier. He could simply leave Stein out to dry and work with the other agents, or possibly they might find a way to help Stein escape, unlikely as that was.

At any rate, he need do nothing for now except draft a message to MI5 disavowing any knowledge of their mysterious prisoner. That would at least give him time to consider what to do next.

Chapter 29

Joseph's heart felt as if it had leapt into his throat. He remained pinned by the gaze of the apparition as it stopped turning and looked down at him. This wasn't at all like the vision they had seen on the road. It had form and detail, and an expression on its face, from the gaping mouth to the mad eyes to the long, gaunt neck that seemed to be stretched by an invisible rope. Joseph could even see the whiskers on the man's face.

Then that face seemed to shift, and the figure slowly descended from where it hung in the air, sinking until its feet were on the floor of the cell. The body was changing too, from the filthy rags of a prisoner to a spotless white shirt and a pair of neatly pressed trousers. The neck contracted to normality, and the face, instead of grimacing in a rictus of pain, now smiled at him beatifically. It was the face of the Prisoner, the man he had seen in his dreams.

And I'm still dreaming, Joseph thought. *My nightmare of Longneck Peter became the Prisoner, who has shared my dreams before. I'm just dreaming.*

"No. You're awake, Joseph. And I'm really here."

Joseph gasped, sat up on the cot, and grabbed his left hand with his right, digging the nails into his palm to drive himself into wakefulness. The Prisoner shook his head. "No. You can't wake up from this. I'm really here. Sorry about the Longneck Peter thing, but he'd been in your dream so strongly, and I can't resist a little touch of theatricality."

"How did you get in here?" was the first thing that Joseph could think of to say.

"Through the wall, of course. It's quite easy for me, just as it would be easy for you, were you to accompany me out of here. I hope you'll wish to do that."

"You're the one . . ." Joseph said slowly. Christ, his mind felt as though it were operating underwater, or under molasses. He didn't understand any of this. "You've been freeing the terrorists, haven't you? I saw you . . . go through the wall."

"I know you did. I felt you as I entered. And of course I saw you as we made our desperate escape. And I summed up matters very quickly. The soldiers were after you, and once they captured you, they would most certainly put you into this prison."

"But how did you know . . . did you find out where I was here?"

"I simply reached out for you, Joseph. The connection between the two of us is remarkably strong, more so than any other I've felt, either while I was in captivity or now that I am free. Ironic, isn't it? I entered your dreams trying to bring you to me so that you could free me, and here I find *you* a prisoner." He looked around the cell. "And in a very unpleasant jail, too. I don't think you'll be getting out by yourself very soon. Even if you should admit to them that you're a member of the Central Intelligence Agency, I doubt they'll believe you."

"You know I'm CIA?"

"Of course. I know nearly everything about you, Joseph. And I know that what you want the most right now, the single most important thing in your life, is your freedom, and that you would do just about anything to get it back. Am I correct?"

"Yes. Of course you are."

"Would that include aiding me—granting me a boon, shall we say?"

"A 'boon'? What kind of boon?" The descent to practicality was bringing Joseph back to his distrustful, cynical self. "I mean, I don't even know who you are. I know you were kept prisoner for . . . a long time. And I know that you can do things that other people can't." He gave a dry laugh. "That much is obvious. But rumor has it that you're not quite Casper the Friendly Ghost, whatever else you may be. If I'm not mistaken, the Catholic Church has called you the Antichrist for over a thousand years."

"Yes, that same Catholic Church that sponsored the Inquisition and condemned Galileo. You know as well as I do that what people can't understand scientifically, they tend to label as the devil's work. So when a being came upon them that their paltry medieval minds could not even begin to comprehend, what did they do? They sought to kill it, and when that failed, they tried to make it powerless."

"And succeeded. Lead was your downfall, wasn't it?"

"It was," the being said sadly.

"So what was the deal—electromagnetic radiation of short wavelengths?"

"It's a bit more complex than that, but you could put it in those primitive terms, yes. It was not, at any rate, magic. There is nothing supernatural about me at all."

"Not even how you can read minds? How you can make people do things they wouldn't normally do? How your commands are strong enough to bring somebody back from the dead, the way you did with Ezekiel Swain?"

"Tell me," the being asked calmly, "do you know Newton's Second Law?"

"$F = ma$. F is the force needed to give acceleration, a, to the mass m."

"In other words, if you push something, it moves. What I do is just the same. I push. Things move. Science, not magic. Your rationalist belief system stands in no jeopardy from me. I'm not the Antichrist, Joseph. Nor am I the Christ. I'm just very much like you, with aspirations and fears and emotions. And I need your help. If I help you to leave this place, can I expect it?"

If, Joseph thought, this man or thing had emotions and fears "just like" him, then he was also capable of hatred and duplicity. He could not promise carte blanche. "What specifically?" Joseph asked. "What kind of help?"

"With your CIA connections, you have access to information that would be valuable to me. I could gather it in other ways, but that would take time and energy. I consider you a valuable resource, Joseph Stein."

"What information? Like I said, I want specifics. Otherwise, I have no choice but to stay here and take my chances. I know that you're involved with terrorism . . . so I just want to know how deep I'm digging my grave."

"All right. If you want specifics, fine. You know from what I've done that I'm no saint. I can tell how you feel about me, so I might as well be honest with you. Fifteen years ago, the British government buried containers of nerve gas somewhere in Scotland. I want that gas. Now, I'm sure you don't know where it's buried, but I'm equally sure that you could find out where it is with a little digging around in your CIA computer files. Even if England didn't share that information with your organization, I'm sure that they came by it somehow."

"Why do you want it?" Joseph asked, a sick feeling in his stomach.

"For the betterment of the world. So. Do you want to come with me? Or would you prefer to stay here?"

It was a Faustian bargain, Joseph knew, but one that he did not necessarily feel obligated to fulfill. He was as frustrated at the circumstances as he was at his moral dilemma. Here at last he was, face to face with the creature who had eluded them all these months, but the situation was much different from what he had imagined. It had become far worse than a simple reversal making Joseph the hunted. He was already caught, and the former Prisoner offered him his only hope of escape.

That was the crux, wasn't it? Agreeing to help this creature, whatever he was, was Joseph's only alternative to staying in prison indefinitely. Better to agree now, he thought, and extricate himself from the web later on. After all, his will was still his own. He could walk away, or *run*, if it came to that, as he felt certain it would. The devil does not look kindly on those who break their contracts.

"I'll come with you," Joseph said. "But I hope it won't be as obvious as your last breakout here."

"Nothing of the sort. You're far enough away from the rest of the prison population so that we won't have to stroll through their midst. No, they'll simply not find you in your cell the next time they look. Another miracle to add to their growing list." He nodded toward the cell door. "I believe we'll go through there first, then walk up the incline until we reach street level, at which point we'll go through the wall. I think that you would find passage through earth even more unpleasant than you will moving through stone. Are you ready?"

"I think so. But you never told me—what's your name?"

"Nothing you would find pronounceable. I suggest you call me Mulcifer. Now, give me your hand . . ."

It was a good thing, Mulcifer thought, that Joseph Stein had followed them to Carlisle and Hixton Prison. During the ride down from Scotland, he had felt the presence of someone else nearby, someone with whom he could establish a rapport, but he had not reached out then. He had wanted to save all his energy for the escape.

Contrary to the belief of his revolutionary comrades, one could not engage in these kinds of activities indefinitely. There had to be time for the strength and the abilities to refresh themselves. But it was best if they thought his powers were always on call. Then they would hesitate to challenge him. And even at his weakest he always maintained enough power to control humans like Rob and Angus, with their puny, easily overcome wills.

When he had sensed the presence of Joseph Stein, just before he had passed through the walls of Hixton to free Kevin Brady, his joy had nearly been overwhelming. In fact, knowing that Stein was nearby had seemed to increase his strength so that his waltz through the walls and cells and hallways had been joyous, and he had swept out the terrorist and turned the other inmates and officers against each other as effortlessly as if he had been instructing a child to throw a stone through a window.

Outside, he had hurried Brady into the van, and they had made their usual breathtaking escape through lines of soldiers grown suddenly and inexplicably quarrelsome with each other, preferring to shoot at their comrades rather than at the fleeing vehicle. They had taken Brady to a safe house, where Mulcifer had privately given him his instructions for two days hence, and then seen him on his way with enough money to procure the essentials.

But instead of returning to the castle and awaiting the glorious day that was intended to free Scotland but would have, Mulcifer knew, quite a different effect, he insisted to the others that they go back to Hixton the following night. "Christ, man, dinna you care how you tempt fate?" Rob had said in anguish, knowing that he could not disobey.

Mulcifer, always recognizing a beautiful set-up line, replied, "I *am* fate," gave Rob's little mind a little *push*, and experienced no further protests.

They had gone back to the prison, and Mulcifer had brought out Joseph Stein with none of the theatricality that had marked his prior missions. Now they were in the van heading back to Scotland, driving north toward Glasgow on the A74, and Joseph Stein was seated in the backseat next to him, wearing the new clothes that they had bought for him earlier that day.

The man was very tired, and Mulcifer also sensed that he was hungry, so when Joseph asked to stop for something to eat, Mulcifer ordered Angus to pull the van off the A74 and stop at the first open eatery they saw. It happened to be a small all-night café that was nearly empty.

They ordered eggs and sausages, and when Joseph said that he had to use the bathroom, Angus started to go with him, but Mulcifer gestured to him to sit back down. "What's with you?" Angus said when Joseph had rounded the corner to the toilets. "You're not afraid he'll scarper?"

"He'd like to, but he won't."

"What did you get him out for?" Angus went on. "Ain't he the one who got caught when you took out Brady?"

"Yes, he is."

"What do we want with him, then?"

"He's going to be very useful, Angus. Don't you be concerned. Yes, very useful indeed."

The men's room had a large enough window to climb out of. Joseph raised it far enough to look out. There was a drop of only a few feet, and a woods that began fifty yards behind the restaurant. He could lose himself in it easily enough, then, when he felt he was in the clear, get to a phone, and dial Laika and Tony at the cottage.

But when he tried to push the window up the rest of the way, he found that he could not. It was not that the window was stuck, but he found himself unable to exert any pressure upon it. His fingers were wrapped around the bottom rail, but he could not bring himself to raise it.

Joseph tried to think of why he could not raise the window far enough to climb through. It had to be Mulcifer. Had the man implanted some fear within him? Was he expecting some huge maw to force its way through the window and devour him, or a hand to crush him?

No, it was nothing like that. As much as he wanted to, he simply could not lift that window, even though he told himself it was absurd. There was absolutely nothing to keep him from just sliding it up and slipping through.

Nothing except Mulcifer.

He took his hands away from the window and looked at them bitterly. If was as if they weren't his anymore, but under the control of someone else. All right then, he thought. The bastard was in the next room, thinking about him, maybe thinking *at* him, or whatever it was that he did.

But he couldn't do it all the time. He couldn't exercise his control twenty-four hours a day. Sometime it would lapse, and then Joseph would get as far away from the son of a bitch as possible. He just hoped it would be before he had to find out where the nerve gas was hidden.

That was information that Joseph knew he could get, and Mulcifer probably knew it too. When it came to chemical and biological weapons, the CIA kept just as close tabs on their allies as they did on their enemies. And the older secrets were, the less securely guarded they seemed to be. The gas had been buried fifteen years before. Joseph could access that data easily enough.

Maybe, he thought, he could pretend he wasn't able to, although he didn't know how far pretense would go with Mulcifer. The man seemed as though he might be very difficult to fool. That would seem to be standard operating procedure for beings who could read your mind and make you do things without telling you.

So he would do what Mulcifer wanted him to, right up until the time he had to dig up the data on the nerve gas. Maybe by then he'd be able to figure out a way to not only resist Mulcifer's wishes, but to turn his powers against him. And in the meantime, he'd be finding out just who was behind the escapes.

But Joseph had the feeling he already knew that. He would have been willing to bet his life that they would go back to Castle Dirk. Though he had suspected it before, he felt sure of it now, and wondered if it was because Mulcifer had somehow put that certainty into his head, shared that knowledge with him.

He sighed. There was only one way to find out, so he did what he had no choice but to do. He went back to the table where the three men sat. Or, he thought, the two men and something else. Something very different, the manifestation of the last words of Conrad's *The Secret Agent*: "unsuspected and deadly, like a pest in the street full of men."

Chapter 30

Something had gone wrong, and there wasn't a thing they could do about it. The last that Laika and Tony had heard of Joseph was a call he had made from a pay telephone several hours before the jailbreak that had freed Kevin Brady. He had followed the van to Carlisle, and two of the three men inside had gotten out and gone into a pub. Joseph had to ring off when he had seen them coming back out with a bag of food.

Along with the story of the escape, there had been news reports that a man suspected of aiding the terrorists had been arrested and remanded into custody. When they hadn't heard from Joseph hours after the break, they feared the worst had happened, and that the suspect was their teammate. No photograph had been released, but Laika was certain that one would be sent to law enforcement agencies, including the CIA. She hoped it would go to Skye rather than anyone else who might recognize Joseph. It was more than possible; it was likely, considering Skye's position in operations. But then, they wondered, what would *Skye* do?

And now, the 6 A.M. news reports told of the disappearance of the suspect from Hixton Prison, a quiet and miraculous escape that had as yet no explanation, although authorities felt that it had to have been an inside job, and several prison officers were being interrogated. Joseph was a wonder, of that neither of them had a doubt, but getting out of a high security

English prison didn't seem to be one of the things his skills would have prepared him for.

And if he had escaped, why hadn't he contacted them? Tony was afraid that he might have been killed in the chaos of the first escape, but Laika refused to consider it.

There was, however, one trail to follow. Although Tony and Laika didn't know where the men from the castle had gone before, they knew now that they had gone to Carlisle shortly before the Kevin Brady escape. It could have been a coincidence, although they had remained alive and healthy by refusing to believe in coincidences. It now seemed all too possible that those in the castle were connected with the escapes.

So all they could do for now was watch the castle and wait for the return of the van. If Joseph's photograph crossed Skye's desk, he would be in touch sooner or later, probably sooner.

At noon, Tony sat on the ground watching the castle and the road into it, all pretense of archeology gone, since they had had no visitors since Molly Fraser to mark their progress or the lack of it. He had prayed countless times for Joseph to come back safely, and hated it when it was his turn to keep watch for fear that he would miss his colleague's return or some other news that would reach Laika at the cottage.

From what little they could establish, the sightings of apparitions had either declined or stopped completely, and further investigation showed no reasons for the occurrences, not even legendary. If Molly Fraser could be trusted, MI5 was having no better luck.

At one o'clock in the afternoon, Tony saw the van returning down the road to the castle. Through his binoculars, he could see only the driver, a thin-faced man with sandy hair, and a heavier man who sat in the passenger seat. Whoever may have been in the back was hidden by the solid panels.

He watched the van as it disappeared into the inner ward, wishing that he could see who climbed out of it. Then he called Laika on the cell phone and told her what had happened.

"Somebody was watching us," Rob said, as he parked the van in the inner ward. "I saw a double flash of sunlight from the top of the ridge to the south, like a pair of binoculars."

"Shite," said Angus. "Who?"

"Maybe those archeology snoopers," said Rob.

"Or maybe," said Mulcifer, "your little friends." He smiled at Joseph, who said nothing, and tried to keep his mind clear. But the more he tried *not* to think about Laika and Tony, the more he found himself doing so.

"What friends?" Rob asked.

"Never mind," said Mulcifer. "All will be answered soon."

"Who the hell is this?" asked Colin Mackay, rising impatiently from his chair as Rob and Angus led the stranger into the small study, with Mulcifer behind them.

"His name is Joseph Stein," Mulcifer said, "and he's one of the three American CIA agents who have been staying nearby and watching over us."

Colin recognized the man. He had been one of the three archeologists he had driven off his land. Only they weren't archeologists at all, were they? "CIA?" Colin asked Mulcifer. "How do you know that?"

"Oh, I know almost everything there is to know about this chappie," said Mulcifer. "But there's not a thing to fear. He won't do anything I don't want him to do."

Mulcifer gestured for Rob and Angus to leave. They glanced at Colin and he nodded for them to obey. Then Mulcifer told Colin about the escape, and how he had seen this Joseph Stein outside the prison. He told about Stein getting captured by the police and of his freeing him.

"But Christ, man," Colin said, "you've brought a CIA agent here. There's no way we can let him go, don't you know that?" Stein looked on edge, but somehow resigned to his fate. Colin was certain that he knew the rules of the game.

"He is a repository of information," Mulcifer said. "One that I want to start drawing upon as quickly as possible. The computer is hooked up to the phone line, yes?"

"To the Internet? Yes, of course."

"Mr. Stein and I will require it. In the meantime, you need to be thinking about two things. The first is if there is another way we can leave this castle beside the main road, one that can't be observed from that southern ridge. And second, we'll need a place where we can store Mr. Stein here when he's not in use. He's much more valuable to us alive than dead."

"What about the other agents?" Colin asked. "Do they know about the jailbreaks?"

"They suspect," Mulcifer said, "but they have no proof. The van was away from the castle during the escapes, so they know that we could have had something to do with it. They have been searching for me, you see, among their other activities, and have, I'm certain, connected the castle to the Templars and probably also to your father." Mulcifer glanced casually at Stein, who looked surprised. "I *am* correct, am I not? Deductions, for a change, rather than exploring your thoughts." He looked back at Colin. "The others don't know he's here. They'll probably realize that his escape could have been due only to me, but I seriously doubt that they'll report you to the English authorities. They want me, you see. This is the third time our paths have crossed, and they're unlikely to do anything that would jeopardize their own contact with me. So . . ." He clapped his hands together. "Let's get to work, Joseph."

"What are you planning?" Colin asked. "What information is he going to provide?"

"You'll know when we have it," Mulcifer replied. "Or maybe a little later. But don't worry—it's all for the cause."

Colin did not offer to supply Mulcifer with a guard over Stein. He knew there was no need. The pair left the room, and Colin thought about what else Mulcifer had said.

There was a large open elevator in the inner ward that had

been used to take supplies down to the cellars. A car or van would fit on it easily enough, and from the first cellar there was an escape door onto the beach. The van would just fit through it, he thought. Then they could drive a half mile north on the beach to an old boat access road that was still functional, and get out onto the main road without being seen by watchers on the ridge.

As for where to keep Joseph Stein, the bottle dungeon would be ideal. It was located in the guardhouse of the northwest tower, and a trapdoor level with the stone floor was the only indication of its existence.

It was actually shaped like a bottle, with a long, narrow opening at the top, and a wider cell beneath, accessible only by a rope or a ladder. Once at the bottom of the twenty-foot-deep dungeon, it was impossible to climb the slanted walls to the top, and even if someone miraculously could, the trapdoor would be locked. It was the only dungeon in the castle, and the only one that was ever needed.

Now for the deeper questions, Colin thought. What were these CIA agents doing just outside his castle walls, and how much of a threat did they pose to his mission? After Mulcifer got through with this Stein, Colin would have to interrogate him and see. As far as Colin knew, he and his organization had not drawn the attention of MI5's counterterrorism division, and he wanted to keep it that way, even if it meant disposing of Stein and the other two agents.

He preferred to keep any violence away from the peninsula, so it was something he would rather not have done. But nothing could be allowed to endanger the cause.

Chapter 31

*M*ulcifer closed the door behind them, and ordered Joseph to turn on the computer. The words were spoken gently enough, but it was an order nonetheless, and Joseph could no more have disobeyed it than flown.

"In 1984," Mulcifer said in his deep singer's voice, "the British government decided to dispose of a large supply of nerve gas. They buried it somewhere in Scotland. That is all I know. What I want *you* to find out is what kind of gas it is, why it was buried, and precisely *where*, along with how it is guarded, if at all. I know you have access to CIA data banks—and since the CIA's deepest secrets were entrusted to you as an intelligence interpreter, you can delve into the agency's deepest cover secrets. So ..." He gestured to the computer. "Delve away."

It took Joseph nearly an hour to find the information. He had determined not to do so, to chase around the data banks, hopping from link to link, never finding the information Mulcifer desired, telling him that it simply wasn't there.

But he found that he could not deceive or disobey the man at all. He was, to his horror, like a ravenous dog sent by its master to bring back the prey, and he could do nothing else.

"The gas is VX," he told Mulcifer. "It's similar to sarin, the gas that was released in the Tokyo subway by Aum Shinrikyo, that Japanese cult, but this stuff is a hundred times more deadly."

"And how does it kill?" Mulcifer asked.

"It screws up the nerves that control certain muscles, like your diaphragm. You can't breath, you convulse, you die. Sarin just dissipates in the air, but VX is thicker. You get a drop on your hand or your face, and you're dead in minutes."

"And supposedly decent, civilized countries use these things?"

"And worse. There's a biological weapon called botox, a toxin made from the botulism bacteria. Iraq has a healthy— or *un*healthy—supply of it. Got it from the United States."

"And why did England decide to bury their supply of VX?"

"Too horrible to contemplate using."

"They finally decided."

"The mills of bureaucracy grind exceeding slow," Joseph said, glad that his cynicism had not escaped along with his will.

"How much of this VX is buried away?"

"Over a hundred canisters weighing about a hundred pounds each."

"The destructive power of a canister?"

"Spread two canisters over a medium-sized city, and you've pretty much got a dead city."

"Finally, where and how is it buried?"

"About fifty miles northeast of here, in Glen Cassley. The nearest town is a little village named Duchally. The canisters were put in a deep cave, which was then caved in with dynamite. The crater that was left was filled in with concrete. And there's still a guardhouse posted there. It's government land, and it's fenced off." Joseph allowed himself a smile. "So if you were able to get through the guards, you'd only have to blast your way through a twenty-foot-deep plug of concrete, and then maybe another fifty feet of rock and debris to get to the cave. You know, I really don't feel too badly about giving you this information, since I know you'll never be able to do a goddamned thing with it, you bastard."

Mulcifer smiled back. "I truly appreciate your cooperation, Mr. Stein. Now to conclude, I want you to develop a map of the area for me, showing me precisely where the cave is, along with the perimeter of the area and guardhouse. Go ahead. I have all the time in the world.''

When Joseph was finished, he printed the map and gave it to Mulcifer, who thanked him and left the room. Alone, Joseph tried to send an e-mail to Laika and Tony, but was unable to type in the address. Jesus Christ, it was as if he were six years old, and someone had put a Net Nanny on his machine. He couldn't do a damned thing other than what Mulcifer told him to do.

In another minute, Mulcifer returned with the man Joseph knew as Francis Scobie, but whom he suspected was the heir, if not the son, of Andrew Mackay. ''I'm finished with Mr. Stein for the time being,'' Mulcifer said. ''You may show him to his accommodations now.''

Mackay and the bigger of the two men who had been in the van herded Joseph at gunpoint through the hallways and into a guardhouse, where a ladder led down through an open trapdoor. Joseph looked through the opening and saw that the chamber below seemed to have been dug out from the solid rock on which the castle sat. ''Do you have anything with a view?'' he asked.

''You're lucky to have the ladder,'' said Mackay. ''They used to just drop them in.''

That night, two men stood watch on the towers to make sure that no one approached the castle, while everyone else slept. Joseph was sleeping on a small mattress that had been dropped down the hole, wrapped in two blankets. It had taken him a long time to get to sleep, for he had kept wishing that he had not agreed to Mulcifer's deal. He had escaped from an English jail, all right, but was now imprisoned in a hole in a rock, with a bucket to piss in. Still, he was exhausted enough to sleep dreamlessly.

There was one person awake besides the guards. Mulcifer had looked closely at the map Stein had given him, comparing it with relief maps of the area. Then he had gone to the store-room, removed the boxes, opened the hidden door, and descended the long, winding stairway. He had no need for light.

In the large room where his persecutors had been meeting for centuries, he closely examined the huge wooden shield that bore the Mackay coat of arms. Then he shoved the table over against the wall and stood on it so that he could easily reach the shield. The catch was where he had thought it would be. If, he observed, you grasped the hand holding the dirk and pulled it hard toward you, an opening would undoubtedly appear in the wall.

For a long time he stood there, his hand on the carved wooden fist. The temptation to pull upon it was strong, but so was his fear. He didn't know what would happen, how easily he could control what was in all likelihood within.

He pushed against the stone wall with his mind, but felt nothing there. Either they were long gone, or, as was also likely, the great slab of stone was sheathed with lead. But the lead wouldn't keep him from opening it should he choose to. It was not harmful to him, only restrictive, limiting. He could open the passageway and find allies obedient to one who had seen more than they ever had, who knew far more of this world from dwelling on its surface, albeit a prisoner, for over a millennium.

Or he could find enemies.

At last he released his grip on the fist. It seemed foolish to take the chance, now that he was free at last, and everything was going so well. Tomorrow would be proof of that. He would drink deep and be sated, at least for a time. He had set his infernal devices, the living bombs he had armed and triggered with electrical impulses, the same way that they would trigger their dumb and lifeless bombs.

He stood there in the darkness that was light to him, and thought about the suffering and death that would come, and was surprised by a brief instant of sanity in which he almost felt some pity for these creatures whom he was destroying. It lasted only as long as it took him to identify it, and then he drove it mercilessly from his mind. Perhaps he had been among them too long, but he had been among those of his own kind all his life before he had come to this world, and he had savaged them as well.

Sanity? Was that how he had actually thought of it for a moment, as sanity? No, it could not be, for to him the twisted *was* the sane, the abnormal the norm, the insane the lucid and clear and rational. He was incorrigible, his behavior and beliefs irreversible. That was, after all, why he was here, banished from his own kind, except, perhaps, for those behind the wall.

Morality did not enter into it. Morality was illusion, and the affirmation of *mortality* the only truth, the sole element of life which made existence worthwhile. And one affirmed mortality by exercising its rights, as inclusively and universally as possible. One killed so that one could say, *I live.*

And only when one stood on a world once teeming with life, and stood alone, could one's purpose be fulfilled. *In the midst of life we are in death?* No, quite the opposite—only in the midst of death are we truly alive.

So it was that he had pushed against, and at times through, the lead. So it was that his spirit had suffered, and his soul had bled in his attempts to touch those who were extensions of his mind, vessels of his blood. So it was that, paradoxically, he had weakened himself in order to feed and give himself strength.

Now he was free. Now the earth was his. Tomorrow it would begin. No one should bless him or curse him or praise him as a dark god. He could not help what he would do. It was his nature.

Chapter 32

*T*he next morning at 11 o'clock, a series of suicide bombings provided London with its worst terrorist attack ever, within a single minute. Struck were St. Paul's Cathedral, Westminster Abbey, Buckingham Palace, the Tower of London, the British Museum, and the Victoria and Albert Museum. The damage in each was extensive, and it was later stated that the bombers could not have positioned themselves in any better location, if sheer destruction was their goal.

The bombers had gone into the interior of each building, except for Buckingham Palace, where the bomber must have stood against the gate. Still, the damage was enough to blow out nearly all the windows of the palace wall facing the gate. Luckily, the royal family were on a jaunt to Balmoral, and not inside at the time. The survival of the royals did little to comfort the families of the 127 spectators and tourists who died at the front gates, however, not to mention the guards, and 48 more badly injured survivors.

The St. Paul's bomber had stood not directly under the great dome, but below in the crypt, next to Lord Nelson's tomb, where the blast would be directed upward, smashing through the floor and into the area beneath the dome. The explosion easily demolished the supporting pillars around Nelson's tomb, so that the arches above crumbled, and the dome itself collapsed inward.

The strategy had been similar in Westminster Abbey. There the bomber had positioned himself between the Chapel of St.

Edward the Confessor and the Chapel of Henry VII, assuring the destruction of the tombs of England's greatest monarchs, along with the Coronation Chair which Edward I had ordered made in 1296, and on which monarchs had been crowned ever since.

The bomber at the Victoria and Albert Museum must have stood in the Gothic Art hall of level A, so that the blast exploded outward from the center of the building. Though protected by more walls, the detonation did immense damage to the delicate works of art, even those not actually touched by the explosive. Afterward, there was scarcely a piece of unbroken glass or ceramic in the entire building.

A central site was not used for the British Museum, however. There the bomber stood in front of the Elgin Marbles, which were reduced to rubble, along with most of the Greek and Roman exhibits, and many of the surrounding rooms.

The Jewel House was the target in the Tower of London. The bomber had apparently been stopped by security people, but had pushed himself onward and gotten as close to the Crown jewels as possible before he set off the bomb. The jewels might have survived in some form, but it would take a while to sift through the rubble of the building. The heavy transparent plates had been designed to stop bullets, not a massive amount of plastic explosive.

But the destruction of the treasures of British culture paled in terms of the loss of human life. Early estimates were placed at 300, besides the 127 who had died at Buckingham Palace. Every site was a major tourist attraction, so many foreigners were killed, along with 40 secondary-school students from London whose ages ranged from 12 to 15.

The bombings had definitely been suicidal, and MI5 quickly estimated that each bomber would have had to have been carrying approximately 50 pounds of plastic explosive to produce so much devastation. When eyewitness reports were compared, it was found that at each of the six sites a stout clergyman had been seen, dressed in a loose raincoat. It would have been possible, experts declared, for men of medium weight to carry 50 pounds of plastic explosive strapped to their bodies under their coats, and detonate it with a simple trigger device when they reached their target area.

Later that afternoon, the letters arrived, postmarked the day before, claiming responsibility for the six bombings. They concluded, as had the others, "We are Scotland."

The British government stated that they would stop at nothing to bring to justice the cowardly and reprehensible organization that was behind these bombings. The prime minister's statement concluded, "If these butchers and murderers think that this government will capitulate to terrorism, and particularly to terrorism of such a fanatical and blasphemous nature, they are dead wrong. They will be found, and they will be made to pay for their crimes against this country and its people, and for its terrible sins against humanity. The destruction of the best of this great country—its churches, its monuments, and its children, whose loss will be felt the worst of all—has utterly doomed the cause of these madmen, and set them beyond the pale of civilized society. Those who set these suicides on their bloody course are monsters, and this nation shall not rest until we are free of them forever, until they and the hatred that bred them are effaced from the earth."

"You bastard," Colin Mackay said, in a voice that shook with rage and terror and sorrow. "What have you done? All those dead . . . children, civilians, churches . . . my God, there's not a man in the British Isles who wouldn't cut off his right hand to put you behind bars!"

Mulcifer stood in the afternoon drizzle that spat down on them where they stood in the northwest tower. He looked at the gray sky and the gently rolling waters of the Minch. "I believe you have that wrong. It's *you* they want to put behind bars. Mr. 'We Are Scotland' himself. They don't know me from Adam. Nor you, as yet." He gave a small shrug. "I don't see why you're so unhappy. The heart of England has been struck a terrible blow. The very spirit of the empire has been grievously wounded, and you are now the head of the most feared terrorist group in the world. You've shown England that you're capable of touching them anywhere, and that you are capable of inspiring followers, allied to you politically only in the most tenuous ways, to die for your cause.''

"But after what you did," said Colin, turning from him angrily, "they'll never capitulate—*never*."

"I gave you what you wanted," Mulcifer said quietly.

Colin whipped about, looking at him with fiery eyes. "And didn't it mean a damned thing to you that you killed children?''

"Would it have meant a damned thing to you if I had specifically targeted a busload of soldiers, and that bus had been used at the last minute to carry a troop of boys and their widowed grandmothers to matins? Oh, you might have wrung your hands, but in the end you would have waxed eloquently about the vicissitudes of war and chalked it off to bad luck. Your problem is that you confuse intent with results.

"And as for meaning a damned thing to me, of course it did. I feel every one of those deaths, my friend, and I revel in them. The younger and more innocent, the more delectable the incense.''

Colin looked at him for a long time. "Maybe I was wrong. Maybe you *are* the Antichrist.''

"Or something even worse," said Mulcifer, his face soft, his eyes dreamy. "Maybe 'the deil' himself, after all.''

Colin shook his head. "No. Like you just said. Something even worse.''

What was this beast? Colin wondered, as he turned and walked away, down the stairs and into the castle. It was a creature who not only had no mercy, but to whom the deaths of children were joyous events. As much as he hated to admit it, his father had been right. The creature was thoroughly, unredeemably evil.

But Mulcifer was right about one thing. His actions had instantly made Colin's group a force, not only to be reckoned with, but to be greatly feared. There was not a terrorist organization in the world that had ever pulled off such a brilliantly orchestrated series of strikes. Yes, it was true that innocents had been killed, but innocents always died in war, as tragic as it was.

Jesus, listen to me, he thought. Just like Mulcifer said. The bastard read minds like books. But then Colin paused and thought that he had never truly felt Mulcifer inside his own mind. He could guess, of course, what Colin was thinking, but not enter him, as he had the others, including the man down in the dungeon, that CIA agent.

He had been meaning to talk to Stein and find out how much he knew, not only about Colin's activities, but about Mulcifer as well. The creature himself had admitted that their paths had crossed before. Maybe Stein knew something that would prove useful, some way to restrain or control Mulcifer. Yet if he knew that, why was he now their prisoner? Still, perhaps there was something he could learn.

Colin got a pistol and went to the trapdoor that covered the bottle dungeon. No one was guarding it. There was no need. He opened the trapdoor and dropped the ladder down through the hole. "I'm coming down," he called, stuck his pistol in his waistband, and climbed through the trapdoor, descending into the dungeon.

Halfway down he clung to a rung with one hand and took out his pistol with the other. "Get over there against the wall," he said, and Stein did as directed. Colin finished climbing down, his eyes constantly on Stein. As he stepped onto the dungeon floor, he gestured with the pistol. "Sit down," he ordered, and Stein sat on the rough bed. "Now, Mr. Stein, suppose you tell me just how much you and your friends up above know about me and my group."

"We know that you've gotten into some bad company," Stein said. "I don't think Kadaffi or Saddam or even Hitler would have aligned themselves with your righthand man. Unless you're *his* at this point."

"We'll talk about him later. What do you know about *us*?"

"Actual or theoretical?"

"Both, please."

"How much we *really* know depends on what your name is."

"And what do you *think* it is?"

Stein looked at him heavily. "Mackay."

"Aye," Colin said, nodding slowly. "Colin Mackay is my name. Now tell your story, Mr. Stein."

"It's a long one," Stein said, and began.

Chapter 33

*T*here was little point in keeping it to himself, Joseph thought. Mackay was a sounding board. He could see how much of what they had deduced was true and what were illusions born of their own imaginations.

He told Mackay about the eleven poisoned bodies that had been found in the burned down hunting lodge in upstate New York, and about the evidence that indicated they might be of great age. Then he told about the man who called himself Kyle McAndrews, and how he had tried to kill the operatives in revenge. "He thought we had caused the deaths of his eleven 'brothers.' "

"And had you?" Mackay asked.

"No. We're not sure who did."

"You hesitated. You suspected."

"Yes. We thought—we *think*—it might have been a man named Daly. A CIA agent who . . . turned. So McAndrews wasn't far from the truth. Only it wasn't us."

"And what happened to this Daly?"

"He's dead. As for the man who called himself McAndrews, we tracked him down and started to question him, but he tried to kill us."

"So you killed him," Mackay said.

"We had no choice."

"Which of you shot him?"

"All of us. We all shot."

"And what happened to his body?"

Joseph took a deep breath. "We couldn't have it discovered. Because of the brand, you see." He eyed Mackay, but no emotions crossed the man's face. "The *Templar* brand. On his chest. Also the fingerprints, and his appearance. We suspected that he was a very old man, in spite of his physical appearance."

"So what did you do with him?"

"We destroyed the body. It's gone, like it never existed."

Mackay smiled bitterly. "The curse," he said softly.

"Masonic?" Joseph asked. "Or is the Templar curse similar? Something about being cut apart and having the pieces of your body scattered to the winds, isn't it? *If* you happen to reveal the secrets of the society. Like maybe telling someone about the purpose behind the Templars' existence. Or even sharing . . . other secrets."

"Did you find anything else on this McAndrews?" Mackay said, as if anxious to change the subject.

"Anything else? Like what?"

"Oh, personal possessions. Anything that would tie into this Templar idea."

"Very little. Some cash, clothing . . . an old knife, that was all." Joseph didn't mention the simple wooden cup in the elegant case that they had thought might be the Grail. Even now it was wrapped inside one of his suitcases at the cottage.

He went on to tell Mackay about their near misses at finding the Prisoner, of their return to Scotland to investigate the ghostly sightings, and finally about their deductions that the prison escapes were connected to the former prisoner. "You know the rest," Joseph concluded. "I was in the wrong place at the wrong time, and your powerful friend saw some potential for aid in me, the same way that he did in you."

"So you've told me what you've seen and done," Mackay said. "Now what have you guessed?"

Joseph took a deep breath, considered what he was about to say, and then figured the hell with it, he couldn't very likely get in any more trouble than hc was in already. "We've guessed that you, Colin Mackay, are the son of Sir Andrew

Mackay, who was going under the name of Kyle McAndrews. That was probably only one of hundreds, maybe even thousands of aliases that he used over the years, because those years were many. Your father, and the other men whose job it was to counter the influences of the thing they thought was the Antichrist, were probably alive back in the 1300s. And I suspect that you're no spring chicken, either. Did your father ever share with you his secret for longevity?''

Mackay's head inclined in the most subtle of nods.

"So how old are *you?*" Joseph asked. "Sixty? Seventy?"

"I've lived nearly a century," Mackay said softly, his eyes faraway, "since I drank . . ." He stopped abruptly, as though he'd said too much, and glared at Joseph. "Go on."

Joseph licked his lips and gestured around him. "This castle, if not this exact room, needless to say, is where the twelve Templars met every decade, for ceremonial or practical reasons, I'm not really sure, but meet they did. Until they all died. Then Colin Mackay took possession, with his merry band of Jacobites, and they set out upon the rather unlikely task of terrorizing England enough so that it would grant Scotland freedom, and blah blah blah for six pages of demands.''

"We're not Jacobites," said Mackay. "No kings, but the people."

"Yeah, whatever. Anyway, you made the mistake I did—you trusted Mulcifer, or, more to the point, you figured you could use him and then betray him, but it didn't turn out to be that easy, did it? Starting to get the feeling you're holding a tiger by the tail?"

"No." Colin Mackay shook his craggy head. "It's broken loose."

Joseph heard the sadness and the regret. "Jesus, what happened? What's he done? Something with the IRA men he busted out, wasn't it?"

Mackay told him then, and Joseph could scarcely believe it. He closed his eyes, but kept seeing pictures of the things Mackay had told him about, and opened them again.

"Haven't you lived long enough," he asked Mackay, "to know that killing people isn't the way to get your political party elected? Haven't you lived through the entire twentieth century, for Chrissake?" He waved a hand in frustration, and hung his head. "So what are you going to do about it?" he said softly. "You going to let him keep on with it?" He looked up at Mackay. "You know what he got from me, don't you?"

"No. What?"

"The location of the nerve gas the British government hid. You think he's going to just use that on military targets? If you do, I got a castle on some nice swampland I'd like to sell you."

"All right," Mackay said angrily, "I don't want any more civilian casualties—I never did in the first place. I don't give a good shite about the treasures of Britain. London could fall into a black hole so long as the people didn't go with it. But this ends now. We're not using any nerve gas, and none of my men are going to help that bastard get it."

"Are you so sure of that? In case you haven't noticed, Mulcifer *does* have a wee bit of influence over most of your crew." Joseph's mouth suddenly tasted sour. "And me, too, I'm afraid. In spades. He tells me what to do, and I do it. Doesn't matter whether I want to or not. There was no way I could keep from getting him the information he wanted. Any idea how he does that?"

"It's the blood," Mackay said. "Before he was captured, he bred with women—rape mostly, I believe. I cannot think he'd ever be capable of any tenderness. Over the centuries, his descendants have spread, marrying, carrying on the blood-line, until his progeny are numerous. But those in the high-lands kept to themselves, married among themselves, unlike the lowlanders. The bloodlines stayed pure. That is why the twelve were all highland men, their ancestry firmly estab-lished—so that there would be no trace of his blood in their veins, that he might have no influence over their minds or souls. The greater his influence, the greater the blood tie, although some people are far more suggestible than others.''

"Well, if that's the case," said Joseph, "I feel both highly suggestible and as though I come from an unbroken line from Mulcifer himself.''

"It's very possible, but according to . . .'' He hesitated, and then shrugged. "According to my father, there's no shame to be felt in succumbing to his commands. However, that didn't stop my father and the others from killing the thing's servants when they could. They may have been helpless, but still, they committed the crimes.''

"And if,'' Joseph said, "I had been ordered by . . . the thing to kill, I would have had no choice? Somehow I can't believe that.''

"Believe it.''

"Someone can't be driven by sheer mental suggestion to commit a crime they wouldn't commit themselves under certain circumstances.''

"He forced you to reveal the location of the gas, and you knew it was possible—*probable*—that he would use it, if he could get it, to kill people.''

"But that was something I might do anyway, just finding information in data banks. There's a difference between that and pulling a trigger or setting off a bomb.''

"You think so, do you, Stein? Well, I hope you're right. And I hope you never have to find out.''

"So do I. Don't let him get the gas, all right? He wouldn't be able to do it alone—he'd need your men.''

"He won't get the gas,'' Colin Mackay said. "Count on it.'' He climbed quickly up the ladder, and Joseph watched as he pulled it up after him. The trapdoor made a loud clunk as it was fitted back into place, and Joseph was alone again.

There might, he thought, be an ally in Mackay, in spite of his alignment with Mulcifer. Joseph knew his chances of leaving the castle alive were small, but if he could do something, anything, to keep Mulcifer from accomplishing more slaughter, he'd count his life well spent. His mind spun with various schemes that Mackay might use to control the creature once again, but at last he had to remind himself that he was not Mackay. He was an ineffectual agent in a dungeon made of stone, and unless he could somehow gain Mackay's ear and trust, he could do nothing.

Then he thought of what Mackay had said about the bloodline connecting him to Mulcifer, and grimaced at the irony of it. This whole thing had begun with the three of them theorizing about the Merovingian bloodline, that hoary conspiracy theory linking Jesus to some latter-day descendant through a supposed marriage to Mary Magdalene.

Now here was a bloodline rearing its ugly head again, but this time it was a bloodline linking Joseph to whatever devil went by the name of Mulcifer.

Chapter 34

*T*ony and Laika had dug in. There was little else to do. If Joseph had escaped from the prison, he would get in touch with them when he could. Tony had seen the van return to the castle, but there had been no sign of Joseph among the passengers. And then the shit had hit the fan.

The six terrorist acts struck them like a strong slap across the face, and the follow-up news made it clear that they were the results of the same Scottish nationalist group responsible for the escapes, the group that was very possibly located in Castle Dirk.

"Laika," Tony said, as they walked behind the cottage, trying to work off some of their excess energy, "we need to do something. If they've got the Prisoner in there, and if he's behind this, my God, we don't know what might happen next."

"What do we do, Tony?" she asked impatiently. "Go to the police? Tell Molly Fraser what we suspect? Get MI5 to send in a SWAT team? If our mystery man is in there, that'll do a shitload of good. You know what happened in Utah—he'll just turn them against each other, it'll be a slaughter, and he'll escape again."

"We can tell them about his . . . powers. Maybe they could find some other way—"

"They'd never believe us. You know damn well they wouldn't. Besides, we still don't have Joseph back, and I'm not going to take a chance on his getting killed in the crossfire if he's in there. Maybe we'll go in after him, you and I. But I don't think it's urgent, not yet."

"How can you say that, especially after what's happened in London?"

"It's especially *because* of that. Look, six terrorists were freed, and six terrorist strikes occurred. We've got every reason to think there's a connection between the two events, and if there is, then they've shot their wad for the time being. If we're wrong, if the castle crew *isn't* involved, then it doesn't matter at all."

"I just feel . . . I don't know, *responsible* for what happened. If we'd shared our suspicions—"

"Stop it," Laika said sharply. "The blood of all those people isn't on our hands. Maybe if we were dealing with anyone else, with someone *human*, it would be different, but this ex-prisoner of ours is beyond humanity. There's no way we can ever guess what we can expect from the sonofabitch, other than blood and more blood. But if it's going to be anything like the last time, he's going to have to set it up first. And before we see any signs of that, Joseph might get back."

As if on cue, they heard the sound of a car coming down the stone road to the cottage. Although it didn't sound like the Peugeot, it was unlikely that Joseph would have gotten the car back anyway. It was nearly dark, and just starting to rain again as they rounded the side of the cottage and saw the vehicle, a large sedan that might have been dark blue, but looked black in the dying light.

The front doors opened and two men got out. They were both wearing khaki-colored raincoats, belts cinched tight at the waist. Neckties knotted like clenched fists sat beneath their white dress collars. Laika didn't know who they worked for, but they looked like pros. Then the man on the passenger side opened the back door, and Richard Skye stepped out.

He gave the drizzling sky a disapproving glance and then offered Laika and Tony his usual unenthusiastic smile. There was not enough effort in it to label it insincere. "Agent Harris, Agent Luciano," he said, with a curt nod to each.

"Good evening, sir," Laika said, her heart racing as she wondered what the man was doing there. "Will you come inside?"

She turned and led the way, and the others followed. Tony came up next to her, looking mildly panicked, but she quickly shook her head, telling him not to say a word. This was hers to handle, whatever it might be.

Once inside, Skye introduced the two men as Agents Finch and Weyrman. Finch was slightly taller, and Weyrman's features were more regular, but other than that Laika didn't see any more difference between them than two dogs from the same litter.

Tony served them all coffee, and after they had discussed the weather and the landscape, Skye asked Finch and Weyrman if they would mind going out to the car while he discussed "some matters" with Agents Harris and Luciano. They took a cup of coffee each, and left with brief nods. Laika was sure they were packing under the raincoats, which they had not removed.

"Now," said Skye when they were alone, "you're undoubtedly wondering why I came all the way over here rather than using other methods of communication. It's simply because I've put two and two together and come up with four, or at least what *appears* to be four. It's not so much the so-called ghostly appearances in this area that have piqued my interest as it is these prison escapes I asked you to look into, with your very limited resources. I received this photograph from MI5 the other day, asking if my people could identify the gentleman."

He passed Laika a black-and-white laser-printed image of Joseph Stein. Laika could see that he was subtly twisting his features, doing his best to preserve his identity.

"Try as he might to make silly faces," Skye said, "I couldn't help but recognize Agent Stein. But no sooner had I received this photograph, to which, by the way, I made no reply, than the news came that this unknown prisoner had also miraculously escaped. Now, from every official report

I've seen, and from those we've intercepted, there is every reason to believe that these prisoners, including Agent Stein, actually passed through solid walls, along with their liberator, in order to escape.

"What's more, it's obvious that these terrorists were freed for the sole purpose of carrying out the six bombings that just took place. So, along with the odd method of escape that is most definitely deserving of direct investigation, I also find that one of my field agents may be somehow involved with the worst terrorist attack ever to strike one of our country's staunchest allies. So my first question, and my only question for now—what do you know of Agent Stein's whereabouts?"

"Nothing," Laika said. "We haven't heard a thing from him, but we're confident that he'll contact us as soon as the opportunity arises."

"If it does," Skye said. "At any rate, I trust that you now understand the reasons for my presence. Now. I've lodged Agents Finch and Weyrman in the town, but since there is an extra bedroom here, I shall be staying with you. It's been a very long day. I was among the many people at Langley who got no sleep last night, and I'd like to regain some alertness before we discuss these matters further."

At Skye's direction, Finch and Weyrman brought in a small suitcase, a laptop computer, and Skye's briefcase, then drove back toward Gairloch. Laika showed Skye the remaining room, and offered him the larger one that she was using, but he declined, saying the smaller room would be sufficient, since all he intended to do was sleep in it.

After getting Skye settled in, Laika rejoined Tony downstairs. She hesitated to say anything, not knowing how much Skye could overhear from upstairs, should he be listening. Tony had only one comment to make, and he did so just loud enough for Laika to hear:

"If Joseph knows what's good for him, he'll just stay wherever he is."

Chapter 35

Joseph had learned to sleep with the light on a long time before. The naked overhead bulb proved no impediment to his slumbers, but the light made him sleep just lightly enough to be awakened by the sound of the trapdoor opening twenty feet above.

He didn't move at first, wondering what it meant. Were they bringing him a meal? Or were they going to kill him? The possibility of both life and death were very real for a hostage held by terrorists, which was after all exactly what he was.

The ladder came down, and Mulcifer scuttled swiftly down it, turning and smiling at Joseph as his feet landed lightly on the stone floor. Joseph didn't know whether to feel relieved or frightened. "Pretty pedestrian entrance," he said. "So why didn't you vaporize yourself and drift through the trapdoor and down to me?"

"The law of conservation of energy rules us all, Joseph. I perform only when necessary. I've already impressed you enough, haven't I? Besides, there's something I need you to do for me."

"What? Walk into Parliament wearing dynamite sticks strapped to my ass?"

"News travels fast, I see." Mulcifer didn't lean against the wall, or make any move to relax. He simply stood there, arms at his side, as if it were the most comfortable position imag-

211

inable. The creature's lack of humanity, in this and so many other things, was disconcerting.

"No," Mulcifer went on, "I don't want you to do anything like that for me. Your goal is much closer to home. You see, Joseph, your mind is like an open book to me. When I care to turn the pages, I know pretty much what you know. I know what you and your two colleagues have learned about me, and I know that your connection to the CIA is among the greatest risks and dangers that I face. I know that you know my weakness, and there are few who do. Therefore, I've decided to eliminate you all."

It was the casualness with which he said it that chilled Joseph most, but he tried to disguise his fear. "That comes as no surprise. I never thought I'd get out of this castle alive. So are you going to do it, or have one of your flunkies do the deed?"

"One of my flunkies, I believe. And you're wrong—you *are* going to get out of here alive. Only you won't be alive for long." Mulcifer reached behind him and drew out a small automatic pistol. "It may not look like much," he said, "but it will get the job done. When you get back to your cottage, I want you to act perfectly natural, like the prodigal returned, glad to see them and be seen, and as soon as you have the opportunity, I want you to first kill Agent Luciano, and then Agent Harris. Then I want you to turn the gun on yourself.

"Shoot yourself in the abdomen first, six inches below the sternum. That should provide a nice, slow, bleeding wound that will eventually kill you. Keep the pistol in your hand, but shoot yourself in the head only if someone else comes in." He held out the pistol to Joseph. "That about covers it. It's got a full clip, so if you happen to miss your friends the first time, keep shooting."

Joseph reached out and took the pistol, but not for the purpose of assassinating his friends. He had no intention of doing anything that Mulcifer had just told him. Instead he jacked the slide, putting a round into the chamber, and turned the muzzle toward Mulcifer. The hammer was raised, the gun ready to fire. "Lead's your weakness," he said. "How about lead bullets?"

"They sting a bit. They're merely projectiles, though. You'd have to have a bullet that would expand to my size and wrap entirely around me for it to do any good. Besides, even if it could harm me, you won't be able to pull the trigger, because I don't want you to. I won't even use that usual villainous bravado and ask you to try. There's no point in wasting bullets. And this way you'll think it's your own choice not to fire. Then you can still maintain the illusion that once you get away from me, your own will can be strong enough to dismiss my order. But it won't be, despite your feelings to the contrary. Those are merely emotions. What I'm dealing with is science."

"You are so full of shit," Joseph said through clenched teeth.

"And you are so full of *me*," Mulcifer said. "But if it comforts you to think, 'Out of sight, out of mind,' go ahead. It doesn't matter what you think. All that matters is what I've put in there." He pointed to Joseph's head.

"Whatever you've put in," Joseph said, "it's not going to stay for long. You can't make me kill my friends. You can't make me kill myself. I have my own will. I'll fight you and I'll win." Then he paused for a moment, his mind whirling with thoughts and strategies. "That's why you're telling me all this, isn't it? Just to implant the idea, to make me think that it's inevitable, when it's nothing of the sort."

"No, I'm telling you because it doesn't matter at all what you think. Thinking has nothing to do with it. You are water. I am heat. With enough heat, water will boil. The water's wish *not* to boil doesn't enter into it. Water has no will. It responds when acted upon."

"You go to hell," Joseph said, his finger trembling on the trigger. But he knew that if he pulled it, nothing would happen.

"I'm tired of talk," Mulcifer said. "It's such a primitive, imperfect method of communication." He turned to the ladder and climbed up it quickly. Joseph watched him go, the gun still clenched in his fist. He waited to see if the ladder would be pulled up, but it was not. Then he lowered the gun and tried to think.

Despite what Mulcifer had said, Joseph knew that he was incapable of turning on Laika and Tony. They had become far more than colleagues. The experiences they had gone through and the secrets they had shared had bonded them together like family. Maybe it was a family that had its little spats and disagreements, but it was a family nonetheless. He would no sooner harm them than he would have killed his own mother or father.

He knew that Mulcifer had been responsible for turning other people against their friends, and even their loved ones. But Joseph refused to believe that the same could be done to him. He was not other people, he was Joseph Stein, and his will was his own. No shoddy hypnotist, even if he did have powers beyond Joseph's comprehension, was going to tell him to hurt his friends and get away with it.

No, Mulcifer wouldn't get away with it at all. Joseph would return to Laika and Tony, tell them everything that had happened, and then they would bring down the might of the whole goddamned British army on the bastard, maybe the whole might of NATO, for that matter. They'd drop so many shells on the castle that Mulcifer would be *covered* with lead, if that was the only way to take him down. "You want lead, I'll give you lead," Joseph whispered, and started to climb the ladder.

But he stopped just before he stuck his head through the trapdoor. What if the spooky bastard had been lying? What if it had all been a set-up just to get him killed, and Mackay's men were waiting above with drawn guns? Mulcifer liked his little games.

Hell, he thought, what if they were? Better to die clean trying to escape than stay down in that pit any longer. Besides, despite his paranoia, Joseph thought Mulcifer had been telling the truth, at least about what he wanted Joseph to do.

The arrogance of the creature was even greater than its powers, and this was one time that its hubris was going to prove stronger than its ability to deliver the goods.

Even though Joseph had expected to see Mulcifer at the top of the ladder, watching him beatifically, no one was there. His pistol at the ready, Joseph left the guardhouse and scuttled through the inner ward to the gatehouse. He didn't want to take the chance of being spotted from the castle, so instead of going through and up the drive to the road that would take him back to the cottage, he hugged the castle wall until he reached the steep stairway, and descended it carefully down to the stony beach.

The rain had stopped, and he started southward on the several-mile walk to the cottage. But he had gone only a hundred yards when he stopped and considered the possibilities.

Though he had no doubt of his ability to disobey Mulcifer when it came to harming his friends, he realized that he had had no doubt that he would be able to disobey him regarding accessing the information from the data banks. True, as he had told Mackay, there was a difference between hitting keys on a computer and pulling a trigger, but just the same, why take chances?

He looked down at the pistol in his hand, and then turned toward the Minch. He drew back his arm, intending to throw it far out into the water, but stopped just as his arm was about to snap forward. He suddenly felt as though the gun was a part of his body, and that to try and throw it away would be like trying to throw away his fingers—silly, absurd, unheard of.

He lowered his arm, the gun at his side again. He realized that he had not done what he had intended to do, and with that realization the fear returned. He tried now to simply drop the pistol, but the fingers of his right hand would not obey him. He snatched it with his left hand, as though he were in some horror movie in which the hand of a killer had replaced his own, and he must defeat its murderous purpose. But he could not drop it from either hand, and he fell on his knees on the rough pebbles, breathing hard.

At last he pushed himself upright, thinking that maybe his legs would obey him, that he could go away from the cottage, just keep walking in the other direction until someone found him or he fell from exhaustion. But he had moved only a few steps northward when he stopped, unable to go further. "Please," he whispered roughly, unsure of what or whom he was addressing. "Please . . ."

His feet would not take him where he wanted to go. He could not drop the gun, could not move away from his targets and his friends. But maybe . . . maybe there was one other thing he could do. As long as he didn't think about it.

Joseph jerked the pistol up, pushing the muzzle against his temple, and tried to pull the trigger.

He couldn't. His finger on the trigger was like stone, the trigger immovable, as if the entire pistol had been cast from iron. For a long time he stood there, the muzzle against his flesh, but no matter how much he wanted to, no matter how often and how insistently he told himself that this was now the only way, he could not move the trigger.

Finally he dropped his arm, fell to his knees, and rolled over on his side, weeping until it seemed that all the moisture in his body had turned to tears. At last, there on the cold, wet pebbles, he closed his tear-filled eyes, and his anguish and sorrow and loss over what he must do exhausted him, and drove him into the dark pit of a restless sleep.

His fingers holding the gun did not relax. They remained clenched around the deadly metal all the time he slept, through what was left of the night, and into the gray light of the next day.

Chapter 36

After he spoke to Joseph Stein, and gave him his command, Mulcifer thought no more about him. That Stein would do as he had been told, Mulcifer had no doubt. Now it was time for something else.

It was shortly after midnight, and Mulcifer first went to Colin Mackay's room and pounded on the door. "I want everyone in the great hall," he told Mackay when he opened his door. "As soon as possible." Then he turned from Mackay and continued down the hallway, pounding on doors and telling the men to come to the great hall for a meeting, and to bring their weapons.

In less than five minutes they were assembled, all fifteen men, including Mackay. "Most of us, two van loads, are going on a little midnight journey, about fifty miles northeast of here. We'll be taking two vans, and if we leave within the hour, I expect we'll get there around three in the morning."

"And do you mind very much," Mackay asked, "if we might inquire where we're going and what you expect us to do?" His voice was dripping with sarcasm, as though he had no intention of allowing his men to participate in whatever it was Mulcifer was plotting.

"Oh, you won't be going, Colin," Mulcifer said. "No, I'm afraid you're going to just have to stay here, guarded by some of your merry men. I figure you won't mind, as we're going to get several canisters of nerve gas, and I know you disapprove of its use."

"Nerve gas . . ." Mackay said. "The hell you are. I said before that we're not using any of that shite."

"And I say we are. Now . . ." He turned to the men. "I'll want you, you, you, you . . ." He pointed to them one by one, including Rob and Angus in the draw, until he had assigned all but three men to the vans. "James," he said, "I believe you and Peter and John will remain here. I want you to guard Colin here."

"I've had enough of this," said Mackay. "All of you, back to your rooms. You're to take no more orders from him."

"Excuse me, Colin, but they have no choice in the matter. Oh, a few of them might, but if they disobey, I'll simply have their comrades in arms shoot them. And that's not much of a choice at all, is it?"

"Rob," Mackay said, turning to his friend, "put that gun away and go back to your room."

Rob closed his eyes, as if willing his body to do what Mackay had said, but Mulcifer knew he couldn't. "I'm sorry, Colin," Rob said, opening his eyes and looking at his friend with pain on his face, a pain that Mulcifer drank in like a gardener delighting in the scent of hyacinth. "I don't think I can do that. I want to, but I just can't."

"That's a good boy. Now—you lot—I want you to keep an eye on Colin here all the time we're gone. Don't let him out of your sight."

"You filth," said Mackay. "Why don't you just drop me into the dungeon with Stein?"

"Because Stein is no longer there, for one thing."

"*What?*"

"That's right—free as a bird. Free to go back and dispatch his two colleagues and then blow a hole in his own belly. Sorry I have to miss it, but duty calls, as it does for all of us. Let's be off. The weapons shouldn't be necessary, but we'll bring them along in case we run into the authorities. What we *will* need, however, is a decent flashlight for each man, extra batteries, shovels, crowbars, and some explosives.

"Yes. We will definitely need explosives . . ."

*   *   *

Angus drove the first van, the Prisoner seated next to him. Rob drove the second. Each van carried five men, and there was plenty of storage room for whatever it was they were getting. They had taken the vans down into the cellars on the big elevator, and then driven them onto the beach through the hidden exit that had been built centuries before to escape from the castle on horseback, then gone north on the beach to an access road.

From there they had driven off the peninsula, then north to Gruinard Bay and east down the southern shore of Little Loch Broom, south through the Dundonnell Forest, and north again toward Ullapool when they reached the River Broom. The crow seldom flew straight in the highlands.

From there they went northeast past the Cromalt Hills, then southeast on a one-lane road. It bore no other traffic at that time of the morning, so the passing places remained unused. Near Rosehall they turned north again, on a vile little road that Mulcifer promised was the end of their journey.

Just past a sad pile that Mulcifer said was Glencassley Castle, they saw a sign that read, ''GOVERNMENT BIRD SANCTUARY—GATE 1 KM.'' Mulcifer ordered Angus to pull off the road, and guided him over a slight rise that would hide the vans from the sight of anyone who might be driving past, though that possibility seemed about as likely to Angus as pissing beer.

But as Angus got out of the car, he saw that there might be more to their location than simple concealment. Less than thirty yards away, hardly visible in the cloudy night, was a mound of earth barely four feet high. It didn't appear to be a natural formation, and Angus had seen enough of them to know that it was a barrow, a burial place that had been dug before Scotland had its own history.

It was one of those ancient places in whose presence Angus always felt a trifle uncomfortable. When he thought about how old these things were, how they'd been built before Christ had walked the earth by men who'd left hardly any other record of their passing, it made him shiver. The stone circles were bad enough, but barrows were graves in which the dead had been placed, and in which their dust still lay.

And those dead had been of a race, ancestors of his own, that was rich in magic and wizardry. Who was to say that those barrows weren't still guarded by the spirits the old Celts had placed there for that purpose? And who was to say that a worker of magic, like this goddamned Mulcifer surely was, couldn't accidentally or purposely bring those old bastards back to life, if they weren't already?

The men fell in behind Mulcifer, who was facing the barrow. Angus couldn't see his expression, but guessed that he was smiling. The prick was always smiling, as if he had the most precious little secret but wasn't going to share it with *you*. Angus thought he acted like a ponce, but that he did it just to piss people off.

"There, gentlemen, is our entryway," he said.

Rob walked up and stood next to him. "You're not saying the canisters are buried in that barrow and left unguarded, are you?"

"No, I merely said it is the *entryway*. Now, let's start digging."

Mulcifer walked to the mound, and Angus followed with a shovel. Maybe he'd be haunted for disturbing the dead, but he had to have something to do to get his mind off their sacrilege. He and the others dug where Mulcifer directed, and at first he began to think that the barrow wasn't hollow, but was composed only of earth that they piled carefully for later replacement. At last, however, the shovels hit stone, and they scraped the dirt away from what appeared to be a stone vault over which the earth had been thrown.

The ancient stones yielded easily enough to their crowbars, and the smell that burst from the sealed-up tomb was not that of recent death. Nothing organic had tenanted that chamber for many centuries. It was an odor of something older. Angus couldn't remember ever having smelled its like before. It was, he thought, the stink of primal secrets.

Soon the entrance was large enough to step through, and Mulcifer entered first, beckoning the men in after him. Angus went in right after Rob. Only five of them fit within the chamber, whose floor was level with the ground. But in the center of that earthen floor was a flat sheet of dull black metal, three feet wide and four long, scarcely a half inch thick. At each of its four corners were heavy stones that nearly came up to Angus's waist.

"Roll them off," Mulcifer ordered, and they did so, although it took four of them, panting and groaning, to roll or slide each of the boulders aside. "Now lift it up," said Mulcifer, "and lean it against the wall."

Angus felt hesitant, as though if he did, something that didn't like its secrets revealed would rise up out of the earth and devour them all. But his feeling gave him no pause, and he joined the others in moving the metal sheet, so heavy that he suspected it was lead, and propping it against the stone wall.

A chill wind blew up through the hole, smelling only of damp stone. They all shone their lights down into the opening at once, and saw a flight of steps leading into the earth. "Follow me, all of you," Mulcifer said, loudly enough so that the men still standing outside heard him as well. Then he walked down the stairs.

Rob followed, then Angus. Angus didn't want to go, didn't want anything at all to do with this Mulcifer, who blew up children and took them to places that surely no one had seen for hundreds of years. But he had no choice. A hundred times before, he had wanted to take out his pistol and just fire point-blank into the shite's grinning face, but he had never been able. Maybe if he worked hard at it, he could put a bullet in the back of the bastard's head.

Angus had heard the prisoners he'd freed babbling that they'd seen Mulcifer taking bullets like bug bites, and some swore they'd done the same thing when they were with him. But that didn't necessarily mean that those prisoners couldn't have died later. Hell, they blew up easily enough, didn't they?

So maybe Mulcifer the Mighty wasn't like Superman all the time, either. Maybe Angus could catch him with his trousers down just long enough to finish him off.

It was a thought that made him a little happy anyway, as the stairway ended and they passed into a low-ceilinged tunnel that led downward at a gentle angle. It seemed hewn out of the rock itself. At no point was the tunnel wider than four feet, or higher than six, so the taller men, Angus among them, had always to move at a slight crouch.

Every hundred yards or so they came across other tunnels branching off into the darkness. Before they reached these junctures, Mulcifer's pace slowed, and he approached them cautiously. It made Angus curious. He had never seen Mulcifer cautious before.

As they moved downward, Angus began to wonder what had made these tunnels. At first he suspected underground streams, but then he realized that water would have smoothed the walls, and these walls were rough, top, bottom, and sides. At one of the cross tunnels, when they slowed, he ran his fingers over the walls, examining them more closely. He saw hundreds of small jagged marks in the stone.

Nothing natural that he knew of could have created the marks. They looked more like chip marks, and a sudden shock went through him at the possibility that these tunnels had been carved by hand out of the solid rock.

What was even more disturbing was the fact that all of the marks seemed to have been made from the descending side of the tunnel, as though the excavators had been working their way *up* from below. That thought made Mulcifer's caution all the more understandable.

Chapter 37

If Angus was any judge, they walked on through those claustrophobic passages for miles. There was no sound except for the scuffling of their shoes on the rock and their labored breathing. Angus's back and neck were getting sore from his constant slouching posture the low ceiling made necessary.

At last Mulcifer stopped at a T-crossing. Angus, just behind him with Rob, could see that to the right the tunnel went steeply downward. They might have been able to walk down, but odds were they would have slid on their arses all the way to wherever it ended up. To the left, only a few feet away, was a cul-de-sac.

"End of the line," Mulcifer said. He pointed to the stone wall of the cul-de-sac. "We'll blow through that. It's only a few inches thick, so plant your charges accordingly."

"Now, wait a minute," Rob said. "You want us to set off charges down here? Christ, man, the whole place could collapse on us!"

"It won't. These walls are very strong. They've been down here . . . well, a long time. Just set the charges straight so it will kick the stone backward, down that shaft, or forward, into what's on the other side. The men can retreat back down the way we came when the blast goes off."

Angus and Rob did as they were told. Rob was good with explosives, and used a stone hammer to chip out small cavities in which to insert the C-4. After he had set three charges in a triangulation pattern and attached electronic fuses, he nodded to Mulcifer, and the three of them joined the other men who had already gone fifty yards back up the passage and around another corner. As Angus ran past the tunnel that went sharply downward, he thought he heard something, like a quick patter of claws on rock. He didn't stop to investigate.

Once they reached safety, Rob pressed the electronic trigger, and the shock of the concussion down the tunnel pushed against them like a quick, strong wind. Even though Angus had placed his hands over his ears, the sound was deafening, and his ears rang with it for a long time after.

The dust took several minutes to settle, and when they went back down the tunnel to the cul-de-sac, Angus saw that much of the stone that had been blown away had indeed rolled down into the steep declivity from which he had heard that odd sound. The cul-de-sac itself had been blown away, and a gaping hole six feet in diameter opened into darkness.

Mulcifer walked up to it fearlessly and stepped through. Rob and Angus shone their lights inside, and saw Mulcifer walking over a pile of rubble down into a cave fifty feet across and another forty feet deep. Its ceiling was fifty feet high. At the far end, where the ceiling sloped downward, was a huge pile of rubble that it would have taken several trucks to haul away.

But what drew Angus's attention most were the metal canisters on one side of the cave. There appeared to be a hundred or more, and they were stacked in four long rows on wide metal racks. Their light green color was not due to corrosion, for the metal still sparkled, and the only dust on them was what had settled from the explosion only minutes before.

Mulcifer continued to beckon the men to come closer and make room for those still in the tunnel. "Come in, come in, gentlemen. Nothing to bite you here. And I don't think we need to be concerned about being disturbed by the authorities. There are the canisters I require. They weigh one hundred pounds each. I really don't want to overburden any of you, particularly on such an arduous journey, so I suggest that two men carry one canister. That will allow us to remove five of them, which should certainly be sufficient for my purposes. Shall we?''

They paired off, Mulcifer and Rob taking the first canister and leaving through the opening. Angus and another man were next. Angus positioned the top of the six-foot-long canister under his left arm and followed Mulcifer and Rob, his partner behind him. Soon they were all winding their way up the gentle incline of the tunnel again.

So this was the gas, Angus thought, the shite that Colin hadn't ever wanted to use. And here he was, disobeying his leader, not his clan chief, perhaps, but someone far more important to him. He felt like Benedict Arnold, another Judas for England. They had lost their purpose now, maybe their entire goal, and it was all the fault of this preening, poncy bastard who called himself Mulcifer, like he was some actual demon from the bowels of hell.

Well, he wasn't a demon, whatever he was. He was alive, and anything that lived could be killed, if only someone had the will to do it.

Maybe now was the time. Mulcifer seemed to be straining a wee bit under his load. It could be that he was concentrating so much on the physical that his guard was down. It would be so easy just to take out his gun and shoot the prick. He could at least try it.

With his free right arm he reached into his jacket where his pistol nestled in its shoulder holster. It was one sweet gun, a Glock 21, capable of spitting out ten .45 slugs as fast as he could pull the trigger, which was pretty damned fast. He tentatively wrapped his fingers around the butt and was surprised to find that he could do it, especially with the thought so strong in his mind of killing Mulcifer. Now, if he could only take it out . . .

He gave it a sharp tug, and it left the holster and rested in his hand, the metal warming to his touch. Then he brought it out and held it in front of him, against his chest. He'd have to be careful to avoid hitting Rob, but if Angus moved slightly to the side, he thought he could shoot past his friend easily enough.

Angus had no doubt that he could do it now. The bastard's guard was down, he was sure of it. He *could* pull the trigger, and he *would*. He raised the gun, gritted his teeth, put pressure on the trigger . . .

And the gun fired, slamming a slug into the back of Mulcifer's head, pushing him forward so that he dropped the canister with a ringing clatter. Rob dropped to the ground, and Angus kept firing, the bullets hitting Mulcifer in the neck, the head, the back, pushing him forward like a puppet, the bullets holding him up like strings as screams burst from him with each shot.

Then the magazine was empty, and Mulcifer, with one final agonized wail, fell straight down onto his face, and Angus heard his skull crack against the stone floor. Mulcifer's fingers and feet twitched spastically, then stiffened, and he was still.

"I'll be damned," Angus whispered in the sudden stillness, slowly lowering his end of the canister to the ground. Not one of the men had drawn his own gun to defend Mulcifer, and now they just stood there, all holding their canisters except for Rob. He still lay where he had dropped, but he was looking from Mulcifer's riddled body to Angus's emptied pistol and back again, hope slowly growing on his face.

"I'll be *god*damned," Angus said, a smile starting to crease his broad face as he walked slowly toward the creature lying on the stone floor of the tunnel. He stood above him, looking down at the back of his ruined head, the white shirt shredded by bullets. Then he crouched down next to him. "You go to hell, you bastard," he said softly.

Mulcifer turned over and smiled. "You first, you chubby Scottish bitch."

Angus felt bathed in ice. For a moment he could not move. Then he scuttled away from Mulcifer until he came up against the stone wall, still holding his doubly useless pistol in his hand. Mulcifer was getting to his feet now, and the damage that the bullets had done to his head and body seemed to be healing as Angus watched, the flesh knitting itself back together again seamlessly. Although the shirt remained torn, the blood that had stained it was vanishing, fading from crimson to pink to peach to the transparency of water.

"What did you think, Angus?" asked Mulcifer clearly and flawlessly from a throat that the bullets had torn apart. "That you could kill me? That somehow your bullets could succeed where all others had failed? That you were Wallace or the Bruce or some other dead Scottish hero whose magic could slay the evil prince? And did you think that I would not be aware of your feelings, your hatred? I knew what you intended, you fat fool—I *allowed* you to draw that gun, to shoot me down. Because I wanted them all to see that doing so causes me no harm, no, not even discomfort. And one thing more—I want them to see what happens to those who disobey."

"You ..." Angus felt his words choke in his throat, but he would not let this vile thing know how afraid he was of it. He pushed the words out, broad and burred and Scottish. "You go and *fook* yoursel'."

"The word," said Mulcifer dryly, "is 'fuck,' and it's one that gentlemen shouldn't use. Therefore, you die no gentleman's death, you shortbread-sucking, *haggis*-gobbling, *kilt*-wearing, jock scotty *McAsshole!*"

Mulcifer's words had increased in volume and intensity, but now he dropped the volume again. "No offense intended, of course. Just as I'm sure you didn't intend to offend me with your little fusillade of lead. Everyone, turn your lights directly on our friend Angus here."

The flashlights that had not already illuminated Angus now shone on him, making it hard to see. "Now, Angus, let's see how those fine Scottish teeth can gnaw through fine Scottish flesh. I want you to chew through the veins in your wrist, Angus. Just ignore the pain and gnaw right through until the blood starts spurting."

Angus looked down at his right hand, still holding the pistol. He didn't think about what he was going to do, not about the horror of it, or the agony it would cause him, or the death that would follow from the loss of blood. He didn't wonder about how he had come to be doing such a thing. He simply did what he was told. He felt no anger, no terror, no desire to strike back at the man who had directed him to oblivion. He simply chewed.

Chapter 38

*T*he ones who felt all the emotions that Angus could not were the men watching him. Rob could only stand there as his friend scraped at the skin over his own wrist, piercing it with his teeth, and then tearing away small bits. The bleeding started quickly, and by the time Angus reached the artery, his face was already smeared red. The pulsing blood struck Angus in the eyes, but he merely closed them and continued to worry at his arm like a dog ripping meat off a soup bone.

After a few more minutes, he toppled over onto his side, but continued to chew weakly until his only motion was the blood that continued to run from the gaping wound in his wrist. His eyes glazed over, and Rob knew he was dead.

"All right," said Mulcifer. "Let's be on our way. We'll leave Angus here." He knelt and picked up the canister he and Rob had been carrying and slipped it under one arm as easily as if it had been inflatable. Then he nodded to Rob to pick up the front end of Angus's canister, turned, and walked leisurely down the tunnel, his head slightly bent.

Rob and the others followed. He could not remember ever feeling so much hatred, and knowing that hatred was what he must *not* feel. If the thing felt it, he might do the same to Rob as he had done to big Angus, and then Rob would never know the joy of avenging his friend, who would have fought a bear with a fork for the fun of it.

So Rob tried to think of other things, of heather and mountains and glens and the beauty through which they had come and through which they would return in daylight with their terrible burden. He hoped that the horror walking ahead of him could not see what was not consciously thought, and then, acknowledging his own dreams of revenge, tried to bury them deep under images of white clouds and blue skies.

When they arrived back at the barrow, early morning light was glowing through the opening they had dug. At Mulcifer's orders, they covered over the hole in the floor with the heavy metal sheet again and shoved the four boulders onto each corner. Then they replaced the stones and the dirt, finally putting the turf back over the bare earth so that unless one looked carefully, the barrow appeared undisturbed.

When they finished, Mulcifer had them load four of the five canisters into the rear of the first van, and the fifth canister into the other. Then he went up to Brian and Henry Baird, two brothers in their twenties who had been among the most militant of Colin's small cadre, and drew them aside, out of hearing of the rest of the men.

He talked to them for ten minutes, and they showed no response other than to nod when he was finished. The Baird brothers got into the second van, and Mulcifer told the other men to get into the first. "It may be cozy, but we're all brothers in the cause of Scottish freedom, now, aren't we?"

Rob drove next to Mulcifer, and the other men arranged themselves three in the backseat and two sitting on the floor in the rear, amid the canisters. The two vans pulled out onto the A837, but when Rob turned west to head back to Castle Dirk, the van behind went east. "Where are the Bairds off to, then?" Rob asked.

Mulcifer shook his head. "Don't worry about them. Just concentrate on the road. You wouldn't want to have an accident with what we're carrying, would you?"

Rob didn't answer. He didn't have to. This monster next to him knew exactly what he was thinking. So Rob watched the road and admired the scenery. The day was bright and fair. The rain clouds had scudded away, leaving a blue sky with wisps of cirrus high above.

God, his was a bonnie land, and he loved it more than life. But he found himself wishing that they had all loved good sense more. They'd shaken hands with the deil all right, but the deil hadn't let go.

Chapter 39

Although he was sheltered from its rays by the cliff, the sun on the water woke Joseph Stein. When he opened his eyes there was a sparkling like thousands of diamonds, and he pressed them closed again, then opened them more slowly. He knew that he had something to do, but couldn't recall what it was.

Not until he sat up did he realize that he held a pistol in his hand. He looked at it for a moment, and then he remembered what he was supposed to do.

He got to his feet and took a deep breath. It was going to be a beautiful day. He looked at the dancing light on the water for another minute, then turned and walked south on the beach, toward the cottage where Laika and Tony waited.

Others waited there too. Richard Skye waited for the woman to leave so that they could all stop lying and he could get to the root of these phenomena and find the one that he had been looking for, the one with all the powers, the one whose might Mr. Stanley wanted to harvest.

Through his ties to MI5, Molly Fraser's name was known to Skye, so there had been no subterfuge in that regard. In fact, some of Skye's agents had worked with her back in the eighties, so he was familiar with her career and skills. She had dropped by this morning with a bagful of scones, just as Skye had been coming down the stairs. It had been an awkward moment for everyone, and Skye had been piqued when he'd learned Fraser's identity, and that she knew his agents' covers and mission.

But they had explained to him how Fraser had seen Stein, with whom she had worked in the past, and drawn the logical conclusions. At least Fraser, who was now a police inspector, had not informed MI5 of his team's true identities, or at least so she claimed. Agents were in the business of lying, and Skye trusted the woman no farther than he could have thrown her.

So they sat and ate scones and drank tea and coffee and prevaricated. The last thing Skye wanted Fraser to learn was anything about the mysterious prisoner. He didn't even want his operatives to know about him, though he strongly suspected that they had already learned, if not actually crossed his path.

The official story from Skye's side was that his three agents were simply here to try and debunk any purported phenomena before the British and American press had a field day with it. Fraser's story was nearly identical, with the proviso that the MI5's presence was due to a scientific interest in the occurrences, and the possibility of discovering new technologies.

It was all bullshit and Skye knew it. From the cynical look on Fraser's face, he was certain that she knew it as well, but wondered in frustration how *much* she knew.

Fraser was telling them MI5's official story about the terrorist attacks on London, the same data that Skye had received just before he'd left Langley, when they heard someone rattling the knob of the back door. Agent Luciano made a quick movement behind his back, came out with a pistol, and walked swiftly into the kitchen. His quickness made Skye feel secure and protected. Luciano was the right man to have in the event of danger.

Agent Harris's hand also held a gun, and she too walked to the kitchen door. "Visitors come in the front," she said, as if to explain the firepower, and Skye nodded approvingly, but still looked around to decide what piece of furniture to get behind should shooting start.

But instead of gunfire, he heard a burst of laughter from Luciano, and the sound of the door opening, and Luciano and Harris babbling happily. Skye and Fraser walked to the kitchen door and saw the two agents patting an extremely disheveled Joseph Stein on the back and shoulders. Stein's stubbled face was smiling gently, and he looked slightly embarrassed as they walked him into the living room.

What should I say? Or should I kill them right away? Now? When they're so happy to see me back, safe and sound? There, Tony put his gun away, tucked down behind his back, right where I have mine. He's quicker than me, but he won't be expecting me to . . . oh Christ, I can't do it, I won't do it.

Skye. There's Skye, and Molly, too. They have to die, too, then. Oh Molly, oh God, Molly. All right, Tony first, then Laika, they're the ones with guns. Then Molly and Skye. Skye never carries. Then myself. All right, but when, when? Now?

". . . They have you? *Was* that you?" Joseph tried to turn his attention to Laika's words. She was easing him down into a chair. "How did you escape?" she asked, as she joined Tony on the sofa only a few feet away.

"Yes, Agent Stein," Skye was saying. "How *did* you escape?"

"I . . ." He knew that he could say nothing about Mulcifer. They couldn't know that he knew him, *more* than knew him, that he was Mulcifer's red right hand. "Yes, the police captured me during the jailbreak, but they let me go."

"Let you *go*?" Laika asked. "But . . . why?"

Because I have to kill you. Because walls can't keep out the one that wants you dead, and neither can my will. I have no will. He was right, he was right. Will doesn't enter into it. He is fire, I am water. I have no choice but to boil.

No! No! I do *have a choice! I don't have to do this, I* don't!

And then the gun was in his hand, and he was pointing it at Tony, and Laika was saying something, saying no, no, fight it, Joseph, you can fight this. We're your friends. Put it down. Just put it down. Don't listen. *Fight* it.

But he could hardly hear her, and he knew that it didn't matter what she said. He couldn't fight. He could only obey.

Fight it, Joseph. Joseph, fight him. *You can. You can. He can't make you do this. Fight him. Give me the gun. Just give it to me, put it in my hand, and you've beaten him, you've won. You can win, Joseph, you can beat him.*

And now she was standing up, coming slowly toward him, and he was trying to keep the gun on Tony, because he was the one he had to shoot first, but Laika was coming toward him.

Maybe she's right, I can fight him, I can win. The fire won't make me boil, no, the water won't boil, not this time, not ever. I can fight him, I can win, I can—

Tony thought Laika was going to do it, but then the pistol went off, and Tony saw the blood blossom on Laika's chest as she fell back, her eyes wide in shock and pain. Then Joseph pointed the gun at him.

Tony threw himself off the couch, yanking out his pistol as he fell, hearing the second gunshot, feeling the bullet graze his shoulder, and then his gun was up and he was firing at Joseph, once, twice, three times, until finally Joseph stopped firing, and the gun dropped from his hand and he slowly fell, his face gone suddenly gray, bloody froth at his lips, landing heavily next to Laika.

Chapter 40

Molly Fraser dropped to the floor, ripping open Laika's blouse to inspect the wound. Tony saw how bad it was before Molly started to put pressure on it. The bullet had caught her on the left side of the chest, piercing the lung and possibly nicking the heart as well. Laika was breathing lightly and shallowly, and Tony could see blood on her lips, too. Dear Christ, he couldn't lose them both.

Joseph was lying on his side, his eyes wide. His breathing was worse than Laika's. Tony knew he would be dead in minutes. Joseph's lips were moving, as if he were trying to say something. Tony lay down next to him until their faces were only inches apart. "What?" he asked urgently. "What, Joseph?"

The words came out like air from a slowly leaking tire. "Save . . . her. Get . . ."

Tony couldn't understand the next word. Hell, he didn't understand any of it. How could he save Laika? In another few minutes she'd be dead from internal bleeding, and so would Joseph. "Get *what?*" he asked.

"Get . . ." Joseph closed his eyes, and Tony thought he was gone, but he was only trying to fight for the word, which came out weakly, but clear. "*Grail* . . . "

Tony didn't know if it was possible, but he knew that nothing else was going to help Laika live. Without a word to the others, he ran up the stairs into Joseph's room and hauled the suitcase from the closet.

There, wrapped in sheets, was the ornate box that they had taken from the spartan room of Sir Andrew Mackay, the last of the Templars, after they had killed him in a shootout. Tony opened it, took out the simple wooden cup inside, and ran down the stairs. It was a wild chance, but it was the only chance.

"What's going on here?" Skye had regained his composure enough to take command, but Tony ignored him. He went into the kitchen, ran water from the tap into the cup, and went back to where Laika lay.

"Hold her shoulders up," Tony said to Molly. "She's gotta drink this."

"A wee bit late for that," Molly said, her eyes on Joseph.

"Just *do it!*" Tony barked, and Molly got her hands under Laika's shoulders and raised her slightly from the floor. Tony held the cup to her lips and tipped it so that the water ran into her mouth. Most of it dribbled down over her chin, but some passed her lips, and she choked for a moment. Then Tony saw her throat working and knew she had swallowed some.

Then he sat back, exhausted spiritually and physically, the half-full cup in his hands. He didn't expect anything to happen. Joseph's mention of the grail was a dying man's delusion, a man so crazy that he'd tried to kill his friends.

Suddenly, Laika's shallow breathing stopped, and there came one long, deep breath, and Tony knew that this was the last, the final escape of air from her dead throat. But then there came another, and another, and he was shocked to see that the wound in her chest was changing, becoming smaller, glistening less with blood.

As he and Molly and Skye watched, the wound healed itself in less than a minute. Only the blood that had been originally shed remained. Laika blinked, propped herself on one elbow, and looked at Tony, then at the cup he was holding, and then at Joseph. She tried to talk, spat out the residue of the blood, and then cleared her throat. "Give it to him," she said, and her voice seemed faraway. "Give him the cup, Tony."

He knew what she meant. Whatever had shot her and tried to kill him, it was not Joseph. But it was Joseph who had told him to get the grail.

"Wait just a minute," Skye said. "Stein just tried to *kill* us."

"That wasn't Joseph Stein," Laika said.

"Who was it, then?" Skye asked, getting between Joseph and Tony.

"It was the man you've been looking for, Mr. Skye," Laika said. "Now, get out of the way. We have to save our friend."

Tony stood up with the cup and gave Skye a look that made the man shuffle aside instantly. Then he crouched next to Joseph and raised his head. God, he hoped it wasn't too late. Joseph's eyes were dull. The blood was running from two of the three wounds, and blood trails snaked from his mouth down over his chin. His jaw was slack.

Tony poured the water into Joseph's mouth, but it simply lay inside like rainwater in a hollow stump. He pinched Joseph's nose shut, pressed his own mouth over Joseph's, and blew, once, twice, three times.

The fourth time, something lurched inside Joseph. The gag reflex at least had come back to life. Tony immediately pressed his mouth on Joseph's again, and blew hard and long, forcing the water down Joseph's throat. At last he heard a slight rattle, and saw the throat muscles twitch.

Then he pushed Joseph upright so the water would run down his esophagus, if the muscles were no longer capable of drawing it down. At least it had not run back out his mouth. "Come on, Joseph," he whispered harshly, using his sleeve to wipe Joseph's blood from his mouth. "Don't you die on me. You smartass sonofabitch, don't you die . . ." He held the cup out to Laika. "Get some more water—I don't know if I got enough down him."

She went into the kitchen, and Tony heard the tap running. "Come on, Joseph . . . *please* . . ."

"What's going on here?" Molly Fraser asked. "I don't understand any of this . . . why did Joseph try to kill us? How did . . ." She gestured feebly to the kitchen, through whose door Laika now returned. ". . . She become . . . *healed* like that?"

"Joseph didn't try to kill us," Laika said. "It was someone inside Joseph. But it was *Joseph* we had to shoot."

Tony had just begun to dribble more water into Joseph's mouth, when Joseph took in a quick, harsh breath. The air stayed in his lungs for what seemed an eternity, then rushed out again with a force that startled them all. Again he gasped in a ragged breath, held it as though his body was being restored by it, and expelled it.

Then his breaths began to come more easily, though the exhalations seemed almost like shudders. Though they had not pulled away Joseph's torn shirt, Tony could see that no new blood was being added to that which already soaked the cloth. The bleeding had stopped.

"That's it," Tony said, "just keep breathing, just keep it up . . ." He unbuttoned Joseph's shirt and saw that although his chest hair was matted with blood, the bullet wounds were not visible. It was as though they never had been.

In another minute, Joseph was breathing normally, and he looked at Tony and Laika and Molly and Skye, his face filled with agony. "He had me," he said, with the same faraway quality that had cloaked Laika's voice at first. "I couldn't fight. I tried, oh God, please believe me, I did try, but I couldn't . . . it wasn't any use. He *had* me . . ."

Then he looked at the cup Tony was still holding, and a rocky smile came over his blood-caked mouth. "You did it," he said. "Thank God. I found out . . . from Mackay . . . that it was what kept them from growing old. When I was . . . lying there, I remembered the legends, how it could restore the dying to life. I hoped you'd give it to her, but I never thought you'd give it to me. I thought you'd believe I turned.''

Laika knelt next to him and put a hand on his shoulder. "We know you," she said. It was all she needed to say.

Joseph reached out for the cup, and Tony handed it to him. He looked at it carefully, studied the water in it, then poured it out into one of the few still unbroken teacups on the coffee table. Then he ran his hand over the inside. "I didn't notice before," he said, "but it's textured. Like there's a coat of varnish, or whatever they used back then, over something textured that's lining the cup. Like . . . like cloth." He poured the water from the teacup back into the wooden cup, then looked up at Molly, "The same kind of cloth that was in the casket? The same kind as the Fairy Flag?"

Tony held up a hand to quiet Joseph, even though he knew it was like trying to get a genie back in the bottle, or the prisoner back into a lead-lined cell. "It doesn't matter," said Laika, as if reading his thoughts. Then she looked at Molly and Skye. "You've both seen so much now that you'll have to know the truth." She touched her chest, drawing her blouse back together. "I can't bullshit my way out of all this."

Chapter *41*

*B*ut maybe she could bullshit her way out of *some* of it, Laika thought. There was no point in telling Skye everything, although he had to know about the Prisoner now. "We've been getting hints of something since our earliest assignments together," she said. "Nothing definite enough to report—just things that we've stored in the backs of our heads."

Then she told Skye about the indications that a powerful prisoner had been held for a long time under deep security, and of their suspicions that he might have been freed and was working with the owner of Castle Dirk, Colin Mackay. Then she looked at Joseph to fill in the rest. She was anxious to hear what had happened to him, and she knew that they were now stuck with Skye, for better or worse.

"This prisoner," Joseph said, "is at the castle. That's Castle Dirk," he added for Skye's benefit. "We've been investigating it on the possibility that the recent manifestations might be coming from there. Colin Mackay is the owner, the son of a Sir Andrew Mackay. We were able to search the castle before Colin Mackay took possession, and what we found in the cellars indicates a connection to the Knights Templar. That's where we found the cup as well."

Laika was glad to hear Joseph's spin. If Skye knew they had found the cup back in New York, he'd know they were withholding more than just suspicions from him.

"Our research into the family and the castle," Joseph went

on, "indicates that both Mackays are incredibly long-lived. The cup's the reason, whether it's the Holy Grail or just because it's treated with some radioactive substance with . . ." He looked at Laika, then down at his own torn shirt. ". . . I hate to say it, but *miraculous* curative powers. And a greatly increased life span."

Skye stood up and walked to the cup, which he picked up and examined. Then he smiled and drank from it, emptying it entirely. "I've learned never to look a gift horse in the mouth. If it's true, wonderful. If not, well, it's only water." He looked at Molly and Tony. "May I offer you a drink?"

Tony shook his head abruptly, and Molly ignored the question. Instead, she got to her feet. "Look, I don't pretend to know what's going on here, but I want to know something. Joseph, you were there the night of the last prison break, and you were captured. I just saw the photo—that's why I came over here this morning, to find out just what was going on, but I couldn't ask point-blank, with Mr. Skye here. *Now* it seems as if everything's out in the open, so I can ask. And I do so with the full force of the British government behind me. How did you escape from that prison, Joseph? And what do you know about the recent terrorist acts against England?"

Joseph glanced at Laika, and she inclined her head slightly, telling him to go ahead and tell them all the truth. After all, she wanted to know as much as anyone.

"I escaped from that prison by walking through walls, hand in hand with this prisoner I've been telling you about." Laika noticed Skye's body tense. "He calls himself Mulcifer, and he freed the terrorists, too. He joined with Colin Mackay as part of his nationalist group, but I don't think Mackay is in control anymore. Mulcifer is controlling Mackay's men the same way he . . . controlled me."

Molly shook her head and raised her hands in the air as if in disbelief. "What are you talking about, hypnosis?"

"No," Joseph replied. "Hypnosis is bullshit. This is the real deal. I don't know how he does it, whether he implants his brain waves directly into your brain or what, but when he says jump, you ask how high. It doesn't work on everybody. Bloodlines have a lot to do with it. Mackay, for example, is untouchable.''

"Okay, okay," Molly said. "So what you're saying is that the people at the castle are the terrorists, the ones who are responsible for the bombings?''

"That's rather obvious, isn't it?" said Skye. "I have another question, Agent Stein. Why did this . . . Mulcifer, is it? . . . Why did he help you escape from prison?''

"He wanted me to find the location of some nerve gas the British government had stored away.''

"And did you?" Molly asked angrily, as if she knew the answer.

"I didn't have any choice. But there's no way he's going to be able to get to it.''

"What do you *mean*," Molly said, "you didn't have any goddamned *choice?* Are you telling me that you gave away my country's secrets to terrorists? Were you tortured, Joseph?''

"No, Molly. I was *told.*''

"All right, I've had enough of this." Molly picked up her coat and walked to the door. "Your immunity has just stopped dead. I'm calling in an anti-terrorist strike on that castle. We're going to capture those men and this Mulcifer you're talking about, and put him in a good English prison and see how fast he walks out of it.''

"That will *not* be a good idea," Skye said. "Please. Just sit for a moment, and let me explain something to you, Inspector Fraser. To *all* of you." Skye gestured graciously to the chair Molly had left, hoping that she would sit down. Otherwise, he might have to shoot the stupid bitch. To his relief, Molly slowly returned to the chair and sat, her gaze warily on Skye. "Thank you. Now, I want all of you to know that I know a great deal more about this prisoner, this Mulcifer, than you suspect.''

Skye's mind was whirling over what to tell and what to

leave out. The primary consideration now driving him was that he must come into contact with Mulcifer. Now that he had finally found him, the last thing Skye wanted was to have the British government get their hands on him.

He had aligned himself with this man Mackay's nationalists, a no doubt small and underfinanced group, despite the magnificent coup they had pulled off with the destruction of London's greatest landmarks. Still, if what Stein said was true, that had been mostly Mulcifer's doing. If Mulcifer had fallen in with Mackay so quickly, how much more quickly, then, would he be likely to join a man like Mr. Stanley, who already had immense power and wealth? Together they could achieve *absolute* power, power in which Skye would share.

And now something was different. Now Skye would not only share in the power, but inherit it. He had seen the power of the cup, and if it had made the Mackays live far beyond their normal spans, why should it not be true of him as well? He would be Stanley's man for another twenty, thirty, forty years. By then he and Stanley would surely come up with an idea of how to get rid of Mulcifer, or at least of how to contain him again.

Then, when Stanley finally died, everything he had would be Skye's, not just for a few years, but for centuries, as long as he was able to keep violent death away. With the power he would have, it would be tricky, but power could buy a lot of loyalty.

But none of these dreams would come true unless he stopped this woman now.

"There is far more to this affair than terrorism," he said calmly. "I know that with the recent attacks upon London, it seems to you that ending such threats as quickly as possible should be your first priority, but there is far more to consider. Not to overdramatize, but the fate of the world could be at stake here. There are tremendous forces at work, and I truly believe that I am the only person who fully understands the situation, and that I can put a stop to it without further bloodshed, if I can only meet with Mulcifer and talk to him in private.''

"For God's sake," Molly Fraser said in disgust, "how do you expect me to believe that? You've only just learned as much as I have!"

"On the contrary, I've had knowledge of this person long before we ever put this current operation together." He looked at Laika and the others. "I couldn't tell you anything about it, though. National security reasons, of course."

"Of course," said Agent Harris, with a snide look on her face that Skye would have quickly wiped from it had it not been for Fraser's presence.

"So if you will remain silent on these matters for the next forty-eight hours, that should give me enough time to meet with Mulcifer and defuse and resolve the entire situation."

"No bloody way," said Molly Fraser, standing up again. "I'm reporting to MI5 now. Even if I fully believed you, which I don't, I cannot delay my response at the request of foreign intelligence agents, as you damned well know."

"Then," Skye said, getting slowly to his feet, "I'm afraid we have no other course but to make *you* the next prisoner in our little drama." He turned to his operatives. "Take her into custody, and search her for weapons."

"You wouldn't dare," Fraser said.

"I would dare much more," Skye said, "for my country, and for the safety of the world."

Laika's first reaction was to tell Skye to take Molly into custody his own damn self, if that was what he wanted. But then she realized that if Molly Fraser's information caused an anti-terrorist strike, what they were going to end up with was a lot of dead soldiers and nothing else to show for it. It would be Utah all over again. All Mulcifer had to do was come into contact with the men and affect a minority of them, and they'd be shooting one another just the way LaPierre's troops blasted themselves to pieces.

Laika didn't know what to do next, but the *first* thing was to make sure that Molly didn't start anything that couldn't be finished. Laika took out her pistol and pointed it at her. "Sorry, Inspector, but I'm afraid we're going to have to make you as comfortable as possible in the cellar."

Joseph and Tony must have read her mind, because they came straight to Laika's aid. "I'm sorry, Molly," Joseph said, "but it's for the best. Just trust me for a while."

Molly held her arms in the air while Laika patted her down. "Trust you. That's a good one, Joseph. Especially in light of your trying to kill us all, and protecting a bunch of terrorist butchers. Oh yes, this is the most stable bunch I've been around in a *real* long time."

"You saw what happened here today," Laika said. "You think that was all a trick? That Joseph and I weren't really shot and near death? Then maybe you'd like to explain just *how* we pulled off that little Siegfried-and-Roy bullshit, huh?"

"No, I . . . I don't know."

"And it really doesn't matter," said Skye. "Get her in the basement. If there are no windows and nothing she can use to escape, there's no point in tying her up, as long as the door's secure."

The operatives removed their supplies from the basement, leaving it empty. While Tony pulled Molly's car into the small storage barn behind the cottage, Joseph and Laika tried to make the cellar as comfortable as possible for Molly. Then they locked her in, and, at Skye's direction, met in one of the bedrooms so that Molly would not hear them.

"I think," Skye began, in a voice even icier than usual, "that there's an awful lot that you haven't been telling me, Agent Harris. We'll deal with that later." He turned to Joseph. "Agent Stein, are you certain that this Mulcifer is in the castle?"

"Yes sir. At least, I believe he was when I left last night."

"I want to contact him. Do they have a telephone?"

"Yeah," Tony said. "Unlisted, but we got the number a few days ago."

Laika cleared her throat. "Sir, believe me, you don't want to meet with him face to face. His powers are . . . well, there's just no knowing what he might do."

"You seem to know a lot about Mulcifer, Agent Harris. Have your paths crossed before?"

"I know that if he can make Agent Stein try and kill us, he can do just about anything to anybody."

"It's very doubtful that Agent Stein and I," said Skye, "come from the same genetic stock. My family has been Nordic. There are no traces of any Mediterranean or Jewish influence that I know of."

Joseph's lips tightened. "When Mulcifer raped women, he didn't ask about their background. Agent Harris could be a relation, for all we know."

"A distant one, I assume," said Skye. "I've heard your concerns, Agent Harris, and I assure you I'll be cautious. But as I said, I know a great deal about this person, and I feel confident that our meeting will be productive." Then he held out his hand for the phone. "The phone number, Agent Luciano?"

Tony told him, and he dialed the castle. "Hello," they heard him say when someone answered. "I wish to speak to someone there at the castle . . . my name isn't important. This person is a former prisoner who was recently released from years of captivity. Many *long* years. I believe he goes by the name of Mulcifer . . . yes, I will." Two minutes passed before Skye spoke again.

"Hello, Mr. Mulcifer, I wonder if it . . . all right, Mulcifer, then. I wonder if it would be possible to schedule a meeting with you. . . . Well, I have a proposition that I think you may be interested in. It concerns recent activities that have taken place in London. . . . Let me just say that I represent certain parties who have a great deal of interest in your rather special gifts, and that a meeting might prove beneficial to all of us . . . I'm delighted to hear it. . . . Wherever you like . . . where precisely would that be? . . . Very well. And when? . . . Yes, that would be fine. Tell me, would it be all right if I brought along a few associates? . . . Excellent. Thank you . . . I'll see you then.'' Skye hung up.

"So how long do we have to keep Inspector Fraser locked up?'' Joseph asked.

"I'll be meeting the gentleman tomorrow evening," Skye replied, ''so she'll have to be our guest until then.''

"You'll be taking us along?''

Skye shook his head. ''Agents Finch and Weyrman will accompany me.'' He didn't give any explanation, and Laika knew that to ask for one would only anger him further. ''Now, if you'll excuse me, there are some other private calls I need to make. Would the three of you mind going outside for a moment.'' It wasn't a question, and the operatives went out through the back door.

"Damn, I'd give a lot to hear that call,'' Joseph said.

"You will,'' said Laika. ''Tony hooked up a recorder. We'll get the other side of the call to Mulcifer, too.'' She put an affectionate hand on his shoulder. ''I'm glad you're back. And I mean, I'm glad *you're* back.''

Joseph shook his head. ''I am so sorry. God, I would have killed you all if . . .'' He looked at Tony.

"I'm sorry, too,'' Tony said. ''It was the only way to stop you. It's a miracle that it worked out the way it did.''

"This time I'll buy that miracle story,'' Joseph said. ''But that doesn't mean I'm converted.'' They laughed softly together. ''I don't know how to tell you what it was like.'' Laika could barely hear him. ''I didn't want to, but I didn't have any choice. I couldn't fight it. I just wasn't strong enough.''

"From what we know,'' Tony said, ''if he can touch you, if you . . . share his blood, like you said, I don't think anyone is strong enough.''

"Somebody's got to be,'' Joseph said. ''I don't think we've got much of a chance otherwise.''

*T*wo hours later, when Finch and Weyrman picked up Skye and drove him to Gairloch, Laika, Tony, and Joseph listened to the tape. The first conversation was with Mulcifer, and Joseph closed his eyes when he heard the voice.

It sent a chill through Laika, too. It was a voice that seemed totally in control, yet also twisted, as though its owner was about to start cackling at any moment over his imaginary— or, in this case, all too real—power. Mulcifer and Skye were going to meet on the beach at the foot of Castle Dirk the following evening at sunset. When Skye had asked if Mulcifer would mind if he brought associates, he had replied, "The more the merrier."

"I wonder what kind of merriment Mulcifer has in mind," Laika said. "I don't envy Skye, and I certainly don't envy Finch and Weyrman. What's the next call, the private one?"

They didn't recognize either of the voices on the following call:

Unknown woman: Yes?
         Skye: This is Skye.
    Woman: Hold on.
Unknown man: Yes?
         Skye: I've found him.
       Man: Where?
         Skye: Scotland. The Gairloch peninsula on the
               northwest coast. I've spoken to him, set

                  up a meeting for tomorrow at sunset.
Man: Tell me where exactly. I'll be there.
Skye: I don't know if that's wise. He can be violent. It may not be safe for you to enter the picture yet.
Man: It'll be safe. And I'll make those decisions. Now where?

Skye gave the man a detailed description of how to get to the beach below Castle Dirk, and the man hung up without another word. Skye continued to breathe into the phone, then muttered, "Shit," and hung up.

"Either of you recognize the other voice?" Laika asked Tony and Joseph.

Tony shook his head and started to try and trace the call, but Joseph looked quizzical. "It sounded familiar to me, but I can't place it. I don't even have an idea of *where* I might have heard it."

"What's Skye trying to do in the first place?" Tony asked. "Talk Mulcifer into surrendering, or something?"

"I'm not sure," Laika said. "But I *am* sure that he knows more about Mulcifer than he's telling us, and he knows *less* than he needs to. It seems to me that he isn't as hot to capture Mulcifer as he is just to *contact* him. Skye's not an emotional man, but he seemed almost anxious to get an audience from the thing. He may have something totally different up his sleeve."

"Maybe he thinks he can use him somehow," Joseph said. "Mulcifer's power is unbelievable. Colin Mackay already tried to harness it and failed. Skye may be next."

"Or the person behind Skye," Laika added. "Whoever he talked to wasn't taking any crap."

"Make that '*le* crap,' " Tony said, looking up from his computer. "The call went to the Hôtel d'Avignon in Paris."

"Don't suppose you can get a room number?"

"No. Hotel switchboard, that's all."

"He sounded American, though," said Laika. "What's in Paris right now?"

"International Commerce Expo," Joseph said. "A few government types would be there, but mostly businessmen. All the movers and shakers . . ." He paused for a moment, then whispered, "Oh, sweet Jesus . . ."

"What is it?" Laika asked.

"The voice on the phone. I think I know where I heard it. Put yourself back a few years, and try and hear it saying, 'It takes a good man to help a good country.' "

"Political ad," said Tony. "What was it, the Republican primaries . . ."

"David Allan Stanley," Laika said. "Oh, my God."

They all knew who David Allan Stanley was. His father had been a billionaire, and by channeling the family fortunes into the computer industry at just the right time, the son had become worth $30 billion.

In 1996 he had gone after the Republican presidential nomination to the tune of $20 million, running on a one-issue platform of a simplified tax code. His lack of any political experience, along with his doughy appearance and absence of any personality that could be captured by video cameras, had doomed his effort. He had won in only one state, early in the campaign, and finished as high as second in only four others. Some said that his loss had embittered him, and though it was true that he had kept a much lower profile since his defeat, no one believed that his hatred of big government and taxes would remain private for long.

Tony rewound the tape and played it again. "That's him," said Laika. "You're right, Joseph."

"I hated those damn ads," said Tony. "I should've recognized his voice. First LaPierre, and now Stanley. What is it about money, anyway? You get a certain amount and suddenly you want to take over the world?"

"I wouldn't know," said Joseph. "I've never had that much. And if this kind of shit is any indication of what you become, I'll gladly do without it."

Laika bit her lower lip, thinking it through. "I hardly think that Stanley would have been recruited by the CIA. That seems to indicate that Skye's working for him now, and not the Company." She hissed out an angry breath. "If Stanley can't buy the leadership of the free world in one way, maybe he figures he can in another."

"But how did Skye get involved with Stanley?" Tony asked.

"For that matter," said Laika, "how did Skye or Stanley find out about the Prisoner? It doesn't matter. What *does* matter is that we get a record of this meeting tomorrow night. If Skye's acting outside the Company, then so are we. And that means we'd better have some bargaining chips. There's a bluff overlooking that beach. Tonight we'll set up a video camera with a telephoto lens. Have you got a shotgun mike that'll pick up that far away, Tony?"

He nodded. "The water sound might intrude, but I should be able to filter it out afterward. There's brush all along there, so we can hide the camera pretty well."

"All right," Joseph said. "When do we go?"

"You don't," Laika said. "I don't want you anywhere near that castle. Mulcifer probably thinks we're all dead, and there's no reason to enlighten him otherwise, so we're not going to take any chance on his picking up your thoughts, or whatever it is he does."

"Maybe we ought to put your head inside a lead mask," said Tony with a grin.

"Then Leonardo DiCaprio and I would have something in common other than looks," Joseph replied.

Chapter 43

*T*he following morning Brian and Henry Baird drove into the town of Stirling, forty miles west of Edinburgh. The two brothers, following Mulcifer's orders, had driven south and stopped for the night. Then they had proceeded to Stirling, the site of the Battle of Stirling Bridge, where William Wallace's band of Scots had defeated the English in 1297.

The Victorians had erected a monument to Wallace high on the Abbey Craig, and it was to this national shrine that the Bairds now went. When the monument opened at 10 in the morning, the parking lot at the base of the Craig was already half full.

One could either take the shuttle bus up the winding road to the tower itself, or walk up its steep incline. The Bairds decided the bus would be better. Otherwise they would have had to carry the hundred-pound canister of VX up to the tower, and might be too tired to haul it the rest of the way up the 264 steps of the narrow spiral staircase to the top.

They each had an automatic, and when the bus arrived at the bottom of the hill, Brian waited for everyone to get off, and then stepped inside and showed his gun to the driver, telling him that he would shoot him if he did not keep everyone else off the bus. Then Brian sat right behind the driver and held the pistol around the right side of the driver's seat, so that it pressed into his side.

The driver told everyone that he was taking no passengers on the next run, and by then Henry was there lugging the canister of VX. The driver helped him take it onto the bus, and then drove them up to the tower, shaking with fear. At Brian's orders, he stopped thirty yards from the shuttle pickup. Several tourists started to walk toward the bus, but Henry stepped out and waved them away, shaking his head, and they obediently moved back to the pickup spot.

Brian yanked the telephone cord out of its socket and pulled the keys from the ignition, then took the driver to the back of the shuttle, where he struck him on the head with his pistol butt and set him on the floor. Then he and Henry put their pistols under their jackets and carried the canister to the main entrance of the slim square tower. On one corner, the outline of the spiral staircase seemed like a huge, off-center pillar soaring up to the great hexagonal spire that partly covered the open observation deck like steepled fingers of stone.

The brothers went inside, past the curious tourists, and turned to the left, where an official asked what they were up to. In reply, Brian struck him down with his right fist and pushed him out of the way with his foot. Then they started up the staircase.

It was so narrow that one man could scarcely pass another, and when Brian, who was in the lead, met someone who was coming down, he told them gruffly to go back up, which they did, getting off the staircase at one of the exhibit floors. Only one man, whom the Bairds encountered just as they had passed the second level, refused, saying that it was less trouble for them to go down a few steps than it was for him to go all the way back up to the third level. Brian took out his gun and told the man that if they couldn't go past him, they would step over him, and the man turned and ran quickly up the stairs.

At last they ascended the stairs and came out onto the top observation level. The wind was blowing so hard that they could scarcely hear the voices of the dozen tourists standing by the stone railings, looking out over the town below and the hills beyond, to the great loops of the River Forth, and far-off Stirling Castle, rising like the spine of a buried giant from its tree-covered foundation of volcanic rock.

But Brian and Henry Baird had not ascended the tower for the view. They went immediately to the side that overlooked the town, and in front of the curious tourists, leaned the canister against the parapet, and opened the valve with a screwdriver. There was no hesitation on their part, just as there was no recalcitrance on the part of the valve. It opened as easily as if it had been made the day before, and VX gas started to rocket invisibly from the nozzle.

The Baird brothers breathed it in and immediately went into convulsions, as did several of the people nearby. When others saw what was happening, they started to run for the stairs, but the gas, swirled about by the wind, caught them, and they too went down, unable to breathe. Only two people who were on the observation deck just beneath were able to get into the spiral staircase and down before the gas followed them. Everyone else above, ten people and the Bairds, died within a minute of breathing in the VX.

But the strong winds at the tower's top proved lifesaving to those below, sweeping the deadly gas out and up, and dissipating it high in the air. What might have destroyed the entire population of Stirling killed only a few high-flying birds, and did not even reach those at the base of the tower.

No one else was killed, thanks to the couple who had survived near the top, and the warnings they gave as they passed each level that someone was releasing poisonous gas at the top. Several people were injured in the rush down the spiral stairway, but a few broken bones were a small price to pay for survival.

Within a half hour, police had arrived and awkwardly made their way up the narrow stairs in their bulky biological containment suits. After they took photographs, they lowered the bodies, tightly wrapped in plastic, down the outside of the tower, and reported to their superiors what they had found.

The radio in Colin Mackay's small room was playing at a higher than normal volume to drown out the conversation that

Colin was having with Rob Lindsay. They were sitting close together, remembering Angus Gunn and trying to come up with a plan to end Mulcifer's reign of terror over their organization.

"I couldn't do a thing to stop him, Colin," Rob said. "I could only stand there and watch as my best friend killed himself."

"Were there some who could do anything?" Colin asked.

"Aye, I think so. It looked like Danny was going to make a move on the bastard, but I saw Michael start to reach for his gun to stop him. I don't know, maybe I even started to myself. But if you and Danny are untouched by the bastard, odds are there are one or two others who go along because they know damn well that Mulcifer will order us to kill them if they rebel. They'd just be throwing their lives away."

"God *damn* it," Colin said, smashing his fist down on his thigh. "Sometimes I think it'd be better to do it and die than to be that monster's slave anymore, which is what you all are, while I'm no better than a prisoner now. And what about Henry and Brian? He sent them off with enough gas to kill thousands. When's the other shoe going to drop on that? And *where?*"

As if in answer, the music on the radio stopped, and a BBC news bulletin reported that terrorists had released poison gas at one of Scotland's great national shrines, the William Wallace monument in Stirling.

Colin went white and stared into space, scarcely able to believe what he was hearing, but knowing that after the attacks on London, this was a mere bagatelle for Mulcifer. He didn't have to see any pictures of the two "suicide terrorists" to know who they were.

"He spat in our faces," Colin said, when the story ended. "It wasn't enough to use us, he had to spit right in our faces." He looked at Rob with fury in his eyes. "There's no place more sacred to us than Stirling, and he knew it." With one mighty swing of his fist, Colin smashed the radio, stopping the music in a shower of sparks. "It ends *now!*"

He went to the door and swung it open. Outside stood two of his men with pistols in their holsters. "All right, if you're going to shoot me to keep me in there, you'd better do it now. I'm not leaving, I just want everyone in the great hall now." He went down the hallway, banging on the doors of the rooms. "Come on, all out! Come with me! The great hall! Up and out with you!"

Within a minute the ten men who remained were standing in the large room. Nearly all had weapons either holstered or in their hands. Colin had no idea where Mulcifer was, and he didn't care. All he cared about was that the beast had put all of them in hell.

"Have you heard?" he cried. "Have you heard what that goddamned monster did? Do you know where he sent Brian and Henry with their canister of gas? To *Stirling*, lads! To the Wallace monument, where they climbed to the top and released the gas, killing ten people and themselves! He's pissed in our pot, lads! He's turned us and defiled us and made us into what we never wanted to be. And now it ends!"

"I hardly think so," said Mulcifer, leisurely walking in through the open door. "These are my men now, Mackay. I'm the one with the hold over them, remember?"

"No, you can't have them all." Colin looked sternly at his men, trying to put a will of iron into them, *his* will. "Stop it here and now. Have no more to do with this beast. The fault is mine. I thought we could control him, that we could offer him what he wanted, and we could get what we needed in return, but I was wrong. Now let's stop him together."

"How?" asked Danny Christie, almost shyly.

"That *would* seem to be the question," Mulcifer said.

"By denying him," said Colin, ignoring the creature. "By refusing him and turning him out. By banishing this second-rate Satan from our souls. We'll do his will no more!"

"Colin," James Menzies said apologetically. "I'm not so sure I can do that."

"Well, *I* can!" Colin shouted. "And Danny, so can you! And there must be others here, too. We're true Scots and strong men, so let's take him and hold him and bind him in that lead coffin I had made, and this time we'll sink him to the bottom of the sea forever!'' He eyed his men intently. ''Who of you here is untouched by him? Who's been holding back out of fear? Don't be afraid now to admit it—Danny, you're not his, are you?'' Danny Christie shook his head.

Then John Caldwell took a step toward Colin and looked angrily toward Mulcifer. ''I'm not his, either, the blackhearted bastard!''

''Ooo,'' said Mulcifer in mock pain. ''I'll remember that.''

''Remember and be damned,'' Caldwell said. ''I've had enough of your shite!''

''That's three strong lads we are,'' Colin said. ''The rest of you lot can see he can't touch us, so come join us, then, or if you can't, leave us be. We're enough to take him down.''

Colin began to walk slowly toward Mulcifer, who backed away, shivering theatrically. Caldwell and Christie joined the advance. Suddenly, Mulcifer stepped past Colin and thrust the two other men back, one with each hand, so that they stumbled and fell onto the floor. Then he grabbed Colin from behind before he could turn around, and held him as securely as if he had been chained in place.

''Enough of this shit,'' Mulcifer said, looking at the other men. ''Kill those two now.''

Chapter 44

Colin Mackay shouted, "*No!*" and tried to break free, but he could not, so great was Mulcifer's strength. He watched in horror as the other men, all eight of them, including Rob and James, took out their weapons and began to fire at John Caldwell and Danny Christie.

Tears streamed down the faces of the men who fired, and their mouths were open and their eyes afire with the agony of what they were doing to their comrades. The bullets smacked into the bodies of the two victims over and over until their faces were red masks and their chests raw plains of blood.

"Enough," said Mulcifer over the gunfire, and though he did not shout, everyone heard, and the firing ceased, leaving in the vast room a silence broken only by the low sobs of the men who had just killed their friends. Rob Lindsay fell to his knees and grasped his head as though it were about to come off, sobbing from his broken heart.

There was another noise that Colin heard, and he couldn't tell if it was the sound of blood running from the two corpses or his own blood rushing inside his head. Mulcifer's arms released him then, and he stumbled forward, falling to his knees beside his two dead, loyal comrades. He touched their bloody heads as though he needed some physical proof that what he had just seen had truly happened, and then he looked up at Mulcifer through eyes clouded by tears.

"Why don't you just kill me too then? You . . . fucking . . ." There was no word left to call him, no appellation bad enough in all the tongues of this world.

"Because I want you to live, Colin. I want you to see what happens next, to appreciate what else I'm going to do in your name, in the name of your precious Scottish independence, and of course in the name of Mackay. I hate that name. Your father was one of the twelve men who persecuted me for seven centuries.

"I would no sooner reach out of my prison, at great pain and effort, to touch a sympathetic soul, than your cursed father or one of his knightly partners in self-righteousness would undo my handiwork, put an end to my long-sought disciple, terminate my pleasure, the only pleasure I ever had. Do you know what it's like to be imprisoned in lead? *Lead?* That dense, flat element which absorbs the dreams that I send out like no other element on this shabby little planet? Do you know what effort it takes me to project a wish, a desire, a *need* through *lead?*

"The agony that your little dogs here suffered was nothing compared to mine, every time that I pushed through. And I had no choice, just as your other pets had no choice but to cut these men down. How can I make this clear to you, Colin Mackay?" Mulcifer crouched and put his face only inches from Colin's. "When you hunger, you must feed. And if you cannot, you must at least try. That is what I did. That is *all* I did. I followed my nature, and your people called me Antichrist and tortured me because of it.

"Nature. Like your red hair or your white skin. My hunger. Nature, Colin Mackay. You cannot deny nature. You cannot keep nature bound in lead forever. And for the sins of your father in fighting my nature, I take my vengeance on you."

Mulcifer stood up. "As for that leaden coffin you had made, that proof of your intended betrayal, it has long since been dismantled, and its pieces sunk in the Minch. You see . . ." He gave a twisted smile. "I *hate* lead." Then he turned to the others. "Take him and put him in the bottle dungeon," he told them. "I'll come to you, Colin Mackay, and let you know what I do next, in Edinburgh, the capital of your great country.''

Colin leapt at him then, with all the anger he could muster propelling him forward, and bore him to the floor. He struck Mulcifer full in the face, once, twice, thrice, and then he was grabbed by the others and hauled to his feet.

Mulcifer stood up as well, seemingly unharmed. He looked annoyed, and Colin was jubilant to see that he had at least been responsible for that. He had surprised the monster, and if he had surprised him once, maybe he could again. ''I'll destroy you yet, Mulcifer, I swear to God.''

''Swear to whatever nonexistent deity you wish. Swear, pray, and curse all you like. It's music to me. So sing your songs of hatred, Mackay, but know you sing to yourself alone. Now, take him away,'' Mulcifer commanded the men. ''I have other things to think about. You are not the only petty nuisance I must deal with today, Colin Mackay.''

*A*gent Vaughn Weyrman pressed his elbow gently against his side one more time. Yes, the pistol was there, all right. Skye had told both him and Finch not to bring any weapons along to the meeting, but Weyrman had disobeyed. He felt naked without a weapon, especially during such an unpredictable operation. Skye would not tell them who they were meeting, how many would be there, and if they'd be armed or not, and Weyrman didn't want to walk into a hostile situation where they were both outnumbered and outgunned. At least the pistol gave him an edge.

The truth was, he didn't always trust his boss. Why would you trust someone who was running his own operation, and paid you bonuses in cash, and gave you cover stories to use if anyone else in the Company got too nosy? Of course, he could put the shoe on the other foot and ask why Skye should trust him. The answer was, he shouldn't. After all, he'd disobeyed his order not to bring a gun.

There was a good reason for Skye's request. He had seen firsthand how Mulcifer, if that was his name, could affect people. At least he wouldn't be able to make Finch or Weyrman shoot each other—or him.

Skye walked down the beach, the two agents behind him. To his left, the sun was setting over the waters, but he kept his eyes fixed on the castle that was growing ever closer. Now and then he glanced down at the pebbles on which he was walking, moving right or left to avoid the contact of his wing-tips with the occasional sharp-edged rock that the waves had not yet worn smooth.

There was no sight of Mr. Stanley, and that fact both relieved and disturbed him. He would have preferred that Stanley not be present, for he was uncertain as to his ability to protect him should Mulcifer prove troublesome. At the same time, Stanley's absence suggested that he might have had some sort of mishap on his way there, and that would be more than tragic. Stanley was not only Skye's meal ticket, but his passport to a life most people couldn't even imagine.

At last they were directly beneath the castle, and Skye had the leisure to observe his surroundings. A stone finger that might once have been the foundation of a pier extended thirty feet into the water. Above them the castle's stone walls loomed down from the hundred-foot-high bluff. Thick vegetation covered the rocks, and a steep stairway zigzagged up the side of the cliff, apparently a route to the castle.

Skye's eyes narrowed as he saw a figure appear near the top of that vertiginous route. It was a tall man with light brown shoulder-length hair and a short beard. He was wearing a cream-colored shirt and light trousers, and came down the steep path with a graceful ease. There was something about the loose yet controlled way the man moved that reminded Skye of Franklin Ames, Skye's mentor in the Company. Ames, now long dead, had drummed into the young Skye the virtues of loyalty and patriotism. Skye's first impression of the man as an ass had never changed, yet his intensity had always frightened Skye.

His reverie was suddenly disturbed by the sound of something moving on the water, and he turned to see a small submarine break the surface a hundred yards off the shore. At first Skye thought that somehow he had been betrayed, but he saw quickly that this was not a government sub, but a personal one. Stanley.

The craft moved toward the shore and stopped next to the stone remnants of the pier. The hatch on top opened, and a man holding an automatic rifle and dressed in a dark pin-striped suit climbed out and stepped onto the finger of rock. He was followed by David Allan Stanley, whose immaculately tailored topcoat and suit beneath could do nothing to disguise the fact that for all his wealth he was one of the most plebeian looking of men.

Stanley frowned as he picked his way carefully over the rocks toward the beach, the man with the gun in the lead. A third man followed, also well dressed and carrying his own weapon. He wore an odd little cap that Skye suspected marked him as the sub's pilot. The three of them reached Skye when Mulcifer was only halfway down the path, and Stanley continued to frown.

"Good to see you, sir," said Skye. "You come in style."

"Stupid goddamn place to hold a meeting," Stanley said in his reedy tenor. "These your boys?"

"Yes sir, Agents Weyrman and Finch."

"They got guns?"

"No sir, they don't."

"I thought you said this guy could be dangerous." Stanley looked up at the descending figure. "That him?" Skye nodded. "Anybody know you're here?"

"No sir."

"Same with me. Didn't let a damn soul know where I was headed. Stakes are too high, we've worked too hard to find this guy. My people probably think I'm meeting with President Chirac tonight."

Skye looked uneasily at the two men with the weapons. Hopefully Stanley could be persuasive enough so that Mulcifer wouldn't get nasty. If the man wanted to dominate the world, David Stanley would be the perfect collaborator.

"His name is Mulcifer," Skye said. "Not *Mister*, just Mulcifer."

"Funny name. Hell, I'll call him Napoleon if that's what he wants."

Mulcifer had arrived at the bottom of the bluff and was crossing the beach toward them, a smile on his face. "Mulcifer,'' Skye said when he came up to them. "I'm Richard Skye. I talked to you yesterday on the telephone."

"Yes, I know," said Mulcifer. He looked at Stanley. "But I'm unfamiliar with this gentleman."

"I'm David Allan Stanley," the man said, sounding annoyed at not being recognized. "And you're Mulcifer?"

"That's the name."

"I just want to make sure we've got this straight before we go any further," Stanley went on. "You're the one the Catholic Church has been holding prisoner, is that right?"

" '*Ecce homo.*' "

Stanley cocked his head. "What?"

" 'Behold the man.' From the Vulgate."

"Okay, whatever. Is it true that you have all these powers that I've heard about?"

"Why not ask the caretakers of St. Paul's Cathedral and Westminster Abbey? You might inquire as to the whereabouts of England's Crown jewels. You might even ask among the dead."

Stanley looked uncomfortable now, and Skye felt on edge. He could have told Stanley what he had seen the day before, but he didn't want Mulcifer knowing that the three operatives were still alive.

"I hear you've lived a long time," Stanley said.

"I have. Longer than you can imagine. And when you spend several hundred years of that time in captivity . . ." He closed his eyes, put up his head, and took a deep breath. ". . . Freedom becomes far more sweet, as do the things you can do when you're free. Now. Mr. Skye said he had a proposition for me."

"The proposition is from me," said Stanley jealously. "I think that a partnership between us could be highly beneficial for both of us."

"Explain, please."

"If what I hear is true," said Stanley, "you are the most . . . persuasive individual on this planet. You can make people do things they normally wouldn't do. What I'm offering you is what you might call a center of operations. I don't have just businesses, but a business *empire*, already in place in dozens of major countries, and in as many governments in third-world countries. If you collaborate with me, if we join my wealth and resources and influence with your abilities, we could shake up the world—*control* it. *Own* it.''

Mulcifer held up a peremptory hand, and Stanley stopped talking. He tilted his head and looked upward thoughtfully, then back at Stanley. "Why?"

''. . . Why what?''

"I need to know why you *want* to control the world."

"Well . . . power . . . unimaginable power and wealth. It's been the dream of every great leader since Alexander."

"And how much wealth do you have now?" Mulcifer asked. "If you sold everything you had, how much cash would you actually have?"

"You mean, if I turned everything liquid? Well, maybe . . . oh, say fifty billion dollars, give or take."

"Fifty billion dollars. And how old are you?"

"I'm fifty-two."

"So if you live through your threescore years and ten— but let's be generous and let you live until eighty-two, say— that's thirty more years of life. That would be one and two-thirds billion dollars a year. Do you really need more money that that?"

"That's not the point—it's the, the *power*."

"No no no, power is what you use to *achieve* the ultimate, but you have no idea what that is. You're merely a greedy little man who always wants more. You want to be able to control any man, bed any woman, have any object you want. You want people to look at your silly, lumpy face and your chubby little body and say, 'There goes God.' " He shook his head sadly. "I really don't think there's any hope for a collaboration between us. Our aesthetic differences are too great.

"Besides, I consider myself self-made, and I have so much fun in the making. As the old cliches say, the joy is in the doing, it's not the destination but the journey, and make sure you kill all the people on the way up so they'll never bring you back down. Why would I want to start at the top, as co-ruler of the world with you? Where would I go from there? And of course there's the best reason of all—I don't like you."

Stanley's face had gone as red as the dying sun, and his jowls were quivering. It was a frightening sight, and Skye would no sooner have spoken than he would have spat in Stanley's eye. So the thought of killing the very man he most feared, with his bare hands, came as a surprise.

Chapter 46

*I*t was as though a suggestion had come to Skye, a voice had whispered deep inside his brain. *Kill him*, it had said. *Kill Stanley. He is stupid and selfish and a pig, and he will only do the same to you when all is said and done and he no longer needs you. You were trained years ago. You still remember how. Do it. With your bare hands. Now.*

It was absurd, and he tried to push it away, but it kept returning. Then he realized that it was Mulcifer.

Mulcifer was inside his head the same way he had been inside Joseph Stein's. To his horror, he also discovered that he was planning the approach, checking his distance from Stanley, taking his hands out of his pockets, moving his shoulder to see if he had enough room under his topcoat to swing his arm freely in the killing blow.

No, he would not do this. Stanley was talking now, saying something about Mulcifer being a goddamned fool, and that if someday it came to the two of them, he knew damn well which one was going to blink, and that if Mulcifer was smart he'd think twice before insulting somebody like Stanley, because even if Mulcifer didn't give a shit about wealth and power, they could buy things, even buy the life of a smart-mouth bastard who was turning down the biggest opportunity of his life, even if that life had been for hundreds of years . . .

And then Skye was next to Stanley, planting his feet, judging the arc, swinging his hand up and across in the knife blade position, slamming the edge right into Stanley's throat so that it crushed the windpipe instantly, ending Stanley's words and choking off his breath.

Then the man with Stanley shot Skye, a quick reaction blast that sprayed across Skye's midsection, lodging three bullets in his stomach before Weyrman jerked out his pistol and shot Stanley's man twice, right over the heart.

Skye didn't see Stanley's man die. His first thought was of the terrible pain in his gut as he fell to the stones, then anger, pure and naked wrath that he had just killed David Allan Stanley, the man through whom he was to have had unlimited power and wealth, all because this man, this thing, this devil named Mulcifer had hopped inside his head and simply told him to.

When he looked up again, he saw the man in the pilot's cap just standing there holding his unraised weapon, a blank look on his face. Weyrman was pointing his pistol at the man and shouting at him to drop the gun, but he didn't, and Weyrman shot him in the head, then swung the pistol around on Mulcifer.

"Go ahead!" Skye grunted out. "Shoot him!"

"No, don't do that," Mulcifer said. "That would be annoying." Then he looked down at Skye, who was trying to press the blood that was leaking out of him back into his stomach. "That was a very nice demonstration, Mr. Skye. Nice to see your old skills haven't left you. Mr. Stanley was becoming quite irksome. Thank you for your prompt obedience." He walked toward Weyrman. "Well, you're the one with the gun. What would you like to do at this point?"

"I . . . Jesus Christ, I . . ." Weyrman seemed near panic, and Skye didn't blame him. It was only the wounds in his gut that kept him as focused as he was.

"Weyrman," Skye said, "get me some help. Call a doctor, for God's sake."

"Are you going to listen to him, Agent Weyrman?" Mulcifer asked. "The man who killed David Allan Stanley, one of the most important men in the world? Why, this man is nothing but an assassin, isn't he?"

"Y . . . yes," Weyrman said.

"So as a representative of the U.S. government who has just witnessed the assassination of a U.S. citizen, would it not be best to arrest the perpetrator?"

Weyrman nodded unsurely. Then he seemed to find strength. "Finch, get that guy's gun," he said, pointing to Stanley's dead bodyguard. "Sorry, Mr. Skye. We're going to have to take you in."

"Take me *in?*" Skye moaned. "You idiot, I'm not going to *live* long enough if you don't get me help! I am *bleeding* to *death* . . ."

But Weyrman went on, as if thinking it through. "You, uh, you brought us here, ordered us here, and we thought it was to capture this individual, yeah." He nodded at Mulcifer. "But then you killed Mr. Stanley, and, and *you* shot the body-guards."

"No no," said Mulcifer, "that won't do at all. Agent Weyrman, both you and Agent Finch *knew* that Mr. Skye was acting unofficially. In fact, you've both been taking money from him for several years now. You've been traitors to your country."

"How . . . how did you know that?" Weyrman asked.

"Agent Weyrman, Mr. Skye's mind is an open book to me. I look in and read what I want." He looked down at Skye's bleeding stomach. "However, I fear this book is in its final printing. At any rate, you two mustn't be allowed to profit from your sins. Come, let's dig a grave."

He led them away from the water and up beyond the stones to where the ground became sandy. There were two shovels lying there, and he told Finch and Weyrman to dig a hole, not too deep, but wide and long enough to hold a body. Although confused, they obeyed, looking at each other several times as if asking why they were doing this.

Back on the stones, thirty feet away, Skye watched them, his hands pressed to his stomach, feeling his life dripping away as surely as his dreams had. He would never be rich now, never be in the position of power not only to tell his

superiors to go to hell, but to put them there. He was dying
slowly, and the experience gave him leisure to think about
things he would rather not have thought about, about loyalty
and patriotism and his country, all those things Franklin Ames
had preached to him about.

Skye had turned his back on those things, and at the end
had lived for himself alone, himself and his new mentor of
greed and power, David Allan Stanley. And then, just like
that, he had killed Stanley. It had been as though the Imp of
the Perverse had entered his mind and had him perform the
single most self-destructive act imaginable. He had all too
obviously underestimated this Prisoner, this being. This devil.

It was only fitting that he be destroyed by a devil, since he
had sold his soul to one, and become a devil himself in the
process. All his sins sat upon him as heavily as the weight of
his coming death upon his heart, and he closed his eyes and
tried to remember what praying was like. He had not prayed
since he was a child, and although he expected it to have no
more effect now than it had then, he prayed nonetheless.

He tried to remember his many sins, and asked anything
listening for forgiveness from them. He prayed for the souls
of the people he had caused to die, not knowing if they might
be there when—if—he crossed from life to death. He hoped
they would not be. Many of them were as cruel and as hard
as he was, and much less forgiving than any god.

Skye wept from the effort of praying, from the pain in his
belly, from the thousand things trying to push their way into
his head and divert him from his last desperate chance, his
last thoughts of piety and repentance and redemption, his last
dying hopes. If he could only put these other things away, he
thought, all these guilts and terrors, if only he could focus
clearly on coming face to face with a kind and forgiving god,
then he would be all right.

He thought about how to do it, and then remembered the
songs he had learned in the Sunday school to which his parents had taken him before he had finally refused to go any
more. " 'What . . . a friend . . .' " he started to say, and then

the tune came back to him, and he began to sing softly, pain coming with every word:

> *What a friend we have in Jesus,*
> *All our sins and griefs to bear,*
> *What a privilege to carry*
> *Everything to God in prayer . . .*

Those were all the words he could recall, but the fact that he had managed to pull them out of that dark corner of his brain where they had been buried for over forty years was miracle enough. He kept singing them softly to himself, over and over again, until he heard the gunshot.

Then he looked up and saw Finch falling down and not moving again, and Weyrman, the pistol in his hand, looking at the body in horror. Skye tried to press harder against his stomach, but his strength was waning, and it was harder to push back the pain. He looked down again, and started to sing some more, the same words over and over again. Then he heard a laugh, and looked up to see Mulcifer and Weyrman standing over him.

"Oh my," said Mulcifer, a broad grin covering his face. " 'What a friend we have in Jesus'? Don't tell me we have a deathbed conversion here, Mr. Skye? I've heard of such things, but never seen one before. You're actually feeling *guilty*, aren't you? But why? Do you really think that you'll see some god after you die, and that he'll judge your actions while you were alive?"

Skye didn't answer. Instead, he forced out the words of the song.

Mulcifer laughed long and hard, and seemed genuinely amused. "I hate to disappoint you, but you'll meet nothing and no one. You will cease to exist, which, for those who have lived, certainly has to be the most dreadful thing imaginable, far more than an eternity of hell. After all, one can accustom oneself to flames, perhaps even enjoy them after an eternity or two. But how does one accustom oneself to annihilation?''

'' ' . . . All our sins and griefs to bear . . .' ''

"Yes, well, you bear your sins and griefs, and Agent Weyrman will bear you."

Pain spiked through Skye's body as Weyrman put his hands under Skye's arms and dragged him across the pebbles and up the beach to the shallow grave. Every inch brought agony to Skye's body, and he tried to ignore the motion, to center on the song and the entreaty behind it, the prayer that neither nonexistence nor torment be his lot.

Then he felt himself falling. It was only a short distance, but the impact of landing was like having a giant fist pounding down on his entire body. He screamed, and the screaming brought more anguish, so that he could only lie there, the hymn forgotten, while the madness that the pain had brought slowly drained away.

Then, while all the world was a red sky before his eyes, he heard Mulcifer telling Weyrman to load all the bodies—Stanley, his two men, and Finch—onto the submarine, then pilot it out into deep water, release all the air, turn off the engine, and allow it to sink.

Skye didn't know whether Weyrman obeyed the directive or not, but when his eyes were finally able to see again, only Mulcifer was there, standing on the edge of the narrow, shallow grave, looking down at him. "I don't know why I've kept you for last, Mr. Skye, while the rest of them sink into the deep, never to be seen again. Perhaps it's because I think you're the worst of the lot, so we have a great deal in common, or perhaps because you've been searching for me for so long that I feel I owe you my presence while you can still enjoy it."

Skye closed his eyes, and tried to sing his song, but was only able to whisper it harshly. " 'What . . . a friend . . . we have . . .' ''

"You have no friends, Mr. Skye." Mulcifer crouched by the grave so that his face was close to Skye's, and spoke softly. "You never did. You die alone and forsaken, and do you know what? Nobody cares. Not one person in this whole world cares that you're dead, just as no one ever cared that you lived."

Sudden anger flared in Skye, and he reached toward Mulcifer's face, his fingers clawed to rip the creature's eyes away. A garbled sound of hatred escaped his throat, and Mulcifer grabbed Skye's hand and brought it to his lips in a mocking kiss. Then he looked piercingly at Skye. "Our blood sang true at the last, didn't it?" he said triumphantly.

For one final moment, Skye thought about how the thing had tricked him, made him hate again, and before he could shift his thoughts back to his mother or Jesus or anything other than the wish to take this monster into death with him, a great weight seemed to fall upon his chest, the air left his body, the darkening sky grew darker, and then he saw and heard nothing at all.

Chapter 47

"I think he's dead," Tony whispered, and listened for a moment longer, but heard only the soft sound of the sand landing in the grave as Mulcifer kicked it.

He and Laika had been watching from the bluff overlooking the beach for the last half hour, from the time that Skye and his agents had arrived. They had agreed ahead of time that whatever happened, they would not interfere. Mulcifer might be able to turn them against each other as easily as he had been able to turn others. And Skye was not worth dying for.

Nor, it turned out, was David Allan Stanley. Tony tilted the camera upward to capture the small submarine as it carried its dead passengers outward bound. The only way they would ever find it once it sank to the bottom was with a bathysphere, and they'd probably have to search the whole North Sea.

Laika and Tony had heard every word, and gotten every piece of action on videotape, including Skye's death blow to Stanley, and the shooting of all the others except for Mulcifer and Weyrman, who was now piloting the sub to his death. Tony continued to videotape until Skye's body was covered, and Mulcifer walked nonchalantly toward the steps that would take him back to the castle. Then, with a shudder, they packed up their gear and returned to the cottage.

Joseph looked grim, and said he had something to tell them, but first Laika told him everything that had happened.

When she was finished, Joseph shook his head as though he could scarcely believe the turn of events. "So Stanley's been running Skye all the time, and Skye was running us in the hopes that some of these seemingly paranormal occurrences we investigated might lead to the Prisoner."

"And they sure did," Tony said. "In spades. So what's your news?"

"Not good. The nerve gas whose location Mulcifer made me tell? They've got it."

"Sweet Jesus," said Laika softly. "Have they released it yet?"

Joseph nodded. "That's the weirdest part. Two of these loyal Scottish Nationalists let fly with this stuff at the William Wallace monument in Stirling. The people on top died, but most of the gas was blown away by the wind."

"This is no coincidence," Laika said. "Mulcifer's to blame. He's too wild a card for Mackay to control. The bastard's toying with him now, playing his little games." She looked hard at Joseph. "Do you think he's got more gas?"

"I'm sure of it. There was a huge stockpile. He wouldn't have gone to the trouble of getting to it for one lousy tank. But the question is, how'd he get it? I haven't heard a thing about any attack on a storage facility."

"Maybe they're keeping it quiet so they won't alarm the public," Tony suggested.

"Negative. MI5 would've informed the Company if that had happened, but there's no mention on our classified sites. They got in and out without anybody even knowing it."

"But how would that be possible?" Laika asked.

Joseph smiled. "Hey, we've seen this guy work. I wouldn't put anything beyond him, would you?"

They sat and talked, with long periods of silence in which they thought about what to do. Then Laika asked Tony a great deal about the castle, getting him to describe every small detail that he could remember. She made Joseph tell everything he knew about Colin Mackay, what he had said, and what kind of man he was.

At last Joseph said, "You know, I hate to say it, but this situation seems downright impossible. The only person who can clear us with the Company was a *traitor* to the Company and now he's dead; we've got a police inspector who also happens to be an ex-MI5 operative in our cellar, a castle full of terrorists up the road, and, worst of all, a being that we don't understand and we can't control."

"Thank God," said Tony dryly, "we're so good-looking."

"And we've got our health," said Laika.

Joseph looked at them disbelievingly as they both slowly started to laugh. Then he joined in, seeing the absurdity of it all, and even laughing at their hopelessness.

Finally, when they were all sitting there breathing hard from laughing, Laika's face went suddenly solemn. "I have a plan," she said. "But first we have to let Inspector Fraser out of the cellar."

Molly Fraser was furious, and when Agent Laika Harris told her that she was free to go and turn them in to the authorities, she stormed toward the door. "But before you go," Harris said, "there are a few more things you should know. First, Richard Skye is dead. He was working for David Allan Stanley, who is also dead, along with four other men. Mulcifer, the thing in that castle that calls himself a man, caused all their deaths, just as he caused the deaths in London. Just as he'll cause the deaths of more—thousands, maybe millions—unless we can stop him. And Inspector, we're the only ones who can. With your help. *Only* us, and only with your help."

By now, Molly had turned and was listening. "Go ahead," she said, her face still angry. "Talk."

Laika Harris did. It took her two hours to tell the astonishing tale and show Molly the videotape of Mulcifer, Skye, and David Allan Stanley on the beach, and the bloodbath that followed.

If Molly had heard the story only in words, she wouldn't have believed it. But the videotape was strong evidence, and

Molly couldn't deny that she had seen two people take fatal wounds and recover fully from them in minutes. The story, as absurd as it sounded, seemed to fit together with the things she had witnessed.

When Laika Harris was finished, Molly asked her and Joseph and Tony Luciano questions for over another hour. It was after midnight when the talking stopped, and Molly sat for a long time, thinking. Then Joseph Stein came over to where she sat, and crouched down next to her.

"Molly," he said slowly, "I know that I shouldn't expect you to believe any of this, but I've known you for a long, long time. I beg you to believe it. Believe it all, and help us."

"Believe the man who tried to kill me," she said flatly, her mind too full. "Who tried to kill all of us."

"The fact that I did a thing like that," Joseph replied, "proves that everything Laika just told you is the truth."

The paradoxical logic seemed nevertheless irrefutable to Molly. It was true. She had known Joseph as well as she had ever allowed herself to know anyone. All these years later, she knew that he would have given his life for her. He had nearly done it before.

She looked at Joseph, then at the others, one at a time, for nearly a minute each. "I think," she finally said, "that I have a number of telephone calls to make."

Molly Fraser made her first call from her car. It was to Martin Leech, her MI5 liaison. After she had talked to him for a long time, she returned to the cottage and smiled grimly at the others.

"He's going along with us. What really got him interested was the fact that the terrorists are in the castle. He wanted to send in a team right away, but I finally convinced him that if he does that while this Mulcifer is there, he's destroying the team. He's assembling the other players now."

"How in God's name did you convince him of Mulcifer's powers?" Laika asked.

"I didn't try. I told him that our inside informant . . ." She glanced at Joseph. ''. . . told us that this one man, the ring-leader, had a control that would blow the whole castle to bits in the event of a strike, and MI5's team along with it, so we have to make certain that he isn't in the castle when we go in.''

''You didn't tell him about Mulcifer's . . . abilities?'' Joseph asked.

''I told him, but if he didn't buy everything, I wanted to make sure that there was a practical reason not to go in with guns blazing. He's getting the elements set up, though he sounded pretty dubious when I told him about some of the things we were going to need. Still and all, he's preparing it. The team and the . . . matériel will be trucked to Dennis MacLunie's land on the other side of the hill from the castle. There's a hollow further west that's not visible from the road. We could gather a small army over there, and no one would see it. It'll all be coming in in disguised delivery and utility trucks that shouldn't draw any attention.''

''Great,'' said Laika. ''Still, the only way this is going to work is for Mulcifer to leave the castle so we can prepare for him—and if we can get Mackay to help us.''

''I don't think that's going to be a problem,'' said Joseph. ''I'd be willing to bet that after the VX attack at Stirling, Mackay will do anything to be rid of Mulcifer, even collaborate with the Sassenachs. But as for Mulcifer leaving, that's the weakest spot in the plan.''

''Maybe not,'' said Laika, defending her idea. ''Remember, the Stirling attack was a failure, at least in terms of the death count that Mulcifer certainly wanted. I suspect his dream was for the gas to sink down over the town and kill hundreds, even thousands, instead of the mere dozen it did. They'll go out again—we're counting on that—and when they do, I'm betting Mulcifer goes with them.''

''He'd have two reasons,'' Tony agreed. ''First, to make sure that his zombies don't screw things up this time, and second, to enjoy the carnage himself. The gas won't harm him, so he could stroll through the streets watching other people die. From everything you've said about him, Joseph, and from what I saw for myself on the beach, I'm sure he won't pass up the opportunity.''

"So we set up surveillance again ASAP on the castle," said Laika. "But the last time the van got out, we didn't see it.''

"Mulcifer said something to Mackay about needing to get out unseen," Joseph said. "Apparently they've got a way, probably onto the beach from the castle cellars. If they went that way before, they'll do it again. Let's watch from the bluff where you shot the videotape. That should give us a good unseen vantage point.''

"Tony and I will have to follow the van," said Laika. "We can't take a chance on getting you too close to Mulcifer again, Joseph. He thinks we're dead, and that's how I like it." She turned to Molly Fraser. "Inspector, Tony and I will have to be ready to take off after them with the dummies. Could you give us surveillance from the bluff until—and *if*—the van leaves?''

"But how will we know if Mulcifer's in the van?" Joseph asked.

Laika thought for a moment. "They can leave the castle unseen, but they've got to leave the peninsula by the main road." She turned quickly to Tony. "Can you set up a camera alongside the road that can image the occupants of the van through the front window, so that Joseph can see it on a monitor here in the cottage?''

"Sure. I'll do it now, while it's still dark, set it up alongside the road about two miles south of Castle Dirk. That should give us enough time to be ready to tail them when they come by here, and if they use an access road to the beach south of the castle, there's no way it's going to be more than two miles from it.''

"And that means," Laika said, turning back to Molly, "that there's no other surveillance necessary. Good. I'd rather have you with us, Inspector.''

"Make it Molly," she said.

*   *   *

While Laika went with Tony to set up the camera on the road, Joseph and Molly drove to the MacLunie property and waited for the vehicles to start arriving. Joseph was, as always, amazed at the efficiency of bureaucracies when speed was truly called for.

A reinforced van, capable of carrying the dozen hundred-pound canisters they had requested, arrived at 0400 hours. Laika and Tony showed up at 0415. They had set up the camera, and had first returned to the cottage to make sure everything was operational.

Two trucks with the strike force pulled in between five and six. The rest of the matériel had been held at Gairloch, where it would wait until they had taken the castle. Martin Leech climbed out of the first van with the soldiers, and went up to Molly. "God, I don't know why I trust you enough to do all this," he said.

"Because I've never steered you wrong before," she replied. "Here's the tape," she said, handing it to him. "Take a look and then bring it back." She nodded toward the three operatives. "They need it."

"They're hardly in a position to be making demands," Leech said.

"Just watch it, Martin. After you do, I think you'll be ready to do nearly anything they want."

Leech's frown deepened, and he went into the van and closed the door behind him. Joseph knew that he probably had the equipment in there to make a duplicate, and would do so as he watched. Fine, he thought. There'd be no way to keep this all from MI5 anyway. Let Langley work it out with them later, assuming the operation was successful, which was still dubious.

When Martin Leech came back out, his face was pale, and he handed the video cassette back to Molly, who gave it to Laika. Then Molly explained the present camera surveillance to Leech, and remained there while the three operatives returned to the cottage in the van holding the canisters.

''I hope to hell they pass muster—if we get to that point,''
Tony said. ''Mulcifer's got to stay away from the castle long
enough to set everything up.''

''They'll pass,'' Joseph said. ''These were original tanks.
They just filled them with something to give them weight.''

''What?'' Tony asked.

''They didn't say.''

Dawn was just creeping over the hills to the east as they
established their final base at the cottage. Tony made a big
pot of coffee, then filled a thermos and put it in the van with
the canisters. Then they took turns watching the monitor that
showed the wireless feed from the camera set amid brush by
the roadside two miles south of the castle. The two who
weren't watching sat in nearby easy chairs, closed their eyes,
and tried to get a few minutes of sleep.

It didn't come easy, but they didn't have that long to wait
for something to happen.

Chapter 48

"*E*ven though you may not know it down there," Mulcifer called, "it's a beautiful day in the beautiful country of Scotland. The sun is shining, the temperature is quite acceptable, and best of all, there's a light breeze. Not a heavy wind, not a dead calm, but a light breeze and no rain, so whatever might be wafted into the gentle Scottish air will blow hither and yon, assuring an even distribution."

Colin Mackay looked up the neck of the bottle dungeon and wished that his arms were twenty feet long so that he could reach up and yank the smiling bastard above down into the pit with him. Still, he said nothing. At least he could keep that pleasure from the demon.

"I'll be going on this little jaunt, and I'll be taking four of your associates along, so if you'd like to say goodbye to them now, you'd best do so. There's no absolute guarantee they'll be returning. They might *like* Edinburgh. I think it's definitely a two-canister city, don't you?"

Christ, Colin thought. Edinburgh, that fine old city. He could keep silent no longer. "Lads!" he cried up to whoever might be able to listen and act. "Push him in! Don't go along with him, push him in down here with me and then close it off!"

"No no no," Mulcifer admonished. "There's only one man among them who could do that, and he's down there, Mackay. Besides, I'd just walk right through the wall to escape. You need more than rock to hold my vengeance—and my joy. Goodbye, Mackay. I'll be leaving your friend Rob and a few others to tend to your needs. And when I return, don't worry, I'll fill you in on every little detail of what happened on this magnificent Scottish day . . .''

There followed the sound of the trapdoor fitting into place, and then silence. Colin Mackay fell back on the mattress and buried his face in his hands. He would have done anything to stop Mulcifer, would have given his life and his soul, if he even had one left. But there was nothing he could do but wait.

"It's a go," Joseph called, looking up from the monitor. "It was him—right in the front passenger seat!"

"How many?" asked Tony, slipping on his jacket.

"At least four. Good luck," said Joseph, quickly hugging them both. Then they were out the door and climbing into the van with the canisters. In another minute, the van from the castle went by on the road, heading south. Tony and Laika waited until it had nearly vanished over the rise, then drove out the stone-covered lane and began to follow.

Joseph watched them go, and thought about giving a quick, soft prayer, but didn't know what to say. Instead, he went to the car and headed north toward MacLunie's land, where Molly Fraser and the strike force was waiting. At least the attack on the castle would keep his mind busy, and they didn't have a minute to spare.

"Mulcifer's out of the castle and heading south," Joseph said to Molly and Leech as he climbed out of the car. "Let's do it."

There were three dozen soldiers, and they already had on tactical gear, as did Molly. "We'll let the troops take care of getting the castle secured," she said, "but we'd better wear the gear just in case of a stray sniper." She helped Joseph slip on a bulletproof vest and a riot helmet, and handed him a British-made automatic rifle.

Then Molly, Joseph, Leech, and three taciturn types whom Joseph suspected were MI5 spooks of varying degrees of im-

portance watched from the ridge as the soldiers climbed into
four of the vehicles. They drove across the field until they
turned onto the dirt drive of the castle, then sped toward it,
coming to a halt ten yards from the inner gatehouse.

There they stormed out and ran through the rubble of the
fallen outer wall and through the narrow passageway into the
inner ward. Joseph heard the rattle of gunfire, and hoped that
it wasn't Colin Mackay who was going down. The troops had
been given the man's description, and had been told not to
shoot any man similar in appearance. It was possible that
Mackay might battle the intruders, but what was more likely
was that he was now imprisoned somewhere by Mulcifer,
guarded by his own former comrades.

The firing lasted less than a minute, then stopped. Leech's
field phone twittered, and he opened it and listened, then said
a few words Joseph couldn't hear and closed it again.
"They've secured the place. There were only half a dozen
men inside. They shot four, and captured two others who
weren't armed." He nodded briskly. "Let's go in."

As they entered the inner ward, Joseph saw the soldiers
standing about, some caring for their own wounded, and others for the wounded terrorists. Two of the terrorists, seemingly unharmed, had been handcuffed to a post. Other soldiers
were running along the walkway of the inner curtain, looking
into every alcove to make certain that there were no terrorists
hidden there.

"We've got a dozen men going through the place, sir,"
the commander, who seemed as relaxed as if he'd taken a
walk in the park, told Leech. "Got three men down, but none
dead. We killed two of theirs, wounded two, captured two
more. Unless the men turn up more, that's all they had in
here."

One of the soldiers came up to the commander. "Sir, found
several containers of VX stored in one of those rooms over
there."

"Good heavens, it *was* them," Leech said, with a grudging

nod to Molly Fraser. Then he turned to Joseph. "I hope your people stay on the ones who got out."

"Not half as much as I do, Mr. Leech," Joseph replied. "I don't see Colin Mackay here, though."

"Left with the van of gas?" Molly suggested.

"Not likely. He'd never stand for it. But I think I know where he may be."

Joseph led Molly and Leech, accompanied by several soldiers, to the trapdoor that led to the bottle dungeon. "If he's there, I want to go down and talk to him first," he said. "I know how badly you want to arrest him, Mr. Leech, but believe me, he's the only one who we can be *sure* might be able to end this. If we don't have his cooperation, we have nothing. I know how you feel about him, but I want him to be treated with dignity."

Joseph looked at two of the soldiers and gestured to the trapdoor. They lifted it, and immediately a voice came from below. "What's happened? I heard shots! What the hell's *happened?*"

At Joseph's silent direction, the soldiers lowered the ladder into the pit, and Joseph called down. "Mackay, it's me, Joseph Stein. I'm coming down." He handed his weapon to Molly, and climbed down the ladder.

At the bottom, he turned and faced Mackay. The man looked terrible, gaunt and unshaven, his eyes hollows filled with worry. "Familiar situation," Joseph said. "Only our roles are reversed."

"What was the shooting about? Did you get that bastard?"

"Mulcifer? No, he's gone off to wherever his next target is. But hopefully my colleagues will be able to stop him."

"He's off to Edinburgh," Mackay said, "and I hope to God they can. But he said he ordered you to kill yourself— and your colleagues. What happened?"

"He didn't realize that one of my colleagues is the fastest gun in the west. As for what happened up above, we brought in a strike team to take the castle. Two more of your men are dead."

Mackay's face balled up like the fists he clenched. He swung around and slammed them both against the wall. "Ah Christ, Christ, did you *have* to do that?"

"You know Mulcifer's power. He turned them into machines, ready to defend this place with their lives. And they did, unfortunately. Your cause is finished, Colin. The soldiers are inside the castle."

Mackay turned and looked at Joseph with eyes so tired, sad, and wise that Joseph thought he seemed every minute of his century-long life span. "My cause was finished," he said softly, "when I first began to search for that deil in human shape."

"That's true. And maybe more than just your cause. You gave him a focus, you gave him opportunity. And he took every advantage of it. There are hundreds of bodies already to prove that."

"What would you have me do?" Mackay said angrily. "I'd do anything, give my damned, worthless life to have what he's done expunged! But I don't know *how!*"

"We have an idea," said Joseph. "And we're ready to go through with it. But you're the keystone. It's nothing without you."

Mackay looked at him suspiciously. "Why?"

"Because you're the only person in this world who we *know* he can't control."

"That's shite. There must be millions of others."

"You may be right. But there's no way to try them out except in front of Mulcifer himself. And we're not going to get a second shot at this. But there's another reason, too. There's nobody living that Mulcifer hates more than you. He looks at you, he sees your father. He'd follow you anywhere to destroy you, even more so if he were to think that you screwed him the way your father and the other Templars did. He'd follow you into hell itself."

"And if that would put him there, I'd be willing to go. Now that you know that, let's cut this shite and go upstairs so you can introduce me to your English friends. And then you all can tell me what exactly it is you have in mind."

Chapter 49

"*T*hat looks like a lovely place," Mulcifer said. "I'm sure you boys must be hungry."

Gordon MacGregor looked at the small restaurant up ahead. It did double duty as a filling station, with pumps out front. The sign showed a picture of an old man sitting in a chair facing the viewer. The painted words read "AULD ANGUS."

As MacGregor pulled into the small parking lot and parked the van at the side of the building, he thought about his friend Angus and the others who had died. He had shot Danny Christie, his nephew, in cold blood, and then had turned his gun on John Caldwell, but the others had already shot him down. And the beast in the seat next to him was the man responsible, and there wasn't a damned thing that MacGregor could do about it.

He knew where they were headed, he knew what they were about to do, and he knew that he would die in the doing of it, and all he could do was whatever this Mulcifer wanted.

They got out of the van, and MacGregor knew that the others were in the same sinking boat. He suspected that Michael Brownlee still had a touch of his own will left, for he hadn't shot at either of the men back at the castle. Still, Michael was a follower, not a leader, and was apt to do what the majority did, even if it was crazed.

It was early afternoon, and there were a few people having lunch inside. MacGregor ordered a sausage meat–and–onion-filled hot roll. It was a humble last meal, but he was hungry for it. It no sooner came, however, than Mulcifer started his games with the patrons.

Tony and Laika slowed when they saw the van pull into the restaurant. When it was out of sight behind the trees that lined the road, he waited long enough for whoever was inside it to get out and enter the restaurant, then resumed his normal speed and pulled into the parking lot.

The van was parked at the side of the building, and they were relieved to see that the driver had backed it in, so that the rear doors were facing the trees. Tony pulled into the open space next to it. The wall before them had only a few small, curtained windows. "Rest rooms. We lucked out," said Laika.

"Let's hope our luck holds," said Tony, "and they didn't leave anybody in the van." Tony looked through the windows next to him and saw no one, but that didn't mean someone couldn't be in the back.

There was no one else in the parking lot, and Tony got out, walked to the front window of Mulcifer's van, and looked inside. No one was there, and nothing else was visible inside. What they were transporting was on the floor, hidden by the seats.

Tony thought it was stupid not to leave a guard, but it made sense from everything he had learned about Mulcifer. The sonofabitch was so arrogant that he couldn't dream of anything standing in his way that he couldn't put down. Well, the sonofabitch was wrong this time.

Laika stood watch from inside their van while Tony went around to the back of Mulcifer's with his picks. Car locks were the easiest things in the world. A feeler pick unlocked it in twenty seconds. Tony examined the door seam for alarms, found none, and opened the back.

He breathed a sigh of relief and whispered, "Thank you, God," when he saw the canisters. There were two of them, the same light green color, the same new sheen, despite their age, and the same stenciled ten-character line of letters and numbers ending in "-VX." The codes weren't exactly the same, but he doubted that Mulcifer or his companions would have been so anal as to memorize them. Four semi-automatic rifles also lay on the floor.

In another few seconds Tony had the back door of his own van open. "Two of them," he said to Laika. "Looks good." He effortlessly slid one of the replacement canisters out and carried it the few feet to Mulcifer's van. He slid out one of their canisters, glad to find that its weight was nearly similar to the one he would replace it with, slid the harmless one in, and took the VX to his van.

Then he repeated the process, but before he closed and relocked the back doors of Mulcifer's van, he spoke to Laika from the rear of the van. "There are other weapons in here. Should I unload them?"

Laika thought for only a few seconds. "No. They won't check the gas, but they may check their weapons beforehand. Finish up."

As he locked Mulcifer's van, Tony knew she was right. If they found the guns empty, they would know they had been made, and they couldn't take that risk. At least thousands wouldn't die from the gas. They needed all the time they could get back at the castle, and if a few more innocent people got shot, it was a price that had to be paid.

Tony got back into the van and pulled slowly out of the parking lot, remembering what one of his trainers had told him during his first year in the Company: "Sometimes you have to get your hands dirty if you want to clean things up." And that was what he had had to do just now. He wondered who those rifles might kill, and then tried to dismiss the thought.

"Nice job," Laika said, as they headed up the road the way they had come, northwest toward Gairloch. "From the time you opened your door to the time you got back in, two minutes flat."

In spite of himself, Tony smiled. There were, after all,

small pleasures to be taken in one's skills. He smiled, too, at the thought of Mulcifer's reaction when he released the gas upon the city of Edinburgh.

But now they had more work to do, and he put more pressure on the accelerator. It would take another few hours for Mulcifer to get to Edinburgh and try to carry out his deadly plan, and probably another four to return to Castle Dirk. They would have to be ready to give him a warm welcome back.

As they came down the A90, Gordon MacGregor had tried several times to wreck the car by steering it directly into an oncoming truck, but he could not make himself whip the wheel to the right. At least they had gotten out of the little eatery near Killiecrankie without anyone getting killed, although there had been a bonnie brawl under way by the time they left, no small thanks to the bastard by his side.

Edinburgh's city center was packed with tourists and slow-moving vehicles making their way along the narrow streets. At Mulcifer's orders, MacGregor parked the van on St. Giles Street, and they covered the two canisters with blankets and then removed them from the van. Mulcifer himself carried one of the rifles, also wrapped in a blanket.

They crossed brick-paved High Street, and then went across an open space and entered St. Giles' Cathedral through the west front entrance. A man in his sixties, dressed in a dark suit and tie, came up to them and looked curiously at their burdens. "May I help you gentlemen?" he asked in an uncertain voice.

"You may," said Mulcifer smoothly. "We've come to deliver the Last Judgment to the city of Edinburgh, and require your assistance in reaching your lovely steeple."

"I beg your pardon?"

Mulcifer shook his head. "What a pity. So near, and I learn that you and I share no blood. I hate to resort to this, but I have a rifle under this blanket, and should you not take us immediately to the top of the steeple without any alarm or fuss, I shall shoot not only you, but everyone else in this lovely building before I'm forced to reload. Shall we?''

The man swallowed hard, but turned and started walking. He led them on a labyrinthine route up stairs and down dimly lit hallways, meeting no one on the way, until at last they came out into the open air atop the medieval central tower of the cathedral. Above them, the multi-pinnacled crown steeple rose majestically. Below were the teeming streets of Edinburgh.

"I very much appreciate your guidance," said Mulcifer, then swung the rifle butt so that it caught the old man on the temple. He went down without a moan.

"Well, my Scottish comrades, let's not waste another moment." Mulcifer yanked the blankets from the canisters. He clapped MacGregor and Michael Brownlee on their shoulders. "Point the nozzle of this tank outward, gentlemen . . . that's the way. Here's your screwdriver to loosen the valves. Now, you two . . ." He smiled at Steven Robertson and Bruce Calder. "Bring that one over here on the other side . . . follow me. A lovely fall day, isn't it? Such a nice, gentle breeze . . ."

While Mulcifer positioned Robertson and Calder on the other side of the tower, MacGregor looked westward over the city past the spire of the Tolbooth Church to where Edinburgh Castle sat on its bed of volcanic rock. It was a beautiful old city. Too damned bad that everyone in it was going to die.

"All right!" Mulcifer called across the tower. "Open the valves!"

MacGregor twisted the valve open, expecting only a painful death. The gas hissed out, and MacGregor was surprised that he was unable to see it. Something so deadly, he thought, should look so, should be green and thick and viscous, but this looked like only air.

The wind blew toward him, and he hitched in a breath, expecting the agony to begin. But nothing happened.

Then Mulcifer was beside him, his face concerned. "Why aren't you dead?" he said wonderingly, then put his hand in front of the nozzle from which the gas was still streaming. "What *is* this *shit?*" he roared, and then turned the canister about and fitted his mouth over the end, inhaling deeply. He removed his lips, exhaled, and then said, "This is not VX . . ."

He sounded exactly like one of the chipmunks in that Christmas record MacGregor had had when he was a kid.

MacGregor couldn't help it. He laughed. It started low, then began to increase until he was howling with laughter, tears rolling down his cheeks. Then Brownlee was laughing, too, and in another moment Robertson and Calder had come over to see what had happened.

"Damn you, be quiet!" Mulcifer said, but the helium was still affecting his vocal cords so that the words sounded several octaves higher than normal.

Calder gave a burst of surprised laughter, and Robertson followed suit, and now all four of them were laughing. If they died in the next minute, it was worth it to hear this thing who had controlled them and who they feared suddenly made to sound absurd and impotent.

Mulcifer, however, was anything but. Gordon MacGregor did not hear his next words with his ears, but inside his head: *You want to laugh?—Laugh all the way down . . .*

Still laughing, he climbed over the balustrade, jumped from the tower, and hit the roof of the nave below. He did not die for several more minutes, and continued to laugh as best he could, knowing that although the jump had been due to Mulcifer, the laughter was his own. He hoped the bastard could hear it.

Mulcifer stared down at the four men thirty feet below. Two were unmoving, but the others were twitching, and one, he thought, was still laughing. Had they betrayed him? Had they switched canisters somehow? Did Mackay have more control over his men than Mulcifer had thought?

Whatever had happened, at least two more canisters of VX were back at the castle. Mulcifer retraced his steps down to street level, and walked calmly through the west end of the cathedral through which he had entered. A pocket of men were standing about looking concerned, glancing upward at the vaulted ceiling of the nave, as though they had heard the impact of the men falling onto its roof.

Mulcifer wasn't concerned. He stepped out onto the street and walked back to the van, got in, and drove north, toward Castle Dirk. He was going to have to have a very serious talk with Colin Mackay.

Chapter 50

When Mulcifer arrived back at the castle at 8:30 in the evening, the sky was still light enough to see. He drove through the inner gatehouse and was surprised to find that there were no vehicles in the inner ward. He was even more surprised to find, when he got out of the van, Colin Mackay standing up on the walkway around the inner curtain, his arms crossed, glaring down at Mulcifer in hatred and scorn.

"Get a bit of a surprise, did ye?" Mackay asked. "Everything not go quite as planned, then?"

"Where are the men who were supposed to be guarding you?" Mulcifer asked, glancing about but seeing no signs of anyone else. The only disturbing thing, besides the presence of a free Mackay, was an unpleasant smell that seemed familiar, but that Mulcifer couldn't identify. "Where are they?"

"I just had to work at it a little, but I soon brought them around," Mackay said. "They're gone. My organization is dissolved, small thanks to you. If you want to use pawns in your twisted little game, you'll have to find them somewhere else from now on."

"What do you mean, you 'brought them around?' "

"I mean I overcame your orders to them, you poncy shite. I got you out of their heads and I sent them away where you can't touch them again."

"That's . . . not possible."

"You don't sound too sure of yourself, *Mulcifer.*" Mackay sneered the name. "What's the matter? Are you scared, now that you don't have anybody around you can turn into your wee zombies? You can't make me smash my head against a wall or chew my veins open, can you? No, it's just man to man now, isn't it? Or man to monster . . . I can never recall your being anything near to a man. You were locked up like a madman for centuries, because that's exactly what you are—a mad *thing*, not fit to be among human beings, and my mistake was to think that you might actually have some emotions, like loyalty and trustworthiness.'' He made a disgusted sound in his throat. ''The more fool I.

''Well,'' Mackay went on, ''it's just the two of us now. And I'm going to do to you what should have been done when your ugly head first entered the light of day. I'm going to do what my father and the other Templars did. I'm going to beat your power down and imprison it. And this time it's going to be forever. But first . . .'' He held up a finger as if in warning. ''. . . I'm going to kick your sick, twisted arse halfway into your guts.''

Mulcifer felt as close to rage as he ever had. First the disappointment with the canisters, then his own tools laughing at him, and now this young fool—young in comparison to Mulcifer, at any rate—and his misconception that longevity made him not only Mulcifer's equal, but his superior.

''You are badly mistaken,'' he told the yapping puppy, as he walked purposefully toward the stairs to the walkway above. ''Simply because you've felt the power of the cloth of sustenance hardly makes you equal to one who it is intended to sustain. You are immortal, Colin Mackay, but not invulnerable. You can live on only as long as you do not come to a violent end. But a violent end is precisely what I intend for you.''

He was only a few feet away from Mackay now, and he stopped and glared at him. ''You mock me for not being a man, but I glory in it. My strength is greater than *any* man's, and if you doubt it, I'll be happy to give you a demonstration.''

He lunged at him, but Mackay sidestepped and hit Mulcifer

in the midsection, three hard, quick blows that would have punched the air out of any man.

But Mulcifer was not a man, and he pushed Mackay back with his left arm. That arm only traveled a few inches, but the strength of it threw Mackay several feet, and his back hit the hard stones of the inner curtain wall with so much force that he cried out in pain and fell.

"First lesson," said Mulcifer, brushing the shirt over his stomach, symbolically whisking away Mackay's powerful blows as if they had been dust. "You'll definitely need more than fists."

He strode toward Mackay with the intention of grasping his neck with one hand and his balls with the others, then squeezing to create both pain and death simultaneously. He would look deeply into Mackay's eyes as he died, and come as close as he could to feeling the man's death.

Colin Mackay shook his head to clear it, and staggered to his feet. Mulcifer was almost upon him. He stumbled backward, and was only inches from the edge when he regained his balance. Mulcifer reached out for him, but Mackay spun away and ran along the narrow wooden walkway.

He glanced back when he reached the northwest tower, and saw that Mulcifer was following him, walking briskly rather than running, as if telling Mackay to go ahead and run, that he would catch him easily enough. Mackay passed the stairway down, but did not take it. That was not his route. He had one direction in which to go, one destiny only, and it was now twenty yards away.

He ran the length of the northern wall, slowing enough for Mulcifer to draw closer, until only a few yards separated them. The timing and the distance would have to be just right. Nothing must go wrong. He had failed so terribly before, but he could not fail now.

Just past the northeast tower, he glanced behind him to see Mulcifer striding across the boards that passed the stairway down. Mackay stopped, grasped a steel lever that jutted up from between the wooden planks, and jerked it toward him. His action took less than a second, too little time for Mulcifer to even wonder about it.

The wooden floor of the walkway opened under Mulcifer like the trap of a gallows. For an instant he hung there as if suspended, then shot downward.

But the creature's thoughts and actions were faster than gravity, and Mackay saw it reach out and grasp the edge of the opening with its fingertips. In another second it had drawn its upper body over the edge and was climbing back onto the walkway.

"No," said Mackay in a low, firm voice, and then louder, "*No!*"

He closed the gap between them just as Mulcifer was straightening up and plowed right into him, grabbing him and pushing him backward so that both of them plunged through the opening, and down toward the now open well below.

As Colin Mackay's body fell with that of Mulcifer's, his final thought was that he had won. Even though he was a dead man now, he had won.

And then his body, still tightly clutching Mulcifer's, struck the molten lead with which the well had been filled. There was a moment of excruciating agony, and then Colin Mackay knew no more.

Chapter 51

"*H*e did it," Tony whispered, looking at one of five monitors inside the control truck. "Dear God, he did it."

Inside the truck, parked on the MacLunie land over the ridge from the castle, everyone's eyes were fixed on the monitor. On its screen was a dim image of two bodies upon what looked like a surface of gray mud. One of the bodies, Colin Mackay's, spasmed, then constricted like a burn victim's, slowly curling up and sinking into the molten lead.

The other body, however, continued to move. It thrashed about as though trying to swim in the thick, tarry mess. Joseph was amazed that Mulcifer could still live in the 630-degree heat of the lead. If Leech, who had been constantly dubious to this point, wasn't convinced that Mulcifer was something other than human, here was the proof.

"Go *under*, you bastard," Joseph heard someone whisper, and realized it was he. None of them knew what would happen if Mulcifer was not beneath the surface of the lead when it hardened.

"628.5," said an army engineer, reading from an instrument panel. It was cooling fast, down a degree and a half in less than 30 seconds.

They had kept the lead only eight and a half degrees above its melting point of 621.5 degrees Fahrenheit, to ensure that it would not take long to cool and harden once Mulcifer had fallen in. The engineers had set up an electric eye to turn off the heating unit that was part of the refractory liner they had constructed for the ten-foot-deep well. Even though the fire-brick would retain its heat for hours afterward, the lead would harden quickly.

But it appeared as though it might be *too* quick. Now the temperature reading was 626 degrees, and Mulcifer was still thrashing about. Leech's eyes were wide as he watched, and Joseph heard Laika say, "Go *down*, damn you, go *down* . . ." Joseph felt like Tony Perkins watching the car go into the swamp in *Psycho*.

"625," the engineer read. Mulcifer's movements were slowing now. His arms looked like they were treading water. His head bobbed, then went under nearly all the way, but he pushed down his arms, and his face, coated with lead, reappeared.

"624." Mulcifer's arms spread out upon the lead as though he were floating on his back. His face was turned upward, toward the trapdoor through which he had fallen, but his eyes were closed.

Then, like a man vanishing in quicksand, he went under, as quickly and completely as if the retributive hand of Colin Mackay had drawn him down, to dwell with him forever in a tomb of lead.

"Thank God," Martin Leech said softly, and Joseph could hear his voice shake. "Thank God."

"Thank Colin Mackay," Joseph said. "It wasn't supposed to happen this way. He sacrificed himself to get Mulcifer into the well."

Leech cleared his throat. "It was his responsibility," he said. "He was the one who used him. All those deaths are on his head, too."

"*Were* on his head," said Molly. "He's paid the price."

"Not enough of one," Leech said, and Joseph thought that in his eyes he could see the dead children of London.

"Would you have him 'nine years a-killing,' like Othello?" Laika asked. "Let him go. He's done more than any of us could." She looked at the panel. "What's the temperature?"

"620," the engineer said.

"How long before it's completely hard?"

"I'd say until dawn."

"I think we should have someone keep an eye on this monitor through the night," Laika said. "I don't want any surprises in the morning."

"And then we'll airlift the whole plug of lead out," said Tony, "and drop it in the middle of the North Sea."

" 'Deeper than did ever plummet sound,' " quoted Laika.

"*The Tempest*," Joseph said. "You're feeling severely Shakespearean this evening."

"There's an element of tragedy to all this," she replied. "We've won, but there have been too many losses." Laika turned to Leech. "No one goes in there until morning, when we all go, right?"

Leech nodded. "Absolutely. I'm not taking any chances with . . . with whatever that thing was."

"Good," said Laika. "I think we could all use some sleep. We'll head back to the cottage and be back at the castle before dawn. Thank you, Mr. Leech. And thank you, Inspector— Molly, for your help and for believing us in the first place."

"It's hard to disbelieve what I saw with my own eyes," Molly replied.

Leech cleared his throat. "There's a lot here that needs to be ironed out, you know. You three aren't going to be able to just walk away from this. We're going to have to . . . straighten all this out with the CIA. There are a lot of unanswered questions."

"And we'll try and answer as many as possible."

"Nevertheless, you'll forgive me, Agent Harris," Leech went on, "if prudence dictates that I put a military guard on you and your fellow agents. I should hate to find the three of you gone, come the dawn."

Joseph saw Tony's back go up, but Laika calmed him with a look. She would have done the same thing in Leech's place. "A reasonable request," she said, and added, with a smile,

"I'd be happy to have someone watch over us while we sleep."

Joseph thought amen to that. He was exhausted. They had spent the entire day preparing for Mulcifer's return, putting into play the plot that Laika had come up with to capture him again. The simpler the better, she had said, and it had worked, with a great deal of luck.

The old well had been the only trap large enough, and the inner curtain walkway passed directly over it. There would have been no time to prepare anything more elaborate. As it was, the engineers had barely finished lining the well with refractory brick, installing the heating equipment and sensors, preparing the trapdoor mechanism, and getting an electric eye rigged up that would trigger the heating elements to shut off, when the van had been sighted approaching Gairloch.

Naturally, they had to be able to see what was happening with their plan, so Joseph and Molly had set up the cameras and microphones that had allowed them to view what occurred from five different angles. When Laika and Tony had returned from Edinburgh, they had helped finish the installation.

But the success of the plot had been dependent upon one man, Colin Mackay. No one could be in the vicinity of the castle for fear that Mulcifer would sense their presence and turn them against Mackay. It had to be the two of them alone, and Mackay had to be able to enrage Mulcifer sufficiently so that the creature would follow him to the one spot where the trap could be sprung.

Mackay had agreed, and had done what was asked of him. And more. "He had a lot of guts," said Joseph, as they drove back to the cottage. "Bad way to die."

"It was probably fast," Tony said. "There are worse ways. And besides, he didn't have to go through a trial. It would be a helluva thing to try and explain."

"MI5 wouldn't have let him go to trial," said Laika. "I think he would have died while trying to escape. There was too much he could tell that they didn't want anyone to know."

"Is that what you told him when you were talking him into it?" Joseph asked.

Laika glanced out the window. "Let's just say I was at my most persuasive. And my most honest."

Before she went home to go to bed, Molly Fraser stopped by the small jail in which Rob Lindsay and James Menzies, the only survivors of Colin Mackay's group, were imprisoned. The two men were sitting in the same cell, and stood up when they saw her.

"What's happened?" Lindsay said. "How's Colin?"

"Colin Mackay is dead," said Molly. "So is Mulcifer. I don't know what's going to happen to you two. That's up to others. I just wanted you to know that he died bravely."

Lindsay sat down heavily on his cot and buried his head in his hands. Menzies came closer and grasped the bars that separated them. "But did he die for Scotland?" Menzies said, a flame in his eyes.

Molly looked at him, anger and pity warring within her. "He died for Scotland," she said. "And I think he died for the world." She started out the door, then turned back. "To-morrow morning we're going to require your presence at the castle. There may be some questions that only you can an-swer, since you were staying there. I can't make any prom-ises, but if you cooperate, it may be helpful to you. Will you go with no protests?"

Menzies nodded, and Lindsay looked up and whispered, "Yes." Molly saw his eyes were wet with tears. She had only spoken to Mackay for several minutes earlier that day, but she could understand how he might be a man worth fol-lowing, and worth weeping for.

Molly went out into the cool night and looked up at the sky. It was clear, and the stars were sparkling overhead. Things were going as well as they could, she supposed. MI5 was in control, the terrorist threat was ended, and the even worse threat to the world was at least contained, if not destroyed. And on top of everything else, there had been no sightings of those strange apparitions for several days now. Maybe everything was going to be all right, after all.

Chapter 52

*T*he next morning, the three operatives gathered outside Castle Dirk with Martin Leech, several other MI5 representatives, Molly Fraser, her two DIs, who were guarding Lindsay and Menzies, and a dozen armed soldiers from the group who had captured the castle the previous day. The soldiers who had taken shifts watching the lead-filled well all night on the monitor had reported no visual change, and the temperature of the lead now read 48 degrees, the temperature of the morning air.

Joseph remembered the two Scots, Rob Lindsay and James Menzies, from having seen them in the castle earlier with Mackay. They looked abandoned, like men who had lost a cause and a leader, and were left with nothing. Still, he tried not to feel too sorry for them. Terror had been their chosen tool, and people would have died at their hands even if Mulcifer had never crossed their paths. As it was, terror had turned around and bitten them in the ass.

The group went through the inner gatehouse and into the inner ward. Then they turned to the right and went toward the northeast tower, and down the narrow opening between the former stables and the blacksmith's shop where Tony had hidden earlier to the small open area that held the well. Several of the soldiers went up the tower stairs onto the platform above, and looked down through the open trapdoor.

The operatives, Molly, and the MI5 people went to the edge of the well, but Lindsay and Menzies held back, and the po-

licemen stayed with them. What lay over the top of the well
was a dark gray, relatively smooth surface of lead, but Joseph
knew full well that that surface went down ten feet. Mulcifer,
along with the corpse of Colin Mackay, was now encased in
a leaden cylinder ten feet in diameter and another ten deep.

"We'll have to remove the walkway above," Leech said,
eyeing the situation. "Then we should be able to attach a
cable and pull the thing right up with a helicopter—the bricks
will adhere to the lead."

"You'd better have a strong cable," Tony said. "That
plug's got a lot of tonnage."

"All the better to sink it deeper," Joseph said, uncomfortable at the close proximity to Mulcifer, even if he was sealed
behind lead once again. To reassure himself of his safety,
Joseph reached out a hand and rubbed it over the flat surface.
It was cool and unyielding, a fitting, permanent prison for a
cold and hard creature.

"What's that?" he heard someone ask, and looked next to
him to see Laika staring fixedly at the center of the well. He
turned and saw a slight rise that he had not noticed before, a
small, fist-shaped lump on the leaden surface, like a nodule
signaling the growth of a cancer.

Then, as they all watched, the metal over the lump started
to crack.

Something was pushing up from beneath, and now pieces
of lead started to separate from the whole and slide down the
incline that had been made. Suddenly, an arm shot out of the
lead, fist clenched.

Mulcifer's arm.

It seemed to Joseph as though he were watching in a dream,
or as if this was some phantasmal movie sequence, like the
end of *Carrie*, or *Tales from the Crypt*, or a dozen Italian
zombie films, where the rotting hand rises forth from the
grave for vengeance. But *this* hand, Joseph saw, as the fist
unclenched and the fingers spread wide, was not rotten, but
whole. Still, Joseph would have bet that it, too, had vengeance
in mind.

A second fist shattered the lead above it, and Joseph realized that all along Mulcifer must have been only an inch or so beneath the surface. "Oh shit, what now?" he whispered to himself as the fists crashed down upon the lead with superhuman strength, cracking the metal over Mulcifer's chest and head so that, slowly and laboriously, he was able to sit up.

Several of the soldiers raised their rifles, but Laika called to them to hold their fire, and Leech wisely reaffirmed the order. Bullets would do no good.

Mulcifer's chest was bare, for the heat of the lead had dissolved his clothing, and the lower part of his body was still encased in lead. It looked absurdly as though he were sitting in a bathtub. But the look of rage on his face as he glanced at the onlookers belied the image of a man bathing.

He leaned forward, and arms like pistons cracked the lead over his legs and hips. He raised his knees, jerked his flesh from the clinging metal, and stood naked before them, his body superbly muscled. His chest did not rise and fall, and Joseph realized that he probably didn't have to breathe at all, or he would have suffocated inside the lead.

" 'To the destructive element submit yourself,' " he cried triumphantly, " 'and with the exertions of your hands and feet in the water, make the deep, deep sea keep you up.' That's from a book given to me by one of my more sympathetic jailers, who thought that I was human enough to appreciate a good book other than the Good Book. He was correct. And I not only appreciated it, I learned from it. The trick, you see, is just to stay near the surface, and let your strength return!

"Now, where should I start?" he asked, looking from one person to the next, as if feeling them out mentally. "So many lives . . ." He looked past Joseph, and seemed to intensify his gaze upon someone behind him. ". . . So . . . little . . . time . . ."

Joseph couldn't take his eyes off the creature. Fear shot through him at the prospect of becoming Mulcifer's puppet once more, and at the thought of being forced to attack his friends. He noticed movement out of the corner of his eye, and thought that someone might be running away, and then it was gone, and his concentration was centered solely on Mulcifer, who was walking across the surface of lead toward him, closer and closer.

And then Mulcifer stopped, and for the first time Joseph saw something that might have been fear on his face. He became aware of a high-pitched sound, faint at first, then growing louder. It was the same sound Joseph had heard in the castle when they had seen the apparition on the road.

Mulcifer looked down at the lead, and it seemed for an instant as though he might have wanted to envelop himself in it again. Then he looked up, and his eyes widened and his mouth opened in terror and protest.

The area in which they stood was shadowed by the walls of the castle, but now it was as if the sun stood directly overhead, beaming down fully upon the well. Joseph looked up toward the source of the intense and powerful glow and saw a cone of what appeared to be pure light descending toward them. He could make out no surface features or texture on the cone as it drew nearer.

The base widened as it reached Mulcifer, and seemed to drop over and enclose him in light, hiding him from view. Then that light increased until it blinded Joseph and he could see no more.

He could not see, and yet he saw, and *knew*.

Then, so loud and piercing that it seemed to come from inside Joseph's head, pushing outward from his brain against his skull, came a scream more fierce, more filled with regret and loss and terror than any he had ever known. It was Mulcifer screaming, and the sound of it held all the power of a mind so strong that it could make men kill what they loved. It screamed of hatred and madness and self, of all the things that, unchecked, damned the species he had sought to enslave and destroy. But it screamed of something else.

It screamed of captivity.

Mulcifer was bound, and this time he would not escape.

Then the light began to fade, and the world started to reappear. Joseph could see the cone rising into the air, and the empty place where Mulcifer, the prideful and demonic, the failed architect of a hell that he had planned for the world, had stood.

As the light rose and dimmed, becoming one with the sunlight, blending into the blue sky until it vanished utterly, a sense of peace that he had seldom known before filled Joseph, peace and comfort in the newfound knowledge granted him by these other searchers, who had at last brought Joseph the truth he had sought.

Chapter 53

"What," said Martin Leech, still in awe of what they had just seen, "was *that* all about?"

"I think," said Joseph, "that it was about all we'll ever see of that sonofabitch."

"Oh, Christ," said one of Molly Fraser's DIs. They all turned around to look at him, and Laika noticed immediately that James Menzies was no longer there. "Menzies," said the man. "He's gone, he's run off—we were just looking at what was happening, didn't even know he'd left."

Molly Fraser grasped Rob Lindsay's shoulder. "Where is he? Where would he have gone?"

Lindsay looked around, disoriented, as if finally realizing that his fellow prisoner was no longer there. "I saw him— Mulcifer—looking at James, but then everything started with the light, and—"

"What would he have had him do?" asked Laika. "*Think*, man! Mulcifer told Menzies to *do* something. What?"

Lindsay's face suddenly looked more shocked than before. "Oh God, the *explosives* . . ."

"There are explosives in the castle?" Laika asked. She felt the tension that had subsided with the disappearance of Mulcifer surging to the fore again.

"Aye! Three hundred pounds of C-4. Colin planted them down under in case the police found us out, set them to blow the castle apart!"

"All right, lead us to them now. Tony, you know explosives." She looked at the soldiers. "Any of you trained?" Two raised their hands. "Let's go then. Everybody else evacuate right away."

"Now, just hang on, Agent Harris," said Leech. "We can't just run off and—"

"Do you know," Laika interrupted softly, "what three hundred pounds of C-4 can do? There won't be a stone on top of a stone here. I'm giving you a chance to live, Mr. Leech. Take it. Besides, somebody's got to explain this to your government."

Leech thought for only a moment, then nodded briskly. "You two men," he said to the soldiers who had volunteered. "Go with these agents. The rest of you, evacuate this castle immediately!"

"I'm coming with you," Joseph told Laika, but she shook her head firmly.

"I saw your face," she said. "I don't want whatever you know to disappear if that bomb goes off. Out, now." Laika turned back to Lindsay, knowing that Joseph would obey her. "Lead the way."

The Scot led Laika, Tony, and the two soldiers inside the castle, down a hall, and into a room where cardboard boxes were strewn near an open closet door. "I was here before," said Tony, helping Lindsay kick the boxes aside. "There's a secret door to the cellars."

They went down the revealed staircase, and at the bottom, in a huge room filled with pillars that, Laika surmised, held up the castle, was the C-4 against the wall. Sitting on the stone floor next to it, beneath a large wooden coat of arms, was James Menzies. He looked as though he had been drugged, undoubtedly Mulcifer's influence, Laika thought. On the floor next to him was a small, black metal box with wires leading to a detonator lodged in the C-4.

Tony knelt by Menzies and looked at the box. "Shit," he muttered. "He set it off. It's rolling. Five-minute timer, down to 3:34." He shook Menzies by the shoulder, but the man's face did not grow any more alert. "You know any way to cancel this? You?'' he asked Lindsay when Menzies did not respond, but the Scot shook his head.

The soldiers knelt near Tony and examined the device. ''Any ideas?'' he asked them.

One of them hissed a breath through his teeth. ''Jerk the fuse out of the plastic and it'll go off right away. Can't stop it.''

''Unless,'' Tony said, trying to take the cover off the box, ''we cut one of the wires inside. One of them's got to be . . . oh shit.''

''What?'' asked Laika.

''It's soldered shut. Forget it.''

''Let's go. Now,'' Laika said. They had already spent twenty-five seconds talking. That left a little over three minutes to clear the castle. The soldiers started running toward the stairs.

''What about them?'' Tony asked, nodding toward the soporific Menzies, with Lindsay by his side, trying to shake his friend into consciousness.

''I'll take him,'' Lindsay said, leaning over and lifting Menzies in a fireman's carry.

''I'll help you,'' Tony said.

''You'll *go!*'' Laika cried, striking him on the arm with a fist. She wasn't about to let him die for a man the British government would imprison for life, if he didn't wind up dead first.

Tony nodded and ran, and Laika followed. She did not look back. She owed these two men nothing.

Rob Lindsay staggered up the stairs toward the ground floor of the castle. James Menzies was two hundred pounds of dead weight on his shoulders, but he would not leave him there. They were the only two left, out of all of brave Colin Mackay's lads, and they would not be parted now, at the end.

''That . . . prison food'll . . . thin you down some,'' Rob told James, not knowing if he could hear him or not. It was just like that bastard Mulcifer to have the last laugh, wasn't it? Sending James down like that to set off the bomb was a rotten thing to do, but that was what Mulcifer had always been, rotten. To the core.

Rob had suspected it the first time they'd met him over in the States, and the piece of scum had never done a thing to disprove that first impression. Rob didn't know where that light had taken him, but he hoped it was far away from this land that he had always loved, and that now he never would leave, unless the blast blew his body out into the Minch and floated him away.

"Nae," he growled to himself. "That's nae way to think. We'll make it yet . . ."

He had been trying to count the seconds in his head, and he had just come out into the inner ward to the count of *nineteen* . . . *eighteen* . . . when the stones had erupted beneath his feet, tossing him and his burden and most of Castle Dirk into the air. His last thought was that he must have been counting too slowly, for he had always been prey to wishful thinking.

Even though Laika, Tony, and the two soldiers were a hundred yards from the castle when Colin Mackay's explosives went off, the force of it knocked them off their feet. They lay where they had fallen, the wind knocked out of them. Then the stones began to fall.

One of the soldiers was unlucky. Laika saw a heavy stone fall directly on his head as he struggled to get to his feet, killing him instantly. Other stones rained down around them, but none found a target, and they managed to join the others who had safely gone beyond the range of the flying debris.

When Laika looked back, she saw that Castle Dirk had nearly disappeared from the earth. Only part of the inner curtain was still standing, and while she looked, that too slowly collapsed in a cloud of gray dust.

Chapter 54

"I felt relief, that was the first thing," Joseph said, in response to Laika's question. He was standing with her and Tony at the edge of the ridge from which they had observed the castle for so long.

Molly Fraser was below with Martin Leech in the ruins, helping him oversee the cleanup by directing the large number of vehicles, MI5 personnel, and soldiers, as well as keeping out the snooping eyes of the media. The official story would be that the Scot nationalist terrorists who had been responsible for the freeing of the IRA prisoners and the attacks upon London and Stirling had blown themselves up in their own arsenal, after having been tracked down by MI5. It was a scenario highly favored by Leech when Laika had suggested it.

"I felt relief," Joseph repeated, looking at the calming waters of the Minch rather than the frenzied activity at the former site of the castle. "There were ... emotions that I could sense from the light—or the beings who had sent it. It was like, I don't know, an instant download, all this data pouring into my brain in one fell swoop."

"Why relief, though?" asked Laika.

"Because I just felt the greatest calm and wisdom, the greatest *sanity* exuding from this thing. Indescribable. I mentioned to you a dream I had when we first came here, remember? Now I know it was no dream. I think it was the same intelligence then—trying to reach me. I had the same feeling then, only not as strong. But this time it seemed as if nothing could ever be wrong again, as though it had come from some far more highly advanced civilization than our own, so much so that it might easily be thought—or *misinterpreted*—as a god.

"But there was more, too. I felt that it was concerned for humanity, deeply. I felt its dismay over what had happened. And its need to . . . restore order. Somehow I knew that it had brought Mulcifer here—and Mulcifer's not its real name any more than that body was its true form. But the being had intended Mulcifer to be contained, held somewhere, somehow, and not ever loosed upon the world."

"Were they the same species?" asked Tony. "The light-thing and Mulcifer?"

"I think so."

"But the light was calm and wise and sane, you said," Laika observed. "And Mulcifer wasn't anywhere close to being that."

"Maybe that's why he was here," Tony suggested. "Because he was insane in his own world, and they banished him." He looked uncomfortable for a moment. "Um, when I say 'world,' am I right? I mean, are we talking aliens here? Is that really what this is all about?"

Joseph smiled. "I can't think of any other scenario that makes sense. And so does that banishment theory. A society that advanced has probably long abolished capital punishment."

"But why would they have put him on a world that was inhabited?" asked Laika.

"Maybe they thought it was safe. And remember, we don't know how long he was here on our world. We can trace him back to the eighth century, but he might have been here long before that."

"What?" said Tony. "Are you implying before there *were* any people?"

"The impression I got was that these beings are incredibly long lived, so I guess it's a possibility."

"There's another possibility," Laika said. "What if the . . . misfits, for want of a better term, were imprisoned here, but underground, deep in caves that had no access to the surface? Remember, there had to be *some* way that Mulcifer got that nerve gas, yet the surface over the cavern was undisturbed."

"Which means that they had to have gotten in some other way," said Joseph. "Possibly underground, through a series of tunnels that Mulcifer already knew of, tunnels that brought them near or into the cavern." He nodded. "It makes more sense that Mulcifer finally found a way out in the eighth century than it does that his peers just dropped him into a populated world. Somehow he found his way to the surface, and as far as the world was concerned, the Antichrist was loosed upon it."

"Okay," Tony said, "so where does the cloth fit into this picture? When we were watching Mulcifer and Mackay's last shootout, Mulcifer said something about 'the power of the cloth of sustenance' that Mackay's father let him use to become immortal, and the implication that it was originally supposed to sustain Mulcifer. He had to mean the cloth that lined the cup. Did he mean the cloth that was dug up here, too?"

"Both," Joseph said. "The question is where the cloth came from in the first place."

Laika took a deep breath of salt air from the Minch. "You give a prisoner a blanket, don't you? Well, what if this was more than just a blanket—what if it gave him warmth, but also nourishment, somehow?" She gave a small, exasperated laugh. "I have no idea of how something like that could work, but I suspect the technology of these critters is a good ways beyond ours."

"You're probably right," Joseph said. "But that cloth provided something else, too. My theory is that it was some kind of sentinel, and its true purpose may have been unknown to Mulcifer, at first, anyway."

"A sentinel?" asked Tony.

"Yes. The same way that seemingly paranormal acts were sentinels to the Templars that Mulcifer's powers were somehow breaking through the lead. We know the cloth is radio-active, and I suspect that there's something else about it that Molly didn't tell us. I could tell she was holding something back. But maybe the radioactivity provided a signal. As long as the banished one was under the ground, and so was the cloth, there was nothing to be concerned about. No messages from here meant that everything was kosher—so to speak.''

''But when the cloth was brought to the surface,'' Tony said, finishing the thought, ''it somehow sent a signal?''

''Right. The earth's crust might have kept the signals contained. But when it no longer covered the cloth—*or* when the cloth wasn't contained in lead—it sent out some kind of S.O.S. to whoever was listening for it in Mulcifer's home planet or galaxy or whatever. Then they'd know that their prisoner had flown the coop, and they'd have to do something about it.''

''This is all getting to be a little much,'' Tony said, shaking his head, more puzzled than angry. ''How can you be sure of this sentinel thing?''

''The pieces fit. The cloth was exposed. I don't know how it got in that lead box that was dug up, but it was taken out and opened up, and I'm sure it's been out ever since. It sent the signal . . .'' Joseph shrugged. ''. . . And they came.''

''The apparitions,'' Laika said quietly. ''The sightings of ghosts and aliens.''

''Exactly. They wouldn't come physically. But the signal that was sent had to somehow travel faster than light. If they could create a signal that did that, it would only be one more step toward sending simulacra of themselves to observe the area from which the signals came.''

''They came from this peninsula,'' Laika said.

''Right. And this is where the observers—these *searchers*—started to appear. Now, we have no idea of what their true forms are like, but they probably sent themselves in guises similar to the indigenous life-forms so as not to alarm us, which accounts for the humanoid appearances. I first saw one of these searchers as my father. Maybe it was able to get into my mind the same way Mulcifer did. Still, there was always something alien about them, the glowing, the aura of light, the sounds. So there are our ghosts and aliens and angels."

"And there's the reason behind the legend of the Fairy Flag," said Laika. "When the clan chiefs waved it before they went into battle, they sent the signal. The searchers came, looking for an escaped prisoner, only to find a false alarm. Still, their appearance probably scared the hell out of the enemy. But this time it was no false alarm."

Joseph looked at the ruins of the castle and the dozens of men picking over it. In his mind, he saw again the cone of light and felt its quieting presence, quieting for all but one. "Yes," he said. "This time they saw that it was real. The cloth came to the surface through luck, or fate—"

"Or God," Tony said.

"Maybe. But this time they really came—physically, I mean. And they set things right."

Laika frowned. "I just had a thought. The Fairy Flag— they learned that it wasn't cut from the piece of cloth that was dug up here. Does that mean then that there are ... *two* cloths?"

They were quiet for a moment. Then Tony spoke. "And more than one prisoner?"

They looked down at the earth beneath their feet, and said nothing for a long time.

Chapter 55

When Joseph, Laika, and Tony walked back to the castle, Molly Fraser came up to them. "Stranger and stranger," she said. "I'm glad you're here to see it. The boys have been digging, and they've gotten down to the source of the blast in the cellar. Care to do a little more exploring?"

"What do you have in mind?" Laika asked.

They followed Molly, picking their way across the rubble until they started to descend into the crater that the bomb had produced. Joseph saw the remnants of the huge stones that had probably been the pillars supporting the castle. In the center of what remained of a stone wall, there was a ten-foot-wide opening caused by the explosion. A cold wind blew up out of it. "Behold," Molly said.

"That's where the coat of arms was," Tony said. "Against that wall. Bomb took it right down."

Joseph walked to the opening. Though the sunlight shone only a short way into it, he could see a tunnel heading downward. He turned back to Molly. "Anyone go in yet?"

"No. They just uncovered it. Martin is getting some men together now to go down." She raised an eyebrow, and Joseph answered for all of them.

"I think you'd have to clap us in irons to keep us out of that hole."

In another few minutes Martin Leech arrived at the bottom of the crater with half a dozen armed soldiers and several MI5 people. Some of the soldiers were carrying bright electronic lanterns, and one of them handed out strong flashlights to the others.

"I'm not altogether happy," said Leech, "over the idea of your coming down with us, but since you've been in on this from the beginning, you might be able to shed some light on things, depending on what we might find, of course."

"We appreciate the opportunity," Laika said, without a trace of sarcasm.

The soldiers led the way, and Leech, Molly, the operatives, and the MI5 people followed. The tunnel narrowed quickly, becoming just wide and high enough for them to walk through single file. Joseph felt claustrophobic, and was unpleasantly reminded of when he and Laika had maneuvered in the narrow space between the walls of the supposedly haunted townhouses in New York City.

It had only been a few months before, but so much had happened since then that it seemed a lifetime. He had learned a great deal in the interim, and he suspected that he had changed as well, but he wondered if it was for the better.

Today he had said things that he never could have imagined himself saying. He had been talking about aliens and mysterious powers and FTL travel, and other things that would have made his acquaintances connected with CSICOP and other skeptics' groups look at him as though he were crazy.

But, he told himself, he had followed the scientific method to draw his conclusions, and damn it, it *was* science that had caused all these things, nothing supernatural. True, it was a science far beyond anything known to humans, but science nonetheless. At least he had that much to comfort him.

They had gone what Joseph estimated to be several hundred yards, always downward, when Laika stopped and looked carefully at the wall. Those behind her were forced to stop as well, and those ahead turned and waited. "What is it?" asked Joseph.

"Have you noticed that this tunnel isn't smooth, the way

it should be if it had been formed naturally? And look at these marks. What do you think?''

Joseph looked closely. He felt Tony against his shoulder, and saw Molly looking at the wall in front of Laika. Then Tony let out a deep breath. ''That's impossible,'' he said. ''Oh man, it *can't* be.''

''What do you *think?*'' Laika repeated.

''They look like chip marks,'' Joseph said. ''Thousands and thousands of marks on all the surfaces, as though this tunnel were chiseled out of the rock.''

''Yeah, that's wild enough. But there's something else,'' Laika said. ''Look closely. Look at the *direction* of the chips.''

''Oh no,'' said Tony after a moment, and then added quickly, ''No no no no no. . . .''

''From beneath,'' Molly Fraser said quietly. ''This was chiseled from beneath.''

''Let's . . . proceed,'' Leech said, and Joseph noticed that his voice sounded rough, as though he were trying to speak over strong emotion. He could understand the feeling. The discovery implied a conscious act carried out over ages, and only deepened the sense of awe that had been growing in Joseph for weeks.

He found himself wondering if Mulcifer had used a similar tunnel to get to the nerve gas. If he had, that might mean that there were more of these tunnels, hundreds of them, honeycombing the subterranean world beneath their feet. He tried to drive the thought away, and concentrated on keeping his footing on the path that was growing ever steeper.

They had gone perhaps a mile when the leader of the soldiers called out, ''Coming into an open space!''

As Joseph stepped into the cavern, he could not hold back a gasp. It was huge. The ceiling was over fifty feet high, and the chamber itself fifty yards in diameter. The walls and floor seemed to be made of the same type of rock that they had passed through in the tunnel for the past thirty feet or so, a flat gray mineral that shimmered in places with a metallic luster. But what was so arresting about the cavern was not its dimensions nor the uniformity of its walls, but what lay in a huge pile in the middle of the chamber.

It was a vast assortment of bones.

The mound of yellow shards rose to a height of ten feet at its center, and covered nearly half the floor of the cavern. Most of them were so old that they crumbled into dust when they were touched, and could not be identified as belonging to either beast or man. But along the edge of the pile, they found a large number of bones that had not yet decayed. Nearly all, however, had been cracked and shattered. Among them were several pieces that had once been parts of human skulls.

"A charnel house far below the ground," Joseph said quietly to Laika, tossing a piece of bone he had just studied back onto the pile. "Why doesn't that surprise me any more than it does?"

"I think it's going to take a lot to surprise us from now on," Laika accurately observed. "What's the rock this place is surrounded with?"

"Galena," Tony said, coming up to them. Then he shrugged. "I got a mineralogy merit badge when I was a Boy Scout."

"Galena, as in lead ore?" asked Joseph.

"Right. I've been seeing veins of it ever since we came into the tunnel. But this is the mother lode." Tony looked across the cavern at the black mouths of other tunnels leading away. "I wonder where those go."

"I'd rather not know," Laika said. "Frankly, I'd be much happier if I hadn't even known about *this* place."

Leech and Molly, both of whom looked slightly nervous, came up to the three operatives. "Any suggestions as to what *this* might be?" Leech asked.

"We've been discussing it," said Laika, "but we have no idea." It was a tactful lie, Joseph thought. He had all too clear an idea of what this lead-lined cavern had been, and why the bones had been there. "I would make one suggestion, however," Laika went on. "And that is that after we leave, you should have that tunnel mouth sealed up permanently. And I'd suggest that you use some alloy of lead."

"*I'd* suggest," said Joseph, "that you do better than that. What kind of lead did you use in the well on Mulcifer?"

Leech turned to one of the men from MI5. "Pig lead," the man answered.

"I don't know much about it," Joseph said. "Is there any purer lead?"

The man nodded. "Pig lead is 99.73 percent lead content. Fully refined lead can have up to 99.99 percent content."

"I suggest you spend the extra bucks and go for the purer stuff," said Joseph. "That .26 percent of crap may be why Mulcifer was able to break through it."

"I'll suggest it," Leech said. "We'll probably want to take some photographs in here first, however."

Joseph looked at the black mouths of the other tunnels, then turned back to Leech. "Use fast film," he said.

As they entered the mouth of the tunnel through which they had come, Joseph held back, shining his light on the other tunnel openings, thinking that in the deeper darkness, he might actually see something, something that might be hesitant to show itself in the bright lantern light. He shone the lights on the tunnel mouths one by one, and for a moment he thought he saw what might have been the gleam of eyes, but then realized that it was only the metallic luster of the galena that saturated the rock.

Joseph turned, shining his flashlight on the ground in front of him, and walked quickly to catch up to the fading lights of the rest of the party. He was twenty feet up the tunnel when he heard a sound behind him, a stealthy scuttling, like a scraping of a hard-shod foot, or a rough hoof, upon the rock. He whirled about, pointing the flashlight back down the tunnel like a gun, and thought he saw something move, dart quickly out of the light's beam.

He stood for a moment, listening, and then he grew very frightened, and thought that he would give anything for a glimpse of daylight, and dreaded the climb back to the surface through the damp and shiny tunnel. He walked backward, keeping the light focused on where he had been. Then, when he heard the footsteps and occasional voices of the others ahead, he turned and ran, ran until he was with them again.

He talked to Laika the rest of the way up, knowing that if he did not respond, she would at least turn around to see what had become of him, and might be able to save him, should something try and take him from behind, and add his bones to the pile that now lay once more in its eternal darkness.

Chapter 56

*M*artin Leech had put an armed guard at the mouth of the tunnel, and had Molly Fraser and an MI5 agent accompany the three operatives back to their cottage. They would pack and sleep there overnight, and at 5 o'clock the next morning they would be driven to Glasgow and put on an 11:30 British Air flight to Dulles Airport.

At Laika Harris's request, Leech had also contacted the CIA, and made arrangements for a Company limousine to pick up the three agents and take them directly to Langley. With Skye dead, and with MI5 having partial knowledge of their mission and its consequences, it was high time to come in from the cold, and see how much colder the reception they got would be.

Two MI5 agents arrived after dark to relieve the first. They remained in the kitchen of the cottage, brewing tea and talking softly through the night. Molly sat with the three ops in the drawing room, and they talked for a long time before Molly finally left at eleven.

Joseph walked her out to her car, making sure that the MI5 agents knew he would be right back. "Thank you," he said, as they stood in the darkness together. "This never could have been resolved if it hadn't been for your believing us and trusting us. Despite everything."

"My pleasure. It certainly made my usual rounds seem terribly dull. Do you think we'll have any more visits from ghosts here on the peninsula?"

"No. The ghosts and the aliens and everything else are gone."

"You know a whole lot more than you're letting on, don't you? I saw your face after Mulcifer disappeared. You looked like a patzer who just realized how to force checkmate in two moves."

"All you need to know—and MI5 too, for that matter—is that there will be no more ghosts, the terrorist threat is ended, and I don't think we'll ever see the . . . person responsible for it again."

She smiled. "Maybe that's all I really *want* to know. There are a few things I wish I could forget, like that cavern." She hissed, and gave a small shudder.

"Just make sure they seal it up," Joseph said.

"I'll do what I can." She leaned toward him and kissed him, briefly and gently, on the lips. "It was good to see you again."

"Same here. I wish we had had time to catch up on things, talk a bit about more than just . . . our work, strange as it's been."

"Me too. I think about you often, Joseph. We did have some lovely times together back in London, when people weren't trying to kill us, of course. Come visit Scotland again, not on business, but for pleasure, aye? I'll make ye a haggis 'twill melt in yer mouth, laddie."

"You've never made a haggis in your life," he said, laughing.

She laughed in return. "It's true, I haven't." Then they stopped laughing, and she kissed him again, holding it long enough for him to put his arms around her and hers around him.

"Goodbye, Joseph," she said, turning toward her car. "God be with you, whether you want Him or not."

They sat three across on the flight home, taking turns sitting in the dreaded middle seat. They slept, but mostly they talked, trying to explain the cavern and the pile of bones in a way that would let them categorize and departmentalize it so that they could mercifully forget it.

But as they quickly learned, there was no light and breezy explanation for a cave full of bones both ancient and modern, and tunnels carved through solid rock from below. They considered the possibility that it was the place of imprisonment from which Mulcifer had come, a leaden tomb inside the earth where his cloth would sustain him. But had he been there for eons, long enough to cut his way upward one small sliver of stone at a time? If so, he must have had the patience of rain wearing down mountains.

"The strong possibility," Joseph said, "and one that I don't like to think about, is that he wasn't alone. The two separate cloths suggest that. And could one being, even Mulcifer, kill all those creatures whose bones were there?"

"He couldn't have," Laika said. "Remember, he'd been imprisoned by the church for over a millennium, and a lot of those bones were far less than a thousand years old." Laika looked out the window at the clouds below. "There's something else about those bones that bothered me. My old anthropology courses are coming back to haunt me. When you find bones like that, which are usually remnants of animal attack, or even bestial humans, there are always signs of eating, knife marks where the flesh has been cut or scraped off the bone, or teeth marks where it's been chewed off. There were no marks like that on those bones. Which leads me to believe that neither the men nor the animals were killed for food."

"For what, then?" Tony asked. Laika turned a meaningful look on him, and he grimaced. "For the joy of it," he said. "Mulcifer's M.O. all the way."

"Mulcifer's," Joseph agreed, "and those *like* Mulcifer. I think he was the golden boy. I think he was the only one smart enough or lucky enough to somehow get out."

"And the rest," said Laika, "if there really *are* more, stayed down there. And are they down there still?" She sighed in the silence that was filled only by the low whine of the jet engines. "What were they to begin with, and what could they have become?"

"All the terrible things that dwell beneath the earth," said Joseph. "All the awful things we've ever imagined."

"Like the Morlocks," Tony said. "In *The Time Machine*."

"Lovecraft's alien monstrosities," Joseph went on. "And Richard Shaver's deros."

"Who were they?" asked Laika.

"Shaver was a pulp writer in the forties. He wrote these stories that he claimed were true, about an evil race of beings that lived in caverns in the earth and caused terrible events in the world above by psychic means. It was absolutely crazy, but a lot of people bought into it."

"After what we know," Tony said, "I'd be pretty susceptible to that story myself."

"I just hope they seal that opening up, and fast," said Laika, again looking out the window at the gloriously blue sky. "I don't like the idea of deros or Morlocks or whatever *real* things might be under our feet. I think I'd just like to stay up here, thank you, high above the ground."

Tony frowned. "And high above all the questions that we're going to have to answer at Langley when we land."

Chapter 57

*T*he limousine took them directly to Langley, where they were led into the office of the Deputy Director for Intelligence, the man to whom Skye had reported. Before entering the office, they were asked to surrender their arms, but they had carried none on the plane, as the agents who searched them discovered.

Inside the director's office, they were seated in three chairs facing the director, who sat behind his desk. Two agents, who Laika Harris was certain were armed, stood behind them. Laika had on her lap the reports she had prepared on the plane.

"Agent Harris, Agent Luciano, Agent Stein," the director said. "You seem to have caused some problems. According to your dossiers, you were to have been working in Asia and the Middle East. However, intercepted FBI reports as well as other intelligence have placed you in the United States. And now we hear from MI5 that they are returning you home after your participation in an operation in Scotland." The director leaned back in his chair and frowned. "Since Mr. Skye cannot be found to give us an explanation, perhaps you'd care to try?"

"I would, sir," said Laika. "I want to tell you the full story, from beginning to end. But first I'd like you to watch this." She took a videotape from her folder and set it on the desk. "It will explain why you haven't heard from Mr. Skye. It will also explain another disappearance, that of David Allan

Stanley, who Mr. Skye was secretly working for—as were we—but without our knowledge, under false directives from Mr. Skye. I think the tape will also help lend some verisimilitude to some of the more . . . extraordinary aspects of my report.''

The deputy director nodded toward the two agents, who accompanied Laika, Tony, and Joseph into a waiting area. A half hour later Laika alone was taken back into the office. She could tell that what the deputy director had seen had affected him. He looked puzzled and angry, as though betrayed.

''Tell your story, Agent Harris,'' he said.

After the other two agents had left the room, Laika told the deputy director everything, from the very beginning. It was what she had told Molly Fraser, but she added all the truths that she had previously excised. There was not an element that she left out of the report. Everything was there. The deputy director asked her questions throughout, and she tried to answer them. But there were some that she could not.

She did not know, for example, why the tunnel from the cavern filled with bones led into the cellar of the Templars' castle. She did not know how a piece of the cloth had found its way into the wooden cup they had taken from Sir Andrew Mackay's room, or how another piece had become the Fairy Flag, or how a nearly complete cloth had come to be buried near Castle Dirk. Nor did she know, from a more practical political viewpoint, if Colin Mackay's organization was linked to any other Scottish nationalists, or to the IRA.

When she had finished, three hours later, she told the deputy director that MI5's Martin Leech and Inspector and ex-MI5 operative Molly Fraser would be able to corroborate the events that they were involved with.

Then Laika was shown to a private dormitory room, little more than a security cell with more comfortable furniture and a private bathroom, in the basement of the complex, while the deputy director questioned Joseph and Tony separately. She had known that he would want to hear the story from all three of them individually, in order to catch them out in any lies. One would be enough to condemn them.

The deputy director had asked her innumerable small details, things one would not be likely to tell, but that one would remember. For example, he had wanted to know what the weather was like during different occurrences, and had made numerous notes of her answers.

She did not see Tony and Joseph again for two days. During that time she remained in her cozy prison, watching television and reading books she chose from a cart that was brought to her. They had also brought her luggage, so that she had toilet articles and a change of clothes. She had no idea of how long she might be there, and tried not to be impatient.

On the morning of the third day, she was brought up to the deputy director's office. He smiled at her briefly, and she hoped that was a good sign. Tony and Joseph arrived a minute later, and they looked at each other reassuringly. If they went down, it would be together.

"A number of people have seen your tape," said the deputy director, "and have heard a brief version of the rest of the story—the director and deputy director of Central Intelligence, the executive director, the President, and several cabinet members. And some decisions have been made. First of all, the events in the tape will not be made public, in the interests of national security, and you three will never speak of them again—or of *any* of the things you have experienced—to anyone without the proper clearance.

"We've contacted both MI5 and the Vatican, and their responses seem to indicate that the three of you have been telling the truth as you saw it. And from what I've heard, there have been no contradictions between any of your versions. I can tell you that we've known about the Vatican's 'prisoner' for some time, but have always maintained a strict hands-off policy, thinking it some sort of religious conflict, and we certainly didn't want to get entangled in anything like that . . . if we didn't have to. But now the Vatican is willing to look at the situation from a less spiritual and more scientific viewpoint.''

The deputy director rubbed an eyebrow with the tips of two fingers. ''I'm not a fanciful man. Some of the things that have happened . . .'' He shook his head. ''Let me just say that I'm glad that there seem to be explanations that we can at least think of as scientific. And since they are the work of science, even science we don't yet understand, as opposed to pseudo-science, we can't turn our backs on them and pretend they don't exist, and that what happened never happened. There seems to be the potential for grave danger here, not only for our citizens, but for humanity.

''No one knows where this Mulcifer has been taken, or if there are others like him who could threaten our well-being. His existence anywhere implies a serious threat to us all. And from what you've seen and learned, there is a possibility that there could be others like him.

''Therefore, the decision has been made to continue the work that the Templars were doing. Mass killings will have to be investigated to determine whether or not an outside influence, such as this Mulcifer, was at work. Supposedly paranormal events will have to be examined and either disproved or a connection might be found to . . . the beings that we may share this planet with.

''You three have already proved yourselves adept at this kind of operation. That you're still alive is proof of that. And your effectiveness is also strengthened by the fact that one of you,'' he said, looking at Joseph, ''seems to have, shall we say, a psychic link with these creatures.''

''I'm not sure if 'psychic' is the right word, sir,'' Joseph said, and Laika had to repress a smile. Joseph being called psychic had to be his worst nightmare.

''Call it what you want,'' said the deputy director shortly, as though he disliked being corrected. ''You have an advantage the Templars didn't. It makes you more effective.''

''And could make the situation more dangerous,'' said Laika.

"There's always a risk, Agent Harris. And the stakes are very high. We feel the risk needs to be taken."

"So do I," said Joseph. "We all do."

"Good. The Vatican is willing to let a secular agency carry on the work of the Templars, and we are that agency."

"What about the FBI?" Laika asked. "Even though we had no choice, we did . . . terminate one of their agents."

"No problem. The slate's already wiped clean, and their search for you has been canceled. You'll be a special unit on assignment from the President, to whom the CIA charter won't be applicable—pretty much what Mr. Skye said you would be, but he lied. Now you'll be able to work legally in this country as well as abroad. So. Do you accept?"

They looked at each other, then back at the deputy director. "We do, sir," Laika said.

He stood up and shook each one's hand. "Thank you for your good work. You're free to leave at any time, of course. You'll report back in two weeks. I suggest during that time you reacquaint yourselves with family and friends and get some rest. Recharge those psychic batteries, Agent Stein."

Joseph smiled weakly. "Yes sir. I'll do that."

"Just one thing, sir," Laika said. "I hope you'll reaffirm to MI5 the importance of covering up the mouth of that tunnel with lead."

"Rest easy, Agent Harris. It's already been done."

Chapter 58

After several hours of debriefing, Laika Harris, Joseph Stein, and Tony Luciano stepped outside into the parking lot where a car was waiting for each of them. Free in the sunlight, Laika gave a huge sigh of relief. "We made it."

"Yes, we did," said Joseph. "And in two weeks we'll be back in harness."

"Do you mind?" Laika asked.

"No. I didn't enjoy every minute of these past few months, but I have to admit that the prospect of shooting down frauds and phonies is very appealing. It's as if the guys from *The Skeptical Inquirer* suddenly got government backing."

"Aren't you afraid we'll run up against another Mulcifer?" Tony asked him.

"I think Mulcifer, at least, is going to be well taken care of. I don't think we'll see him again. But as for others, I don't know. I'd tell you to just shoot me again if I get taken over by one of them, but we don't have the cup anymore."

"The Company?" Laika asked.

"I have to assume so. After we told our stories and were taken to our little cells, it was conspicuously missing from my luggage."

"Probably in better hands now," Tony said. "Maybe they'll take it apart and see what makes it tick. How about that—think we'd get the credit for the elixir of life?"

"You'll never see it," Joseph said. "HMOs have got too strong a lobby."

"I guess this is goodbye for a while," said Laika, unlocking her car. She turned back to the two and embraced them one by one.

"Aw, okay, group hug," said Tony, embracing both Joseph and Laika again. "I just hope they're not watching us from the windows."

"You know they are," said Laika, breaking the embrace. "They'll like it. Strong bonding."

They could have said more, but they didn't have to. They knew how they felt about each other. They knew each other's loyalty and love. It would be there when they met again, and it would keep them strong.

As Laika drove away from Langley, she glanced into the trees, almost expecting to see dark figures moving furtively against the browns and golds of autumn leaves. It was her favorite season, and she was glad she hadn't missed it here. She and her mother could take some long drives and walks together. She needed to clear her head, get rid of a lot of ugly pictures.

And she needed to stop hoping that the deputy director had been telling the truth, and that the black, open mouth of that damned tunnel that she couldn't stop thinking about was really sealed tight, and that pile of bones, and the things that had put them there, were down in the darkness and would stay there.

When Laika Harris was driving toward Maryland to visit her mother at 4:30 P.M., it was dark in Scotland. If anyone had seen the figure running through the night, they might have thought him a short and stocky man, barely five feet high, with a barrel chest on which no hair grew. He was naked, and though he looked only thirty years old, he was, in fact, much, much older.

He had left his cloth behind, the same cloth that had sustained him for all those years. He would not need it now. When the sun came up in the morning, its light would supply his needs.

He was free, free at last. The others had chosen to remain below, and now they were trapped once more. One day, perhaps, they would join him again.

But for now, he was the only one of them whose spirit had not been crushed by the constant darkness and the surrounding and all-encompassing rock. He was the only one with the courage to slip through into a world far more vast than the one in which he had lately dwelt, but nothing when compared to the worlds and suns and moons through which he had roamed so long ago, roamed and fed his soul that had been starving too long.

There was no thirst in his mouth, nor hunger in his stomach, but both thirst and hunger were in his soul. He had no idea of what this world had to offer him, but he would soon learn.

He would soon teach.

Author's Note

*G*airloch and the peninsula named after it are used to fictional purposes in this novel. There is no Castle Dirk, nor any specific model of it, and certain liberties have been taken with the actual physical properties of the peninsula.

The Mackay clan has also been used fictionally, and the author offers his deepest apologies should any member of this proud and splendid clan (of which the Williamson family is a sept) feel that I have sullied its name in any way. Such was certainly not my intent.

My apologies and thanks are also due to Clan Macleod for the borrowing of their justly famous Fairy Flag legend.

I would also like to thank Diana Gill, Stephen S. Power, and Jimmy Vines for their valuable assistance during the writing of this book.

Readers wishing to further investigate the reality of the paranormal will find much of worth in the following books: *The Encyclopedia of the Paranormal*, edited by Gordon Stein, Ph. D.; *The New Age: Notes of a Fringe Watcher* by Martin Gardner; *An Encyclopedia of Claims, Frauds, and Hoaxes of the Occult and Supernatural* by James Randi; *Why People Believe Weird Things: Pseudoscience, Superstition, and Other Confusions of Our Time* by Michael Shermer; *The Demon-Haunted World* by Carl Sagan; and the publications of the Committee for the Scientific Investigation of Claims of the Paranormal (CSICOP) at *http://www.csicop.org*.

SEALS

THE WARRIOR BREED

by H. Jay Riker

The face of war is rapidly changing, calling
America's soldiers into hellish regions where
conventional warriors dare not go.
This is the world of the SEALs.

SILVER STAR
76967-0/$5.99 US/$7.99 Can

PURPLE HEART
76969-7/$6.50 US/$8.99 Can

BRONZE STAR
76970-0/$5.99 US/$6.99 Can

NAVY CROSS
78555-2/$5.99 US/$7.99 Can

MEDAL OF HONOR
78556-0/$5.99 US/$7.99 Can

MARKS OF VALOR
78557-9/$5.99 US/$7.99 Can